T. J. Armstrong was born in Essex in 195_. __ _
Languages at Oxford and studied Philosophy at London
University. He now teaches in Canterbury. His first novel
Walter and the Resurrection of G., was awarded the Authors
Club Best First Novel Award.

Praise for *Cecilia's Vision*:

'[Cecilia's] story of love, loss and redemption plays out the
conflict between love of the world and the senses and the
ascetic's rejection of appearances ... The book gives us a
glimpse into a parallel world of spiritual enquiry'   *Time Out*

'What makes *Cecilia's Vision* superior to most monks-and-
murder novels is the care with which the religious and political
context is established'   *Mail on Sunday*

'[An] absorbing tale that evokes a real flavour of the period,
and offers a glimpse into an unearthly world beyond'
                                      Big Issue in the North

'Armstrong's work contains much material similar to *Ivanhoe* –
there are heretics burned, beautiful Jewesses, wicked lords and
evil Templars – but he writes in a different key and avoids all
Scott's mistakes which so jar on the modern ear ... The
unfolding mystery draws us inward and onward, likewise the
parallel story that Cecilia tells is utterly fascinating, a wonder-
fully convincing picture of what a woman's life might have
been like in the late twelfth and early thirteenth centuries ...
Armstrong has not simply researched his period – though he
has done that remarkably well – but he goes much further,
supplying an insight into the workings of the medieval

mind . . . Scott wrote about early nineteenth-century people dressed up in the garb of a Merrie England that never existed. Armstrong, by contrast, writes about England as it really might have been; his characters convince as genuine medieval people and it is this that makes his novel such a richly rewarding one'   *The Tablet*

And for *Walter and the Resurrection of G.*:

'Ambitious . . . leaves the reader in no doubt about his ability . . . fresh, touching and intelligent'   *Daily Telegraph*

'Gripping . . . shades of Herman Hesse and John Fowles'
                                                   Independent on Sunday

'An intriguing adventure of the hermetic imagination across time, T. J. Armstrong's first novel compels attention through its twinned story-lines and leaves a strange afterglow in the mind'
                    Lindsay Clarke, author of *The Chymical Wedding*

Cecilia's Vision

T. J. Armstrong

review

First published in 2001
by REVIEW

An imprint of Headline Book Publishing

First published in paperback in 2001

10 9 8 7 6 5 4 3 2

ISBN 0 7472 6738 3

Typeset by
Letterpart Limited, Reigate, Surrey

Printed and bound in Great Britain by
Clays Ltd, St Ives plc

Headline Book Publishing
A division of Hodder Headline
338 Euston Road
LONDON NW1 3BH

www.reviewbooks.co.uk
www.hodderheadline.com

'edelen herzen z'einer hage'

ACKNOWLEDGEMENT

My immense gratitude to the following for their kindness, support, and excellent advice during the writing of *Cecilia's Vision*:

Gwen Armstrong
Jennifer Armstrong
Michael Bainbridge
Mary Berg
Peter Berg
Peter Brodie
Joan Deitch
Ulrich Genzler
Mary-Anne Harrington
Simon Lowe
James Nunn
John (Slide) Pike
Ben Reid
Ilserose Sayer
John Sayer
Olivia Stephens
Timothy Stephens
Claudia Vidoni
Dinah Wiener

Prologue

December 1261, Barreham

FOR TWENTY YEARS I have lived quietly, as curate of this small Kent village, alongside the woman I love, preaching, caring for the sick, yet secretly engaged in the Work. I had believed that my life would continue in this way until my death. But then I received that disconcerting visit from the Dominican friar. The moment I saw his long, dark form striding up the hill towards my house, I knew something difficult was about to take place, that my life would be changed. I had been a Dominican in my youth, but I joined before Pope Gregory published the bull called the *Ille humani generi*. This was the decree that empowered us to hunt down and try heretics. Before then the word 'inquisition' was unknown, and the Dominicans' reputation as merciless 'hounds of God' (*domini canes*), snuffling after heresy and burning all who stood in their way, was not yet made.

The visitor introduced himself as Brother Johannes and as soon as he entered my house, he handed me a wooden box. He said he wanted to know what I made of its contents. My hands trembled with fear as I prised off the lid, which was nailed in place. Inside, bedded in straw, I found a pair of small chalices, studded with precious and semi-precious stones. Below the chalices were three bundles of manuscripts tied with string. I took out each in turn and inspected them. The first was in my own hand, and the second in that of my

1

old friend and teacher, Brother Thomas. They were notes on the interviews we conducted some twenty-seven years ago with a woman who went by the name of Domna Cecilia. I recognised the third bundle too, though the last time I saw it had been long ago.

'It seems, from your reaction, that these are familiar to you,' said Brother Johannes, suddenly jolting me out of dream-like memories of former years.

'Oh, yes,' I nodded.

'Perhaps you would care to explain,' he pressed me.

I hesitated. 'It would take a very long while,' I replied, as scenes from those days began to crowd in on my mind with dazzling clarity.

He reflected for a moment or two. Then he said, 'You are skilled at writing. Perhaps you should write down your explanation. I shall return in three or four weeks. In the meantime, you must make no attempt to leave this village. You will be watched.'

I knew his like well enough to understand there was nothing more to be said on the subject. I offered him hospitality but he refused, saying that he needed to continue on to Canterbury, which lies six or seven miles to the northwest of Barreham. As soon as he departed, I abandoned myself entirely to the study of the manuscripts he gave me and writing the following report.

Chapter One

THE STORY BEGAN on the eve of the Feast Day of Saint Dionysius of Alexandria in the year of Our Lord 1235, when Brother Thomas and I arrived in Canterbury to investigate the old woman called Domna Cecilia, who lived beyond the West Gate. Thomas had asked me to be his assistant. We both imagined this would be just another humdrum matter. Thomas probably hoped I would carry out the bulk of the work whilst he got on with the philosophical enquiries which were so dear to him. I am sure he did not suspect that this investigation would bring his studies to such terrible fruition.

In those days Brother Thomas was already a puzzling fellow. He was in his mid-thirties, plump, delicate and bald-headed. On occasions he would give way to fits of listless melancholy, drinking to excess or else staring into space for hours, quite inactive. Then he would be fired with enthusiasm again, studying ferociously, learning new languages, and constructing philosophical systems, such as the one set out in the third manuscript the stranger gave me, and which will survive him long after we are quite forgotten. I had first met Brother Thomas five years before the events I am about to describe, when I was a fourteen-year-old oblate at the great Monastery of Saint Alban's. There was an immediate empathy between us, and we would spend long hours together discussing Thomas's work. Later, I used to pride myself that I was one of the few to understand his true reasons for leaving monastic

3

orders to live with Alyssa, his common-law wife, and I visited
him as often as I could at Ellethamwolde near London.

As we travelled the pilgrim route, Brother Thomas
explained that the commission to investigate Domna
Cecilia had come from Lord Rufus, who had the castle at
Ellethamwolde and who claimed to be close to the King.
Lord Rufus provided the house which Brother Thomas had
shared with Alyssa since leaving the Dominican Order.
Brother Thomas lived largely from the legal work he
carried out for Lord Rufus, and he and Alyssa also taught
Lord Rufus's children. As we rode on, Brother Thomas did
not go into detail about Domna Cecilia, but chose to
reminisce about the travels he had undertaken in his youth
to the schools of Paris, Milan and Regensburg. He was
particularly taken by Regensburg, he said, whose grand
merchant houses were taller than any such buildings in
England, and more magnificent than many spires built to
the glory of God. This talk of Regensburg was, of course,
no coincidence.

We arrived at Canterbury just after midday, as the bells
rang out for Sext, and we followed the pilgrims to Saint
Dunstan's Church where, fifty years earlier, King Henry II
had begun his penance for his part in the murder of
Thomas Becket. Then we entered the city via the West Gate,
above which the Church of Holy Cross is built, and led our
horses on past the Eastbridge hospital, and the large stone
house of Isaac the Jew, which was to become so familiar to
me. However, we did not follow the crowds of pilgrims
directly to the Cathedral but went straight to the Priory
stables; we left our horses there before returning to the
Forum, and to the house of William the Cook, where
lodgings had been prepared for us. The rooms were cold
and draughty, but the straw was fresh, and there was a table
and chair, and a bed for Brother Thomas, who said we were

better off here than in the Priory guest house, where greater comforts were to be had, but where we would be constantly disturbed.

Brother Thomas had been to the Cathedral on several occasions and knew a number of the monks. He went off to try to find Brother Theodor, the librarian, who shared many interests with him. I was very excited because I had only been to Canterbury once before, and I hurried to join the crowds thronging round the tomb of the Holy Martyr, in order to offer my prayers. Then I returned to our lodgings where I got on with my task of preparing the wax tablets, the parchment, ink and quills, so that records of our investigations could be drawn up according to the custom. Brother Thomas returned after Angelus and we ate together at an inn in the city. I remember little of what we discussed other than Thomas saying he was disappointed not to have found Brother Theodor, who had ridden out on business two days previously but had not returned.

The next morning, after High Mass, we walked out through the busy streets to Domna Cecilia's house. It was an imposing stone building, three storeys high, beyond the West Gate; it towered above the other ramshackle dwellings, with their stench of excrement, rotten straw and cries of animals and babies. Thomas said the original building might once have formed part of an old Saxon defence system. Ragged red and white roses bloomed from bushes on either side of the front door.

As we approached the house, Thomas stopped suddenly and touched my sleeve. I soon saw why. Standing on the opposite side of the road were two massive, bearded men, both of whom had hideously deformed mouths and noses, and glared at us. Thomas nodded towards them, but they ignored us. So we carried on to the front door, pushed at it, and entered the shadows of the windowless lower floor of the house. It was strewn with straw, and a goat and hens were kept there. The hens flapped and squawked as we closed the door behind us. We waited for a moment or two until we were certain that the men outside would not trouble us, then we crossed to the wooden steps and started to climb them. I remember to this day the scent of sandalwood which suffused the building, mingling with the smells of the straw and the animals. This was the start of my pilgrimage, dissimilar perhaps to the pilgrimage to the shrine of Thomas Becket, but one of overwhelming significance to me.

A woman with long curly raven hair opened the latch to the door at the top of the steps and welcomed us into the first room. We took her to be Domna Cecilia's servant; she had piercing dark eyes which darted nervously, and a tall slender figure which was lent an enticing nobility by the long black dress she wore. Her face was drawn and austere, but her features were very beautiful. She must have been in her late twenties but she could have been much younger. She did not speak, but gestured that we should continue up to the top level of the house. Thomas tried to thank her, and asked kindly if this was a convenient time to visit, but all he got by way of a reply was a shy smile. The woman's presence unnerved him, not least, I supposed, because she was so attractive. His puffy cheeks and scalp glowed a delicate pink.

In this first room, the immediate impression was one of cleanliness. The walls were whitewashed, and the boards beneath the fresh rushes were spotless. The most striking object to catch my eye as we entered the room was a chalice, fashioned out of dull, shining gold, once sharp edges now worn smooth, and its stem fixed with semi-precious stones. It stood on a table laid with a white linen cloth. Thomas raised an eyebrow to communicate his awareness of its ostentatious display, which was out of character with the rest of the house.

Behind the chalice was a chart. The central motif was an androgynous figure whose head, hands and feet pointed a perfect pentagram which was in turn ringed by a circle. Overlying the pentagram were systems of triangles labelled with Hebrew letters, twenty-two in total.

In the upper room, to which the woman led us, we saw Domna Cecilia for the first time. I shall never forget the impression she made on me. Half in shadow, her back towards us, she was staring out of the window. I was dazzled by the brilliant light that framed her and struck by the straightness of her bearing, the length and beauty of her hair flowing loose down her back, its colour uncertain against the sunlight. For a moment I wondered if there had been a mistake, if we were in the presence of a much younger woman.

Slowly, she turned towards us. Behind her, through the window, I glimpsed the Cathedral in the distance, shimmering gold and white in the brilliant sun against the crystal blue of the sky, with the same azure light that glowed in Cecilia's eyes. Her features and her demeanour had a timeless quality. Unlike most people of her age, she had neither gained fat, nor had she grown haggard; her face maintained the contours of youth yet very fine wrinkles, and a sternness, particularly around the mouth, gave the impression of a calm, a dignity, as though her features had been carved in wood, lightly painted, and fixed with some precious oil or balm.

I looked round the room and made a mental note of its contents. Against the wall to the right of the window were a simple bed, a spinning-wheel and a distaff. Above the bed was a shelf with three or four loosely tied books. Next to them, marjoram, moonwort, clover and other herbs hung to dry. A peace, a glimmering white, suffused the objects in the house. The wall opposite the window was bare but for two simple pottery piscinas hanging from shiny nails; each

7

piscina was about the size of a human hand, and bore symbols I could not make out. They contained water which reflected the sunlight, causing tiny bubbles of light to dance about the room, interleaving like pale flames with the tawny beams glinting from the amber necklace Cecilia wore over her black woollen dress. I sensed a spark of energy, of recognition, between her and Thomas when, momentarily entranced, Thomas's eyes followed the mosaic of coloured beams, and her gaze crossed his.

There were four chairs in the room. Three were rudimentary, backs hewn from a single beam of wood. The other was a folding chair, such as nobles, high-ranking clergy and persons of royal birth use to signify their office. Its arms were carved with representations of lions, griffins, serpents and butterflies, and the legs with motifs of roses intertwined with lilies. This was the chair on which she beckoned Thomas to sit. I was directed to one of the simple chairs to his right whilst Cecilia took up position opposite us. The last chair, to Cecilia's right, was for the woman called Alazaïs, whom at first we took to be a maid or domestic, since she was often absent from the room, and never joined in our conversations.

'My friends,' said Domna Cecilia, 'you are welcome. How kind of you to come.'

'Thank you,' Thomas replied. 'This is my assistant, Wilfridus. He will take records of our conversations. You know why we are here?'

Following his cue I took out from my bag the wax tablet and stylus I used for jotting notes. Cecilia's reply puzzled me, for she did not answer in Latin, but in a Saxon dialect still common in England, though it seemed quite out of place in the mouth of someone whose appearance was as noble as Domna Cecilia's. 'Of course. I have been looking forward so much to meeting you,' she said to Brother Thomas. 'You are my listener.'

Thomas leant forward, blushing with surprise and anger. I knew that his mother had been of Saxon origin, though his father was of Norman stock. Perhaps Domna Cecilia had deliberately touched some raw nerve. But how could she have known?

'Perhaps we should speak Latin,' he rebuked her.

'Nothing could bring me greater pleasure,' she replied in that language, which she spoke with a light South German accent, 'than to address you in the flower of tongues. But forgive me,' she went on. 'You have both travelled a long way. You must be hungry and thirsty.'

Alazaïs responded by going to the next room and returning with wine, an infusion of vervain, bread, fruit and dishes of delicately spiced vegetables, some cooked, some raw. Thomas's eyes lit up. He was a sensuous man, taking great pleasure in choice food and good wines. I noted the absence of meat, also that Domna Cecilia did not eat with us. Refusal to take food with outsiders was a common trait amongst the heretical sects we were called to investigate in the days when I was a Dominican. As Alazaïs passed round the platter on which she had displayed the food with courtly refinement, I noticed Thomas gaze after her. Food was not the only carnal appetite which troubled him. Cecilia's half-smile made it plain that she had noticed his reaction.

In order to win Cecilia's confidence, Brother Thomas chatted about our journey from London. Alazaïs remained silent, whilst Domna Cecilia nodded vivaciously for a while and smiled generously at Thomas's jokes. Then she interrupted him and said, with a sudden coldness, 'Before we begin, perhaps you would like to tell me what you expect to find here.' Taken aback by her sudden assumption of authority, Thomas and I glanced at one another. There was such a focus of concentration in her gaze, such a force of energy in the expression on her face that depictions of saints in their glory came to my mind, with large, painted eyes, and framed by jagged aureoles of spiritual power. 'Are you seeking wisdom or knowledge,' she said, 'power or justice?' She pronounced each of these words carefully, savouring it so that for a moment its essence became a perceptible presence in the room. With that, she tilted her head to one side, and the sun illuminated her features with light like that of flames the colour of opal and agate licking the faces of heretics and martyrs burning at the stake.

Thomas returned her stare, remaining calm, whilst I shuddered, feeling like a blind man on the edge of a precipice. 'It is my role to ask questions,' he replied.

'Oh, I am sure you will,' she said. 'And I look forward to answering.' Satisfied, I supposed, that she had unsettled us, Domna Cecilia mollified her tone, and continued kindly, almost tenderly. 'I do understand,' she said, 'that it must be a very delicate and difficult matter for you to be entrusted with the task of interviewing me. You should know that my only wish is to help you. For me also, what we are to discuss is of grave importance.'

Thomas nodded, and I dared hope that her words might be genuine, and that this matter, which was already beginning to make me feel uneasy, might be settled quickly. Yet I remembered something Thomas had once warned me about, that apparent cooperation can hide subtle and pernicious stubbornness of spirit. 'Perhaps,' Thomas said, 'you might tell me something of your childhood.' This was a favourite ploy of his, for he believed that few lie about their childhood; if an investigator can observe the movements of the subject's animal spirits as they tell the truth, later it is easier to detect lies.

'Very well,' she began. 'I was born in Regensburg in the year of Our Lord 1173. One of my earliest memories is that

10

high in the wall of Regensburg's old Cathedral, the one they have apparently torn down recently to make way for a building in the new style, there were gargoyles depicting monsters, some beaked, some lion-like, crouching over men's heads, clasping the men's shoulders with clawed or pawed hands, possessing them, triumphing over them. Yet the creatures were invisible to their human victims, so when the waters poured from the men's mouths, these men imagined, I thought, that this happened by their volition. Do you not think, Thomas, that this is a sign of all human speech, and writing?'

She left a silence, to gauge the effect these words had on us. It was Domna Cecilia's habit to use images in her speech, and at times it was hard to be sure when she was describing real things and when she was hinting at patterns hidden from the eye. Did she really believe that all men and women are possessed by devils, or that our speech and actions are involuntary, or that what we say and write does not originate in our minds, but in forces speaking through us, despite us? And if so, what did she mean to imply about the nature of these forces? Anyhow, Brother Thomas took up the challenge and commented, 'Surely, that would be to deny our freedom to choose.'

'Perhaps so,' said Domna Cecilia, pleased, I thought, that she had provoked a reaction from him. Then her tone changed suddenly as she asked, with friendly curiosity, 'Tell me, do you know Regensburg?'

'I studied there briefly,' he replied, his normally mobile features quite unflinching. He wanted to make it plain that he was not to be drawn. His lips remained set in the same smile and the plump flesh of his face stayed wrinkled with kindly attentiveness, his eyes narrow with concentration. I knew from our conversation on the way to Canterbury that he thought highly of Regensburg, and I wondered why he did not seize the opportunity to communicate his enthusiasm to Domna Cecilia.

'Perhaps you could tell me about your parents,' he said.

'My mother was from a merchant's family,' Cecilia replied, 'one of those who built themselves tall houses. On the top storey of our tower my maternal grandfather stored precious merchandise from the East, and at the height of his power he controlled a small army of men, to protect his goods from robbers and swindlers. Regensburg is, as you know, Brother Thomas, a city where learning and invention are much prized; many famous scholars gather to debate religion and philosophy, and mills have been constructed in the steep valleys of the hills nearby, on the streams which drain into the Danube. This river is the source of the city's wealth, for the ships travel there with goods from distant countries: precious metals from the lands of the pagan Slavs, rare furs from Novgorod which lies in the frozen wastes of the North where the sun never shines, and silk from the misty Eastern lands of Cathay. The trade is so abundant and varied that some say there is no worldly desire the merchants of Regensburg cannot satisfy, if only one has the money to pay.

'My own father was not a merchant but a knight, related to a noble branch of the Welf family. Though he did not bear their name; he boasted that his lineage was even more noble than theirs. He held a fief with a small castle just north of the city, in a village called Salleran. My family's claim to glory before God and man was the chapel they had built and decorated with lovely pictures of the Virgin, Mary Magdalen and Saint Catherine. But to pay for this chapel, my paternal grandfather had run up debts, and the solution was for the eldest son, my father, to take a merchant's daughter as his bride. This was my mother, whose wealth and beauty more than compensated for her obscure lineage. Some were surprised at the match, since in Regensburg, as everywhere else in the world, wealthy merchants look down on those who owe their wealth only to birth, and vice versa. Yet there was more to it, for I am sure my mother and my father married for love, the sort of love of which the troubadours sing.

'My father,' she went on, tilting her head to one side, and half-closing her eyes, as if to evoke his form in her mind's eye, 'was a dreamer, full of fun, and always enthusing about some new plan, like joining a crusade, or else there would be some trading venture which he thought would restore our fortune. Whenever possible he would be off hunting in the forests, and many friends and companions would come to our castle where they would eat and drink until late at night. He would invent endless stories for us when we were children, about quests for treasure or beautiful women, or the Graal. Whenever he told such stories I always conceived of him as the knight, and myself as a young maiden, like Obilot in the Parsifal story, and my mother as the most beautiful woman in the world, radiant with virtue. I realised only later that some of his stories had a hidden meaning, and that they might explain more about his departure to England.

'My father had friends everywhere, amongst nobles and townsfolk, clerics and Jews. He loved the festivals at Regensburg, at Easter, Christmas and Whitsun, when nobles and their people would come from throughout the Empire, and there would be music, dancing, processions and colourful festivities of every kind. I also remember meeting people from Rome, Greece, Hungary, Russia and even brown-skinned men from distant India. Maybe it was from these experiences that I acquired the idea that all men and women are brothers and sisters, and that we have much to learn from one another.

'Many of my father's friends were musicians; some of their names are still famous, and their songs still sung, though they are long since dead. I remember how my father would sing to us too, and he began to teach me the flute, the psaltery, and the fiddle. It was from him that my love of music came. This is a song I have from him.'

In a gentle voice, she sang:

> 'Du bist mîn, ich bin dîn;
> des solt du gewis sîn.
> du bist beslozzen
> in mînem herzen:
> verlorn ist daz sluzzelîn:
> du muost och immer darinne sîn.'*

'I was seven when I saw my father for the last time,' she continued, glancing at Brother Thomas, who was, I could tell, taken by her singing. 'As I said, he was a member, and active supporter, of the Welf family, so when Henry the Lion fell into disgrace, and Bavaria was given into the hands of the Wittelsbachers by the Emperor, he was forced into exile in England.

'My father left my mother and myself behind in Regensburg, though most of our lands were confiscated. Just before he left he talked of a chalice, an old family possession, he told my mother, its origins stretching back to King Solomon, the Kingdom of Jerusalem, perhaps further, to the very beginnings of time. It was rightly his, he said, and it would restore our fortunes, if only he could find it.'

'Did you believe him?' Thomas interrupted. He was clearly interested in this story of the chalice, and my first thought was of the one Domna Cecilia had so ostentatiously placed on display for us. They seem a long while ago now, those days when the great clans of the Staufers and the Welfs vied for supremacy in South Germany, both nurturing ambitions to be sole heirs to the Crown of the Holy Roman Empire.

---

* *You are mine, I am yours/Of that you may be sure;/In my heart/You're locked away,/The key is lost/You'll have to stay. (Anon)*

'At the time I dared hope,' Domna Cecilia replied in answer to Thomas's question. 'We all did. But then hope was soon thwarted, for my grandmother told us the news that my father had died, in the year of Our Lord 1181, in Canterbury. I have not given up my quest to find his grave, Brother Thomas. Perhaps you will be able to help me with this. As to my mother, I recall her clearly in the days after my father's departure. Suddenly she seemed cold, brittle, like a living skeleton beneath a thin covering of skin, with eyes that stared joylessly even if she tried to force a smile for me. It was only a matter of time before she fell ill. Some said she had a fever, but the old Polish doctor who used to visit us had a better word for her state: melancholia. I thought perhaps her heart was broken. Infusions he prescribed, of mugwort, moonwort, buttercup and juniper, only aggravated her condition. I did what I could to comfort her, for I believed there was a better life beyond this, and this thought consoled me. But try as I might, I did not have enough love to give my mother. She died within a year.

'After my parents' death, my grandparents looked after me for a while. But they were growing old and I felt that I was a burden to them. The days I spent on the third floor of their tower-house in the Wahlstreet were endless. I was a quiet girl, not much given to games and the usual things of childhood. It was after my mother's death that the visions first came.'

'What kind of visions?' Thomas interrupted.

Cecilia tilted her head to one side. 'I would imagine that I was able to converse with my dead mother, that she could hear me, and that she appeared to me. Or else I would think I could see the Virgin Mary in her glory, surrounded by unworldly creatures like those depicted in the portal of the Irish monks' church in Regensburg.

'Sometimes too I would look out of the window at passers-by, and it was as if I could see light shining around them, like a rainbow, whose colours each held a special significance.'

'And do you still have these visions?' Thomas interrupted, his voice surprisingly harsh.

'Oh,' said Cecilia, 'I have had many visions. As to whether I believe in them, that is a different matter. In any case, my two pleasures in those days were going to church, and secondly, lessons with Sister Margarete, whom my grandparents paid to teach me the rudiments of Latin. She was from the Mittelmünster, the poorest of the three Benedictine houses for women in the city, but the one at which the ideals of the monastic life were taken most seriously.

'My grandparents, busy, practical people, were quick to understand the inclinations of my spirit, and that life with Sister Margarete at the convent might suit me better than continuing as a hanger-on in a merchant family. When it was proposed that I should go with Sister Margarete, and stay until I was of marriageable age, no one objected. I certainly did not.

'For many young girls, the régime at the Mittelmünster would have been unbearable, for strict reforms had been introduced: we were to attend each office, rising at midnight for Matins; the food was simple, the hours of silence were long and there were few opportunities to leave the Convent. Yet to me, this life was Heaven on earth. I could spend hour after hour lost in reading, improving my Latin, delving into Greek, studying the notation of musical sounds, practising my singing, and meditating on devotional texts. Soon I had mastered most of the books taught for the trivium and quadrivium. My learning was, I suppose, ahead of my years, but I did not realise this at the time. Many of the older nuns mothered me; only a few were unkind on occasions, I suppose because they had grown bitter with life. Amongst the younger nuns, though I was the youngest by far, I found true companionship and a real striving after learning, for there were several at that convent who knew of the writings of Hildegard of Bingen, who had died twenty years or so before, yet whose ideals influenced many convents beyond her own in Rupertsburg.

'It was in those days that I learnt to illuminate manuscripts. The famous Monastery of Prüfening was not far away and as soon as my own gifts became apparent, I was allowed to take instruction from one of the younger monks. His name was Andreas, a tender young man scarcely older than twenty. When we were together I would blush and tremble and when we were apart I would think only of him, my flesh craving his. I discovered how frail a stuff I was made of. I never thought it possible then, for I was very young and untried in the ways of the world, but now I suppose my feelings could well have been reciprocated. He arranged for me to see the magnificent book copied and bound for the Abbess Uta, so precious that it was encased in gold; he taught me how to copy in the style of this book as well as in the newer style Otloh had learnt from the Tegernsee, which brings figures to life, so that they seem to move between the seen and the unseen world. One day Brother Andreas simply disappeared from the Monastery. I was never told why. There was never anything between us.'

'And your visions continued?' Brother Thomas pressed her.

'Ah, Brother Thomas, you are more interested in my visions than my loves. Very well. It was the custom for us to perform music set down by monastics, like Hildegard of Bingen, and the delicate music of the Ambrosian rites favoured at Milan, which we had special dispensation to sing. Sometimes then I would feel like Saint Augustine, who describes how tears streamed down his face at the beauty of music. An older girl I admired, Sister Veronika, often sang solos. She was a quiet, thoughtful young woman with a voice which soared like a bird's in the highest registers, and then could fall suddenly, low, full and sweet, the notes always true, ornamented without excess, seeming to come from a world shimmering with blue and ochre light. One day in the chapel, as I sang the antiphon with the chorus, and other nuns played flutes, psalteries and viols, Sister Veronika's voice leapt high, weaving breathtaking patterns above the other sounds like the lines in the luminous wall paintings of lilies and the Saints, and suddenly I felt myself shaking like a leaf, as if involuntarily resisting a force which I knew was about to break into the childish freshness of my experience. I thought I was surrounded by jagged patterns, like the dog-tooth arch of the vaulting above the chapel, yet these patterns were living, a chrysalis of trembling, wrapping round me like an egg. Then, breaking into my mind like a spiritual memory, I glimpsed the distant glow of an unearthly, blue and starry light shining from somewhere beyond, and this light became a cocoon in which was the form of a woman, singing like Sister Veronika, though she was not the same, for the woman was timelessly beautiful, deep blue and gold light shining from her.'

At this point Cecilia fell silent; fleetingly, in my mind's eye I thought I glimpsed the form she described.

I looked over towards Brother Thomas, wondering what his reaction would be. I saw that the tension had gone from his face, and his eyes gazed towards an indistinct point before him. Suddenly, he shook his head, and there was a look of resentment in his eye, as though he had been unwittingly duped, but his voice remained calm as he prompted her to continue with the words, 'And how did you interpret this vision?'

'At first I was unsure,' Domna Cecilia replied. 'I wondered if it was the blessed Virgin, or Hildegard, or some Saint I could not identify. Or perhaps, I thought, it was my dead mother calling to me.'

'And what did you do about it?' Thomas asked her, firmly now.

'I told the Abbess,' Cecilia replied, smiling broadly. 'She advised due caution regarding such experiences, particularly in view of my youth. I obeyed, of course.'

'And now,' I said. 'You know what the vision was?'

'Oh, yes,' she replied.

'And what do you make of it?'

'I try not to judge,' she smiled. 'That is your job, not mine.' There was a subtle arrogance in her modesty. Clearly, she was throwing out a challenge.

This is where my notes finish for the first day. I remember Domna Cecilia saying that she was tired, and asking if we might continue another time. It was getting late. The autumn sun had set and moonlight was already shining through the window on to Domna Cecilia's face, illuminating it as if she were a statue in a candle-lit church.

I could see that Thomas too was tired. We stood up to take our leave. As we did so, a black cat with staring yellow-green eyes slipped past me, its smooth fur brushing my feet as if with a chemical charge. It kept well clear of Brother Thomas as it crossed the floorboards and jumped on to Cecilia's lap. Thomas was visibly disconcerted by the cat, but he thanked Domna Cecilia most courteously for her hospitality.

We made our way down the dark staircase, past the chalice which seemed to glint, eerily, almost disdainfully, with a light of its own, and out into the bleak streets, beneath a night sky where tawny shreds of clouds raced low and menacing beneath the three-quarter moon, obscuring the stars.

Brother Thomas led the way silently, deep in thought, striding with considerable vigour despite his heavy build.

'Tell me,' he said, 'what did you think of Domna Cecilia, Wilfridus?'

'She sang beautifully and I understood what she meant about her visions.' I stopped myself from going too far and we walked on in silence for a while towards the Eastbridge hospital and the bridge over the Stura. 'Did you deduce anything from what she told us?' I asked.

'She mentioned the Welf family. If she is connected to them, then Frederick, the Holy Roman Emperor, will not be well disposed towards her, since he is a Staufer.'

'But surely she is too poor to be of any concern to the Emperor?'

'She is from the Empire. Her father was noble. Who knows? Great families never forget.'

'And the chalice?' I pressed him, as we huddled in our cloaks against the cold, and continued along Saint Peter's Street and past the silent Jewish quarter, with its opulent stone houses, towards the towers of the Cathedral, which rose above the town like a giant, ghostly reliquary.

'The precious stones with which it is set,' he said slowly and carefully, 'are, I am sure, chalcedony, opal, moonstone, emerald, ruby, topaz, alexandrite, cat's eye, pearl and lapis lazuli.' I was taken aback by the certainty with which he reeled off the list of stones, since neither of us had had time to look that closely at the chalice. Then he said, 'Did you notice anything about the way Domna Cecilia smelt?'

'Smelt?' I repeated. I cast my mind back. I thought of the atmosphere which breathed round her when she spoke, a sense of peace, of wellbeing, so that I had not wanted to leave, even though we had been with her for the greater part of the afternoon. Her scent, when I came to think of it, was not what one normally associates with an old woman. Rather, there was a youthful freshness about her so that, for a moment, in the half-light of the upper room, it was easy to imagine her as she was some forty or so years ago, at the age she described herself in her story. It had something about it of newly mown hay, or linden blossom, a youthful fragrance.

'The way a person smells,' said Brother Thomas since he could see from my face that I understood, 'is always indicative. Anger, lust, godliness, each has its own particular smell.'

'I meant to ask you,' I said. 'Wasn't it Saxon that she spoke to begin with?'

'My dead mother's tongue,' Brother Thomas replied. 'Domna Cecilia could not have known. The gift of tongues has many forms. Only, it is the gift most easily mimicked by the Evil One.'

Chapter Two

THE NEXT MORNING we were to visit the Prior, John of Sittingbourne. I knew of him only what others knew, that he was generous in granting misericords to those who liked to ease their lives with feasting and strong wine, and that he was jealous that the Pope had given the Archbishopric to the austere and unworldly Edmund Rich of Abingdon. John avenged himself by continuing to live lavishly in the magnificent palace whenever Edmund was absent. Before that fateful visit, however, we attended the service for the Feast Day of Dionysius which was celebrated in the Quire of the Cathedral. The awe-inspiring symmetry of William de Sens' building, the exquisitely sung chant, and the incense-filled, dull amber light, transfixed by glimmering red and blue beams from the stained glass, together formed a single essence and reminded me of Domna Cecilia's description of her childhood.

After the service, as we walked out through the cloisters, across the Green Court through leaves which swirled at our feet, past the brewhouse and the bakehouse, whose own fragrance mingled with the homely scent of woodsmoke curling from the town, I saw a beautiful young woman, aged about eighteen, running towards the almonry gate. She wore the clothes of a wealthy townslady and her long black curly hair streamed behind her. I remember this clearly. It was as if I recognised her, even then.

At the Palace, we were welcomed by one of the younger monks who introduced himself as Brother Andrew. He had long eyelashes and that hurt, almost feminine look I had often seen in those favoured by certain men in high office. He led us up the steps beyond the main hall to the Prior's private rooms. The room in which we were received was brilliant with wallhangings embroidered with signs of the Saints and depictions of apes and curious beasts such as are described in the books of the pagan Romans. Prior John himself was a massive man, larger than life, his face and body rippling with fat, but strong and decisive in his gestures. He fiddled with papers on his desk, then looked up, grinning disarmingly, and signalled to us both to sit down.

'So,' he said, addressing me first, 'you must be Brother Wilfridus from the Dominican house in London. You are most welcome. I have heard nothing but good of you. And you,' he said, turning to my master, and fixing him with a penetrating gaze, 'must be Brother Thomas.' Then he picked up a letter from his desk and brandished it saying, 'Well, well. This is what Rufus writes about you. You are learned, having mastered not only Latin and Greek, but also some Arabic and Hebrew. However, you are a religious given to lusts of the flesh, an investigator of the faith of others, yet your own faith is uncertain; and though you are a ministerial, owing strict allegiance to the bureaucracies of Church and court, you would rather be writing your own philosophy, verse and music, if only you had the time, and perhaps talent. Is that correct?'

As he finished reading, the Prior shot me a sideways glance, kindly and conspiratorial. Was he trying to undermine Brother Thomas and win my favour? Was he poking fun at Lord Rufus, the man who supplied Brother Thomas with the legal work which brought us here? I shuffled uneasily, and cast my eyes down. Brother Thomas, however, gave the impression of being unruffled. 'There is some truth in those words,' he said. 'They could apply to many men, and much more is true about me besides.'

'My dear Thomas,' said the Prior, 'your clever answer speaks volumes. Of course, you have studied at the schools in Paris. Do remember though, self-doubt may be a virtue, yet it is rarely appreciated – it reminds others of the emptiness in them. Why, looking at you sitting there, even I might doubt myself! Anyhow, tell me, how are Alyssa and the children?'

I was growing more uncomfortable by the minute. The Prior was playing on one raw nerve after another. 'They were fine,' Brother Thomas said, clearly nervous now, 'when I left them in Ellethamwolde.'

'Good, good,' said the Prior, raising an eyebrow to communicate both that he was a man of the world, and his distaste. 'You are, of course,' he went on, 'perfect for the job of investigating Domna Cecilia. But there has been a complication. At Swiffeld,' he went on, studying Thomas's reaction, 'not far from Dover, there is a Templar house. This morning, our Brother Theodor was found there, dead. His work here at the Priory was to check entries in the rentals, keep the records up to date, and chase up monies owing. That was why he was at Swiffeld, since the Templars' house is on our land – you can imagine what a treacherous lot they are when it comes to paying dues. He was found hanging from a beam, by the feet. He had been gagged; when the gag was removed, they found his mouth had been stuffed with pebbles.'

'How did he die?' Brother Thomas asked, pity and curiosity vying to mould his expression.

'He was hanged by the neck first. They strung him up by the feet afterwards. At least, that is what the Brother said who brought the message. Apparently the pebbles were placed in his mouth only after he died.'

'Do you think the Templars murdered him?' Thomas asked rapidly.

24

'Who knows?' the Prior shrugged. 'Of course, they deny it. Needless to say they will carry out their own investigations. However, I wondered if you would be kind enough to ride out there, perhaps today. I would value your opinion.'

Brother Thomas hesitated, as if making a difficult calculation. Then he nodded slowly, graciously, as if acknowledging that he had no choice. 'Of course,' he said. 'I should be delighted to help in any way I can.'

'I know your immediate concern is our friend, Domna Cecilia,' said the Prior, 'but you cannot be with her every hour of the day.'

'Of course not,' said Thomas. 'We shall leave as soon as horses can be made ready. I am afraid that ours had a rather gruelling time of it yesterday.'

'Brother Andrew, see to it, please,' the Prior commanded the young monk who had shown us in. Smiling at the Prior, but pointedly avoiding our eyes, he turned on his heels and left the room. 'As one who was a Dominican,' the Prior said to Thomas, as if simply to while away the time, and giving no hint that his question might be linked with Brother Thomas's investigations, 'perhaps you could tell me something about this Cathar heresy which has possessed so many people in the regions round Toulouse.'

'Of course,' said Brother Thomas, his eyes lighting up. The various heresies springing up in different lands were much discussed by the clergy in those days and nothing pleased Brother Thomas better than to discourse on the theological distinctions between them. 'The Cathars believe that there is not one God but two – one good, one evil. They believe that the evil god created matter and that the good God is pure spirit, beyond matter. They do not believe, as we do, that this world is redeemable. Rather, they believe that divine souls are trapped in matter by the evil god, that they wander from one living being to another throughout the cycles of life and death. The only hope of release is to become a "perfect one", which is their name for a Cathar Elder. They alone have the right to call God Father. They do not believe that Christ was made flesh, for all flesh is evil. Therefore souls are saved by Christ's message, not by His Death and Resurrection.'

'I know that,' the Prior tutted irritably. I saw Brother Thomas recoil and I wondered if he had fallen into some subtle trap. Certainly, the Prior had gained ascendancy over him, for Thomas's bearing was deferential in a way I had rarely seen before. 'I know the stories about how hard the heresy is to detect and condemn, how their elders act like saints and talk like philosophers. The question is whether you think there is any chance of the heresy taking root in England.'

'I have come across only isolated cases,' Thomas replied. 'Most recant immediately when they realise their error. Generally, the rest are mad; only a few are evil, and they have to be condemned for what they are.'

'Very interesting,' said the Prior. 'Perhaps I should warn you not to be drawn in by Domna Cecilia. In such cases too much sympathy can be a dangerous thing.'

Shortly after Terce, having chosen two aging but serviceable horses from the Priory stables, we set off to Swiffeld via the cattle market, then out along the Dover road past the leper community of Saint Lawrence. As we reached the open countryside on the road towards the town of Bridge and the Elham Valley, Brother Thomas asked, 'What do you make of the Prior?'

'Impressive,' I said, uncertainly. A squall blew in from the sea chasing clouds low overhead.

'The most basic lesson,' said Brother Thomas, 'is that those who burn most bright often have another side to

26

them, a brooding darkness.' He fell silent.

A little later, I asked Brother Thomas to tell me how he knew which jewels were fixed to the stem of the chalice we had seen at Domna Cecilia's house. I have already written that Brother Thomas was intensely interested in occult philosophical systems. As he explained to me, for the first time, how he suspected that the stones which studded Domna Cecilia's chalice would conform to such a system, squawks of sea-gulls taking refuge inland mingled with the cries of the rooks and the crows, filling the skies with a noise like the shrieks of the damned. The system, as I later came to understand it, is based on the following list of correspondences between numbers, the Hebrew alphabet, and precious stones:

0	Aleph	Chalcedony
1	Beth	Mercury, opal, agate
2	Gimel	Moonstone, pearl
3	Daleth	Emerald, turquoise
4	He	Ruby
5	Vau	Topaz
6	Zain	Alexandrite
7	Cheth	Amber
8	Teth	Cat's eye
9	Yod	Pearl, peridot
10	Kaph	Amethyst, lapis lazuli
11	Lamed	Emerald
12	Mem	Beryl, aquamarine
13	Nun	Snakestone
14	Samekh	VITRIOL
15	Ayin	Black diamond
16	Phe	Ruby
17	Tzaddi	Glass, crystal
18	Koph	Pearl
19	Resch	Chrysoleth
20	Schin	Opal
21	Tau	Onyx

I pointed out that there could not possibly have been so many stones on the chalice we saw, but Thomas appeared to ignore my question. So I asked something else. 'Do you suspect that Domna Cecilia is an adept of the occult or that the Prior meant to imply she was a Cathar?'

We had just passed through Barreham, where I now live, though it is hard for me to associate my memories of those days with this place, for they seem to belong to a different world. We were riding past the mounds along the wayside of the chalky road, some great, some small, marking the places where warriors lay buried, from times so long ago that now no one remembers their names. Brother Thomas sighed and shook his head as if he were talking to a complete fool. 'We shall assume nothing until we have evidence,' he said. 'Besides, you should know by now that no one can be an occultist *and* a Cathar. The two are contradictory and incompatible. Occultists see divine systems in matter. Cathars see chaos in matter and think the divine is quite separate, outside and beyond the created world.'

By the time we arrived at Swiffeld it was raining and I was drenched through. The Templar property there consisted of a huddle of buildings set round a chapel. Behind them was an open area where decaying remains of military apparatus, horse jumps and straw men for jousting practice, created an impression of desolation.

The Master, Father Wibert, showed us to the refectory, where we were to join the others for their main meal of the day. Father Wibert was skeletally thin, one eye only shining bright in greeting, for the other was closed over with a growth of skin, so that it looked like the shut eye of a lizard. The other Brothers to whom we were introduced in the shabby hall were old, each deformed in some way: one was hunched double with age, grinning a toothless grin, another was gnarled, like a living mandrake, one was bald and had a vast belly, another had a face so overgrown with hair he looked like a wolf. It was as if time were wreaking revenge on them since they had cheated death in battle. The memory of them still fills me with a cold horror, mingled with pity.

The wind howled as we ate together in the small refectory. The Templars talked about Brother Theodor, whom they professed to love for his yarns about intrigue at the Cathedral Priory. Brother Rainer, the wolf-faced monk, was the one who had found him hanging, since it had been his turn to keep the Matins vigil.

Brother Thomas joined in the talk about Theodor, how tall he was, those powerful eyes, the fierce eyebrows, how carefully he had drawn up lists of the lands, houses and businesses in Canterbury which owed dues to the Cathedral Priory. He mentioned Theodor's passion for cataloguing books in the Cathedral library, his interest in systems drawn up by the Ancients, an interest he, Brother Thomas, shared. As he spoke, and as his words made Brother Theodor's memory vivid, Brother Thomas looked round from one face to another – hoping, I supposed, that some flicker of an eye might betray guilt. I tried to surmise what might be going on in the minds of the Templars, but their faces seemed fixed, as if chiselled in stone, and I could deduce nothing.

Father Wibert described what had happened two evenings ago. They had eaten together just as we were eating, he said. Then, after Compline, Theodor had volunteered to keep the first vigil of the night and the others had gone to bed, just as we soon would. No one had suspected anything until Brother Rainer, who was to relieve Theodor just before Matins, found his corpse hanging from the beam. He called the others immediately. The corpse was laid out; an exorcism was performed and messengers were sent out to inform the appropriate authorities about what had happened. One of these was the Prior.

After the meal, Brother Rainer took us to the chapel. Inside, the walls were bare except for two crude wallpaintings, one of an eagle, and the other, next to it, of a winged angel standing on a crescent moon, surrounded by stars. The rain was still torrential and the wind groaned unabated outside as Brother Rainer showed us first the rope, then the beam from which Theodor's body had been found hanging, and then the corpse itself, which lay on a trestle-table in front of the altar, the rope-burns clearly visible round the feet and the neck. The face was bluish and bloated from the pebbles which had filled it. The pebbles had been removed and were set out on the sill of the window behind the altar in two circles which touched so as to form the Arabic sign for the number eight, or for infinity, depending on the point from which they were viewed.

Immediately, I thought of the occult systems which so interested Brother Thomas, and wondered if there was some message encoded in this arrangement. I watched as he counted them. There were twenty-one stones in total, which I thought curious because such systems are usually based on the number twenty-two. In silence, Brother Thomas gestured that there was a gap in the arrangement of stones in the lower circle, as if one of the stones had been taken away, destroying the symmetry. 'The mouth, Wilfridus,' Thomas said suddenly. 'Perhaps you should look, or feel inside.'

I noticed Brother Rainer recoil, just a little. I shuddered but forced myself to do what Brother Thomas had told me. I tried to move the stiff flesh of the face. The light beard growth felt uncanny against the skin of my fingers. Rigor mortis made it impossible to prise the mouth open further without doing violence to the lips and jaw. Breathing in deeply to quell my nausea, I thrust a finger between the stiff, cracked lips, grazing my skin against the sharp teeth. Under the dry, reptile-like tongue, I found another stone and passed it to Brother Thomas. Smiling with grim satisfaction he placed it at the point in the figure of eight where there was a gap. 'The eleven,' he whispered, as if to me. Brother Rainer overheard, of course. The look of shock and concern in his eyes was unmistakable.

We returned to the main hall, and Thomas interviewed each of the Templars in turn. Each denied any knowledge of why or how Brother Theodor might have been killed. I was impressed by the one-eyed Father Wibert, a Prussian converted to Christianity in early manhood, who spoke flawless Latin and French. When he had finished answering questions about Brother Theodor, he went on to talk about his own youth, and how he lamented having to leave the Holy Land where he had fought alongside King Richard.

The storm still blew as we went to sleep in the room where Brother Theodor was to have slept. While Thomas, for whom a sound sleep was apparently a birthright, lay snoring, I spent an uneasy and wakeful night, wondering if Theodor's ghost might return at any moment to whisper to me of his fate, or if that same fate might await Brother Thomas and myself.

When at last I slept, I dreamt of the beam from which Brother Theodor hung. In my dream it glowed an ochre yellow. Then I was in the Cathedral, but it was filled with weird fruit and peculiar vegetables, as if the stone had burgeoned, and the flagstones were fertile with flowers. In the Nave, pillars were stamen-shaped and wrapped with leaves from which gleaming flowers peeped; the roof's vaulting became the veins of arching ferns, suggesting weirdly arithmetic patterns. I set down these dreams as soon as I woke, which is how I remembered them. At the time, they seemed to hold some prophetic significance, just beyond my grasp.

* * *

Next morning, as a pale, sulphurous sun peered from behind misty clouds, we attended Mass and then Terce with the Templars, who mumbled their way through the offices without music and without enthusiasm. Poor Brother Theodor's corpse was beginning to fill the air with the smell of putrefaction, so it was a relief when, shortly after Terce, three monks and four lay Brothers, who had set off just before dawn, came from the Cathedral Priory with a horse-drawn cart and a coffin, to accompany Brother Theodor to his last resting place in the Cathedral cemetery.

Just before we were to leave, Father Wibert walked up to us, his cape flapping wildly in the wind; he grasped Brother Thomas's arm tightly and said, 'You are sure to suspect us of this killing, but you would be wrong to conclude that we are guilty. Someone will come to you who will explain. Meanwhile, you should go to Isaac the Jew, who lives in the stone house opposite Saint Helen's, on the corner of Hethenmanlane on the other side of the river to the Eastbridge hospital. He will be able to tell you more than I can.'

Despite Father Wibert's words, there was nothing to stop me from drawing the obvious conclusion that the Templars had killed Brother Theodor. As we rode off, I told Brother Thomas what I thought. He merely shook his head and refused to speak, I supposed, because of the presence of the other monks and the biting cold.

We arrived back at the Cathedral Priory in time for the evening meal. I was served food amongst the ordinary monks and their servants whilst, on the high table, Brother Thomas ate in style alongside John of Sittingbourne and other guests richer, more noble, or better connected than I ever hoped to be. As darkness fell outside, the exquisite food and wine, the honeyed smell from the beeswax candles, the guffawing of the monks, the geometric and organic shapes of the stone walls and the vast hearth flickering ochre and gold in the shifting light, fused to create the impression of something alive, engulfing and corrupt.

That night it was my turn to sleep soundly, and I did not hear Brother Thomas come in late.

Chapter Three

THE NEXT MORNING, before we went to see Domna Cecilia, Brother Thomas sent me into town to buy food for breakfast, and it was then that I met Michael for the first time. The weather was much milder than the previous day. The town was already coming to life as I made my way through the winding streets. By the Palace gates servants were sweeping leaves into piles with their long brooms of bound birch twigs, peasants were leading animals to market, traders were setting out their stalls and low in the sky, the morning sun cast long kindly shadows.

Coming towards me, framed in the morning light, was a youngish man, tall and athletic, with strikingly broad shoulders and long curly brown hair. He was dressed like a peasant, in a ragged tunic, baggy breeches and startups (shoes laced at the front with pegs nailed to the soles), which gave him an ungainly appearance. He clutched a small bundle of parchments in an outstretched hand, trying to attract my attention. Canterbury is, of course, crammed with jugglers, hawkers and tinkers, and I would probably have ignored him, had it not been for the brilliant glint in those brown eyes of his, like the colour of autumn leaves, shining youthfully amber from his tanned, bearded and smiling face. 'Brother! Brother!' he called. 'Come here!'

Stopping in spite of myself, I asked him what he wanted, but not as harshly as I would have liked, for there was something disarming, perhaps even comical about his bearing. 'You are the assistant of Brother Thomas, aren't you?' he said.

I was taken aback, not expecting anyone outside the Cathedral precincts to know who I was. 'That is as may be,' I said. 'What do you want of me?'

'You should see these,' he said, ignoring my hostility. He handed me a bundle of some twenty or so pieces of parchment, cut into rectangles, about two inches by four, warm, almost organic to the touch. On each was a peculiar, brightly coloured picture. On one, for example, a fish-like monster snapped at a great wheel; on another was an angel amongst stars, surveying the earth and pouring a fluid from one urn to another; another depicted a horned creature holding two naked men bent and cowered in chains. They reminded me of drawings I had seen amongst Brother Thomas's papers.

I feared however that they might be idolatrous, demonic even, that the mere touch of them might affect me with some spiritual pollution, so as he handed them to me, my hands recoiled and I dropped them, then I watched helplessly as they drifted with an eerie slowness towards the muddy ground. When I looked up I saw that a small crowd had gathered, mostly young, poor people, outsiders, with the same distant stare in their eyes as that of the man who had accosted me. I suppose I feared their reaction, so I bent down to pick up the pieces of parchment, in a higgledy-piggledy order, and I handed them back to the man. He chuckled, and looked round, as if sharing some secret with the others. 'Have you a silver coin?' he asked me.

All I wanted now was to get away, so I handed him a silver penny, though I could ill afford to part with it. Theatrically, he peeled off the top four pictures from the bundle. 'Look!' he said, pointing at each of the cards in turn, and I noticed that, despite his shabby clothes, his hands and fingers were clean and well kept. The first picture showed a noblewoman on a throne, the second was a man hanging from a gallows, the third was a skeleton culling bones, and the fourth was of a girl and boy rising from a tomb, looking towards a sun which bore human features. 'This,' said the young man, 'is what the pictures foretell. First an Empress, but not an Empress of this world. Then, the Hanging Man and the realms of Death. Then Judgment, yours or hers.'

As he spoke, those standing round him began to laugh, whether in sympathy with him, or just to mock me, I did not know.

Angry and unsettled, I strode off, back to our lodgings, but did not tell Brother Thomas about my encounter as we set off past the Jewish quarter and then along Saint Peter's Street, out by the West Gate towards Domna Cecilia's house. The streets of Canterbury were still muddy from recent late-summer showers. The market was in full swing and from the Forum to the West Gate we had to push our way through hordes of pilgrims, hawkers, peasants and dogs. Scents, sweet and acrid, fresh and earthy, shouts, cries, snatches of hymns and bawdy songs mingled with the brilliant swirling colours.

At Domna Cecilia's house we were welcomed again by Alazaïs, who led us upstairs and served us wine, olives, and a delicate sweet dish made of almond butter and juniper. Thomas tried to engage Alazaïs in conversation but she made no attempt to reply. Her silence was disconcerting, so it was a relief when Domna Cecilia joined us.

'Perhaps,' said Thomas, 'you might tell us more about your life at the Convent.'

'What I recall most of those days,' she began, 'is the echoing, bell-like laughter of the younger nuns in the cloisters and the pure lines of the music we sang together, now like angelic voices calling from far away. I wonder what you think, Thomas. If you once experience truth and beauty, and that experience is taken away from you, does something of it remain with you always, to act as a guide and a fixed star, or does its absence make the rest of your life intolerable?

'Those days often come back to me still, for they formed all my better qualities: my knowledge of languages, of music, the philosophy of the Ancients, and the teachings of the Saints. I felt not so much that I was learning, but rather that another world, a truer world, was calling to me, the world of Plato's eternal forms perhaps, or the world in which the souls of the unborn dwell, before they come to earth.'

Thomas raised an eyebrow at this point. 'You believe in Plato's doctrine of eternal forms?' he asked, with an ambiguous warmth of tone in order, I supposed, to catch her out, for Plato's view was essentially pagan.

'Saint Augustine of Hippo,' she replied, 'said the study of grammar is the first step in the passage from material things to immaterial things. What do you think, Thomas? Is music part of the corrupt world of matter, or is it of the eternal world of the spirit?'

Thomas was on familiar territory here, for he loved to discourse on such subjects. But to his credit, he refused to let himself be drawn. He replied, 'That is a difficult question. But it is your views that are our concern. Could it really have been the case that you wished to renounce the world at such a young age?'

'Very much so,' said Cecilia. 'I dreamt I might be granted the strength to follow the example of Saint Aurelia, who hid herself away in a cell above the Andreas Chapel at Regensburg, in order to give herself entirely to her meditations. Alas, it was not to be. I dreamt too of undertaking a journey to the Rhineland, to Rupertsburg, where Hildegard had been Abbess. My old friend, Sister Margarete, had been there, and had known the Abbess Hildegard. Her descriptions of the Rupertsburg Convent took on a life of their own in my mind, melting together to form a beacon, a world shining with the light of a lost Eden. In my imagination, the Rhine Valley glowed emerald green, gold and white with ripe corn; the Rhine itself flowed with the clarity of spiritual waters which, at rare moments of contemplation, refresh the spirit. I imagined the learning to be had at such a convent, studying the mystery of numbers, and their correspondence with music and the movements of the soul. Whenever I had the opportunity to read Virgil and Ovid, or meditate on the resignation of Boethius, as he waited for death, true to his philosophy and his religion, I would always wish to be transported to Hildegard's Convent, for I imagined that there my understanding of such things would be more complete.

'One morning, when I was thirteen, something occurred which gave an intimation of what was to happen later in my life. I was copying the book of the Apocalypse in the scriptorium when I was called to the rooms of the squat, hunchbacked, but urbane Mother Beatrice, the Abbess, whose good sense and concern for her nuns I admired, even if she had little time for flights of fancy or religious excess. She was not alone. One of the priests who used to say Mass for us was there. I was nervous of this man. He was blind, with only a few wisps of white hair on an otherwise bald head. His clothes were white, though he was not a Cistercian. To my shock, as I entered the room, he fell to his knees in front of me, half mumbling and half chanting in a language I did not understand. I felt an irresistible quaking within me. At last he rose, placed his hands on my head, as if in blessing, and said, "Truly, daughter of Jerusalem, one day, the Kingdom will be yours."

'I was too frightened to speak as, slowly, the old man stood up and left us. As soon as I had recovered my composure, I asked the Abbess what he had meant by his strange words but she led me back to the scriptorium where I continued to copy manuscripts in silence. I received no reply.'

'Which year was this?' Thomas interrupted.

'It was 1188; Jerusalem had fallen to Saladin the previous year. Outside the gates of Regensburg, armies were already beginning to gather which were to set off on that ill-fated Crusade with Frederick, our Emperor.

'A week after my encounter with the blind priest, I was called to the Abbess's office. I remember her clearly as she sat on a tall chair behind the massive desk she loved, though it dwarfed her. "I have bad news," she said. "Are you ready? Two days ago, your grandfather died, of a fever. I have only just heard, and the funeral, I fear, has already taken place. You should pray for him. He was a good man and a fine Christian. Be consoled that he is reunited now in Heaven with your grandmother, and others he loved."

' "Why was I not told?" I asked.

' "It was the wish of your closest surviving relative, Lord Stierenfurt. He did not wish to disturb your peace. Not then. Now, though, he has changed his mind. He has a castle near Würzepurc in a village that bears his name. Tomorrow your uncle will take you there in a horse and cart. Just think, my young friend," she repeated, as if this might console me, "a horse and cart! What style!"

' "When will I be returning to Regensburg?" I stammered.

'There was pity in the Abbess's eyes as she said, "I fear that you will not be returning. Lord Stierenfurt will wish to use the remainder of your dowry for its intended purpose. You are young, my dear," said the Abbess, averting her gaze from mine. "It is right that you should know the world before you reject it."

'I did not despair, at first. Indeed, the next Tuesday morning, when the cart driven by one of Stierenfurt's men turned up at the Convent for me, to take me to Franconia, through the rolling forests and vineyards that translucent spring day, I dreamt of a noble life, such as I had heard of in epics and romances. Perhaps some knight might offer me his service, yearn for me, fight for me, and take me to live with him in some splendid castle.

'The manor house at Stierenfurt could not have been further from the castles of my dreams. It was just next to the village of Stierenfurt, on a low hill surrounded by a rough palisade and earthworks, as if an attack were expected at any moment, though there was still peace in the land then. The house consisted of the dilapidated remains of a stone fort, shored up against the elements with brick, wooden planks and local flint. Against these remains a large wooden house was built, likewise in a poor state, and attached to this in turn were numerous ramshackle extensions, outhouses and a makeshift dovecote. The only dignity was lent by a great eagle perched on the top of the stone tower. It flew away at our approach.

'Awaiting me at the house, huddled outside in the drizzle, were people of whom one or two were familiar from my early childhood, but most quite unknown. They were pitiful creatures compared to the lovely companions of my convent days. As they led me into the dark hall where they had just eaten, the rancid, sweaty odour of their bodies mingled with the stale cabbage smell of the soup they had just been eating, and which still bubbled in a great cauldron over the fire in the centre of the room to the right of the entrance. The older men were loud drinkers, or else shuffling wrecks clearly not long for this world. The older women were mostly frightened, sheep-like creatures; only one or two chattered incessantly, spitefully eyeing the others. The younger women stared at me, holding on to their menfolk as though I might cast a spell on them. The men stared at me, some grinning, some with disdain. Their clothes, hands and faces were dirt-stained, and in my clean, monastic clothes, I felt alien, separate and afraid. I suppose I seemed aloof, which would have made matters worse.

'Stierenfurt was fat, short, ugly, and vain. He came up to me, grabbed me from behind with one hand, and lifted up my chin with the other, laughing raucously, and repeating, "Didn't I tell you? Pretty as a picture!" The women looked away in disgust, as though I had brought this humiliation upon myself. The menfolk crowded round to stare at me, but Stierenfurt raised a hand, warding them off, saying, "But not for you, my friends, not for you! With her looks, she will fish out an excellent husband, and play her part in increasing the fortunes of the family. What do you think, Tobias?" He was addressing a painfully thin young man with a spotty face, who was staring nervously, like the rest, but who held himself to one side. "Why, if I were not married myself . . ." Stierenfurt leant over me, and pressed his mouth hard against mine; he had been drinking strong white wine, and his breath reeked of stale meat and onions. His foul lips stank of the decay of the pleasures of this world, a way of life of which I had heard, but never thought to experience.

'From then on, each waking moment was a torment, and my dreams teemed with dark anxieties. I spent my days in a draughty room, on the second floor of one of the low towers in Stierenfurt's house, staring at the swans gliding on the river beyond the palisade, anxious about the constant threat of humiliation, for so often I was paraded in front of Stierenfurt's so-called friends, and forced to serve them drink and food, as Stierenfurt blurted gross comments about my appearance, my virginity, what a joy I would be to bed, and so on. A few decent men would blush, and attempt to defend me, but most would joke lecherously with Stierenfurt, and cause me to feel, despite my prudishness, like a common whore, waiting only for the right price to be named.

'Somehow, I maintained my dignity, but with every breath

I missed the joy, the companionship, the light and the learning at the Regensburg Convent. It would seem to me that the chapel there had been thronging with angels, peering from between the pillars. How I yearned for the hours of silent study, the freedom to roam at will through the thoughts of the Ancients, and the poetry and music of lost ages as I turned the pages of the huge tomes in the scriptorium. I could not understand why my angels had deserted me.

'A curious vision came to me in those days, which then I believed was no more than a product of my melancholic imagination. In the vision I saw myself walking across a field swaying with dusty gold brown wheat, amidst which clover grew and poppies bloomed, whilst roses and myrtle-blossoms glowed in the hedgerows that surrounded the house towards which I was moving. The air was laden with the fragrance of blossoms. Around the house, with its low, sloping roof, butterflies played, radiant flowers entwined and birds darted from gable to gable. Yet, as I entered the cool, dark interior of the house, I felt only the pressure of sadness that this abundance of life was not enough to warm the sick girl who was lying on a low bed in a dark room to the very rear of the house. The sandalwood-shuttered window which looked out over a vegetable garden let in just enough light to pick out the colours in the flowers which decked the walls and simple furniture; the girl's long blonde hair woven with herbs and charms spread over her pillow, and her lips red like a pomegranate gave an appearance of health, though her face was pale and her eyes hollow.

'When the vision first came, I believed that I was seeing my own death. In the vision, I would walk into the room, I would approach the girl, and hold her hand. Sometimes she would return a weak half-smile. Then she would be still, cold to the touch, at peace, dying, and I would weep silently, because I knew that, despite her youth and despite her beauty, she would not stay long in this world. That vision haunted me, Thomas, though I never guessed the hellishness of its implications.

'When Stierenfurt was not there, my domestic duties were light, for his wife, a timid woman, had enough servants, and I spent much time in the bare room where I slept, dreaming, reading, and attempting to pray. Here there was no music other than the songs and hymns I hummed quietly to myself, and no books other than an ill-copied Vulgate Bible, which I found in one of the side rooms, and with which I spent so many hours, that eventually I came to know much of it by heart. In the house there was nothing of any beauty, for Stierenfurt frowned on art, writing and music as frivolous. He was interested only in his lands and animals, disputes with neighbours, exploiting his peasants, and the acquisition of wealth.

'My most persistent suitor was the Junker Tobias; he was about twenty-five and wealthy enough, but horses and falconry were his only topic of conversation. I would blush whenever I saw him and of course Stierenfurt would see in this a reciprocation of the young man's passion.

'I considered running away, back to Regensburg, but I was too proud to risk rejection without a dowry, and began to give up hope. I had not been eating enough anyway, and had grown emaciated. Now I lost my appetite entirely, and drank only a little water each day. No one noticed, of course, until I collapsed with a fever, and was confined to my bed where I was visited by terrifying dreams when I would imagine Tobias, my uncle, and my cousins touching me, forcing me to perform obscene acts.

'Other dreams would come too, when I would float through the air, like a bird through milky-white clouds, or high in the aether above the earth, yet still able to look down on myself, as

I lay on my bed. Or in other dreams I would be in vast libraries, where the study of manuscripts would open fissures in time, through which I would fall into worlds not of the present, but of the past, or of learning, where mathematics, metaphysics, music and poetry would form landscapes more real than the world of matter. Perhaps you have a direct understanding of such experiences?' she asked, staring fixedly at my master. Brother Thomas returned her gaze, and made no response. I admired this, for it would have been a mistake, I thought, either to condemn or condone her, especially when I remembered conversations we had had together about the occasional sense one has of falling through time, when listening to music, or reading the works of the Ancients, sometimes even in prayer.

'For fourteen days,' Domna Cecilia continued, apparently unruffled by the lack of response, 'I was nursed by a girl a little older than myself, called Dorothea, whose father was a noble of similar status to Stierenfurt. She was a ward at the court of Leuchtenfels. I was very fond of her, though there was an important difference between us, since it was no secret that her aim was to find a husband. For that reason, she loved life at the court. Her favourite topic of conversation was a certain Davidus, a rich young knight who was often present there. Poor Dorothea doted on him and described him using words like those one reads in romances.

'She was full of admiration for the lord of that court, the Graf of Leuchtenfels. You have probably not heard of him, Thomas, though he was well known in the land then, a strikingly tall man, stern-looking, very strong.' Cecilia hesitated for a moment, a look of pain clouding her eyes. 'In any case,' she continued, 'Dorothea would tell me about how in his youth he had travelled with the crusading armies to Damascus and fought there; she spoke of his skill as a soldier, and how magnificent the tournaments were

44

that he organised. He and his wife were magnanimous too, always welcoming singers and painters to the court.

'As for the Gräfin, Dorothea described her as a tall, beautiful noblewoman whose skin was pumiced white as snow; she was dedicated to the courtly arts of music, dance, poetry, tapestry and embroidery, of which she had learnt much whilst travelling with her father through North Italy and Aquitaine. She had a cruel side too, Dorothea added. As I lay there, drifting in and out of consciousness, Dorothea's depiction of the court was so vivid that I saw it clearly in my mind's eye, as if glimpsing in advance what would bind me to that place. What must it be, I wondered in my innocence, to love a man of truly noble mind, spirit and bearing?

'To do Stierenfurt credit, introducing me to Dorothea was a clever ruse since her zest for life restored my own. She was not prudish. Unlike my nun friends, she expressed sinful thoughts with such good humour I wondered if life had more to offer than I had imagined. As I recovered, she brought a double-bowed psaltery, and the two of us would sing together music I knew from the Convent, and songs popular at the court, which gave expression to the desires of which we spoke. I was heartbroken when the time came for her to leave, but my strength had returned.

'Another fourteen days passed. Then, quite out of the blue, Stierenfurt called me to him in the main room of the house. To my surprise, I found him grinning from ear to ear. "I can see why you are not interested in Tobias," he said. I felt myself grow rigid with fear, for such conversations would invariably lead to some humiliation for me. "You are right," he went on, surprisingly calm. "You can do much better for yourself than him. I have been talking about you to my friend the Graf of Leuchtenfels. He says that if you wish, you may live at the castle for a while, and seek your fortune. Many a fine knight passes through that court." Stierenfurt winked at me in his coarse way.

'Quick to calculate where my advantage lay, instead of sulking silently, my usual reaction to him, I said, "Uncle, I do understand your good intentions toward me, and I am very grateful to you."

' "So that is settled then," he replied. "The Gräfin is coming tomorrow. We'll just have to see what she thinks of you. Off you go now. I must discuss this with your cousin."

'I left the room, but I overheard him as, turning to his wife and sons, he hissed between clenched teeth the one word, "Hussy!"

'Sure enough, the Gräfin of Leuchtenfels herself and a small entourage arrived the next morning. I rushed out into the green fields beyond the courtyard to welcome them. The Gräfin was riding a splendid white horse. She wore a woollen dress, dyed deep red, with yellow trimming, and embroidered with motifs of roses and hyacinths. Over the dress she wore a cloak lined with ermine and fastened with a clasp fixed with a blood-red ruby. Her hair was long, grey-blonde, and plaited with summer flowers; her bearing was so dignified that she might have been a goddess of love or of nature. She had a guard of six men and a wagon for everything a woman like her might need on such a journey. Riding just behind her, acting as her lady-in-waiting, was my friend Dorothea. I was overjoyed to see her again.

'That afternoon the Gräfin ate with us in Stierenfurt's hall, though it was more like a glorified barn with its scruffy rotting wood and the gaps between the timbers. Stierenfurt behaved like a fool in front of the many guests he had invited from amongst his extended family and other local knights and ladies. He talked incessantly, boasting, dropping names, and causing the company to cringe at his comments about women. The dinner was more distinguished by its quantity than its quality; Stierenfurt stuffed himself and drank too much. I sat there, in silence, not knowing where to look, fearing that Stierenfurt's peasant-like behaviour would spell the end of my hopes of escape. How could the Gräfin ever dream of accepting me at her court on the recommendation of such an oaf? I did not even dare try to catch Dorothea's eye.

'The Gräfin was impeccable throughout, dignified, unruffled, laughing at Stierenfurt's buffoonery, but with no hint of mockery, nor yet of condescension. Her eyes were inscrutable; her sideways glances made me wonder whether she was laughing with Stierenfurt, or at him. There was a certain melancholy about her, which added to her courtly grace, so I wondered what burden of care she must bear with her through the world. I wondered too if it was true what Dorothea had said about her, that she had a side to her that was cruel and ruthless. But I did not dwell on such dark apprehensions, for it was April, and the sky was an azure blue, blossoms bloomed on every twig and birds filled the air with song. The scents on the breeze were a call to freedom and pleasure, pilgrimage and music.

'By the time the conversation turned to me, Stierenfurt was drunk. The theme of his vulgar chatter was what pleasure I might bring to the marriage bed. Sneering, he mentioned too my monastic education and my interest in music. "Charming," said the Gräfin as her lofty gaze fell upon me. "I should love to hear her sing and play."

'Stierenfurt offered excuses, fearing embarrassment, for neither he, nor the members of his family present, had ever heard me sing before. However, Dorothea was quick to fetch the psaltery, and she accompanied me as I sang a love song about the bright rose in bloom, a lover's love, birds singing in the wood, and how, if a woman's lover were to leave her, so would the joys of summer too.

Mich dunket nihts sô guotes   noch sô lobesam
sôdiu liehte rôse   und diu minne mîns man.
diu kleinen vogellîn
diu singent in dem walde: dêst menegem
    herzen liep
mir enkome mîn holder geselle,   ine hân der
    summerwunne niet.*

'As we sang, Stierenfurt, who had drunk too much strong white wine, fell asleep and began snoring. The Gräfin, unperturbed, smiled at us when we had finished, glanced askance at our host, and said, "It seems you have Orpheus's gift. Tell me how you think life at a court such as mine might be conducted?"

'I looked back into those penetrating grey eyes of hers and said, "I would not presume to know, but I have studied the words of the blessed Hildegard, who maintained that the life of an earthly court should reflect that of the Courts of Heaven."

' "Do you know," said the Gräfin, "I used to correspond with the Abbess Hildegard, and I even met her on one or two occasions. That is just the kind of thing she would say." By now I was speechless with astonishment and admiration. The Gräfin leant towards me and whispered, so that the other guests would not be able to hear, "Don't worry, my dear child, you will soon be free from this place."

'All that night, I could scarcely sleep for excitement. Next morning, over breakfast, the Gräfin presented Stieren-furt with an amphora of wine, a gift from the Graf, who remembered my uncle with some affection from times when they had soldiered together. As far as my departure was concerned, that clinched it. Stierenfurt pretended he

---

* *Nothing seems so good to me, or as worthy of praise/As the bright rose, and my lover's love;/The little birds/Which sing in the woods bring joy to many hearts/If my noble lover leaves me, all my summer joy will be gone. (Anon)*

was sorry but anyone could see he was only too pleased to get rid of me. I left that very morning.

'You see, Thomas, how quickly sorrow can turn to joy, and of course vice versa. But then comes the question: which of the two, sorrow or joy, is the true essence of our lives?'

This is where my records end for that day.

Chapter Four

THE NEXT MORNING we had planned to go to the scriptorium in order to look up the rental agreements regarding Domna Cecilia's house, and I was to see if I could find any genealogies which included her family. As we were about to step out of the front door, the lay Brother who ran the lodging house handed us a letter. It was sealed with red wax stamped with the image of a lion, which was Lord Rufus's sign. Brother Thomas grew pale as he read it, and his hands shook as he passed it to me. I still have that letter, so I can reproduce its contents in full:

My dear Thomas,

I trust that you are well and that your investigations of Domna Cecilia are progressing to your satisfaction. I write to pass on instructions from High Authority. For reasons of State, which are and which must remain secret, you are to provide, by whatever means, evidence on the basis of which Domna Cecilia shall be found guilty of heresy, any heresy, so that, if deemed necessary, she can be burnt. Also you are requested to seek out and report on a text called the Hermesis *which you will find either in the library at the Christ Church Priory, or in the scriptorium at Saint Augustine's Monastery. I know you, Thomas, and I know of your faithfulness and loyalty. Therefore I entrust you with these tasks, which you should fulfil with due alacrity,*

Your Rufus.

We both studied the text together. Then, after a lengthy silence, Brother Thomas said, 'Let's eat something. The library can wait.'

Food was often Brother Thomas's first thought when a problem needed solving, or if he was anxious about something, so we walked out into the chilly, empty, early-morning streets. Brother Thomas remained silent as we crossed the Forum. 'What does he mean by the *Hermesis*?' I asked.

'I have heard of it,' he replied. The finality in his tone made me drop the subject immediately. I was aware that his reticence did not stem from ignorance, and I knew better than to press him on the subject of the occult. We reached an inn in Mercery Lane which was just opening for business. It was quite empty, so Brother Thomas led me into it, and we sat in a corner at some distance from the fire, so that we would not be disturbed, and ordered bread, cheese, onions and ale.

'Have you ever seen anyone burn at the stake?' Brother Thomas said, as we ate. I shook my head. 'It is not the custom in England,' he continued. 'Hanging is more usual. I saw burnings during my travels. I recall an old man at Rheims, witty and charming as he was marched across the town square to the pyre before the Cathedral, but who cried like a little boy as soon as the flames were lit at his feet. Then in Cologne there was a young woman accused of heresy, who was dragged by the hair, screaming for mercy; she had all but fainted for fear and exhaustion by the time they had her tied. But as the flames began to burn, her screams were so pitiful that the crowd stopped jeering, and I am sure that many would have run to rescue her but for the soldiers standing guard. She was burnt by what they call the *petit feu*. The executioners are careful that their victim should neither be strangled nor choked by the smoke. Flames lick a long time round the feet and legs, until they are quite black, and the stench of the flesh can be smelt by everyone, including the victim, who is often conscious, and capable of speech, even after the skin of the legs is burnt away.'

I felt my stomach turn. 'Surely there is mercy,' I said, naively perhaps. 'Surely God protects those who do not deserve to suffer.'

Brother Thomas nodded. 'There was a man,' he said, 'who was burnt in front of the great Cathedral at Worms. Calmly, they say, he stated and restated his innocence, praying aloud for his persecutors, rather than for himself, all the way to the stake. His lips moved in prayer even as his skin blistered red; when the flames released the ropes which bound his hands, he raised his arms as if to bless the crowd. Many said he was wrongly accused, that angels came to protect him, and conveyed his soul to Heaven. It is believed by some that a person's indwelling spirits, good or evil, are revealed in the flames as they are parted from the flesh, and the soul of the sufferer is judged, for some utter pitiful cries for forgiveness, and foul obscenities break from the mouths of others, as they rail against their accusers, foaming at the mouth, spitting and grimacing.'

'What of Domna Cecilia?' I interrupted.

It is early days yet,' Thomas sighed. 'We do not need to judge. At this stage we may still stick to the facts. We should ask ourselves why Lord Rufus mentions burning, rather than hanging, and we should bear in mind that they clearly want a public trial and execution, when it would have been easier to have her taken away and killed secretly. Few would have noticed and fewer still would have cared.' I wondered, as Thomas spoke, if he was missing the point, and if the Prior really meant to imply he thought that Domna Cecilia was guilty of heresy.

'There is one element of her story,' I observed, 'that I have difficulty in understanding. I presume that the Graf and

Gräfin of Leuchtenfels were powerful people. Why should they have taken an interest in someone whose position was as lowly as Cecilia's?'

Brother Thomas nodded. 'Logically,' he said, 'the problem has to lie with the premise. Perhaps Domna Cecilia's position was not as lowly as we assume. That would explain their wanting a burning.' I shook my head, unable to follow his train of thought. 'You understand the attraction of burning?' he added.

'I don't see . . .' I began.

'Relics. There are no relics. A public trial, a burning, no relics. It is worth considering. Perhaps,' he said, 'the question is not *who* Domna Cecilia is, but rather who people *think* she is. It would be wise,' he went on, changing the subject, 'if you were to call on Isaac the Jew when we have spent an hour or two in the library.' He gestured vaguely towards the Jewish quarter, in the opposite direction to the Cathedral. 'Isaac is well versed in Canterbury's financial life. He is involved in the running of the Mint and the Exchange. I have come across him a few times via Lord Rufus. If you could arrange for me to visit him, there is a chance he may be helpful to our cause.'

With that, we set off back along Mercery Lane, across the Forum which was quite lively with tradesmen now, and towards the Cathedral where the bell was ringing out to signify that Low Mass was over. We went directly to the Cathedral library, which was reached via the great cloister. It was in a long, narrow hall, and in the semi-obscurity the rows of varnished shelves and cases which divided the area into alcoves seemed to recede into infinity.

Brother Andrew, the Prior's favourite clerk, was there, and he took it upon himself to show me round the library, whilst Brother Thomas got on with seeking out the rentals relating to Domna Cecilia's house. The library was quite remarkable. There were the usual collections of books on the liberal arts, but much more besides. The Greek collection was vast, including many works of the Church Fathers, and there were ancient texts in Hebrew and Chaldean. Other texts were in Saxon, French, Provençal, German, Lombardian and Spanish. Many bore the mark which showed they had once been in the possession of the Knights Templar. Andrew also showed me scrolls on which were odd pictures of eyes, fish, bulls and creatures that were half-man and half-cat. No one, said Brother Andrew, could understand these pictures. In addition there were copies of music from distant parts of the world, using many different kinds of notation, some from as far away as Greece, North Africa and the Lebanon. The sheer quantity of the knowledge was giddying; it left me feeling melancholy, for no human life could be long enough to take in so much. I envied Andrew that he lived in this place and had constant access to these books.

Next, we went together to ask the librarian, Brother Alfred, a squat, elderly monk with a round belly, if he had heard of the *Hermesis*. He shrugged, then made the gesture to indicate that this was a pagan work, putting his hands to his head to look like rabbits' ears and wriggling his mouth and nose. 'I know of the work and we once had a copy,' he said. 'But now it is no longer available.'

'Why is it not available?' Brother Thomas demanded, surprisingly aggressive.

'It was borrowed,' said Alfred.

'By whom?' Thomas snapped. His sudden assumption of authority bore fruit.

'The Prior,' Alfred replied. 'Or someone close to him. There is no point in upsetting such people,' he mumbled.

Thomas shrugged. 'You don't know anything about the book?' he asked Brother Alfred.

'I never read it. Magical mumbo-jumbo, I should imagine.

Nothing suitable for a young man like your friend,' he said, gesturing towards me. 'At his age he should stick to the Gospels. The soul is a precious thing.'

'Really?' said Brother Thomas. Then he turned to me and said, 'Well, Brother Wilfridus, time to look up some genealogies.'

After an hour or so we had discovered that Domna Cecilia's family had indeed once been considered both ancient and noble. Domna Cecilia's real name was Maria-Thea Cecilia von Palviezen. In his papers, the Abbot of Bellapais in Cyprus referred to her as Hildegunde, though this was a code name he took from the old Latin poem 'Waltherius et Hildegunde'. The family claimed direct descent from the Merovingian line, who in turn were thought to descend from the Kings of Jerusalem in Old Testament days. No evidence was provided, and I must say that I was not particularly impressed, since there can hardly be a noble family anywhere in the world which does not pretend that its origins stretch back to King Arthur, or Ancient Greece, or Troy, or the Old Testament.

Shortly before High Mass, Brother Thomas came over to my desk. He showed me a book, which was not the *Hermesis* but which purported to know of its contents. It claimed, for example, that the *Hermesis* described:

> . . . *how the age in which we live is dark, for it is the Age of Kings, an Age built on lies, since the earth and her riches are the heritance of all men and all women. Therefore the Age of Kings will come to an end, and Light and Reason will rule through the Councils of Seven, chosen neither by birth, nor wealth, nor by inheritance, or grace, or favour, but by the men and women for whom they will be responsible. Then there will be no need for nations, nor estates of man, nor ranks, nor differentiation between men and women* . . .

These words shocked me, since they attacked so much that we hold sacred, and I understood why the librarian should have been so cagey about our enquiry.

The rest of the book was nothing more than a shambolic collection of texts by various authors, some on the preaching of de Fiori, and others on numeric systems predicting the Age of the Holy Spirit, the Last Days, and the coming of the Antichrist. Some glosses suggested that perhaps the Antichrist was to be an Emperor of the Holy Roman Empire, implying that Frederick himself might be that wonder-worker. It spoke too of the 'True Empress' who would rule before the coming of the Antichrist.

Thomas and I spent an hour or so studying these writings, shielding our eyes from the morning light which poured in through the window, trying to find a common thread, wondering if there were grounds for anyone to conclude that Domna Cecilia might be this Empress. Yet the texts were vague, and seemed only to contradict one another.

At last the bells rang for High Mass. As we walked together through the cloisters with the other monks Brother Thomas said, 'By the way, I discovered that the house Domna Cecilia lives in belongs to Lord Rufus. It is curious that he never told us this, don't you think? Perhaps he is lending it out to the authorities in order to impress the King.'

I nodded, uncertainly.

After Mass we went to Domna Cecilia's house.

As soon as we arrived, Domna Cecilia told the woman called Alazaïs to serve us food: bread, fruit and salads. The food she brought was typical of what one might expect to find in a southern country, but not in a place like Canterbury. I wondered how they had managed to acquire it. Alazaïs served us, but as usual remained quite silent. Neither she, nor Cecilia, ate with us. When we had finished, Domna

Cecilia continued with her story.

'You have experienced love, Thomas,' were her first words, and I recall that she talked, not as if to an interrogator, but rather to a pupil struggling to grasp an important lesson, 'otherwise you would not be my listener. Women have been burnt, you know, for tempting clerics. But what do you think of love between the sexes? Is it a sign of God's presence in our nature? Are its origins angelic? Or is it a trick of the flesh, of the dark realm of matter, set to ensnare our souls?'

Thomas did not recoil at this, but smiled, holding his head slightly to one side, as if to say that he understood perfectly her attempts to make him comment inappropriately, but that he would not be drawn.

Cecilia returned Thomas's smile, content to let the questions hang in the air. 'I was telling you,' she continued, 'about the day I set off from Stierenfurt to the court at Leuchtenfels. The journey took two days. The sudden joy was overwhelming, to be free from Stierenfurt, from his poor, sheepish wife, from his lecherous, uncouth sons, and to have escaped the endless stream of wine-swilling, vulgar visitors. I shared a horse with Dorothea, and the two of us laughed, chatted and sang as we rode through forest paths and open fields, through tiny hamlets and lonely peasants' dwellings. We breathed in the scents on the warm, spring air, and the blossoms of the trees seemed to fall around us like cascades of future loves. "*Welcome, sweet summer weather,*" we sang. "*The winter was long, and we have had enough of its cold.*"* How dignified and haughty we looked whenever a young man stared at us, and how we laughed and giggled as soon as he was out of earshot.

'That day was so full of joy; only when we stayed the night at an inn near Nuorenberc, a terrible vision came. I heard a

* *Willekomen, sumerweter süeze!/Der winter sî lenge!/Er hat sîner kelte uns benüeget.* (Göli)

droning, a grinding, which filled the night air with dread. Then I looked up and saw the source of the noise: insects like dark, flying crosses, or keys, signifying death, black with massive stings, were everywhere in the sky, large ones moving in relentless straight lines, smaller ones sweeping hither and thither; from the bellies of the large insects, black eggs rained down upon the land, and where they fell, fires burst forth like dark, hellish trees, sucking under-ground people and buildings, churches and city walls, even innocent children, for these eggs contained the seeds of the destruction of the world. Meanwhile, from the smaller insects fires, like lightning, spat forth in streams of flashing light. I thought I had seen a vision of the Last Days, but I told no one of it, not then.

'I was still troubled by the vision when we arrived on the evening of the second day. The castle of Leuchtenfels was magnificent, looming before us against the sunset, flags flying from parapets, noble trees standing guard, and as we came closer still, I saw the crowds of ministerials, knights and ladies, nobly dressed, young and old, coming out to greet us, and then accompany us over the drawbridge to enter the main courtyard.

'The day we arrived was the Feast of Saint George; during the evening meal in the hall, which was decked out with flowers and bunting, I sat with Dorothea, sipping nervously from the soup scented with mallow, picking at guinea fowl and fruit, overwhelmed by the radiance of laughing, smiling people from all walks of life: noble, clerical and peasant. Entertainers came too: jugglers, acrobats and singers, some performing bawdy ballads, and others offering refined courtly songs in the latest fashion, such as I had seen written down, but never imagined I would hear in such company. One sang a song about a girl who says that when she stands alone in her shift, and thinks of a certain knight, then her colour blooms like the rose on the thorn, and her heart is troubled by sad moods:

> 'Swenne ich stân aleine   in mînem hemede,
> und ich gedenke an dich,   ritter edele,
> sô erbluot sich mîn varwe   als der rôse an dem dorne tuot,
> und gewinnet daz herze   vil manigen trûrigen muot.'*

'After the meal, I was led to the Gräfin, whose dress was like that of the Queen of Angels, and who spoke to me in such a charming, courtly way, that I could not imagine there might be any harm in her. Then I was taken to the cosy little room on the second floor of the tower which served as the *kemenate*, or women's quarters, which I was to share with Dorothea and another girl called Lisa.

'The next morning, Dorothea, Lisa and the Gräfin herself explained the work that was to be done in the household: sewing, cleaning and serving food were the basic chores. In addition, we were to supervise the children and catalogue and copy books and parchments stored in the library, for the Graf was an avid collector of manuscripts, even though he had little time to read from them. He was particularly interested in genealogical writings though there were many books on law, philosophy and theology too, as well as poetry from pagan Rome and brand new collections of courtly songs. Needless to say, I devoted many spare moments to that library. The days that followed were long and busy, but I greeted each new task with pleasure. I discovered that I had a gift for teaching the younger girls and boys; even the menial tasks refreshed my mind, and I would reflect on the Gräfin and her high ideals. Stories of the courts of Aquitaine were her model, where music, love and the service of ladies were

---

* *When I stand alone in my shift/And think of you, noble knight,/My colour blooms, like the rose on the thorn/And my heart is troubled by many sad moods (Der von Kürenberc)*

considered the highest virtues.

'My life at Leuchtenfels was, for the first few months, a time of blossoming and happiness. The lessons I had learnt at Regensburg stood me in good stead. I had taken to heart the Abbess Hildegard's writings about the reflection of the divine in the ordering of our worldly lives, how our temporal courts, if filled with music, joy, dancing and learning, might reflect the celestial orders. It even seemed, at times, as though these ideas might become reality. In the Gräfin's private chamber, where the treasure caskets and the finely worked chess sets fashioned out of ivory and gold, quartz and jade were kept, I would sit with her on brightly embroidered cushions, and read copied texts of philosophical works by Hildegard or romances like *Waltherius et Hildegunde* and *Tristan and Isolt*.

'I would teach the Gräfin sacred chants I knew, particularly those in the new style, where two melodies are sung at once in harmony, and we would reflect on the merits of these compared with the old chants, like those we sang at Regensburg, where a single line can be so ornamented, and so subtle in its shape and flow, that greater richness of meaning can be implied than in the sounding of notes together. Meanwhile the Gräfin would teach me courtly songs from Aquitaine by well-known singers like Vidal and Ventadorn, and new German crusading songs like those of Friederich von Husen, who was, alas, soon to meet his death on the Crusade to Jerusalem alongside our Emperor, Barbarossa. Many of these songs I found so stirring that I almost wished I had the powers of a man, so that I too might go on a Crusade to free Jerusalem for Our Lord, and help usher in the Last Days. When I talked to the Gräfin, she would often stare at me with huge, burning eyes, as if there were a secret understanding between us, and she would speak in praise of the Welf, Henry the Lion. Now I know what she must have believed, and why I was so favoured.

'Often, when I was with Dorothea and Lisa, one of the young knights would smile at me, and make it plain by his bearing that he wanted me. I would, of course, greet such attentions with stern and haughty looks. Dorothea and Lisa teased me, saying for example that I would do well to take such a man. "I cannot," I would say, "for I have no dowry to speak of," upon which the other girls would laugh. Then, you see, I was innocent, though I soon learnt to perfume my hair with musk, cloves, muscady nuts and cardamom, and to chew aniseed, fennel, or cumin, to sweeten my breath.

'I realised how many young women really behaved when I found Lisa in floods of tears one evening. She was pregnant. I did not chide her, but behaved coldly towards her. I told Dorothea I could not understand how Lisa could have been so stupid. Far from agreeing with me, Dorothea looked at me, eyes narrow with disdain and said, "You have no idea what love can do." Of course she was right. Poor Lisa was driven from the court and returned to her village in Thuringia. Some said she drowned her baby the moment it was born, and that she was hanged as punishment for this. Others say she went to live in the hills with the wild people.

'Perhaps once or twice in a lifetime, one meets someone who possesses a quality, a nobility, which is not of this world, but seems to come from elsewhere. Such people often have a special understanding of music, or poetry, or love. I once knew such a man, Thomas. I dreamt of him again just the other day; that was one of the ways I knew you were coming, my listener. In the dream, he spoke the words, "Not long now." There was such peace in that dream, and such a terrible awareness of loss when I woke. Now his songs are known throughout the world and few would be surprised that I was drawn to him. Yet then he was a vagrant youth of eighteen, with long unkempt hair, and deep brown eyes, which had a haunting look of yearning.

'The first time I saw him was late one autumn afternoon. We had just been preparing the food for the evening meal. Some of the men had already started drinking and there was quite a crowd in the great hall, chatting about the day's business and the Graf's announcement that he was to organise a tournament, where joy and pleasure would reign supreme, so that the Graf's generosity and nobility would be known for ever.

'Unexpectedly, the Abbot Maximilianus from the nearby Cistercian Abbey turned up. He had with him the young man I just described. He was carrying a fiddle and according to the Abbot Maximilianus he knew a great deal about courtly song. As at most courts, the people are greedy for entertainment, but as soon as they get any, they would rather chat amongst themselves, or find fault. So it was then. The young man sang and played his heart out, but very soon the visiting nobles, townsfolk and servants were laughing and joking, almost drowning him out.

'I was curious, for his voice had depth and resonance to it, yet it was sweet and expressive. He sang a variety of songs, on many subjects from crusades to love. Yet it was his last song that stuck in my mind, a piece that he had composed himself, redolent of sadness and longing for ideal love. I still recall the textures that wove before my mind as he sang, as if I were glimpsing another world through flames flickering like a phoenix, a destiny half grasped, something to do with the gold and brown of autumn leaves, and falling. I tried to catch the Gräfin's eye, for I thought that she had understood. In any case, she graciously thanked the Abbot and the young man, who left the court, apparently dejected. It was months before I saw Walter again, but now and then his voice would come to mind, as though he were already part of me, for this was the only potion needed to make me love him.

'My life at the court of Leuchtenfels soon settled into a pattern,' Cecilia continued. 'I was always busy, working with the Gräfin on some project or other, and I was too naive to see that, as her favourite, I could not expect to enjoy the confidence or sympathy of those who might have become my friends. I lost myself increasingly in the daily round of tasks: sewing and weaving, looking after the younger children, cataloguing works in the library, studying when I could, talking to the Gräfin about the conduct of the court, reading to her, and planning feasts and music for noble visitors. I myself would often sing or play at such occasions.

'Sometimes, during the course of that long winter, rumours about Walter der Ouwe would reach us, that he had taken up the life of a wandering musician, that he had been arrested and imprisoned in Babenberc, and that he had powerful protectors.

'When he did turn up at the court the following year, I was not surprised in the slightest. It seemed the most natural thing in the world. It was a spring day, and the heat cast a curious stillness over the land. I was walking the ramparts of the castle, where I would go in the afternoon for fresh air and views of the bustling town below. Staring into the crowds of those milling around the entrance to the castle, I saw him. His hair was long and knotted, and he wore scruffy clothes, rips and tears in his brown woollen jerkin, and his frayed breeches baggy with wear. He might have cut a ridiculous figure but for the pride of his bearing, and those autumnal brown eyes glinting in the sun from his fine, gaunt features.

'He raised his eyes towards me and smiled, as though we

both knew in advance the drama we were to enact, and were glad, despite the pain that was inevitably to follow. That moment of mutual recognition seemed to last an eternity. At last, the spell was broken; Walter merged again with the crowds and I, as if in a trance, walked slowly down the winding stone steps to the gate, where poor pot-bellied and bald-headed Petrus was on duty. By the time I arrived, Walter had already introduced himself to Petrus, but Petrus was giving him a hard time of it, convinced Walter was just a vagrant. I arrived in time to confirm that Walter had already played once at the court, and that the Gräfin was very taken by his music. I suggested that perhaps the Graf might be pleased at the prospect of some entertainment. Reluctantly, Petrus sent me to the Graf, who was in the middle of some difficult business in the great hall. Fortunately, this meant he welcomed any prospect of diversion.

'I went to fetch Walter, in order to present him to the Graf, and as I accompanied him from the gatehouse, across the yard, past the stables to the keep, Walter's manner was as polished as if he had practised the courtly arts for years: his speech was refined, witty and peppered with Latin phrases, and his comportment was noble and dignified.

'As he entered the hall, I saw Walter look round again with awe, for the walls were splendid with luxuriant tapestries; orchids we had gathered stood in vases on table-tops and chests; meadow flowers and new rushes covered the floor; seats were strewn with delicately embroidered cushions, and there were magnificent shields above the hearth, one of which had been captured by an ancestor of the Graf during the pilgrimage to the Holy Land when Jerusalem was taken. I presented Walter to the Graf, the Gräfin and other nobles. There was an obviousness about that moment too, a tranquillity, as though everyone, including Walter and the Graf, divined the inevitability of what was to follow.

'The Graf asked Walter to sing there and then. Walter began with the last song he had sung so many months before. Deep within me, his voice struck that same resonance, and it cost me some effort not to betray my feelings when the Graf announced that Walter was welcome to stay at the castle, to help with the courtly and military training of the younger pages, the library and, of course, music. Later that day, the Gräfin, other ladies, and I, helped fit Walter with a new set of clothes. From then on he was the object of my every thought and dream; knowledge I had gleaned until then appeared only confusion; anything I saw that was not him, hurt me, and life weighed heavily when he was not there. Yet when I did see him, I would blush and grow pale by turn, for love, when it is unspoken, has a way of declaring itself by painting our faces.

'It is time, Thomas, for us to finish now. I am tired and I am sure you have business to attend to. But before you go, I should like to sing you that song Walter first sang to me.'

A stillness settled in the room. In the fall of her long hair I glimpsed something of the girl Cecilia had once been. The autumn sky over the town beyond her window was a deep, crystal blue and I noticed smoke from townhouse rooftops drifting up through the still air towards clouds which were purple and gold in the light of the low autumn sun. Cecilia stood, slowly, majestically, walked over to a chest next to the hearth, opened it, and took out a fiddle. Sitting down again, and placing the fiddle on her lap, she played the opening notes of a melody, and then accompanied herself, singing in a low, but hauntingly pure voice. The song was a simple declaration of love, in the old style, where the poet says he has chosen his lady for her beauty, and when he looks into her eyes, he has a feeling in his heart as though dawn were breaking.

'Ich han si fur alliu wîp
mir ze vrôwen und ze liebe erkôrn.
minneclîch ist ir der lîp.
sêht, durch daz so hab ich des geswôrn,
daz mir in der welte niht
niemer solde lieber sîn:
al aber si min ouge an siht,
so tagt ez in dem herzen mîn.'*

That is where my records end for that day's interview. We exchanged courteous greetings and walked out of the quiet of her house into the hubbub of the town. Darkness had all but fallen. As we approached the West Gate, I looked up towards the moon and saw a black cat, just like Cecilia's, leaping vigorously from one housetop to the next, just below the constellation of Sagittarius.

---

* *I have chosen her before all women/To be my wife and my love./Everything about her is beautiful./See how I have sworn therefore/That in the whole world/Nothing should ever be dearer to me:/Whenever she looks into my eye/Day breaks in my heart. (Heinrich von Morungen)*

Chapter Five

AFTER MASS, NEXT morning which was sung exquisitely by the monks, Brother Thomas made his way back to the scriptorium. I was to go to Isaac the Jew's house, in order to arrange a time for the two men to meet, but before setting off, I lingered for a while in the Quire. The atmosphere of Canterbury Cathedral was quite different from that of any other I knew. There were times of day when the broad ambulatories round Saint Thomas's tomb bustled with pilgrims. Men and women from each walk of life came, some still dirty from their travels, and others decked out in clothes of the latest fashion, coming to worship at Becket's shrine, chatting excitedly as they queued to lay gifts and offerings to the Saint; yet there were other times, like that morning for example, when the air was filled with an eerie presence, as if the warmth of prayer fought in vain to traverse the beams of cold light which criss-crossed the stern, geometric space.

Leaving the Cathedral I made my way through the cloisters, out through the new gate, across the Forum and then right to the Church of Saint Helen, opposite which was the Jewish quarter and Isaac's house. His was the largest and most impressive dwelling outside the Priory precincts, built of stone and three storeys high, in the latest Italian style, with its own courtyard.

I knocked on the massive wooden door which was opened by a servant, an elderly woman with short dark hair. I explained who I was. She disappeared into the shadowy interior of the house but soon returned, saying that Isaac was willing to see me immediately.

Walking into Isaac's house was like walking into a dream. Though the sun shone through the narrow stone windows, light from bronze lamps danced over luxurious tapestries and rich furniture. Tables, chairs, cupboards and chests were fashioned out of the choicest woods and exquisitely carved with eagles, rams, owls, orbs and sceptres; each object would have been fit for a royal dwelling. Logs burnt in a hearth engraved with floral motifs.

Isaac was sitting at a desk on which were spread charts and tables. They were written in Hebrew script. Since he was a merchant, I assumed these were the tables of his accounts. Isaac was in his early forties then, tall, jovial, his tousled hair already grey. He was dressed plainly enough, his one concession to vanity being the pointed shoes he wore. 'It is very kind of you to call,' he said, standing up to greet me. 'I was just about to pour myself some wine. Now you must join me.' He led me into a small room behind a curtain. Here there were incense burners, charts, statues of gods and goddesses from, I supposed, the ancient world, an immense candle-holder with seven branches studded with rubies, and furniture even more admirable than in the first room.

Wine and bread were brought to us by Isaac's step-daughter, Myrrah. She was seventeen years old and so graceful it took my breath away. She had long curly dark brown hair, which was uncovered, dark eyes, and skin as fine as porcelain. She wore a long loose gown of green silk, tied with a white sash, attached to which was an aumonière of shiny purple silk.

'So, you are the assistant of Brother Thomas?' Isaac asked me. I nodded. 'Have you met Lord Rufus of Alencis yet?'

'No,' I replied, 'but I have heard a fair amount about him from Brother Thomas.'

'I know him because I have a lot to do with the Wardrobe, the King's inner court,' Isaac continued. 'Financial matters. You can't miss Lord Rufus, with his extravagant clothes and his bright red hair. He has a finger in every pie imaginable.'

'Why are you telling me this?' I asked.

Isaac drew his fingers over his short white beard, an habitual gesture of his. 'For Brother Thomas's sake. I know he is close to Lord Rufus, or believes that he is. But he should be careful. This makes him vulnerable. Perhaps you should look out for him.'

'I shall do what I can,' I replied, torn between suspicion and pride that I had apparently been taken into Isaac's confidence. 'Do you work exclusively in financial affairs?' I asked. I noticed Myrrah raise her eyes and smile, kindly enough. I realised that my question was a stupid one.

'It is the only trade permitted us Jews,' Isaac said, with perfect good humour. 'Perhaps you have heard of my fellow moneyer, Benedict, whom they call the "Little Jew"? He once had a grand house in London. That was some thirty years ago. King John confiscated it and gave it to the Earl of Surrey who is still there. Benedict hopes for its return, of course, but I do not hold out much hope. Meanwhile, the two of us run the Exchange which you will have passed on your way here.' There was no bitterness, only humility, in Isaac's voice, and this drew me to him. 'We are fortunate here in Canterbury,' he continued. 'We even have our own synagogue, just behind my house, where my people can pray and settle disputes according to the laws of the land which was taken from us over a thousand years ago.'

'When would it be convenient for Brother Thomas to call?' I asked, not wishing to outstay my welcome.

'Tomorrow at this hour,' he said. 'On his way to Domna Cecilia's house perhaps.' I was bemused, since I had no idea anyone outside the Priory was aware of our investigations. 'I am very fond of Brother Thomas, by the way,' Isaac went on, as if to reassure me. 'He is content to live with questions. He does not snatch at answers.' I found myself smiling back at Isaac, aware of a certain sympathy between us, for this was exactly the quality about Brother Thomas that drew me to him, though I would not have been able to put it so succinctly. Myrrah too gazed up at me, and again I felt a yearning dizziness as I admired the perfection of her face and eyes.

'Yes,' I said, vaguely.

'You will have met the Prior too,' Isaac continued, as if making small talk. 'I know him well. The Jews of Canterbury and the monks of Christ Church have long been close. My father often spoke of the time sixty years ago when Archbishop Baldwin besieged the Priory with the King's soldiers because of the dispute about the proposed college at Hackington. Extraordinary! The Archbishop claimed he disapproved of the monks' luxurious life-style. But the Jews of the city supported the Priory and not the King. They risked their lives smuggling food for the monks. Yet then my father paid over a hundred pounds towards the release of King Richard. Why do you think that was?'

'I really don't know,' I replied, trying to concentrate on his words rather than Myrrah's eyes.

'Perhaps that is something you might reflect on. Brother Thomas speaks highly of you. He regards you as his prize pupil. But we must not detain you any further. I presume, by the way, that you have heard the news about Swiffeld?'

'The murder?' I said, presuming this was what he meant, because it was common knowledge by then.

'Not just that,' he said. 'It seems since then the other Templar Brothers have left. At least, the place is deserted.'

'How do you know this?' I asked, perhaps too forcefully.

'In my position I have to understand the ebb and flow of power. The Templars generally know more than they pretend.

They have access to secret rolls of royal lineages, astrological charts, prophetic texts.' As he spoke, there was a mocking twinkle in his eye. 'However,' he went on, 'their knowledge is often flawed, since they have it at second hand. Ask me again in three days. By then I shall have found out more. Did you look in the lower chapel while you were at Swiffeld?' I shook my head. 'That,' he added, 'is a shame.'

Isaac said nothing more. I glanced towards Myrrah who sat quietly, eyes cast down. For whatever reason, I wished to avoid appearing foolish in front of her, so I did not ask any more questions. I thanked Isaac and Myrrah for their hospitality and took my leave.

I set off towards the Cathedral. Near the church of Saint Mary Bredman, striding towards me amidst the crowds, I saw the man who had told my fortune two days earlier. I had taken him to be a vagabond, so I thought this was just a coincidence, and averted my eyes. Looking round after he had passed, to my bewilderment I realised that he was making for Isaac's house. I saw the heavy oak front door open to him, and he slipped inside. Stronger than curiosity, another feeling came, which I had not experienced before with such irrational vigour: envy. Though I had only ever seen her the once and for so short a time, I was jealous that any handsome young man should be near Myrrah.

As I walked back to the library, and the bells rang out for Sext, Isaac's words about Swiffeld continued to haunt me. I resolved to ride out to Swiffeld that very day. At the Cathedral I looked for Brother Thomas but was unable to find him. One of the monks said he had headed off to Saint Augustine's Monastery and I presumed he was looking for the *Hermesis* there. I left him a message explaining where I was going and why, and I arranged to borrow a horse from the Cathedral stables. I knew it was wrong to act without Brother Thomas's knowledge. Perhaps it was my feelings for

Myrrah that unsettled me, inspiring me to unaccustomed heroics.

As I set out through the cattle market and on past Saint Lawrence's leper colony into the open country, the afternoon sun shone brilliantly and autumn leaves shimmered like golden flames in the afternoon light. My journey to the town of Bridge was uneventful, the road being practically deserted. Beyond Bridge, as I rode through the mists of the wooded valley between Barreham, indeed past the very house where I live now, and Denton, home of the Vaudabon family, I heard behind me the dull pounding of a horse's hoofs. I pressed the pace of my own horse, so that the low sun flickered giddyingly between the bare boughs and through the spiky branches of the trees; rooks squawked, taking to the wing as I passed. The horse I rode was past its prime, and not built for speed. The rider soon caught up and drew alongside me. My heart beat fast for I feared attack from robbers, then it beat faster still as I realised who the rider was: the vagabond fortune-teller whom I had seen enter the house of Isaac the Jew. His clothes were finer now than when I saw him earlier in the day. Perhaps he had changed at Isaac's house. Moreover, the horse he rode was magnificent. I wondered how he came to be in possession of such a noble creature.

However, I was not pleased to see him. His handsome features, and his leonine confidence unnerved me. Besides, I could not account for his desire to interfere with my business. Was his interest rooted in idle curiosity or something more sinister? His words of greeting did not allay my suspicions about him. 'Wilfridus,' he said, 'what a coincidence to find you riding the same road as myself. Perhaps you are on the way to Swiffeld?'

'You believe in coincidences?' I answered coldly. I became aware of crows croaking in the trees above us.

'I was there yesterday,' he said, ignoring my jibe. 'The place is deserted. Not a soul to be seen.' Even as he spoke I felt my neck hair bristle with foreboding. 'If I may accompany you, I know my way round. Perhaps I can help.'

'Very well,' I sighed.

After a lengthy silence, as we rode on through the woods, he pointed towards a path leading to the left. 'The land out that way,' he said, 'belongs to the Ratlings. Aeliz, the wife of old Lord Alan, was cured by Saint Thomas when she drank the water tinged with his blood, even though Lord Alan had been an embittered enemy of Becket during his lifetime.' I did not respond. 'Do you think the barons really are planning a rebellion?' he asked, changing the subject.

'Why?' I replied. 'Are you a rebel?'

'No more or less than you,' he countered. Then he added quietly, 'Of course, some believe that beneath the ebb and flow of worldly power there lie other forces which few understand.' Again I pretended to ignore this pronouncement, though I noted the similarity between the turn of phrase he had used and that of Isaac earlier in the day. After a silence, as we rode deeper into the muddy forest, he said, 'My name is Michael, by the way. You know, the King is coming to Canterbury soon.'

This was the first I had heard of the King's visit, and I was not best pleased to hear it from this man. 'I thought the King was spending the winter at Windsor. How do you know otherwise?' He remained silent. 'Your prophetic powers, perhaps?' I said, trying to provoke him.

He smiled as if to a naughty child. The fine weather was clearly not going to hold. Clouds were rolling in low and fast from the sea. It would not be long before the first downpour of rain. 'It is easy to mock,' he said at last. 'But you have met the Empress. Why would you be riding out to Swiffeld were it not for the Hanging Man?'

We rode on in silence until, at last, we reached the open road sloping down towards Swiffeld. As we approached the Commandery the rain abated a little and I caught a glimpse, through the thin cloud, of the sun on the horizon, a sickly yellow ghost of its former self.

We dismounted and led our horses round the Commandery. There was no chanting from the chapel, no movement, no sign of life – just an uncanny calm beyond the gusting of the wind. We walked first to the empty stables where we tied our horses. Then we went to the living quarters, and the dining hall where the long table and the benches gathered dust in the gloom. The buildings were deserted. The memory of the faces of the Templar Brothers I had met here before was like that of a vapid dream.

Finally, Michael led the way to the chapel. Within, the light was poor because the windows were high and the day was so dull. There was no sign that the offices had been kept, no hymnal or Bible open, no residual scent of incense. We stood there, looking at the tall, dusty pillars, the altar in front of which poor Brother Theodor had been laid out, and the beam from which he had hung. I glanced at Michael; there was a compelling seriousness in his look which reminded me of Cecilia.

'Have you ever heard talk of the Sacred Geometry?' he asked suddenly.

'Of course,' I replied, thinking he meant the numerological theories applied to geometry and architecture most schoolboys learn.

'Then what I have to show you will be of interest.' He said nothing more but led the way to a low door to the west end of the chapel. It opened on to gloomy steps leading downwards. In the crypt the only light came from tiny slit windows at the very top of round arches which rose to just above ground level. Michael took a tallow lamp from behind the altar. When he lit it, shadows danced across the rounded dog-tooth arches carved in the style of the last century. One was decorated with the sign of blindfolded justice and another with a fantastic lion. The crypt's simple symmetry was like the Cathedral's, only squat and in miniature. 'This part of the chapel is only rarely used,' he said, 'for example when new Brothers are admitted, or for special services when dignitaries of the Order visit from abroad.' Next, he gestured to me to follow him behind the altar. He cleared away a layer of dusty straw and withered sunflower heads to reveal a trap door, which he lifted open.

We descended a ladder, one rung at a time; the flame of the lamp lit the chalky walls of the shaft as warm drafts of air rose hellishly from below out of the darkness. At the bottom of the shaft was a large chamber, hollowed out into the chalk. In the middle of the floor were the remains of a fire; the flickering lamplight revealed small piles of charred bones.

Nervously, I bent down to inspect them. The floor of the cave was chalk, and I saw that lines cut into it intersected at the point where the burnt bones lay. Trembling involuntarily, I traced them and discovered, as I had feared, that there were five such piles, equidistant from the centre of the fire, and that the lines formed the diabolical shape of a pentagram. I crossed myself, and pronounced under my breath a prayer of exorcism, to ward off any evil forces which might still linger there.

Two tunnels led away from this chamber, one to the east and another to the west. We peered into the entrance of the tunnel leading westward; its floor reaching down, I thought, to the very bowels of the earth, or to Hell itself. The tallow lamp began to splutter. 'This tunnel leads to Dover,' Michael said as the cold flames danced over his bearded face. 'Some say it was burrowed by former rulers of the land, before the time of Moses. Others say it was burnt into the earth by the fallen angels, when they were driven from Heaven at the beginning of time, when the Devil, in the form of a dragon sweeping the firmament with his tail, and scattering the earth with precious jewels from his forehead, took a third of God's creatures, and entrapped them in flesh. There is nothing here in any case. Perhaps my suspicions are unfounded. We'll try the other tunnel.'

I felt my skin creep. This story of the Devil was from the Apocrypha, and it was favoured by certain heretics. Returning to the central chamber, where the ladder led back up to the crypt, I found myself fascinated and allured by the dark eye of the entrance opposite. 'Would Brother Theodor have known about these tunnels?' I asked Michael.

'Almost certainly,' he said, his voice echoing in the dank, subterranean air. 'Maps are kept in the Cathedral library, and he would have found them sooner or later. It is possible to walk underground the full distance from Dover to Canterbury.'

We crouched to enter the tunnel which led to the east. Michael followed behind, lighting the way with his tallow lamp. We had walked no more than ten paces when an appallingly familiar stench reached us, the stench of death. I looked towards Michael, whose features were taut with foreboding, and walked on, with a sensation of moving through the dark entrails of some vast, fallen creature, until we reached the source of the smell. Hands tied, each in a sitting position, heads slumped grotesquely forward, backward, or lolling to one side, immense gashes in their necks, were the bodies of the Templars; the only ones missing were Father Wibert, and Brother Rainer, the man whose beard grew thick on his face like a wolf's.

Oppressed by the foul air and the horror of the grisly sight, I pushed past Michael, and stumbled back to the main chamber, where the pentagram was cut into the floor. Michael was following close behind me. Numb with terror, I began climbing the ladder into the crypt, then up into the main chapel and out into the open air. I waited for Michael in the gloomy twilight despite the blast of cold wind and freezing rain. I could not face going back in.

When he emerged, Michael looked, as far as I could tell, no less horrified than I was. 'Who could have done such a thing?' I said, the dark wind bearing my voice away towards the copse of jagged trees by the road.

Michael shook his head. 'There were threats,' he began. I had the distinct impression that he was scared of me. 'But perhaps you should return now,' he said, 'and inform the appropriate authorities. I need to carry on towards Dover.'

Only too pleased to have a reason to leave that place, I went to fetch my horse. By the time I returned, Michael had re-entered the chapel. I could see, from the light of the lamp inside, that he was taking something from the leather bag he carried. He held the object, which was long and thin, to his lips. I called to him, against the wind, to say that I was leaving. But the only reply I got was the sound of the flute which he had started to play. I grew suddenly angry, because I thought he was being discourteous, though he probably could not hear me because of the wind.

I rode off, spurring my poor horse furiously, as if speed might drive the sight of the dead Templars and the sound of Michael's flute from my mind. It was only when I reached the high ground and a misty half-moon began to peer through the thin clouds above the tumuli which line the Downs, that I recognised the melody Michael was playing. Cecilia had sung it during the course of my previous visit.

I slowed down a little, my strength draining from me as I reflected on the lives those Templars must have lived: their youth spent in the Holy Lands, the radiant colours of those mysterious places, the terror, vigour and joy of the battles, the wisdom and learning they would have acquired. Those memories were pitifully lost now, never to be retrieved in this world, unless by some miracle of divine intervention.

When I looked up towards the moon, it seemed to glow an uncanny red and, just for a moment, I saw the Prior as a terrifying devil, with wide, red, staring eyes, and metal hooks in his ears and lips, flailing wildly around him and tearing down the fabric of the Cathedral because he could not bear the harmony of its architecture. I had no idea where this image might have come from, but it haunted me each second of my dark journey back to Canterbury. I tried to think of Myrrah's beautiful face to comfort me, but the rest of the journey was a long struggle through gnawing cold, greyness and fatigue.

When I arrived in Canterbury I looked for Brother Thomas, but he was nowhere to be found. Despite the vision of the Prior I had experienced on my way back to Canterbury I asked to see him, and was shown to his brightly lit, tapestry-hung rooms by Brother Andrew who, as ever, was attending him.

The Prior was welcoming at first, and by no means disconcerted as I apologised that Brother Thomas was not with me. 'How good of you to call,' he said. Brother Andrew eyed me with suspicion. 'You know, I don't think I have seen Brother Thomas today either. But my dear Wilfridus, you seem to be in something of a state. Have a goblet of wine and tell me what I can do for you.'

Unctuously, the Prior poured exquisite wine for me into a plain, silver goblet, and I told him what I had just discovered. The smile gradually faded from his face. 'We'll send people out there immediately, of course, and inform the Templar Commandery at Dover. This is an appalling thing to have happened. Who do you think could have been responsible?'

Even then, something about the Prior's reaction made me

feel uneasy. There was shock in it, but no surprise. 'I have no idea,' I said.

'What do you make of your new friend, Michael?' he said, when he had instructed Andreas which monks and lay Brothers should be sent to Swiffeld.

'I would not say that he is my friend,' I insisted, sensing the hostility towards him in the Prior's tone of voice. I went on to tell him how I had come to know Michael.

'How do you think he knew about the murders?' the Prior asked.

'He mentioned rumours,' I replied.

'Nothing more than that?' interrupted the Prior. 'That sounds highly suspicious. If you ask me, the man is implicated somewhere along the line.'

I forced a smile, pretending to admire the Prior for his superior powers of deduction. However, I was certain that Michael could never have been guilty of such a crime. But how, without evidence, was I to convince the Prior of this, particularly since he seemed more intent on accusing Michael than lamenting his Christian Brothers? We continued to discuss the matter, inconclusively, until it was time for Compline. I walked down the stairs with the Prior, then the two of us went our separate ways.

Chapter Six

THE NEXT MORNING, before we went to visit Domna Cecilia, we attended High Mass during which obsequies were said for poor Brother Theodor, who was to be buried directly afterwards. Throughout the service, my mind was drawn to the top of the tall acanthus pillars, to the precise point beneath the north transept from which, some fifty years ago, de Sens had fallen. Time and again, as I sat through the service, my mind would dwell on that fall, and I would see him, now as an autumn leaf, now as a parchment, now as a ghostly figure, tumbling downwards, as if his shade were trying to call to me, to warn me that I should fear becoming involved in the secrets that had killed him. Another thought obsessed me too: Myrrah. For the shape of her lovely face was reflected in each contour and line in the Cathedral where there was grace or beauty.

After Mass we went directly to Domna Cecilia's house.

'I presume,' Domna Cecilia said to Brother Thomas as soon as we were settled, 'that you wish to know why I spoke so much last time about Walter von der Ouwe. Today, I shall explain.

'In those early days at the court we spent much time apart, for while I was busy in the women's quarters, or *kemenate*, Walter had to master such diverse arts as riding, swordsmanship, falconry and archery. He excelled at the latter, for as a boy he had learnt how to make and shoot the kind of bow

80

cut from yew used by the English. However, we did see each other most days, either at meals or in the library, where we would often work together in the evening. Walter had studied at the famous cathedral school in Babenberc until the fire in the year 1185; we talked a great deal about the work of the Abbess Hildegard, whose writings he knew well, and whose ideas he prized above many others. We conversed too about Virgil and Ovid, whom we had both read, and about our ideals of how life at court should be conducted.

'Some afternoons the Gräfin would invite us both to the private rooms above the great hall, where the court's treasures were kept in delicately carved chests, and where the Emperor Barbarossa himself had once been received. When Walter sang there, amongst the opulent tapestries, as the sun shone through the narrow window, so that the light reflected on the dazzling chalices, jewellery and other precious objects displayed round the room, I imagined that I was in Heaven itself. The Gräfin had a large number of musical instruments in that chamber, including rebeks, lyres, flutes, fiddles, lutes, psalteries, harps, and a brand new hurdy-gurdy; I was astonished at the speed with which Walter mastered each, and drew from it something of the same sweetness of tone that was in his voice.

'One afternoon, when Walter had been at the court only a few days, the Gräfin stopped me on the way to the library, and said, "Tell me, what do you think of the new singer?"

'I blushed. How could I tell her that he was all my joy, and all my sorrow? "He sings well," I said. "He is gifted. And learned. But . . ." I struggled to think of something negative to say, "perhaps a little arrogant, above his station."

' "Do you think so?" she said. "Yet you have eyes only for him."

' "And he has eyes only for you," I replied, trying to make light of the situation.

'She was in no mood for banter however. "I am sure," she continued, "I need hardly remind you of your noble birth, and that our aim is to find you a good husband. You would be foolish to throw yourself away on a penniless vagrant, no matter how talented."

' "Of course," I said, casting down my eyes.

' "Besides, we have someone in mind for you."

' "May I ask who?" I said, my quivering voice betraying me.

' "No," she replied. "First I must speak to your uncle. Meanwhile, do be careful of that singer." The last words were delivered with a severity which deterred me from asking more.

'Walter flourished at the court, acquiring the arts of war as completely as those of music and poetry. I knew that many women would have been pleased to take him as a lover, yet I am sure he was unaware how attractive he was, for I never saw him react to the charms of the other ladies, beyond showing them due regard and respect. I suppose this must have infuriated them.

'The two of us often sat together at supper. Our conversation was purled with high-blown ideas: honour, fidelity, moderation, right-living, words which seem tainted now, in our century, but which then shone resplendent like jewels, conjuring a brilliant world of fine-living and of virtue. I suppose I must have seemed very self-righteous, and hopelessly naive. But in those days modesty, innocence even, were praised, by some at least.

'Also, Walter and I would meet in the library after supper, which was in a separate part of the castle, in the vaults beneath the chapel. Though alone, we respected the rule of silence, for whilst reading, thinking and dreaming, we knew a closeness which speech would have shattered. This faculty of sympathy between us was perhaps a closer bonding than the physical act of love, which can entail an ironic separation; throughout the years of our parting, this sympathy never left me, and I suspect the same might have been true for Walter.

'Still, there were moments, in the library, late at night, when I would catch Walter staring at me, and I would experience, with a vivid intensity, stirrings of the flesh. I would wonder if Walter had ever known a woman. It was said that young men at court regularly indulged in such adventures. I believed that he had not done so, and prayed that this should be the case. Sometimes I did imagine bearing children for him, risking my life so doing, for women are justified, I had read, by braving the danger of childbirth, just as men are justified by risking their lives in battle. Walter filled my thoughts, my dreams and my days, for wherever I went, I would see him, in the gardens, the great hall, the chapel. Such ease of access and such innocent love! Can you imagine, Thomas? And so unlike the dark years which followed. It is curious, do you not think, that much of our conversation was about the divine order and the universal harmony which the Abbess Hildegard saw in her visions. Yet the love between us which this talk engendered was the source of so much discord and emptiness. Some say love is like the precious stone alexandrite, glowing green by the true light of day, but red by the covert light of lamps and fires. I am sure you understand this, Thomas.

'One evening, the following spring, as we sat playing chess, applying the new rules whereby the Queen is allowed to move more than one square at a time, Walter talked of a linden tree not far from the castle, a tree which, he said, when stirred by the spring breezes, and with golden sunlight pouring through its leaves, was not like just any tree, but an ideal tree, the pure, platonic idea of what a tree is, perhaps, in the eternal realm. It was, I suppose, with a sense of resignation, a sense of prior knowledge that I stole away, one evening, to meet him there. In the towns and villages on my way, the boys had been out gathering flowers for the girls they wished to marry, and Walter had done the same for me.

'At first we talked, nervously, about the affairs of the day, the news of Henry II of England's lonely death at Chinon, far from his children, who had turned against him. Some whispered that this was a divine punishment for his treatment of Thomas Becket. The bleakness of the spirit of our times weighed on me like a dark sea, whilst Walter, his deep eyes, his gentle speech and his art seemed to offer a more luminous world into which the two of us might escape. With a lyrical melancholy he talked that night about his past, about a Jewish teacher whom he had seen burn, his days studying in Babenberc, a fellow singer killed in a cruel accident, and his ambitions at the court.

'All the time we spoke, and as the sun set, the weather was mild, zephyrs played and myriads of tiny flowers dotted the forest floor. A massive translucent moon rose through the trees and, one by one, stars appeared, as though the angels were lighting their candles. The sky was so clear, and the celestial bodies seemed so perfectly ordered it was almost as though one could see the crystal spheres separating the various realms of the heavens. Walter sang me a song from Aquitaine: 'Can vei la lauzeta mover/De joi sas alas contra.l rai'.*

'We lay together by roses and orchids, near a meadow where watercress grew beside shallow ponds.

'When I had given myself to him, I asked Walter if I was his first. He told me about a girl he once loved, but who had left him inexplicably. I felt torn apart, for I wanted to be his first love, yet I glimpsed a darkness, an emptiness, not beyond him, but within. I felt desperate. Part of me wanted to leave

---

* When I see the lark beating/Its wings for joy against the sun's rays . . .

him, there and then, to have nothing more to do with him. Then I rejoiced that I had sacrificed my innocence to the love I bore him, for I imagined that together we might struggle against the darkness I sensed. A foolish thought, as I know now, but to love him was such sweetness, such joy, Thomas, that even now the memory of it sets me trembling. I felt transported to a world where spring lasts for ever, with its flowing rivers, its bird song, its radiance and heady scents of blossom and new corn, and I weep for gratitude that ever I experienced such joy.

'If only we could have stayed there longer, like Tristan and Isolt in their lovers' grotto, nourished only by love and music, and with the birds of the forests as our servants and musicians. Afterwards, as we lay together, I remember, a nightingale did sing in the tree near us. At last, when the moon was high in the sky, I crept back to the castle, like a guilty thing of night.'

For a while Cecilia fell silent. The autumn sky over the town beyond her window was an infinitely deep blue and I glimpsed smoke from rooftops drifting up through the still air towards the few clouds which were purple and gold in the light of the low autumn sun. Cecilia then stood and walked over to the chest next to the hearth, as she had done before, opened it, and took out the fiddle. This time, she played a slow introduction in the style of the Saracen, until my mind was quite giddy with the swirling patterns conjured by her playing, and then she sang the well-known song about a woman lying for the first time with a man on a bed of grass and flowers, beneath a linden tree, while a nightingale sings above them. Feelings of joy and modesty are uppermost, for the woman does not regret giving herself, but wishes no one else to know, apart from the little bird. I recognised the song as being Walter von der Ouwe's.

Daz er bî mir laege, wessez iemen,
(nu enwelle got!), sô schamt ich mich.
wes er mit mir pflaege, niemer niemen
bevinde daz, wan er und ich,
und ein kleinez vogellîn,
tandaradei,
daz mac wol getriuwe sin*

As she sang I experienced a feeling of falling through time, as though I were present, through the power of the music, that evening so long ago. I looked up nervously towards Brother Thomas, wondering if his reaction had been similar. He was staring, vaguely, as if glimpsing bright scenes in the air in front of him, memories perhaps of his own loves. Alazaïs by contrast sat hunched, head bowed, as if embarrassed or afraid.

When she had finished playing, Domna Cecilia simply placed the fiddle on the table in front of her. Brother Thomas looked up but did not speak, nor did he respond in any way, other than to readjust his sitting position. In the same gentle, lilting Latin, Domna Cecilia resumed her story.

'The winter and spring of that year at Leuchtenfels, the year of Our Lord 1190, were spent preparing for a Whitsun tournament, which was to be the most magnificent in the land. There was much talk of our Emperor's Crusade, and publicly everyone supported him, boasting that they would soon be following him to the Holy Lands.

'Walter and I made the most of the few opportunities we had to be alone together, in the castle, in the town, and in the countryside beyond, for love was both our sickness and

---

* *If anyone knew that he lay with me/(Heaven forbid!) I would be so ashamed;/What he did with me, may no one ever/Know of, apart from him and me/And the little bird/Tandaradei/Who will be true to us. (Walther von der Vogelweide, 'Under der linden')*

86

our physician. Of course I thought no one knew about us. I was so naive. When we met, our talk was mostly of our ideals, of music and religion. We strove to be just excellent friends but despite our best intentions passions of the flesh were irresistible. Perhaps our noble discourse was a mask, but I do not think so. His joys were my delight; my sorrow was his pain.

'I knew how tenuous my position was at court. I had no power over my future. At any moment I might be married off against my will, sent packing back to my uncle, or disgraced. I was no longer at peace with myself. Trivial tasks brought no happiness. My only consolations were music and Walter, for their common essence was not, I believed, of this world, but derived from somewhere above, beyond and at odds with it.

'By spring the oscillation between yearning and despair led to a melancholy which could be dispelled neither by the daily chapel services, nor by any friendship, not even the dance-like comings and goings of the housemartins nesting in the eaves outside my window.

'One day, just before dawn, as I slipped down the stairs from Walter's room, darting from shadow to shadow across the courtyard, I heard footsteps. Someone was coming towards me. I tried to hide, pressing myself against the wall, but it was no good. A giant shadow loomed, and I felt a massive hand placed on my shoulder. I looked up, trembling with fear, into the face of Friderich, the old soldier who kept the night watch. "Oh," he said, "it's you. Come along." He wrapped me in his great cloak which was lined with sable, and led me to my own room. "Don't be afraid," he said. "I understand."

'He told no one about us but selflessly became our love's only friend, helping us pass lovers' messages, diverting attention from meetings, and warning us when the dawn light meant time for another tearful parting. Then he would whisk me down passageways, past stables, and round the back of the kitchen to my room, huddled in his cloak against the cold and chance encounters. In addition to our caresses, and our idealistic talk, Walter and I would invent songs about our love and our plight, including some about Friderich, who was such a good friend to us, warning us when dawn was about to break, or if there was any danger. Some of these songs are still well known, though no one knows how they came into being.

> Owê, sul aber er iemer mê
> den morgen hie betagen?
> als uns diu nâht engê,
> daz wir niht durfen klagen:
> 'owê, nu ist ez tac',
> als er mit klage pflac,
> do er jungest bî mir lac,
> nun tâget ez.*

'The preparations for the tournament,' she continued, 'were difficult and time-consuming. The Graf had invited so many guests they could not be accommodated in the castle, so tents were set up outside the walls, tents of many different colours with bright buntings, each corresponding to the arms of the noble house to occupy them. The mêlée was to be the climax of the festival, and it was to take place on the Monday, in accordance with the Truce of God still valid then, which forbade fighting from Tuesday until Sunday. But from the Wednesday when the guests were to arrive, until the following Tuesday when they were to leave, there were to be displays of arms, extravagant banquets, open air Masses

---

*   Oh, woe, will he forever more/Have to wait for morning?/If only night would stay here/To save us from moaning,/'Oh, woe, the day is breaking':/These were his words/As he lay beside me,/Now the day is here. (Heinrich von Morungen)

organised by Bishop Otto himself, and of course much singing and dancing.

'Walter composed many songs for the banquet and the two of us practised them together. These were perhaps our closest moments together, the communion of music being more intense than fleshly coupling. We were foolishly optimistic, daring to believe that this tournament would be the making of us both, that Walter would distinguish himself in some way, either as a musician, or in the jousting, like Gahmaret, Parsifal or Lancelot in days gone by, that he would gain a title, some land perhaps, and that then I would be his wife.

'On the Tuesday before Pentecost in the year of Our Lord 1190, the guests finally began to arrive. I served at the banquet. The next morning I was to practise music with the Gräfin in her private chamber. However, we were not alone as usual. In the room with us was one of the most massive men I had ever seen. He had a great, unkempt beard, a balding, wrinkled head and shoulders like an ox's. His clothes were those of a knight, but they were dirty because he had been exercising since the early hours in preparation for displays of arms and the mêlée. Neither he nor the Gräfin offered any explanation for his presence, and it was not my place to ask. The man eyed me leeringly as I sang, smiling with a mouth from which half the teeth had been knocked out, and the rest were a detestable yellow.

'At last he stood up, thanked the Gräfin in a gruff voice, but courteously enough; he took my hand, and tried to draw me to him. His hand was gnarled and rough, and I started back. He had firm hold of me, and he would certainly have pressed his mouth against mine if the Gräfin had not shot him a stern look. The man left, grinning, and I was about to express my outrage when I saw that the Gräfin's face was aglow not with shock, but with pleasure.

' "Well," she said, "he does seem to like you."

' "Who is he?" I asked, feeling the blood drain from my face.

' "If you are very lucky," she said, "your future husband."

' "Does he always treat women like that?"

' "Most far worse, I dare say. He is a hardened fighter. The number of battles in which he has excelled, throughout the Empire, Spain and the Holy Land, are countless. And you know what such soldiers are like with women. But he has acquired admirable wealth, and whoever marries him will be able to count herself more than fortunate. Besides, perhaps he has a gentle side, which you will be able to cultivate. If not, then you might reflect on the words of Our Lord, that those who live by the sword, die by the sword. It will not be long before you are a wealthy and sought-after widow." There was a cruel ring to her voice, as though she knew the devastation her words would wreak. I still hoped against hope that the Gräfin was my friend, but then she said, "By the way, you know young Walter has written a song about a linden tree?"

'I knew nothing of the song, not then, but a vicious glint in her eye, and the memory of the evening with Walter when we became lovers, froze me with foreboding. This was her way of telling me she knew about us, and that she would act against us.

'During the course of one of our last meetings before Whitsunday, Walter confided to me he suspected that many of those present were in fact supporters of the Welf, Henry the Lion, and that the tournament was a secret rallying point for them. Because of my father's sympathies, I did not flinch at this. Besides, the machinations of the great ones seemed to take place in spheres an infinite distance above those in which I moved. I did not suspect how much my father's allegiance, and his claims about himself, had bound me to

90

the Welf cause, and the difficulties a match between myself and Walter might therefore cause. Meanwhile, of course, no one could have guessed that within a month the Emperor Barbarossa would be dead, drowned in the River Salef, beyond the Taurus Mountains.

'I tried to put the conversation with the Gräfin from my mind, but that evening my worst fears were confirmed. I had just finished serving the soup and meat in the massive tent in front of the castle. The weather was hot and still, the night clear and starry. The sweet smell of the horses stabled across the courtyard mingled with the succulent odours of food and the perfumes the women wore. How nobly the women were dressed, and how gallantly the men behaved towards them. That festival might have been Heaven on earth for one like me, but my thoughts were set on Walter and the hopelessness of our love.

'Soon, it would be my turn to sing, and I was about to withdraw to the women's quarters in order to fetch my fiddle and prepare mentally, for the quiet courtliness of the songs I performed required my full concentration if I was to gain the guests' attention over the hubbub, the chit-chat about horses, jousts, tournaments and love-matches.

'Just as I was about to leave, the Graf, who wore a silk cloak lined with marten fur and embroidered with gold, stood up and rapped the table with a chain-mail gloved hand to bring the company to silence. "On Monday," he announced, "there will be a joust followed by a full mêlée. All men over the age of fourteen are invited to participate. There will be two parties. Mine will be led by Walter von der Ouwe, and the other by Johannes of Ulm. These two men will open the conflict with a joust. May God give joy to those who fight nobly!"

'Everyone stood to cheer at this. Walter was borne up on the shoulders of his grooms, who idolised him; Johannes stood on a chest, and bellowed that all fine drinkers should fight on his side. Only I stared on in horror mingled with foreboding, for Johannes of Ulm was the massive, bearded, bear-like man who had tried to kiss me in front of the Gräfin. Walter would be no match for this seasoned warrior. I sensed some deeper purpose to this announcement, and feared for Walter's life.

'I have no idea how I managed to sing that night. I kept glancing at Walter and von Ulm who were sitting next to each other. Von Ulm had his arm round Walter's shoulders; as I sang, the two of them stared at me, nudging one another like old drinking companions. I wondered if each knew the claim the other had on me. Yet I was relieved. Walter was just like Tristan, for he had a way of charming all men, even very rough military men. When I had finished singing, I saw Johannes slap Walter on the back in a gesture of friendship, so hard that he knocked the wind out of him. As soon as he could breathe again, Walter joined in the laughter. I should have felt relief at their comradeship, but I was close to tears.

'By the Saturday, I was so overwhelmed with the oppressive feeling that I was already living in my own past, that I took to avoiding Walter. Perhaps I was hoping to reconcile myself in advance to the void about to overshadow my life. To poor Walter, I must have appeared hurtfully aloof. Those days were an endless torment, serving, smiling, singing, fending off would-be admirers, sick at heart and dizzy with heat and foreboding.

'At last, on the final Sunday, there was a grand procession through the town after the Whitsun Mass. Noblemen and noblewomen had come from throughout the Empire. The weather was warm and the sun shone brilliantly, but when the Gräfin or one of her entourage pointed out such and such a knight because of his looks or to recount his exploits in battle, or if someone singled out the finery worn by a lady,

I was so distracted that I understood nothing, not even jibes aimed at me.

'The first part of the afternoon was given over to displays of horsemanship and weaponry (no fighting because of the truce), and towards the end of the afternoon the nobles rode out with falcons. At last the time came for the great banquet, the last before the mêlée on the Monday.

'I watched the men carefully. There was Walter, smiling and charming as ever as they returned from the hunt. I served at the feast, special dishes from the East: dates, pistachios, apricots, shallots which come from the land of Ascalon, lozenge-shaped sweets made of ground almonds, and dried fruits perfumed with rose water, aniseed and ginger; then there was partridge, pheasant, pigeon, boar, venison, every kind of vegetable, sauces containing the rarest of spices, and fruit from many different lands, some oddly shaped and with a curious bitter-sweet taste. I was possessed by a feverish dizziness and realised, too late, that I had eaten very little over the previous few days, despite the fact that I had spent much time preparing and serving food for others. I ate a little then but the food was so rich it turned my stomach; it was tainted, I thought, with the sickness of this world.

'When the guests had eaten and drunk their fill, the Graf announced that Walter would sing, and the people fell silent, for Walter's music was much praised, and since he was to lead the mêlée the following day, many were eager to hear him, in case it should be for the last time.

'I was already unsteady on my feet and shaky with tiredness as Walter embarked on his usual repertoire. Then, smiling at me, for everyone to see, eyes gleaming with love and hope, he began to sing the "Under der linden" song, the last verse of which I sang to you earlier. It was the first time I had heard it.

'The beauty of Walter's singing, the evocative power of the

words and the sweetness of the melody brought back to me that evening of our first love, the linden tree, the stars, and that darkness which still possessed me, so vividly, with all the yearning and irreparability of our love, that I stood stock still, forgetting who I was and where. Then the tent and everything in it began, slowly, to spin; there was a rushing sound as golden, ochre and brown textures twisted, like a whirling eddy of autumn leaves, or the brushing of an angel's wing, and then there was blackness as I fell into a dead faint. The last thing I remember was looking at the Gräfin whose features seemed to grow suddenly old in the light glinting from the cat's-eye stone of her brooch.'

By then, it was almost dark outside and Alazaïs was lighting the tallow lamps. Just for a moment, the deep blue light in the room pulsed with the textures of the scenes Cecilia had described. Her cat jumped up and settled in her lap.

After a lengthy silence, we took our leave and set off towards the Cathedral.

We had just left the Jewish quarter to enter Mercery Lane when I heard someone call Brother Thomas's name in a deep, hissing voice. At the same time, I felt something touch my shoulder. I started and glanced round to see a bony hand resting there. Turning fully, I found myself staring into a pair of fierce, piercing eyes, blue like lapis lazuli, set in a face thick with hair, like a wolf's. The man seemed ready to spring at me at any moment. Shocked, I realised it was Brother Rainer, one of the Templars from Swiffeld, the one who had discovered Theodor's body, but who himself had not been found amongst those killed later.

'You just be quiet and listen, young man,' he said to me. I was transfixed by his cold, blue eyes. There was a sneer in his voice as, turning to my master, he said, 'I have words only for you Brother Thomas. *Do not forget the eyes of the Assassin. We know where your woman and your children are. Domna Cecilia must be spared. Do not forget the eyes of the Assassin . . .'* Suddenly the old Templar burst out with a cackle of cruel laughter, and pushed me backwards, so that I almost knocked Brother Thomas over. Before I had recovered my balance, the man had darted off into an alley.

I started to run after him, towards the High Street. 'Take no notice,' I heard Brother Thomas call behind me. 'Besides, you will never catch him.'

That was true enough, for the Templar seemed to have vanished into thin air. 'But you heard what he said about your wife and children,' I protested.

'There is nothing we can do,' said Brother Thomas. 'Not at this hour. Let us sleep.'

We emerged from the dark street into the Forum. The silver and grey Cathedral towered against the deep, dark sky which was the colour of amethyst. We returned to our lodgings. Brother Thomas was oddly still. I tried to convince myself that the Templar's behaviour was merely deranged. Yet his words echoed in my mind, gnawing like acid, and the memory of his fierce, deep eyes would not leave me.

'We should report this to the Prior,' I said to Brother Thomas as we settled down to sleep.

'What good will that do?' he asked patiently.

'Brother Rainer should be treated as a murder suspect. You heard how he threatened your family.'

'That, surely, is reason enough to be careful of the Prior too.'

I lay awake wondering how Brother Thomas was able to keep so calm about Rainer's threats. Eventually, I fell into a deep sleep, but when I woke next morning, it was to find that Brother Thomas had gone. He left a note asking me to continue the investigations as best I could. He, meanwhile, had set off to Ellethamwolde to make sure that Alyssa and the children were unharmed.

Chapter Seven

I T FELT ODD to be on my own, and I was very worried about Brother Thomas and his family, since they were my dear friends. Nonetheless after Mass I set off to the library and read all the archives and journals I could lay my hands on relating to the years leading up to the death of William de Sens: the death of Becket, the siege, and the great fire in 1174 which made necessary the rebuilding of the Cathedral Quire. I studied de Sens' plans, and his book which explains the number relationships he used. He claimed these patterns were present both in living things and beyond this world too in the uncreated world. Central to the pattern was the number twenty-two. I attended the Cathedral offices with the other Brothers, staring round me in wonder at the magnificence of the architecture, as its mysteries began to unfold.

I remember distinctly how, just after Sext, as I worked in the library, lost in thought and wonder at the breadth of de Sens' vision, I felt a light touch on my shoulder, then a quiet, gently accented voice close to my ear whispered, 'Perhaps this is what you are looking for.' A musk-like scent breathed round me as I turned and found myself looking into a pair of wide brown eyes. The young woman was wearing a hooded overcoat which hid her hair and her figure so that, from a distance, she could have passed for a young man. She placed a book on the desk in front of me, smiled kindly, and raised a finger to her lips to signify that I should neither speak, nor make any attempt to follow her.

I was sure it was Myrrah, though ever since she has always denied being in that library, and my memory of that moment certainly has the quality of a dream. I was about to run after her but then I saw that the book she had placed in front of me was the *Hermesis*. I began studying it, and was entranced by the tables of correspondences it contained, between heavenly creatures, the stars, animals, plants, metals, the human body and the ages of man. At the end of the text were tables of genealogies which I was just about to study when the bells rang for Nones. I attended that office, my mind swirling with the patterns I had glimpsed in the text, and with an irresistible yearning for Myrrah. I might have resisted the charms of her physical body, or of her spirit, in isolation. But to sense the two in one, how could I have stopped myself from loving her? Or was I in the thrall of a dream, or some other insubstantial power? For when I returned from the Cathedral, the text was gone. The librarian insisted that the *Hermesis* was not in the library, and that no one had entered the library at the time I was convinced I had seen Myrrah.

I spent the whole of the rest of the evening and the next day in the library, reading whatever I could find, hoping against hope that the *Hermesis* would reappear. I learnt a great deal, but everything seemed disconnected, and by Compline on the second day, my mind was in turmoil. Even as we processed out of the Cathedral, I knew I would not sleep if I went to bed, so I slipped out of the precincts to drink at the inn where I had been with Brother Thomas. My excuse to myself was that I might catch sight of Brother Rainer, the Templar Brother who had threatened Thomas. I suppose I must have spent about an hour there before setting off with the intention of returning to my lodgings.

I was about to cross the Forum, which was deserted but for a few drunks and poor folk, some asleep, others staring with pleading, fearful eyes, huddled in alleyways where the wind bit less fiercely, when I saw a couple walking towards the new Priory gate. For a moment I thought it was my obsessive and amorous mind that made me believe that the young woman was Myrrah. Then, from the way she moved and the shape of her shadow against the Priory wall, I became increasingly convinced that it was her. Moreover, her companion had long curly hair and wore a large cloak with a fur collar. I was certain that this was Michael.

Again the sequence of events is like a dream. No one attempts to stop them as they walk through the gate towards the massive Cathedral brooding against the sky like a great bird of prey. I follow them into the Precincts and see Michael and Myrrah's shadowy forms move along the wall of the monks' graveyard towards the campanile, then thread their way through the shadows of the windswept cemetery like spirits of the night, darting and gliding, imperceptible unless one knows they are there. Reaching the wall of the Cathedral, they enter the North Stair Tower, one of those still remaining after the great fire and the rebuilding some fifty years previously.

Uncertainly, I follow, speculating wildly about their intentions. A part of my mind is feverish with jealousy, perceiving this as some perverse lovers' tryst. Then I imagine they are on their way to a secret meeting with one of the Brothers, or perhaps even the Prior himself. But to what purpose? And again, why a wealthy Jewess, and a man who is, as far as I can tell, little more than a tramp?

In the gloomy, geometric silence of the dark Cathedral I wait for a while at the bottom of the tower. The movement of dark shadows behind its narrow windows betrays that they have reached the level of the old council chamber, with its flaking wall paintings, in disuse since the fire. I hesitate, myself keeping to the shadows, so that they will not see me, and I stare hard at the small windows of the tower, thinking about William de Sens, what further secrets he might have built into the numerology of the Cathedral's construction, wondering why he left this tower intact, whilst most of the rest of the Quire had been demolished. I think about Michael and Myrrah huddled together on that dark stairwell.

At last, there are signs of movement in the Cathedral. The first monks are starting to gather for Matins, the office, loved by some and cursed by others, which every night interrupts our sleep, but which guarantees and symbolises the continuity of prayer and the quest for light through the darkest of hours. I wait for the monks to file past and follow them into the Quire, taking up position in my allotted stall, from which I can just see the South Tower. Tensely gripping the wood of my lectern I follow the service, looking round to see if any of the Brothers might, for some reason, be eyeing me suspiciously as I check the tower where I know Michael and Myrrah are hiding in case there are signs of movement. The monks seem sleepy and bleary-eyed except the Prior, whose eyes gleam in the candle-light. On two occasions I am so sure that he is staring quite deliberately at me, that I avert my own eyes. There is no sign of Michael or Myrrah.

By the end of the office I have decided what to do. I make sure that I am amongst the last of the Brothers to process out of the Cathedral. Just before we reach the door leading to the cloisters I turn left into the shadows of the Nave, walking quite normally, and head into the shadows. As I hoped, no one challenges me as I take up position in the darkest corner from which I still have a view of the tower and the door through which I saw Michael and Myrrah enter. My excuse, that I am undertaking a private act of penance by keeping an all-night vigil, is not needed. The Brothers with whom I exited are too sleepy to notice me.

As soon as I am convinced that the Cathedral is deserted I

make my way back into the Quire towards the South Tower, and slip through the door, determined to confront Michael and Myrrah directly. I decide that if there is a good reason for their presence I will not report them to the Prior. Otherwise, I will have no choice. Step by step, I make my way up to the old council chamber. I push at the door which creaks on its hinges. There is just enough light from the moon outside for my eyes to make out the charred walls, the flaking remains of the wall paintings, and the few sticks of furniture. Otherwise, the chamber is quite deserted. Then I hear the sound of feet scuffling on the stairs above me.

I return to the staircase of the tower and follow the sounds spiralling upwards through the chilly darkness towards the passageway leading into the gallery, some fifty feet high, which looks over the main part of the Quire. There is no sign of Michael or Myrrah, and I begin to wonder if their phantom-like presence is not just a product of my jealous imagination.

I have reached the dark corridor now and, head crouched forward, feel my way along with both hands. Suddenly, the wall to my left seems to melt away, my feet slip on the smooth stone and I feel myself keeling over towards the warm, dark void, hands flailing. I have reached the point where the passage opens out into the triforium gallery. The magnificent forms of the Quire below begin twisting towards me, blue-grey and lethally geometric in the dim moonlight. Just opposite is the point from which William de Sens fell sixty years before. For a moment I imagine myself plummeting, just like him, through the emptiness, turning over and over in the void until that final thud, followed by nerve-racking pain. But just as I am about to fall, I grab hold of a pillar, regain my footing, and steady myself.

Shaken, I am about to give up hope, but then, through the darkness, on the opposite side of the Quire, I see, just for a split second, shadows move along the gallery, heading towards the staircase leading downwards. They must have followed the horseshoe of the Corona above Saint Thomas's shrine, where the treasures offered to the Saint glint in the dull light like trophies of forgotten battles. I feel vulnerable, frightened and giddy as I make my way round. When I reach the other side, it is a relief to exchange that uncanny light for the dusty, stone-scented blackness of the North Tower stairwell which Michael and Myrrah must have descended just a few minutes before me.

I reach the exit to the Quire, on ground level, where the door is ajar. But this staircase leads down further into the Crypt. I choose to continue the descent. My decision is rewarded by a faint glow of light and the murmur of an unfamiliar chant rising through the chill, dark air towards me. I expect, any moment, to brush into Michael and Myrrah. There is a faint scent in the air which at first I take to be hers, but then recognise to be the burning of incense.

I emerge into the main part of the Crypt where the statue of the Madonna stands. I look round. Everything is quite deserted. There is an indistinct ochre light gleaming from just in front of the altar which is situated at the very east end of the Cathedral, below the Corona. At last I recognise the chant, which is that of the Rite of Milan, the rich and ornate Ambrosian line with which Cecilia claimed familiarity from her childhood days.

I make my way silently from pillar to pillar until I reach the altar of the Madonna. Here I crouch and look through the small windows at the back of the tomb into the East Crypt, its massive, sternly symmetrical pillars supporting the whole weight of the Corona above. Standing in a semi-circle in the centre of the Crypt are five men wearing green chasubles over white robes, and a further two, lay Brothers in the usual grey habits. The men in green each wear silver chains round their necks, but they are hung, not with crosses as pendants, but interlocking rings, one silver, one gold. I recognise three of the men. There is Prior John, Brother Andrew, his favourite clerk, and Father Wibert, the Templar whose corpse had not been found amongst the others at Swiffeld. I do not recognise the other two men in green.

The two men dressed as lay Brothers are holding crowbars, ropes and winches. I realise that the men are standing round a hole in the floor. Flagstones have been removed and next to the hole lies something dull brown, green and grey: a lead coffin. The Prior, who has been leading the chanting, which I now recognise from the words to be a rite of exorcism used when opening the tombs of the dead, stops singing and nods to the two lay Brothers. They step forward, take a crowbar each, force the lid open, and place it to one side. Within the coffin I can make out the dusty remains of a skull and the rich apparel which clads the decomposed body. The five green-robed men step forward to inspect the sight. Father Wibert shakes his head, as does one of the two men unknown to me who has long silver hair.

Prior John gestures to the two lay Brothers. One of them climbs into the hole, so that only his upper body is visible. The chanting begins again as the other lay Brother hands his companion a shovel and then replaces the lid of the lead coffin. There is a tense silence as the shovel clicks against the stony earth, and the others look on.

At last, there comes a thud, and a scraping sound. The lay Brother in the hole looks up, smiling. Some time elapses as more earth is shovelled out of the grave, and then a contraption made of sturdy wood with a system of ropes and pulleys is brought out from behind a pillar, positioned over the hole, and used to raise another coffin, likewise lead, buried under the first. This coffin is set to the right of the hole, the ropes are detached and the lid opened. All seven men look in. This time it is Father Wibert who reaches inside, and pulls out a wooden casket, about three hands in length. He prises the casket open. He holds up its content, a chalice wrought in heavy, yellow gold, and simply set with large jewels, emeralds, rubies and lapis lazuli, glinting in the light of the candles as if it were rejoicing at its release from the darkness. It is not unlike the chalice I had seen in Domna Cecilia's house. Prior John signals to the men in brown that they should reinter the coffins, then he takes charge of the chalice, replacing it in its casket. Prior John finishes the chanting of the exorcism, and then intones appropriate passages from the Office of the Burial of the Dead.

Only when they have finished are the lay Brothers dismissed. The Prior and his remaining companions begin chatting informally as they move slowly towards the treasury. I try to justify the Prior's action. There was probably a good reason for appropriating the chalice. Perhaps because of its great value. Perhaps because it had some special significance. But then there was the question of what the Templar Brother was doing there, and why the chalice had been buried in a grave containing two coffins.

I am just beginning to consider how best to get out of the Cathedral and back to my lodgings without being seen when there is a flurry of movement, footsteps and shouting. A figure wrapped in a large cloak is rushing towards the group of men as they amble to the treasury door. Taken by surprise, they offer no resistance. The cloaked man pushes over two of the men, then punches the Prior in the stomach so that he doubles up in pain, releasing the casket which the man seizes from him. At that point it should be possible to see the attacker's face, but he is wearing a mask. However, from the man's long, curly hair, I am convinced he is Michael. I wonder where Myrrah might be.

Before anyone has time to react, the masked man has turned on his heels. Rather than making for the door leading into the cloisters and attempting to escape via the Green Court he heads back to the North Tower. Suddenly, I realise the danger I am in. If I am found hiding behind the altar I will be implicated in the theft. But what am I to do? I cannot risk walking to the Green Court, nor can I follow Michael up into the tower. Instead, I crouch as low as I can, tucking myself into the area beneath the altar, which has a curious, sweet, tomb-like smell of its own.

I huddle, shivering, in silence, and the stony darkness engulfs me. For what seems an eternity I listen in dread to the scuffling of feet and urgent voices reverberating in the sanctified air around me. I imagine Michael and Myrrah, and their pursuers hurrying hither and thither, up and down the stairwells, to and fro along the endless passageways in the walls of the Cathedral. Meanwhile, I feel like a disembodied spirit trapped in the stone, just as some say the human spirit is trapped in this world of blind matter. The cold eats its way through my clothing like a relentless, dull pain.

At last, the sound of the voices dies down. With infinite care and slowness at first, I ease my way out of my hiding place. My limbs are leaden with cold. It is quite dark. Step by step, I move through the gloom of the Crypt, staying as close as I can to walls and pillars. The skies must have cleared, for moonlight pours in through the high clerestory, crisscrossing the round arches with deep blue and silver light. I feel that I am in a mysterious geometric forest, haunted by ghostly angels of the Ideal.

I think of possible hiding places in the Cathedral, the passageways in the walls, the great, bowed area under the roof, the altars and tombs, the tunnels leading from the Crypt. The possibilities are infinite and I conclude there is little chance that Michael and Myrrah will have been caught.

At last, I have reached the door which leads into the cloisters. I ease it open. The grounds of the Priory are still and deserted as I make my way back to my lodgings. I throw myself on to my bed and for a few hours I sleep a nightmarish sleep, living and re-living the events of the last few hours.

The next morning at Low Mass in the Cathedral there was an unsettled atmosphere, a furtiveness and shuffling as troubled looks passed from one monk to another. Even the boys from the small Priory school had quit their usual boisterous behaviour and scampered by, sullen and silent. It was a rainy day, a chilly harbinger of winter, and the cloisters offered only scant protection from the strong wind as I followed the procession leaving the Cathedral.

So far, no one had confronted me about the events in the Cathedral the previous evening. What troubled me most was that I would not have been able to offer a coherent explanation for my presence there. I was there by chance, yet Brother Thomas was not the only person who would have insisted that there is no such thing.

However, after Mass, just as we were entering the cloister by the water tower, Brother Andrew, of the long eyelashes and girlish complexion, caught up with me and tugged at my sleeve. He was red in the face, agitated. 'Prior John wishes to speak to you,' he whispered.

My heart sank. 'Do you know why?' I asked.

'I'll walk with you,' he mumbled. There was sympathy in his voice and I thought that, if I had the skills of Brother Thomas, I might know how to make the most of this situation. Yet with each step I took, fear gripped me more firmly. He led the way through the Dark Entry. The spiralling pillars on the east side, their capitals carved with fantastic beasts, dogs, apes and devils, were like living things in the rain, albeit deformed. We crossed the open courtyard and were immediately drenched through. In the Palace itself we left puddles of water on the stone floors, soaking the fresh rushes. I stood at the foot of the stairs while Andrew went up to announce my arrival.

There was a long wait before I was summoned to the elegantly draped chamber, where the extravagantly robed Prior John was waiting for me. I entered, my head bowed, expecting a confrontation about my presence in the Cathedral and the theft of the chalice. Yet the Prior's manner was not what I had expected. He stood up, walked over to me, and slapped me on the back. 'Come now, Wilfridus!' he exclaimed. 'Whatever is the matter with you? Are you ill? I have good news!'

I felt like a condemned man reprieved just before hanging. 'Forgive me,' I said.

'I know Brother Thomas is away, but I have information,' said the Prior, 'about the murders at the Templar house in Swiffeld. It is important that you should pass it on to him as soon as he returns. We think we know who was involved.' I tried to analyse Prior John's gestures, his expression and the tone of his voice; there was no indication that he was playing a game of cat and mouse, nor that he was deliberately working to set me against my master. Nor was there any intimation that the previous evening he had been the victim of a violent theft. Whatever his faults, the Prior was a subtle man. 'Our suspect has been seen around Canterbury since the murders,' he continued. 'A good-for-nothing so-called Franciscan. Like all ragamuffins with mystical pretences these days! A fine excuse for treason!'

'Treason?' I repeated, fear and bewilderment mounting within me. The image flashed before my mind of a case I had heard of recently: a church dignitary convicted of treason who had been bound, then covered with iron weights, and starved until, one by one, the weights broke his bones, and he was crushed to death.

'He and other malcontents in his circle are suspected of spying for Louis of France; apparently, he is out to find treasure, a chalice of some kind, which is supposed to convey mysterious powers. Ridiculous of course, but you can never tell what might drive such people.' Nothing in the Prior's manner betrayed his interest in the chalice, and his urbanity was such that I would never have guessed that he had held it in his hands only a few hours ago.

I took a deep breath. 'What has that to do with the murder?' I asked.

'Murders,' the Prior corrected me. 'You forget the Templars are a military Order. If anyone understands invasion plans of other nations, then they do. There are many who would kill for their knowledge of such things as the precise layout of the tunnels beneath this county.'

'What is the name of the man you suspect?' I asked.

'Michael,' replied the Prior, staring hard into my eyes. 'He is connected to the Jewish family that lives in the great stone house opposite the Church of Saint Helen.'

'I am surprised,' I began, trying to hide my utter bewilderment. 'Brother Thomas had another suspect in mind. Brother Rainer, the Templar who claimed to have found Theodor's body and who himself escaped the killings.'

'Interesting,' said the Prior thoughtfully, 'that he should come up with such an idea.'

Encouraged by the Prior's apparent interest in me, I blurted, 'Brother Thomas was threatened two nights ago. He was told that his wife and children might be at risk if he fails to find Domna Cecilia guilty.'

'His *wife?*' repeated the Prior, raising a disapproving eyebrow.

'Concubine,' I corrected myself, and the Prior winked conspiratorially, as if to communicate that at least we two, unlike Brother Thomas, were above the temptations of the flesh.

'I see,' he said. 'However, I think you and Brother Thomas will discover as your work progresses that there are grounds to suspect Cecilia of heresy, and you should do nothing to obscure this fact. Moreover, this Michael fellow will certainly provide a far more fruitful line of enquiry than Brother Rainer. Even if he is still alive, he will almost certainly be out of the country by now. They pick up curious habits in the East, these Templars, what with their potions, and the leaves they smoke.'

The Prior intoned these words with such a kindly, paternalistic authority that I would never have imagined he was lying through his teeth. Besides, I was relieved that no mention was made of Myrrah.

I returned to our lodgings to find Brother Thomas there. He looked tired and shaken as he sat at the table, pouring himself ale from the pitcher.

'Did you find Alyssa?' I asked.

He shook his head.

'And the children?'

Again, the same reaction.

'Did you find out what has happened to them?'

'I have no more idea than you,' he said. 'I saw Lord Rufus. But I shall explain later, after we have visited Domna Cecilia. In the meantime, I am sure that you have much to tell me.'

We left immediately. Brother Thomas's mood was sombre, and I did not dare press him about Alyssa, but recounted in detail my meeting with Isaac, the events in the Cathedral the previous night, and the words I had exchanged with the Prior earlier that morning. Brother Thomas listened in silence, nodding occasionally to encourage me to keep on with my narrative, but I could tell that his mood was continuing to darken.

Chapter Eight

WHEN WE ARRIVED at the house, Alazaïs served us food, and Domna Cecilia continued with her story. As I write now, so many years later, with the documents in front of me from so long ago, it is curious to see that same neat hand which is still my own, that same Latin, and certain quirks of expression I have come to recognise as my own, even when I am trying to express the thoughts of others. I wonder at how still, how timeless, words on the page are, how inadequate they seem to record the perturbations we suffer in our lives. I suppose it is that stillness we seek, those of us who write, and who read, for the writing comes from a part of us which is unchangeable and untouched by external events; it belongs to the eternal, unseen world, a world of intense beauty, yet which has the power and the propensity to destroy: a world which Cecilia understood so well.

'I was telling you,' Domna Cecilia began, 'about how I fainted that evening I heard Walther's "Under der linden" song for the first time. I woke before dawn to find myself alone in my room, feeling utterly cast out and rejected. Nothing in my monastic education had prepared me for the panic and terror which, slowly but surely, overwhelmed me. I sobbed uncontrollably. I tore at my hair, pounded my fists against my face and body, and threw myself on the floor, writhing in despair. Over and over I tried to get out of my room, but the door was bolted on the outside. That night seemed to last an eternity.

'At last, just before dawn, Dorothea did come, whether out of friendship, or to gloat, I was beyond caring. I plied her with questions and she told me what had happened the previous evening after I was carried out of the hall. She explained how Walter and Johannes von Ulm nearly came to blows because of me, but were separated on the orders of the Graf who reminded von Ulm that he and Walter were due to lead the jousting in the mêlée the next day. Von Ulm threatened a fight to the death. Walter stood his ground, saying he would not relinquish me. How he must have loved me, to risk his life for me like that, yet I felt so small, and so unworthy.

'Dawn came with a gnawing terror. My mind teemed with images of Walter dying one pitiful death after another at the hands of his more powerful opponent. In despair, I thought of the terrible damnation they said awaited those who died in tournaments, how demons swoop in the air above the jousting field, waiting to scoop its victims' souls to an eternity of fiery torment, for their death is a sinful one, unsanctified by the rites of the Church. I tried to pray, but these terrible images would not leave me.

'Now my honour was lost, I wanted only to run through the castle's dark passageways to Walter, to throw myself before him and beg him not to take part in the fight. But the door was bolted and Dorothea said soldiers stood outside, barring the way. In my heart I resolved that if Walter were to die, then I would take my own life, for I would rather burn with him in Hell than suffer his loss in Heaven or on earth.

'Walter's "Under der linden" song imprinted itself on my heart. The gentle, lilting melody, and the delicate structure of the words had something in them of Walter, something I could not bear to lose. Even as Dorothea taught me the words of the final verses (the song was already on everyone's lips), it seemed not that I was learning it, but rather recalling it. When Dorothea left me I sat at the window of my room, looking out across the jousting field as the grey, desolate light spread over the cloudy sky above; I sang the song repeatedly, as a lone lark trilled somewhere overhead, oblivious of my sorrow. If only, I thought, I could hold Walter close again, as I held that song in my mind.

'I watched the preparations for the tournament, then the start of the Mass, with the priests in their exquisite robes, the horses decked out in their finery, the opposing parties, on either side of the altar, and the Graf and Gräfin between them. I wanted to be there. Dorothea had gone. I called out. No reply came from the soldiers. I pushed at the door and found it was no longer bolted. Swiftly I pulled on my finest dress and, though my hair was uncombed and my face tear-stained, I ran down the winding steps, ducking beneath the low beams, out across the courtyard, through the arched gate and towards the field. I must have looked like a wild thing but I did not care. My only thought was that somehow I might throw myself at the feet of the Graf, or Johannes of Ulm, beg them, sacrifice myself to any design they might have for me, if only the fight could be stopped and Walter allowed to live.

'They were waiting for me. The moment I began to try to force my way through the crowds, girls who had once been my friends flocked round me like harpies and men-at-arms barred my way. I had to view the preparations from a raised patch of ground some distance from the altar and the field of combat. I was beside myself with fear and distress.

'Over to the left, I could see Walter, as he prepared for battle. Unlike his opponent, only his gloves and hauberk were chainmail, otherwise he preferred leather for greater mobility. As he made ready, he chatted to his comrades,

Simon and Herbert. I see him now, just as I did then, so graceful, tall, hair swept back just before he put on his helmet, and then the great surcoat over his hauberk. I remember the noble assurance of his movements, that strong, rugged face suffused with dignity and gentle power, lilies blooming at the far end of the field where he mounted his horse. Now, as then, I perceive not just his physical self, but the whole texture of his life: an interweaving of beauty and despair, profligacy and yearning, and some final resolution perhaps, glimpsed only through flames; I see him beneath the low, scudding clouds through which the sun shoots fierce shafts of golden light, and there, at the opposite end of the field, is the silhouetted figure of Johannes of Ulm.

'Now, with the movement of cloud shadows rolling over fields on a summer's day, Walter and von Ulm are riding over the emerald green of the grass glittering with dew. Slowly, they turn to face each other, and charge. Their pace appears to quicken only at the last minute before they clash. There is an explosion of colour and a whirl of movement in the sunlight, a din of horses neighing and lances crashing against shields. The tumult subsides yet Walter is still mounted. He has survived the first blow. I look on, quivering with such emotion that I forget myself. I am not there. I am only what I see and feel.

'Both men ride away for another pass, but to my horror, von Ulm turns early. Ignoring the rules of knightly combat, he charges Walter from the rear. Walter hears the hoofs, pirouettes crazily, just in time to deflect von Ulm's lance, then swinging round his own, catches his opponent a giddying blow to the head. The crowd cheers Walter now as he rides in pursuit of von Ulm. Anger and relief flood through me.

'Walter is too courtly to press an unfair advantage. He allows his opponent to prepare for the next pass but when the time comes von Ulm charges with his lance aimed at Walter's mount. Walter, caught unawares by this low, snake-like tactic, sees the tip of von Ulm's spear pierce the flank of his rearing horse, then run into the flesh of his own leg. The wounded animal collapses beneath him. Clasping his thigh, Walter falls to the ground. I press my hands over my eyes, and taste the salt tears as they run down my hands and into my mouth. I force my eyes open to watch as von Ulm drives his horse round in a tight circle, intending to trample Walter, who rolls out of the way just in time. My stomach knots. I can feel the pain in Walter's leg as he drags himself to his feet. Again, von Ulm turns, more leisurely this time, taunting Walter with his lance. It is as though he is about to run it through my heart, and I pray that it might be mine, and not Walter's.

'The next charge seems to last for ever. At the last moment Walter, suddenly nimble, jumps catlike to one side yet does not avoid the lance altogether. Instead, he traps it between arm and shoulder, but the thrust lifts him from his feet and he is carried backwards for some ten yards and only breaks free by swinging his sword-arm round over his head; his sword sweeps through the air like the sail of a lethal wind-mill; the blade crashes down on the shaft of von Ulm's lance. There is a sickening crack and Walter falls to the ground, lying motionless on the grass, hand and leg covered in crimson blood glinting beneath the sun, writhing like a wounded animal. For a moment, I hear his music again, the fruit of that lovely and harmonious body, and shudder for fear I might be hearing his soul pouring from it.

'Von Ulm grasps for his sword. But his arm flails desper-ately like the broken wing of a wounded bird, a dark, steaming shadow pouring from it, his blood, his life-blood. There is a gasp, followed by an uncanny silence as we see the helpless agony on von Ulm's face; Walter's blow has severed the hand which lies on the grass, crabbed like a stranded sea-creature, still clasping the shaft of the lance. In my mind, horror mingles with numb relief.

'Twice, von Ulm, still mounted but teetering like a massive tree just before its felling, tries to charge down Walter. The first time, Walter steps aside. The second time he grabs hold of von Ulm's foot, and is dragged backwards, splattering the green grass with scarlet until, at last, with a terrible clatter, von Ulm drops from his horse.

'I pray that this might be an end but still the fight is not over. Von Ulm somehow clambers to his feet, then totters like a drunkard towards Walter, who looks on, sword in hand, dazed, transfixed by the dreadful sight; yet he is too courtly to run through a wounded and defenceless man. Von Ulm, heedless again of the mercy shown him, lumbers relentlessly towards Walter, embraces him in a terrible bear hug, and tries to squeeze what remains of Walter's life from him as dark, hot blood streams from his wrist. At last, von Ulm's strength fails him, and he falls backwards, defeated. Walter, still standing, steadies himself by placing a foot on his foe's chest; a cheer goes up from the crowd.'

Domna Cecilia paused at this point and Alazaïs went out to fetch more food and wine.

'Both men were borne from the field,' Domna Cecilia continued as soon as Alazaïs returned, 'and the Graf charged me with the care of them, since I was the cause of the fight. Walter was given a room in the East Tower, and von Ulm lay in a low, vaulted chamber next to the chapel. I nursed Johannes von Ulm throughout those last few days of his life, despairing that the mixture of mandrake and aconite with which I treated him was powerless to stop the gangrene from rotting the open wound on the stump of his arm; nobly, he mustered his strength to confront his new enemy, Death.

'On the first day, I remember he received a visit from a priest with tawny eyes and head that was quite bald. Thereafter, Ulm took to quizzing me about religion, the forgiveness of sins, and the life everlasting. I grew to respect his undaunted, child-like spirit. Only later did I connect the priest's visit with rumours about Walter, since some believed he had a special role to play in the unfolding of history, of the Last Days.

'Just two days before he died, von Ulm asked that Walter should be brought to him. Walter came hobbling across the courtyard on a pair of makeshift crutches, uncertain what to expect. Von Ulm greeted him with tears in his eyes, reached out with his good hand, and touched Walter on the forehead, then me, and begged us both for forgiveness, saying that a special destiny was vouchsafed us, and he was foolish to have intervened, though he had done so in ignorance. I did not understand his words. Even now they are not clear to me.

'When I was not with von Ulm, I was with Walter. For the first day or so he had lain in silence, drifting in and out of consciousness as I watched over him. I felt we were close as never before; through the silence our souls reached out and touched; I sensed again that in some essential way, in some realm glimpsed only as a shimmering presence, we were one.

'After the first two days, Walter began, slowly, to recover. He received many visitors. Noblemen and ladies came to praise his skill as a horseman and a singer. His songs and his story were all the talk. Like fools we dared hope the Graf and Gräfin would grant us some reward, land perhaps and permission to marry. How naive I was.

'On the Monday morning, exactly one week after his victory, the day after von Ulm's funeral, I was on my way as usual to visit Walter, only to find my way barred by Friderich the nightwatchman. He told me kindly but politely that I was to see Walter no more. I asked him why. Propriety was the reason he gave. Now that Walter was recovering, he said, it would be unseemly for us to be alone together.

'All that day I was desperate with worry, trying to understand who might have given such an order and why. By the evening I had decided that the only course of action was to go directly to confront the Gräfin. We had not talked since the tournament. Her coldness towards me was palpable and I had been too nervous until then.

'In the evening I sought her out in the private upper chamber where we had spent so many happy hours together practising music, reading and talking of our ideals of courtly life; it had been a place of such joy, vibrant with music and laughter and beauty. Now, however, she greeted me not with a smile, but with a sneer. Though the objects in the room were the same, the casks, the tapestries, the musical instruments and the chess sets, they were alien now, and the atmosphere was bleak and sullen.

'I tried to disregard this, concentrating only on what I had to say. "Walter," I said, "has been brave and loyal. I am here for his sake, though he does not know I have come. I wish to know if you think the Graf might grant him a fief, and let me be his wife."

' "You fool!" the Gräfin snarled. "Such arrogance! Take your request to the Graf. See how *he* reacts!"

'I still thought the Graf a just man, and trusted that he would understand, that he would explain the Gräfin's odd behaviour towards me, so I went to the great hall. There I found him, sitting on his folding chair, playing dice with someone I did not recognise, a man with long white hair, wearing striking red and white clothes, like those of a priest. The only light was from one lamp on the table. The rest of the hall was in darkness. "What are you doing here at this time?" the Graf asked gruffly. The white-haired man raised an eyebrow and looked me up and down, then turned to the Graf.

' "I have come," I said, "to request permission to nurse Walter von der Ouwe again, and ask you to grant him sufficient means that he might continue to serve you and that we might marry."

'The two men exchanged conspiratorial glances. "We were just talking about you," said the Graf. "I shall give you my reply later." The white-haired man guffawed, causing the lamp light to flicker.

' "I am very grateful," I said, as politely as I could, though I felt frozen with fear. The white-haired man leered at me again, and reached out a hand to touch me. This hall had once been Heaven on earth to me. Now the reeds on the floor were mildewy, the light of the tallow lamp danced sickly yellow over the faded tapestries, and the stench of urine was rank. Decay seeped everywhere.

'I pulled away from the white-haired man's grasp, walked as calmly as I could out of the hall and crossed the courtyard which now seemed a ruin fit only for ghouls. Slowly, I climbed the wooden stairs to my own room, high in the tower. I threw myself on to the bed, and sobbed. Then I tried to read, or to pray, wondering what the Graf had meant, but the sense of dejection and evil overwhelmed me.

'After an hour or so, I heard footsteps on the stairs to my room, followed by a loud knocking at my door. It was the Graf. He was alone, and he was drunk. "This is my reply," he said. "You want Walter – you can have me first." I was frightened, and backed away. He eyed me. "I said, you can have Walter if you have me first." He laughed cruelly. I shook my head. "Well," he hissed, "if not willingly . . ."

'He was a strong man. I tried to fight back, but there was nothing I could do. He grasped my arms, pinned me against a wall, and then dragged me on to the bed. He hurt me,

Thomas, but worse than the pain was the terror. My hopes, my illusions were stripped away and violated too, and as he possessed me, so too I was possessed by the horror of the void with which I am now too familiar. He spoke only once, and I have never forgotten his words. "So," he said, "if you are with child, no one will know whose it is."

'When he went, after what seemed an age but was probably only a few minutes, I did not dare leave my room. For a day and a night I sobbed and I ate nothing, drinking only the stale water from the jug by my bed.'

At this point, Domna Cecilia fell silent. Just for a moment, the deep blue light in the room pulsed with the textures of the scenes she had described. Her cat jumped up and settled in her lap. We had sat with her for the greater part of the day, breaking only once for the lunch served by Alazaïs. Now, the winter sky beyond the narrow window was growing pale as the sun set. I could see shreds of tattered clouds tinted ruby red now in the sunset, sailing past with an ironic aloofness; the room had grown gloomy and shadowy. It felt as though we were in a hermetic vessel, sealed off from the normal flow of time and the impinging of external events.

We sat in silence for a while, then Alazaïs went to fetch tallow candles, which she lit, so that eerie shadows danced across the room. Domna Cecilia's eyes glowed an unearthly ochre in the half-light, whilst Brother Thomas's puffy features took on a drawn pallor. Alazaïs placed a hand on Domna Cecilia's shoulder and bent over her, to comfort her.

'Why do you think,' Brother Thomas pronounced kindly and carefully, 'the Graf behaved in such a way towards you?' Domna Cecilia remained silent. 'Was it unbridled lust, perhaps,' Thomas continued, 'a desire to punish you and Walter von der Ouwe, or was there some deeper motive, something perhaps to do with the priest you said was with him earlier in the evening?'

Alazaïs looked angrily at the two of us. She said nothing but there was no doubt that she thought these questions were out of place. Domna Cecilia was not weeping, but she was visibly upset. After another lengthy silence she said, 'Tomorrow, or the next time you come, I shall attempt to explain, but it is no easy matter.'

This is where my record of the day's interview comes to an end. Thomas and I returned to our lodgings. We walked in silence, both of us, I suppose, imagining and re-living the story Domna Cecilia had just told us.

Only when we settled in our draughty room, and lit candles with the intention of writing up our notes, did Brother Thomas recount to me what he had experienced in the days when he had been away. He drank a good deal of wine as he talked. His story made an odd impression on me. When I had finished writing up my notes on Domna Cecilia, I realised that I was still wide awake, so I recorded Brother Thomas's story too, as though he were the subject of an enquiry, like Domna Cecilia.

I am glad now that I have these papers, particularly in view of what Brother Thomas had to say about the boy Geraldus.

This, then, is Brother Thomas's story as I set it down.

Chapter Nine

'As you know, I left early in the morning,' Brother Thomas began. 'I had been unable to sleep because I was, and still am, so anxious about Alyssa and my children. As I rode, I kept thinking about the last time I was with them, when we said our farewells and you and I, Wilfridus, travelled together to Canterbury. I re-lived our parting, the last words we spoke, the light catching my children's hair, my last glimpses of our few common possessions through the open door, and the clouds rolling across the sky above the Thames. I had sensed then that this was no ordinary farewell, that the simple, domestic moments we shared might never return. I did not know, and still do not know, why this might be.

'You know the theory,' he continued, 'that each of us possesses numerous bodies, in addition to our material bodies: the spiritual body, seen by God; the sideral body, on which the stars act; the mental body, which is the seat of thought; and the elemental body, by means of which our essences are projected into the aether. You remember too how we have discussed the idea that there might exist a grammar of the human soul, just as there is a grammar of language. If this is true, it will explain how I feel bound to Alyssa, and how I love her, Wilfridus, how our bodies complement each other at so many levels beyond the carnal. The nature of this love is one that Domna Cecilia appears to understand well, and if ever I had a wish for you, Wilfridus, it is that one day you should experience this too.'

I remember that, even as he spoke, I could not stop myself from thinking of Myrrah.

'This is why I rode fast and anxiously,' Brother Thomas continued, 'unaware of my surroundings, reflecting that I would know no peace until I was certain that Alyssa and the children were safe. As I rode, I thought repeatedly about Domna Cecilia's story about Walter. That she should have told us about this no longer seemed a coincidence but part of a pattern. I had the same feeling about the events involving the boy Geraldus, which are being talked about everywhere now, and which I witnessed at first hand. Something is about to happen, Wilfridus, and I only wish I knew what this is to be.

'Because I rode so fast, I reached the Medway by midday. From the ford where I was to cross I could hear there was a commotion nearby. I followed the shouts and screams to a riverbank downstream, where men were dragging something out of the river, a human figure in sodden clothes. There was a girl standing aside from the crowd; I asked her what had happened. Nervously, she told me that Geraldus, a cousin of hers, eleven years old, had been sitting on the river's edge, upstream by the road, stoning frogs. He lost his footing, and slipped into the water. His friends had laughed at first. But their laughter soon ceased as they watched him drift with the current, face down, until he got tangled in reeds. It was from here that they had just pulled him to the bank.

'I went over to the group to get a closer look. The child lay lifeless. As rain poured down from the bleak, grey sky, and more and more common folk came to gawk, they placed him on a rough stretcher and carried him to the church. I took this to be a bad omen and, since there was nothing I could do to help, I resolved to stay no longer. As I walked away, I heard the priest urging the people to have faith in Saint

Thomas of Canterbury and to pray.

'Throughout the rest of my journey I thought constantly of that lad, sitting on the bank of the river one minute, throwing stones, just like any other boy of his age, then the slipping, a sense of helplessness perhaps, the cold water engulfing him, the desperate struggle for air, and then . . . ? Would it have been like entering a world of dreams, blackness and repose, a long, shadowy wait for the Resurrection of the Dead? Or would his soul have flown directly to God for Judgment? I thought of my own little family, and prayed for their safety. I thought of Cecilia too, of the tenuous hold we have on this life, whose few precious sweetnesses are so hard for us to relinquish.

'The rest of the journey home was uneventful enough, and I arrived at Ellethamwolde after sunset on the third day, my horse and I exhausted, the ground hard with frost. In the distance, from the top of the hill overlooking the village, I could see the masts of the ships and the dark, winding waters of the Thames, reaching over barren mudflats to the east, bringing back memories of my childhood. You can imagine the sight, can't you, Wilfridus, since you have been there so often. To the west were the myriad flickering lights of the towers and pinnacles, churches and halls of the City of London. In the deep blue starry sky, the moon hung, massive, more like an enormous pale pearl than a heavenly body.

'As I kept going down the hill, past the church, and towards our house just beyond the centre of the village, I reflected how fortunate we had been, Alyssa and I, to have known the happiness we had shared, yet how vulnerable we were too, for if ever we failed to please Lord Rufus, this could so easily be swept away. As the familiar sights crowded in on me, the ten years we had lived here formed a perceptible shape in my mind: the first years of studying and teaching together, then the children coming. I thought how our love was not unrequited like the troubadours', how it did not have the ecstasies of the mystics, though there was passion in it, but how its basis was a deep friendship. Forgive me if I repeat my belief that such love is superior to the loves sung by the poets and visionaries.

'Walking past the church, through the huddle of sleepy houses up the lane, I began to fear the worst. Acrid smoke curled from other rooftops, and the light from lamps and fires could be glimpsed through windows and cracks in doorways. Yet no light shone from our house, and no fire burnt in its hearth. My heart beat fast as I drew closer. I called out Alyssa's name, hammered at the window, then shook the door in frustration, unable to open it because of the inside latch. Eventually, I had to force the hinges. Inside, the darkness was unbearable. I found the tallow lamp on the chest to the right of the door and lit it. Walking round the two simple rooms, I was greeted by the usual household objects, each with their memories of moments I had shared with Alyssa.

'In the far room, where we slept, the bed was as she left it each morning. There was no sign of violence, or of anything sinister, no food left uneaten, or chairs knocked over. There was no message about where she might have gone. Even the bundles of manuscripts we had copied, Latin poets, extracts from Aristotle, Boethius and the like, and the three books we had managed to keep for ourselves over the years, two Gospels and Hrabanus's treatise on the liberal arts, were undisturbed in the chest.

'I found the flagon of wine in the alcove by the steps which led to the small upper room, lit a fire, and started drinking, stuffing myself with the remains of the bread, onions, cheese and salted pork I had with me from the journey. I drank too much, hoping to ease the pain of missing Alyssa. Eventually, I was lying alone in our bed, desperate with worry about her, sobbing myself to sleep in the cold and dark.

'I was woken not long after dawn by the sounds of neighbours setting about their daily tasks. Joseph, the fish merchant, was on his way to the market by the Thames and Fredemund, the scribe, whom you know, Wilfridus, was chopping logs. I had a foul headache from the wine, and re-kindled the fire before drinking some ale, and picking at the remains of my bread for breakfast. At last, stepping into the freezing cold, I forced a smile and called out to Fredemund, "Hello! You will never guess. I come home unexpectedly to see Alyssa and the children – and they aren't even here! So much for slaying the fatted calf. Do you know where they've gone?"

'Fredemund stood up from his chopping and greeted me, grumpy as usual, but avoiding my eyes. "It is good to see you, neighbour," he said. "No, I do not know where your lady is."

' "How long has she been away?" The wind was cold, and sea-gulls screeched overhead. I resented having to drag the information out of him.

' "Just two days," he said, nervously shifting from one foot to the other.

' "Well? Did she leave against her will? Who did she go with?"

' "Soldiers," he said at last, and my heart sank.

' "Soldiers," I repeated. "Whose soldiers?" He shrugged. There was no reason why he should know. "And the children?" I asked.

' "The children too," he replied in a tone which expressed sympathy, but conveyed also that he would rather not talk to me any longer than necessary.

' "You don't know any more?" I asked.

' "As you are aware, neighbour," he went on, "it does not do to enquire too closely, not when the country is ruled by foreigners."

' "No," I nodded. "Perhaps not." The jibe was meant for me, of course, because Lord Rufus was close to the Poitevins.

' "If you'll excuse me," said Fredemund, "I must take the wood in, and then I am expected at the Abbey."

' "But of course," I said.

'That morning I approached everyone in the village I could find, and they told me the same story. Two days previously, a group of soldiers had come first thing in the morning, and led Alyssa and the children away. There was no suggestion of resistance or mistreatment. No one seemed to know, or perhaps they had not dared find out, who commanded the soldiers. Nor did anyone have any inkling where my family had been taken, other than that they had been led off in the direction of London.

'By mid-morning, my head was pounding. I left my home at the castle stables and, sick and exhausted, I set off on foot to follow them. It took most of the rest of the day to trudge my way over wet meadows, through drenched woodland paths and along dank village streets until I found a poor boatman, hunched and gaunt, to row me across the river, in between the mudflats and the massive ships, anchored because of the low tide. The boatman let me disembark at the moorings to the west of the Tower of London. That enormous castle glowered over the river, a sinister reminder of worldly power. I walked through the fields towards Westminster and the tall stone houses where the King's ministerials have their chambers.

'Hoping to find Lord Rufus, I called at the Wardrobe offices. An officious young man wearing a Benedictine habit told me to wait. To my relief, he returned to tell me that Lord Rufus was present, and that he would see me straight away. The young man led me upstairs to the second floor, past armies of clerks, record keepers and dispatchers, ultimately controlled now by Peter de Rivaux, des Roches's nephew, and ushered me at last into Rufus's magnificent room, which was finely furnished and hung with tapestries woven with exuberant emerald greens and golds. There was a bright red carpet in front of Rufus's desk, on which his favourite dog was curled up fast asleep.

'Rufus stood up. "Ah, Thomas!" he exclaimed, smiling broadly, his blue eyes gleaming from his freckled face. "It is splendid to see you! Tell me, have you ever read this?" He was not, as I had supposed, engaged in administrative work, but reading John of Salisbury's *Poetria Nova*. "It is superb!" he said. "The man's Latin is almost as good as yours . . ." You can imagine, Wilfridus, a typical backhanded compliment coming from Lord Rufus.

' "Have you not heard?" I interrupted. "Alyssa and the children – two days ago. Soldiers took them away from our house at Ellethamwolde."

'He looked puzzled. "That is the first I have heard of it," he said.

' "So it wasn't you?"

' "No. Besides, why should anyone want your . . . ?" He could not find the words to describe those I love. "You thought it was me, or the King?"

' "They were taken by armed men."

' "That could have been anyone," he said. "Have you any other indications?"

'I told him, Wilfridus, about how we had been threatened the previous evening, and the Templar's words: "*Do not forget the eyes of the Assassin. We know where your woman and your children are. Domna Cecilia must be spared . . .*"

'As far as I could read Lord Rufus's reaction, he was genuinely shocked. After a tense silence, he asked, "Have you enough evidence against Domna Cecilia?"

' "Perhaps," I said. "I would rather wait."

' "Because of that ridiculous Templar?"

' "No, because we are not sure."

' "Truth ought to play a role, I suppose," Lord Rufus mused in his worldly-wise way, though he was clearly concerned. "But there are other considerations, as I wrote in my letter. Now, you aren't going to let me down, are you?"

' "I thought," I replied, "that you wanted a public conviction with clear evidence. That will take time."

' "We cannot wait for ever," Rufus warned me. "You know Domna Cecilia came to us directly from Languedoc? There has been a spate of abductions and murders lately, attempts to foment political unrest, not just the Templars . . ."

' "What has that to do with Domna Cecilia?" I interrupted

' "The victims all have links with Domna Cecilia," he said. "Like Alyssa."

' "You are trying to tell me," I said disbelievingly, "that Domna Cecilia is responsible for the abduction of Alyssa and my children?"

' "There might well be a connection," he said. "My point is that you are wasting your time here in London. I am sorry about Alyssa and your children, and I promise that I shall go through the pipe-rolls myself in case a royal order was given, unknown to me. But in my opinion, your best hope of finding them will be to bring this Domna Cecilia business to a speedy conclusion." Lord Rufus began shuffling the papers on his desk. I was unable to tell whether this last observation was supposed to contain a veiled threat. In any case, it was clear to me that I would get no more information out of him, and that I really had no choice. It would be foolish to lose his good will. I bade him goodbye. Just as I was about to leave he said, "By the way, I shall be riding to Dover in a day or so. I am sure we shall meet soon, while I am in Kent."

'I set off past the site where the King's masons will soon be starting work on the new Abbey Church. You know, Wilfridus, they say that its walls will be paper thin, held up with buttresses like angels' wings, with windows high, delicate and pointed, and narrow pinnacles striving heavenward. When completed, it is to rival any of the magnificent new buildings of Paris. Imagine what secrets might be encoded in the proportions of such a building, Wilfridus, secrets of the correspondences between sacred numbers in the Bible, in the stars of the heavens, the orders of angels, of animals and of matter itself, perhaps too of the ordering of the Ages of Man, the lives of kings, and the numbering of days before the End of Time.

'Next, I took the road by the beach, following the bow in the Thames, past the houses crammed with curials, town-loving lords, affluent foreigners, money lenders, clerics, and then the squalid rookeries of the poor folk whose lives are filled only with begging, hunger, whoring and drinking. Each street corner I turned, every inn where I stopped for food, every stranger's face I saw caused me torment, for I thought that any moment I might see Alyssa.

'The emptiness inside me grew bitter and consuming as I took a ferry over the Thames. I spent the night at my house at Ellethamwolde, making further enquiries in the morning, none of which came to anything.

'So it was that yesterday at Nones I was following the stream towards the village where the boy Geraldus had drowned stoning frogs. Ironic, I reflected, how much stone-thrower and frogs had in common, both dispatched into oblivion by blind forces beyond their control. As I approached the village, I heard the chanting of the *Te Deum*. Despite the wind and the rain, huge crowds had gathered, monks, priests and lay people, carrying crosses, and torches smoking against the grey sky. They were processing from the river, where the boy had drowned, and up to the church. The people's faces were rapt in religious awe, curiously pale, eyes hollow as they gazed up towards the cloudy heavens, heedless of the rain, as if glimpsing a world beyond the skies. I asked a sallow, hunched young man, with dark hair and blue eyes, what was going on.

' "Sir," he said, eyeing me suspiciously, "you must be the only person in the whole land who does not know. There has been a tremendous miracle. Geraldus, the drowned boy, has been raised from the dead. All night long he lay in his parents' house. Then the priest came, and prayed for him in the name of Saint Thomas, sprinkling him with a tincture of aloe. At that moment Thomas, the holy Martyr of Canterbury appeared, and the life sprang back into the boy. He stirred, and groaned, and sat up, and asked for water, would you believe it, as if he had not drunk enough already, and he asked for fish to eat too! Look, there you can see him!"

'Sure enough, at the head of the procession, dressed in white like a king, and sitting on a chair borne upon the shoulders of four young men, was a boy, grinning, waving to us. Following the procession, I asked more questions of the people there. Everyone confirmed the story. There seemed no doubt that Thomas, the Saint and Martyr, once a statesman, a man of power and war, had looked down from Heaven, and performed this miracle.

'I don't know why, Wilfridus, but as I rode on, a terrible sadness overwhelmed me. Too tired to continue my journey, I ate at an inn yesterday evening, in Chilhamme, and stayed there the night. I rose early before rejoining the pilgrim route to this place. I could not stop thinking about the boy Geraldus. As we approached Canterbury, and as the dead stone of the Cathedral loomed into sight, I asked myself repeatedly what it had to do with Resurrection. There is no need for you to say anything, Wilfridus. Perhaps you had better forget what I just said, for I am not in the best of spirits. I shall try to sleep now. The situation may be clearer to me in the morning.

'Just one more thing,' he added as he got into bed. 'The

chalice you saw disinterred two evenings ago – I will wager that the precious stones which stud it are amethyst, emerald, beryl, snakestone, black diamond, ruby, pearl, chrysoleth, opal and onyx. There is a story that chalices of this nature were fashioned in Israel, before the birth of Christ, at the time of the Sacred Kings. The distribution of the stones themselves has a hermetic significance.'

I asked Brother Thomas to explain, but he was already asleep, or at least pretending.

Chapter Ten

NEXT MORNING, WE attended High Mass, and then went to Domna Cecilia's house, but taking a roundabout route, walking via Saint Mary Northgate past the vineyards near Baggeberri, where skeletons of houses still stood gutted after the fire some ten years earlier. The trees and buildings, the very earth beneath our feet, oozed dankness. Then we turned back towards the town via Weterlok Lane, and crossed the Stura by the Mill, with its great wheel, which belonged to the Abbot of Saint Augustine's Monastery.

We arrived at Cecilia's house to find the roses had been stripped of their last petals by the rain and the autumn winds. The two men with deformed mouths were still there, sitting outside. They nodded to acknowledge our presence and let us enter. Cecilia's house appeared to be empty. No one answered when we called out her name. Unbidden, we went up the stairs to the first floor where we hesitated for a while in the semi-darkness.

Then came the noise of something, someone, stirring in the room above. Brother Thomas took the lead, walking quietly up the narrow stairs to Domna Cecilia's room where we found her. She was sitting on her chair by the window, distaff in hand, head slumped forward, motionless. I could not tell if she was asleep, or dead. Gently, Thomas pronounced her name, at which she looked up, and her large turquoise-blue eyes stared fiercely from the symmetrical whorls of fine lines, like those of an all-seeing, avenging angel.

'I am sorry,' Brother Thomas said, 'for disturbing you.'

'How strange,' she replied, 'to be asleep in the daytime, as if already one were not of this world. Of course, I was expecting you.'

'Where is Alazaïs?' Thomas asked, and I found myself wondering about the motive for his question.

'Ah, Alazaïs. She has gone to buy food.' Cecilia sighed condescendingly. Then she added, suddenly full of sympathy, 'You seem shaken, Brother Thomas.' I wondered if perhaps she did know something about the disappearance of Alyssa and his children.

Thomas gave nothing away, but deflected the talk from himself. 'Who are the men I keep seeing outside your house, with their scarred faces?' he asked.

'I thought you would have known that better than I do. They have been with me ever since I came to England,' she said defiantly. 'They were appointed by Peter de Rivaux. I am allowed nowhere without them.'

'And Alazaïs?' I asked.

'She comes and goes freely on errands. They know she will not go far. Perhaps you have not realised,' Domna Cecilia said, tilting her head to one side, 'that Alazaïs is mute.' A strained silence followed which was broken by the sound of footsteps on the stairs. Alazaïs appeared, out of breath, gesturing apologies for her lateness. She served us wine, bread and a dish made from figs and saffron. She smiled charmingly and brushed against Thomas, her face so close to his, that I knew he could smell the sweetness of her breath. I wondered what she expected to achieve by this.

'Perhaps you would like to continue with your story,' said Brother Thomas at last to Domna Cecilia, when the food was served.

'Very well,' she said. 'I had reached the point when the Graf violated me. Afterwards I spent a night and a day wretched and alone. On the second evening, Dorothea came. She had been told I was ill, and I lacked the courage to tell her the truth. She said she had heard Walter was making a good recovery. However, there were men posted outside his rooms who let in no one but Friderich, so she had not seen him. The Graf and Gräfin had announced that they were to leave these lands for a while, to go on pilgrimage, probably to Santiago de Compostela. Other courtiers too were preparing to leave. The daily rituals, even the services in the chapel, were grinding to a halt. It seemed that the courtly virtues were fleeing the castle, to be superseded by some darker rule.

'For the next week I did not leave my room. Dorothea was the only person I saw. I never told her what had happened. Perhaps she knew. In any case the two of us became friends again. She brought me food of which I ate only very little, since I felt so ill, so distressed.

'At last bitter news came that my uncle, the Lord of Stierenfurt, had arrived and was to take me away. I gathered together my few belongings. Stierenfurt came directly to my room in the *kemenate* to fetch me, his eyes burning red with rage. "You have let us down, completely, the whole family," he snarled. I doubted he knew the whole truth but it would have made no difference if he had. At least I was not alone as I walked through those once cherished buildings for the last time. I did not ask where we were going as I followed him down into the courtyard. A horse was waiting for us, and seeing I was in no fit state to walk, my uncle grudgingly let me mount it. There was no one to say goodbye, no Graf, no Gräfin, no friends and no Walter, only the cold, speechless walls, and the desolate whirring of the flags and bunting still flying from the tournament, tattered and scruffy now.

'We travelled mile after mile through the rolling country-side, up into mountains where only sheep grazed, over the

134

plains resplendent with wheat, and the valleys fat with vine-yards where towns and villages nestled alongside glittering rivers. The weather was balmy. In the villages, young men and women were out, playing games and dancing; twice I saw young men offering flowers to girls. Once, we surprised a courting couple in the forest. I thought of Walter, and felt so isolated, so excluded.

'From the first, my uncle made it clear that he had no more respect for me, speaking only to bark orders. My status was to be that of the lowest servant. A good marriage would be impossible now. No convent would want me. I began to despair.

'We travelled until late on the third day because my uncle wished to save the cost of a night's lodging. That evening, we were walking through a deep green oak glade; the setting sun, a brilliant orange-yellow, cast a web of dazzling beams through the dark criss-cross of boughs and branches, and there was a scent of hyssop in the air. On the path ahead of us, silhouetted against the sun on the crest of the hill, amidst the poplar trees which grew higher than the oaks, was a man on horseback, noble and knightly in his bearing, like a vision of something holy or fatal, a harbinger of the Beyond, or of Death.

'Suddenly the rider pressed his horse to charge down the hill towards us. My uncle, who was leading our horse, started backwards. It was too late to flee. I began to fear that the man was a thief. As it happened, I was not wrong, for he had taken from me everything precious I possessed; or rather I had given it to him. It was Walter. Recognising him, my uncle turned beetroot red with anger. "What do you want?" he shouted.

'Walter, tall and poised in his saddle, showed no deference but remained calm and courteous, which of course enraged my uncle even more. Walter's voice came as if from a great distance. "I wish to talk to your niece," he said. The hateful memory of the Graf and what he did to me returned like a dark presence separating me from Walter, though I loved him.

' "You bastard, you fool, you seducer and thief," my uncle screamed. "You'll hang for this when my men catch you. They'll chase you throughout the Empire, and the Bishop will have you flogged and . . ." I could take no more. I shouted to Walter to follow me, turned my horse and rode off at full gallop, leaving my uncle apoplectic with impotent fury.

'Trees rushed past me and the darkening air made my senses spin; I rode up a hill into the forest and then down into another valley, forgetting myself for a moment, a disembodied spirit in the turmoil of movement. By the time my horse grew tired, the sun had set and the first night-mists were already beginning to weave uncanny forms over the forest floor. The moment of unreality was fleeting, of course. My memories soon returned, and with them that oppressive hopelessness. I slowed the horse and it was not long before Walter drew up alongside me.

'We rode on for a while, in silence. When we dismounted, Walter tried to talk to me, but as we led the horses deeper and deeper into the forest, it was again as though Walter were part of another world, one far away, or that he were a phantom of himself, to whom I should not speak. He explained how he had heard of my departure, how he had seen neither the Graf nor the Gräfin, for they had not visited him, how the castle was deserted, and how Friderich, the nightwatchman, had given him money to come after me. Walter reproached me for leaving him, accusing me that I no longer loved him. Slowly, it dawned on me: no one had told him what I had become at the hands of the Graf. The darkness creeping over the forest engulfed me too, a cold,

136

isolating numbness, rising like hemlock, or a dark ocean in which I was drowning. After another long silence I told Walter why I had left the castle.

'Walter tried to comfort me, but at his touch my spirit doubled up in pain. I studied his face. Gentle and noble though he was, in his features I read compassion and disgust, pity and disappointment. I was no longer his. I was another's. I was no one's.

'Now, I am sure that Walter would have loved me, despite the Graf. He said he wanted to marry me, to care for me. But even if Walter had accepted me, I could not, then, have accepted myself. The hurt done to me seemed to contain a dangerous germ of evil with which I would have to cope alone for fear the contagion might spread to others.

'I tried to find the words to explain this to Walter, but then came the din of men shouting and dogs barking in the distance. We mounted and rode on deeper into the forest, through dark glades where tall, mossy trees grew beside grassy banks, letting our horses splash through streams so the dogs would lose our scent, up hills where the trees were sparser, and the tiny closed buds of flowers mirrored the stars of the night sky with their tips of white and yellow.

'When the horses grew tired once more, and there was no more sign of pursuit, we slowed down, dismounted and walked on, leading our horses. Walter talked, doing his best to evoke happy times we had shared. I said little, for it was as though I were enveloped in some dark cocoon. I tried to lose my present self in the dank shadows of the forest, and give myself to the luminous essence of our lost life at the court. But always the aching knowledge would return of that world's extinction.

'We walked up a steep hill emerging from the forest. Walter fell silent and soon we were moving, ghost-like, through moonlit scrubland dotted with large boulders, bathed in the silver light, a landscape not of this world, but of some more perfect, more fragile realm. In front of us, at the very top of the hill, was an old castle, approached by means of a small bridge over the bottomless shadow of a moat in which mists swirled. Beyond the bridge rose a defensive wall, framed by two symmetrical towers. Behind the wall stood the silver-grey parapets of the keep, the narrow spire of a chapel, and a mast from which no flag flew.

'Walter said that this was Hohenfeld, that the lord who lived here had died childless some ten years before, leaving it to the Church, which had placed it in the trust of Carthusian Sisters who followed an extremely strict rule, like the Carmelites. There was a kindly peace about the solemn buildings. As we drew closer, I felt the place calling to me that it was to be my home.

'Walter rode ahead and knocked at the gate. After a while it was opened by a tall, thin woman, noble and gentle in her bearing, her kind face half-lit by the candle she held. This was Sister Ursula. Walter explained that we were travellers, and that we were seeking shelter. Sister Ursula said that the rules of the Convent prevented men, other than the priests officiating the daily Masses, from entering its gates. It was agreed that Walter would sleep rough outside, and they gave him food and blankets. I was offered a cell for the night.

'The austerity of the house was, as I discovered, extreme, but this did not mean to say that its members were unwelcoming, or aloof, nor did it mean that they neglected their duty of Christian charity to those in need. That night I was a recipient of such charity. Sister Ursula understood my distress, encouraging me to talk as much as I wanted, though she seemed to understand my feelings in advance. It was as though the cocoon surrounding me was melting, and I was still speaking as the bell struck for Matins at midnight. I have rarely spoken so much about myself,

Brother Thomas, before or since – until now.'

I remember distinctly, and I recorded it in my notes, the appearance of Brother Thomas and Domna Cecilia during the course of this interview, for I thought they looked at each other with the eyes of lovers.

'Sister Ursula and I prayed together at Matins,' Domna Cecilia continued. 'Like many contemplatives, she was an intensely practical person, and after the office she led me to a cell and explained that my choice was threefold: I could go into the world with Walter, seeking love through immorality, and glory in a life of chance; I could go to my uncle and beg forgiveness, seeking honour through humility, and salvation through subservience; or else, and I blessed her for this, she said I could stay with them in their house, for they thought I would be suited to the life there. I could earn my keep, she added, by copying manuscripts, and growing food with the others.

'I returned to the chapel where I spent some hours in prayer, until I fell asleep, there on my knees. When they woke me, I took the habit they offered me, and professed myself one of them that very dawn.

'Walter arrived shortly after I had been received. He was bedraggled from sleeping rough, face and hair glistening with dew as he stepped into the simple visitors' room, with its bare, white-washed walls, vaulted ceiling and rustic furniture. If Sister Ursula and the Abbess had not sat with us, I would almost certainly have failed to keep my resolve, for I never saw Walter, or anyone, look more lovely, more loving or more in need of love.

'I suppose I had expected anger, words of protest, pleading, but Walter sat in utter humility, nodding his assent to everything I told him, though I understood that my words must be breaking his heart, as they were breaking my own.

'When I had finished explaining that I wanted to stay in

the Convent, slowly, silent and defeated, yet infinitely kind, he stood up, smiled, bowed a gentle farewell, turned and walked away from me and my love, without looking back, without a word. How easy it would have been to run after him. But his solemnity, the presence of the two older women, and some involuntary paralysis, stopped me from doing so.

'When he had left the room, I walked over to the window, now brilliant in the early morning light, and watched him ride away, towards the sun, down the hill, into the glittering forests, their gold and green mingling, refracted and distorted in the tears which filled my eyes. That,' she concluded, 'is how my life at the Carthusian house began, a life dedicated to a quest for the ideals of purity and beauty, which I had lost in this world, and now hoped only to glimpse perhaps in some other realm.

'The search for God through the *via negativa*,' she said, 'can be austere and terrible, though Saint Denis argued that it was preferable to the affirmative way, for God transcends being. For the disappointed, the hurt and despairing, however, the practices of the Carthusians can be a ritual suicide: the loneliness kills the mind, and the lack of nourishment kills the body. In our Convent the castle buildings were divided into small cells, mostly at ground level. Each had its own garden where, individually, we grew fruit and vegetables for sustenance. In warmer countries, the Carthusians whom we imitated each cultivate all their own food; we, however, needed the supplies of bread and soup each day from the kitchens to survive. We ate no meat and I am sure that the early deaths of some Sisters were due to starvation. However, I would not deny that those who are healthy in spirit can live long years on very little food.

'We spent every weekday in total solitude,' she said, pausing to eat from the food set out for us. This was the first time she had done so. Brother Thomas looked towards me, raising an eyebrow, and nodded gently, indicating that I should note the fact. 'All monastic offices, other than Mass,' she went on, 'were said or sung alone in our cells. Only at dawn each day did we catch a glimpse of each other on the way to chapel. Yet even here, wooden partitions separated us. On Sunday afternoons and special Feast Days we met in the former great hall or, if the weather was fine, in the orchard behind the keep. Here we chatted, exchanged observations about our reading and contemplation, and assured ourselves that every member of the community was well and in good spirits. Ironically, after a week of looking forward to human contact, its reality would often disappoint, and I would not be sorry to return to my cell. On the way back, each Sunday evening, we would collect books from the well-stocked library to be our companions throughout the next six days.

'I grew to know every inch of my cell; even now I remember cracks in the masonry, knots in the grain of the wooden shelf and flaws in the weave of the linen altar cloth, as if they were old friends. Time soon lost its meaning. Days came and went. It was like being in love: in love with loss.'

'I fail to see,' Brother Thomas interrupted suddenly, 'how such a life could have been suitable for a girl of the age you were then.'

'That,' she replied, 'is because you men think women are driven only by passions of the flesh, that we want only men and children, for you ascribe your own desires to us, and blame us for them. My passions had been quite stilled by my experiences at Leuchtenfels. Certainly, prayer would be interrupted by memories of Walter and the Graf, inspiring a turmoil of self-pity, disgust, lust, yearning and regret. Yet I learnt to detach myself from these feelings, to contemplate them as if from a distance, to wait quietly for their clamour to subside, until they became powerless to swallow me.

Perhaps to strive for lost purity is nobler than to possess it naively.

'Friendships I made at Hohenfeld were very precious to me. There was Sister Ursula, my spiritual guide, who was familiar with the Carthusian way from her travels in the Holy Lands and who helped me understand the numerical systems describing our greater bodies. Then there was Sister Violetta with whom, on special Feast Days, I would practise singing. Like Veronika, my old friend in Regensburg, she understood the musical principles of the Ancients and was adept at the performance of the new harmonic sacred music. At High Feasts, the two of us would sing in the exquisitely painted chapel, and as the candles shone in the midst of the incense smoke curling towards the emerald and gold of the vaults and ceilings, and our voices soared over the chanting, I thought I glimpsed Heaven itself.

'One hot June morning, returning to my cell from Mass, and looking forward to the hours of study in front of me, I saw Sister Ursula coming towards me, her usual smile clouded with concern. It was a Tuesday, a day of silence, yet she spoke, saying, "The two of us must go to the Abbess immediately." She took my arm and we threaded our way through the vegetable plots, where the plants were suffering in the mid-June heat, as were the two of us. "You must prepare yourself," she said, "for bad news."

'At the gatehouse we found the Abbess waiting outside, wringing her hands. She was a short, thin woman, with silver hair, and a deeply lined face, from which stern but wise eyes shone. I had never seen her in such an agitated state. "Come with me," she said, and led me, not to her own cell as I had expected, but to the vaulted basement room below the one from which I had said farewell to Walter. She sat opposite me, with Sister Ursula next to her. "We have had a number of visits recently," she said, "from your uncle, the Lord of

Stierenfurt. He has always known you were here, of course. For a while he was content with the arrangement, and even helped us financially. Now, however, his attitude has changed."

' "Do you know why?" I asked. Sister Ursula shot me a stern look, for it was none of my business to interrupt.

' "Your uncle wields considerable financial power," the Abbess went on. "Through negotiations with the Bishop he has acquired the fief to this land from the Church. We dared hope he planned to protect us. Now, however, he has threatened to close the Convent unless you are removed from here. There would be nowhere else for us to go. Legally, I fear that he has the right to carry out his threat."

'After a silence I said, "Such meanness of spirit is typical of him."

' "How do you wish me to reply to your uncle?" asked the Abbess, looking over her shoulder and frowning nervously. "You may refuse, if you wish."

' "There is no decision," I said. "Life anywhere will be hard to bear after the joys I have known here. But to know you are here . . ."

A harsh, male voice boomed suddenly, "That is fine talk from someone who calls herself religious, after everything I have done for you. There is nothing more to say. She is coming with me, now!" From a side room where he had been eavesdropping, the bloated figure of my uncle appeared; scowling through piggy eyes set deep in his blotchy, rubicund face.

' "Forgive me, Uncle," I began.

' "Get changed immediately," he said, "out of that ridiculous outfit. We are leaving. Put this on." He thrust a bundle into my hands. His voice jarred cruelly after the months of silence, and the gentle voices of the nuns. Yet their stillness was within me, and I felt that I possessed more power to cope now than before.

'The Abbess nodded towards Sister Ursula, who led me to the room from which he had just emerged. "I am sorry," she whispered.

'In the bundle was a dress, in the latest fashion, garish dark red, tight-waisted and short-sleeved. The couvre-chef was the same lurid colour but the tunic was green and decorated with overlapping circles of dark blue. I hesitated. Then I considered the threat to the Convent. I knew my uncle was capable of lashing out to hurt anyone who stood in his way. I took a deep breath and put the new clothes on, reflecting that he must have paid a good deal of money for them, since they were brand new. I thought they made me look like a whore.

' "You look lovely," said Sister Ursula; there was something in her voice, and in her gaze, that unnerved me.

'My uncle rubbed his hands when he saw me. "With looks like that, we might find a man for you yet," he said. "Memories are short. After your months here, people will have forgotten your indiscretions. There is a promising suitor," he gloated.

'In silence, too numb to weep, I let my uncle lead me out of the castle gate, to where his men and horses were waiting. I did not once look back as we rode into the forest, through that same glade where I had last walked with Walter. Now, it was alive with June flowers: Saint John's Wort, marigolds, and dogroses; birds sang gloriously, like choruses of heavenly souls. The world beyond the Convent, which had been monotone and insubstantial in the moonlight as I left it, was vivid now, animate. Despite my fears, a part of my soul leapt for joy, as the wind blew in my hair and as the horse moved beneath me.

'By the end of the day, when we arrived, exhausted, at

Stierenfurt, my uncle was grumpy, complaining about his back, his legs, feeling giddy, how his head ached, how he was doing this for me, and how I should be grateful. I said nothing. I was not going to be drawn into an argument with him.

'At the manor house, my cousins, Stierenfurt's sons, were waiting for us: Marcus, a fat slob like his father; Richard, a gaunt young man of twenty or so, always sulking and whinging; and Simon, a sad creature, not unpleasant by nature for he was too dull, but easily led by his brothers. The soup was the same as ever: I was mocked just as before when I refused their wine and the game they had hunted; the comments about my appearance and what I would be like in the marriage bed were as intolerable as before. But now there was a difference. They were unsure of themselves, but I was sure of myself. They were in awe of me. I was no longer the little girl I had been when I first arrived at their house. Now I had my memories. My memories were me. A small triumph, but not much consolation, for I knew how readily awe can turn to spite.

'Daily life resumed just as before. My uncle spent much time riding about his lands, collecting rents, and using his authority to settle legal disputes. He worked hard. Perhaps I learnt to appreciate him more, if not to love him; his awful fits of violent rage made that too difficult. However, I came to understand that he was not an evil man but a simple man bearing burdens beyond his capacities, pitiable almost as he took consolation in food and drink, lost and alone, like an overgrown boy. Besides, I understand now that often his actions were not impulsive, as I believed at the time, but that they were determined by those who were superior to him and who, for reasons you have perhaps fathomed by now, Thomas, took a special interest in my fate.

'After three weeks, there were stirrings in the house and

I learnt that visitors were to come. Amongst these visitors I was to meet my future husband. He was called Martin Palviezen. He was an eldest son and stood to inherit considerable fiefs, held indirectly from the Wittelsbachers, near Würzepurc. Martin's father was called Albrecht. They lived in a good-sized manor house, and possessed many cattle, sheep, vineyards and much arable land, with plenty of serfs and yeomen to keep the land well cultivated. Their family was of yeoman stock and had no noble title. Sadly, Martin's mother had recently died after a long and difficult illness. This, at least, aroused pity in me for Martin. Otherwise, my uncle spoke so well of him that I found it hard to believe.

'From time to time, news reached me about poor Walter who now lived a dissolute life as a travelling player; he drank heavily and drifted from one inn to another, and one woman to another, keeping company with the scum of the earth. I tried to tell myself that those with the highest ideals are most prone to despair, but I was torn. I hated Walter for being untrue to me and our ideals. Yet I felt responsible.

'The night before I met Martin was hellish. I refused food, locked myself away in my room, tried to study, to distract myself in some way, but I failed. I lay awake, as the wind howled outside, and wild animals bayed from distant hills.

'When morning came, it was almost a relief to find that I possessed, after all, the strength which comes from resignation. I washed, dressed and went down the stairs to see that my uncle, and the female members of the family, were well turned out in their best clothes. My cousins were in their hunting gear, out to provide fresh game for the guests. The servants were sweeping and cleaning, and new reeds were strewn on the floor. The old soup had been poured away and fresh was being prepared: a rare honour.

'At about mid-day, the family arrived, and I saw Martin for

the first time. He was a tall, gentle, good-looking young man, only two or three years older than I was. It was apparent from the start that he knew nothing of the courtly arts, for whenever he saw me, he would cast down his eyes and blush. When he did speak to me, it was only about the family land, how it was farmed, what animals they had, how yields had increased now that they ploughed with harnessed horses which were so much faster than oxen, and such matters. He chatted a little too about his military training with the Bishop of Würzepurc's militia. He knew how to ride, but had never attended a courtly tournament, let alone fought in one. His knowledge of religion was scarcely rudimentary. Of singing, poetry, reading and writing, he knew little, and of Latin and Greek he knew nothing. Yet he was a good man, and a kind man. I tried being haughty, then sullen, then boastful of my learning. When I was rude, Martin was diffident. When I showed off, he did not hide his admiration. It was impossible to be spiteful to him. He was uneducated, just as my cousins were uneducated. Yet he had none of their vulgarity; whatever I did only caused him to dote on me the more. He was in my power, even though I did not want that power.

'I had read somewhere that for a man and woman truly to love, it is necessary not only for their angels to be compatible, but their devils too. I knew from the first that I could not love Martin, not with all my heart and soul, not as I loved Walter, and not as a woman should love her husband, for I looked down on him. I never met another man who could measure up to Walter's beauty, both outward and inward. It would have been so much easier if Martin had been cruel, or stupid like my cousins, or even ugly. Yet he was none of these things. I was unable to despise him. On the contrary, I pitied him, well aware how easily pity can be mistaken for love.

'As the days wore on, I grew close to his sister also, and

spent a lot of time with her. She was called Marianne, and was brown-haired and brown-skinned like her brother. She was a quiet, thoughtful soul. What struck me most about the two of them was their openness. My uncle's mind was closed to new ideas. The same was true of my cousins. Yet Martin and Marianne would engage in each new conversation, each new situation, with a generous curiosity, so that when I spoke to them, for example, about my life in the Convent, or my studies, rather than try to put me down, they would listen carefully, full of real interest.

'As their stay wore on I found I was leading a double life. By day I was happy with Martin and his family. Their good will and kindness was charming and contagious. Even my uncle and cousins began to adopt their ways. I was hardly ever mocked now, and if a cousin tried to bully me, then Martin would spring to my defence. In the morning Martin would go off hunting with the menfolk, and I would get on with domestic chores with Marianne, or else we would sit and sew, or chat, or I would tell her about life at court, or I would read to her. Then, in the afternoon the men would return, and the feasting, drinking and laughter would begin, but it was all in good part.

'My uncle was quick to notice that I too was making an attempt to be pleasant, and would smile at me with something resembling kindness, as if to tell me that he had always meant well. I began to understand that, by his lights, his intentions towards me probably had always been good.

'But then the night would come, and the fleeting happiness of the day would evaporate. I would think back to my life at the Convent, to my music, my singing, to my studies. Marriage to Martin would surely exclude this. But most, my mind would turn to Walter. I would wonder where he was. In my dreams I would hear his voice as he used to sing at Leuchtenfels, and I would think of his speech, his wit and learning, that melancholy look in his eyes, that penetrating gaze, the gaze of someone constantly seeking. He was my first love and, I realised, my one and only true love, the only man I could and should have married, yet who was now probably for ever lost to me.

'I suppose I did love Martin. But as a brother, not as a husband. When the day of the wedding was fixed for the first of the following month, I could not find it in me to object. Somehow I smiled through the circling feelings of physical revulsion, disgust at my own ingratitude, yearning for Walter and despair.

'I felt guilt towards my uncle too, who was boasting to his friends about what a grand affair the wedding would be. He had already run up such expenses that he would never forgive me if I backed out. I racked my brains but could think of no escape other than point blank refusal, or running away and consigning myself to an insecure life in the forests, as a beggar or thief, or worse. But this would be to drive me even further from the life I sought than marriage to Martin.

'One day, I was sitting alone with Marianne. We were working on some tapestry and chatting about this and that. Eventually, we came to talk about men, and her experience with them. It turned out that she had none. Suddenly, I saw my opportunity, and grasped it. Simply, without lies, without exaggeration, I told her about what had happened between myself and Walter, and then with the Graf. I watched as the poor girl's face turned every colour. It was evident that she knew nothing of my past, and I surmised that Martin also knew nothing. I began to smile to myself, hoping against hope that I might have found a way out; a phrase from the Gospels came to me: *The truth shall set you free.*

'I spent some time that afternoon with Martin, alone. He was so happy, just back from the hunt, proud to be accepted by people he considered to be his social superiors and, I suppose, looking forward to marrying me. I did not allow myself to feel sorry for him, for that would have been to do him an injustice. Something I appreciated about him, and you must forgive me if you think it is wrong for a woman to speak thus of a man, was his purity, not just in the way that men are accustomed to think of women, but in the way that Christian de Troyes wrote of Parsifal, as *un chevalier pur et fol.*

'That afternoon, as we sat together in the hall of the castle, while the other men were outside skinning a deer they had killed, and the women were at their sewing or starting to prepare the evening's food in the kitchen next door, he told me of the new horse he hoped to buy, and of the cart he was having built by a wheelwright in Würzepurc. Outside, however, lightning flashed in the sky, from a storm brooding over the hills in the distance. Eventually, from far away, there came the deep rumbling of the thunder. The wildness of the weather, of the world beyond, contrasted with the security of the domestic scene I was sharing with Martin, sitting at the table, the smoke rising from the hearth, the first tallow candles lit, a scent like myrrh hanging in the air. I felt an intense tenderness towards him, such as a mother feels for a child. But I did not truly love him. Walter's presence was almost tangible, and I knew that even if we were never to meet again, I could not have betrayed his memory, not then.

'For an hour or so before dinner we went our separate ways.

'How sad the change was that had come over him and his father when they returned. Marianne must have told him. The whole evening they said nothing; they failed to respond to the usual jests of my uncle and my cousins, and refused wine. My cousins tried to cheer them with bawdy jokes which could not have been more out of place. My uncle grew increasingly sullen, sensing something was amiss. My cousins then became unpleasant towards our guests, and might have picked a fight if my uncle had not scolded them. This gave the guests the opportunity to retire to the upper room where, as a special sign of honour, they were accommodated.

'My cousins carried on drinking, and my uncle eyed me suspiciously, but fortunately he had drunk too much to read the situation aright. I went to my room as soon as I could, crossing the courtyard in the pouring rain, the thunder clouds rolling so fast towards the house that they seemed intent on sweeping it away. I threw myself on to my straw mattress and lay awake, listening to the storm, cursing myself, feeling that I had been abandoned by God and man. I must have fallen asleep, because I woke to a morning which was radiant, as if the storm had never been.

'I ventured towards the main part of the house where I was told by one of the younger girls that Martin, Marianne and their father had left, just before dawn. I went straight back to my room and tried to decide what to do. I could not face my uncle, but I did not have to wait long before he came. There was a battering at my door, and he stepped in, with two of his men. I had expected the usual rage. But he was horribly calm. He stared at me. "You told them," he said.

'I cast my eyes down. "I could not live a lie," I replied.

' "No," he said, "and nor can I. I have done everything I can for you. Here!" He threw something at me. It struck my shoulder and fell to the ground. It was a purse. A few coins spilt on to the floor.

' "I do not want your money," I said, turning away to hide my tears.

' "It is not mine," he sneered. "It is from your grand-parents. They put it aside for you. For your safe-keeping, a small dowry. I am finished with you. Get out of here within the hour. If you do not, I shall not be responsible for my actions. As it is, I have these men with me to restrain me. Now, go before you do any more damage!"

' "You should have been honest from the start," I hissed, unaware that his apparent calm masked a dangerously violent rage. He started towards me, grimacing and raising his fist. I feared for my life, but then one of his men held him back, and he remembered himself. He turned on his heels, and strode out of the room.

'Sick with fear, I gathered up the money, made a bundle of the few clothes I had, and walked out of the castle, into the village, and set off to Würzepurc. I soon realised what it was to be a young woman alone in the world. Wherever I went I was followed by men of all stations, from peasants to nobles. Each tried their luck with me, and called me every name under the sun when I rejected their advances. I was set upon by thieves as I entered Würzepurc, and it was only by running as fast as I could into a crowd that I managed to hang on to my money. I remember passing a gallows where a dead man still hung, swaying in the breeze, eyes wide open as if able to see into other worlds. As I made my way towards the city centre, men tried to lure me into inns, and women turned away from me, some even spat in disdain. I longed to find some way of wearing monastic clothes again, with a hood to cover my long hair.

'Finally, I went to the palace, and asked to see the Bishop. You see, my faith in worldly powers, including the power of the Church, was intact then. The palace was high on a hill, above the plain where most of the newer settlements were. A garrison was stationed there and I had to run the gauntlet of soldiers too. The soldiers were present in the city in such profusion because the new Emperor, the Staufer, Henry VI was resident.

'Eventually, I got an audience with the Bishop, who flirted with me to begin with. Then, when he realised who I was because of my connection with Stierenfurt and the Leuchtenfelser (though I did not tell him everything), he organised for me to stay at the Unterzell, the Premonstratensian Convent by the city wall. I was to live there for the next few months, unaware that by doing so I was serving a political, as well as a spiritual purpose.'

At this point Cecilia fell silent.

'I thought you said you married the man called Martin,' said Thomas.

'I did not lie to you, Thomas,' she said. 'I did marry him. And when the time comes, I shall tell you how I came to kill him. But the truth takes time to tell.'

These words of Domna Cecilia's were intended to shock, and they did. However, it was growing dark outside. Alazaïs had returned and was lighting tallow candles. Domna Cecilia's face was stern in the dancing flame-light and it was clear that she felt she had spoken enough for one day, so Brother Thomas and I took our leave from the two women and set off back towards the Cathedral by the West Gate.

Chapter Eleven

A s we approached the Eastbridge hospital Brother Thomas
said he wanted to call on Isaac, and ask him directly
about his views on the chalice, and what he knew about the
man called Michael. I looked forward to the luxury of being
in Isaac's house again, with its wealth of exotic objects, its
opulent scents and gleaming colours. I was in awe of Isaac,
because of his graceful manner and evident knowledge.
Most of all, I looked forward to seeing Myrrah again, not
that I had any hope of winning her. To bathe, briefly and
adoringly, in the light of her presence would be enough.

'You know,' said Brother Thomas as we crossed the bridge
by the hospital, 'that Isaac is involved in the King's finances?'
I nodded. 'You are probably aware too that the Treasury is in
an appalling state. The King lacks money to pay for soldiers,
yet he desperately needs to fight in Wales and in France.'

'Everyone knows that,' I said. 'Why are you telling me?'

'The chalice,' said Brother Thomas.

'You mean,' I said, 'that the King might have ordered its
disinterment?'

'That is one possibility,' Brother Thomas replied. 'Another
is that the Prior might have dug it up to keep it from the
King.'

'Or to keep it for himself,' I suggested cynically.

'You surprise me.' Brother Thomas smiled, evidently
amused, despite the terrible pressures which weighed upon
him.

'But surely the King would not believe there was anything special about the chalice,' I said.

'The King,' Thomas replied, 'cannot afford to disbelieve. He will not wish to end up like his grandfather, Henry II, dying alone and unattended in a foreign land, nor like his father, King John, who perished leaving behind the most terrible debts, and London occupied by the French.'

As we approached Isaac's house, I plucked up the courage and asked, 'Do you think Domna Cecilia will confess to heresy?'

Brother Thomas turned towards me and said, 'She is old but she is not frail. Her spirit is strong. I doubt that she will confess voluntarily.'

'That means,' I said, 'that if they are determined to burn her, she will be tortured first.'

'I understand,' said Brother Thomas. 'I know how you feel. It is not so much that they will beat her, abuse her, break every bone in her body, though these things are terrible enough. What if she did confess under those circumstances? I have seen how a forced confession can destroy the spirit as surely as fire or the hangman's noose destroys the body.'

As he spoke, it was as though I could see Domna Cecilia before me in the darkness, her dignity, her repose, the ageless perfection of her features, and those eyes. Thomas was right. The breaking of Domna Cecilia's spirit would be even more terrible than the breaking of her body.

Despite the cold and the dark, the streets were crowded with torch-bearing pilgrims, merchants and hawkers as we arrived at Isaac's house. Brother Thomas knocked several times on the front door but there was no reply.

Frustrated, we walked to the back of the house, where the Jews have their synagogue. Though only a stone's throw from the main street, everything here was so still, so clean, that I felt like an interloper in a foreign land. One or two Jewish men, distinguished by their long hair and the skull caps they wore, avoided meeting our eyes and took refuge in their various houses.

We tried the door at the rear of Isaac's house, but it was locked. The shouts of the town-criers and the bustle of the busy streets were uncannily distant in the darkness. 'There are no lights inside the house,' Brother Thomas whispered.

I waited for Brother Thomas to decide what to do. Then I saw one of the Jewish elders, Benjamin, walking purposefully towards us, a small, squat man, with long white hair and angry dark eyes staring from behind hooded lids wrinkled with age. 'What do you want here?' he snarled.

'Father Benjamin,' said Thomas. 'Where is Isaac?'

Benjamin spat at our feet. 'You dare to address me as one of your priests?' he hissed. 'I am no father to you.'

'I don't understand,' Thomas answered, his voice calm, but his eyes full of concern.

'Look,' said Benjamin, pointing with his stick at Isaac's house. He tugged at Thomas's sleeve and led him to the window. I followed and peered inside after Brother Thomas. Everything in the house, the exquisite objects, the splendid carpets and tapestries, was wrecked. Furniture was smashed, chests ransacked, and the walls daubed with spiteful words.

'When did this happen?' Thomas stammered.

'This morning.'

'Were they hurt?'

'Who knows?' he replied. 'Myrrah was not there, apparently. I saw Isaac being led away.'

'Where to?'

'How should I know where you people take the likes of us?'

'Who did it?'

'Osbert's men.'

'Thank you,' Thomas muttered awkwardly. Benjamin

strode away from us and, shamed and perplexed, we set off back to the Precincts.

'Who is Osbert?' I asked him as we reached the Forum. This was the only coherent question I was able to frame. All I could think about was Myrrah.

'Sir Osbert is the man who runs the royal castle beyond Saint Mildred's.'

'So there is royal authority for the arrest?' I asked, trying to reassure myself that, at least, if they had been arrested officially there was some chance that Myrrah would be treated appropriately.

Brother Thomas raised his hands in a gesture of helplessness and rage. 'It could have been anyone,' he said. 'The King, the Prior, Lord Rufus, Sir Osbert himself. There is only one way to find out. We'll go straight there.'

So, unexpectedly, I found myself striding through the dark streets, back past Isaac's house, which was guarded by soldiers now, and then out along Ottomannelane, at the end of which, massive and foreboding, exuding a rank atmosphere of cruelty and power, the tall square walls of the castle loomed into sight beyond the narrow rows of wooden houses. It served as a barracks as well as a royal prison. Soldiers were kept here in case Louis of France should try to invade; they were vulgar and violent men of the lowest kind, drunken wrecks most of them, tired of waiting, tired of doing nothing, brawling their only diversion.

At the portcullis we were greeted by Sir Osbert, the Keeper, a vile little toad of a man. I was not certain at first, but the more time we spent with him, the more sure I was that he had been one of the men dressed in green at the Cathedral that night, present at the disinterment of the chalice. After a good deal of surly prevarication he led us to a ground-floor cell where Isaac sat, hunched.

The conditions in which Isaac was kept were relatively good. There was a lamp, a table and chair and fresh straw. I supposed he would be paying Sir Osbert handsomely for these privileges.

'My old friend,' said Thomas, embracing Isaac warmly. 'What has happened to you?'

Isaac returned Thomas's embrace. Though he kept his composure, I thought he was close to tears. 'I was warned that they were coming,' he said, 'but I did not want to leave.'

'Who warned you?' Thomas asked.

'Michael knew. He took Myrrah away, so that she would be safe, but I refused.' I felt relief mingle with a pang of jealousy at these words. 'They came at midnight, hammering at my door, and threatened to have me hanged if I did not let them in. I put up no resistance,' he said. 'They had no reason to be so harsh. But they would not say what they wanted from me. Perhaps you know. Why have I been taken to this place? What is to become of me?'

'Have the Prior's men been here?'

'No,' he said. 'No one.' There was a pleading tone in his voice I would never have thought possible at our previous meeting.

'I think,' said Brother Thomas, 'that the Prior believes you are in possession of secret knowledge. Something to do, perhaps, with the chalice that was taken from him.'

'I know of rumours about a chalice which is supposed to be buried in the Cathedral,' said Isaac. 'It belongs to our people – it always has. It was a sign of kingship, and still is, even when it was in the hands of the Romans, and the Merovingians.'

'Did you know that it had been disinterred, and then stolen?'

'Of course not,' said Isaac.

'If you tell me the truth,' Brother Thomas said kindly, 'we

can help you. But that is the only way.'

Isaac sighed. 'Look at me,' he said. 'How could I help you?'

'Perhaps you could tell me something of the secret Work in which your father was engaged.'

'My father's people often used to work with those at the Priory, in the days when the monks of the Cathedral were wise men of the old sort, before the new breed of monastic came along.'

'I once heard it said that your father could turn beryl to aquamarine, and that he knew much about the transmutation of metals, and of correspondences between herbs, metals, planets and the constellations,' Brother Thomas said, as I looked on, quite taken aback by his words.

'I am a moneyer, first and foremost,' said Isaac. 'I was interested for a short time in the matters you mention, but I met with little success. Besides, much knowledge has been lost since my father's day.' I caught Brother Thomas's eye. It was clear from his look that he thought Isaac was lying. But we could hardly blame him.

'So why would the Prior be so interested in you that he has had you arrested?' Thomas insisted.

'For one thing,' Isaac said, 'he owes me money. You know, he has only one aim in life, to gain the Archbishopric which he considers to be his by rights. It is within his power to force me to lend him money, and then to ruin me. He has even threatened my daughter.'

'I believe it was through you that he found where the chalice was buried, in the Cathedral.' This was Brother Thomas at his best. He had hit the nail on the head. Isaac's reaction was so sudden and so transparent there would have been no point in his denying it.

'It was Myrrah,' Isaac conceded. 'Her understanding of

such matters is astonishing. I would never have managed on my own.' My heart missed a beat to hear Myrrah praised in this way.

'What about Michael?' Thomas insisted. Poor Isaac appeared exhausted, broken, and I could not understand why Thomas was pressing him quite so hard. Surely this could wait until we had got the old man out of prison.

'Very well,' he said. 'I shall explain, though you have probably guessed already. Michael is my son. He was always a great source of anxiety to me. Even as a small child his spirit was restless, impossible to satisfy. When he was as young as six I would find him praying to your Christ, his rebellious nature eager to test what answer he might receive. In debates at the synagogue he would expound Christian and Islamic doctrines and philosophies which fly in the face of our people's traditions. This was why, five years ago, when he was seventeen, I permitted him to go out into the world, to travel, to find whatever he was destined to seek.' My relief that Myrrah and Michael were brother and sister almost made me forget where I was. Now, I dared hope.

'And when did he return?'

'Just two weeks ago now. He is a young man with a great capacity for love as well as learning. Besides, he is blessed with very special gifts, no matter what his other faults might be. Perhaps this is why he returned, because something is about to unfurl.'

'You mean the chalice?' Brother Thomas asked.

'Perhaps,' said Isaac. 'You must understand that my heart was full of joy to see him again, and to know that the faith of our people meant something to him.'

'I have heard a rumour,' Brother Thomas interrupted, 'that there are seven such chalices in the world, and that those who possess them have power and wisdom also, so that the very existence of the world depends on the prayers of these people. Is there any truth in this?'

Isaac looked from one of us to the other. 'There are meanings within the meanings. Besides, there are certain matters about which it is best not to enquire too closely. Remember the fate of William de Sens. Some say he was too liberal with his knowledge.'

Thomas reacted with surprising ferocity. 'That is not the point,' he snapped. 'My aim is to help the living – not least *you*, my friend.' Then he added, with sudden tenderness, 'You must forgive me. Alyssa and my children have gone missing. I am overwrought. I don't know who might help me.'

'I am sorry,' Isaac said, shaking his head, an exhausted sadness in his voice. 'I did not know.' His words were cut short by a rattling at the door of the cell.

Sir Osbert and two guards burst in. 'It is time to leave,' he bellowed.

'We have the right to stay as long as we want,' said Brother Thomas.

'Not according to the message I have just received from the Prior. I sent word about your visit. Prior John is not best pleased.'

'There,' said Brother Thomas, turning first to Isaac, and then to me. 'We have learnt something.'

The two guards grabbed our arms and we were half led, half dragged along the dark, foul-smelling corridor and shown, across the drawbridge to the street. We walked back to the Forum in silence except for the one sentence Thomas spoke. 'How, Wilfridus, in a world like this, can I hold on to hope for Alyssa?' I could think of no reply.

When we got back to our lodgings, Brother Thomas lit the lamps. I remember sensing an odd atmosphere in the room, as though someone else had been there. As soon as there was enough light, we found on the table, weighted down with pebbles just like those stuffed into Brother Theodor's mouth, two pieces of parchment, each densely covered with writing. Too tired, at first, to react other than mechanically, we read the story which I am able to reproduce here in full, since I am still in possession of that document:

There was a man with only one eye in the middle of his forehead. He had three daughters. The time came for them to marry and the first suitor to present himself was a King, the King of the Crows. 'I will marry any of your daughters,' said the King of the Crows, 'for each is lovely. They may choose between them which of the three will be my bride.'

The two older daughters laughed and sneered at the bird-man's offer. The youngest, only ten, was not even told of it. When he found out, the King of the Crows flew into a rage, and pecked out the father's one and only eye.

After the anger left him, and he saw the lovely girls' grief at the devastation he had caused, the Crow King repented. 'By the skills I possess,' he said to the father, 'your sight can be restored to you, but only if one of your daughters changes her mind.'

Immediately, the youngest daughter offered herself to save her father.

As soon as the marriage took place, the father's sight was restored. The wedding feast was sumptuous, and afterwards crow servants led bride and groom to a magnificent castle, far away, on an island in the middle of the sea.

On the wedding night, the King of the Crows explained himself to his new bride. 'I and my people are not really crows,' he said. 'We only appear so, for long ago a spell was cast on us by an evil sorcerer. But you can save us. You need only wait seven years, until you become a woman. But in the meantime, you must never seek to know what I really look like.'

The girl waited. Throughout that time her only friend was an old washerwoman. At last, desperate with impatience, on the eve of her seventeenth birthday, the girl searched the King's possessions, until she found his portrait. What a charming young man he was! How she looked forward to being his wife! But then, with a flash of lightning and a clap of thunder, a terrible form appeared before her, the same sorcerer who had first banished the King. Beside him was the Crow King, still in his crow form. Realising how she had let down her lovely husband, she began to weep.

'Now you will be chained to the top of that mountain!' said the sorcerer to the Crow King. With a pitiful squawk, the King of the Crows flew away to the mountain-top to which the evil sorcerer pointed.

The washerwoman tried to comfort the weeping girl. 'Here,' she said, 'is a golden knife, and here are iron shoes. When you have walked enough to wear out the shoes, your husband will be saved.'

The girl walked year after year, through the country where the sun always shines, and through the country which belongs to the moon. Once she met a wolf, which she had to kill with the golden knife. After that, wherever she walked the grass would sing, and grow blue, wearing away at the iron shoes.

At last she was walking barefoot. She picked some of the blue grass, which enabled her to cross the sea to the island where her husband was banished. Here she met another wolf which she had to kill with the golden knife. The rock where her husband was chained was guarded by two more wolves, one white and one black. She killed them both with the golden knife, thus freeing the King and his people from the spell and from his chains.

Together, they lived happily ever after.

Thomas and I pored over the story by lamp-light and then discussed it. He was convinced that it had nothing to do with the usual astrological, alchemical or kabbalistic systems. I could make neither head nor tail of it, especially since my mind kept turning towards Myrrah. Though I had only ever met her on two occasions, she already seemed to be part of me.

That night Brother Thomas passed on to me his knowledge of the system of correspondences between the heavenly bodies, precious stones and musical notes. They are as follows:

0	D		Aleph	Chalcedony
1	A	Sun	Beth	Mercury, opal, agate
2	E	Moon	Gimel	Moonstone, pearl, crystal
3	B	Venus	Daleth	Emerald, turquoise, salt
4	F♯	Jupiter	He	Ruby
5	C♯	Mercury	Vau	Topaz
6	G♯	Sagittarius	Zain	Alexandrite
7	E♭	Mars	Cheth	Amber Kephra
8	B♭		Teth	Cat's eye
9	F	Pisces	Yod	Pearl, peridot
10	C	Capricorn	Kaph	Amethyst, lapis lazuli
11	G	Leo	Lamed	Emerald
12	D	Aries	Mem	Beryl, aquamarine
13	A	Saturn	Nun	Snakestone
14	E	Aquarius	Samekh	VITRIOL
15	B	Dragon	Ayin	Black diamond
16	F♯		Phe	Ruby
17	C♯	Taurus	Tzaddi	Glass, crystal
18	G♯	Cancer	Koph	Pearl
19	E♭	Gemini	Resch	Chrysoleth
20	B♭	Scorpio	Schin	Opal
21	F	Virgo	Tau	Onyx

Throughout the night these patterns, memories of the shapes of the Cathedral, Myrrah's face, and the crow story returned over and over, echoing in my mind, stirring dim, uncertain thoughts and connections.

Chapter Twelve

T HE NEXT MORNING, after Mass, we walked through freezing drizzle to Domna Cecilia's house. We were welcomed by Alazaïs, who served us wine, bread, and a salad made with cress, melons and herbs.

Domna Cecilia began by asking, provocatively enough, 'I wonder, Brother Thomas, just how reconciled you are to the powers of this world, to the hierarchies of Church and State.'

Brother Thomas pointedly disregarded this and said, 'You were about to explain what happened after you left Stierenfurt for the second time.'

'Indeed,' she said. At this point her cat jumped on to her knees. As she told her story, I often had the impression that she was talking to the animal, rather than to us. 'Today I shall tell you about my time at the Unterzell, the Premonstraten-sian Convent at Würzepurc sacred to Saint Cecilia, and about my first pilgrimage. Tell me, Thomas, do you think I would have made a good Abbess?'

'Undoubtedly,' he replied, smiling with sudden warmth, as though some complicity between them had been rediscovered through her question.

'Then you are wrong. I came to discover that the gift I possessed in abundance was not, as I had believed, an inner stillness, but self-control. I was able to live the life of a monastic, not because I was at peace, or because I loved, in the true sense of the word, but because of an immense arrogance, through which I was able to discipline myself.

165

Within, however, my spirit was restless beyond measure. It dawned on me, but only slowly, that the silence of the monastic life would, if I left other aspirations unassuaged, merely eat away at my soul, and leave me one of those sad, withered creatures, mean-natured and sour, that one so often finds creeping along the corridors and cloisters of religious houses, alongside those lovely people who really have found some truth, some light.'

I smiled at this description which fitted any number of monastics I knew, whose old age was a fearful, arid time of regret and resentment. Then I caught the warning look in Cecilia's eye and shuddered, glimpsing myself perhaps as I am now.

'Life with the Würzepurc Premonstratensians was quite different,' she continued, 'from the one I had shared with the Hohenfeld Carthusians. The régime was much more relaxed. We were allowed visitors, silence was kept in the mornings only, wine was drunk with meals on Holy Days, and study, music and singing were encouraged. Travel from one convent to another was permitted on the slightest pretext. The Convent possessed considerable wealth from fiefs held in surrounding lands. I was not always convinced that this money was put to the best possible use – the glorification of our buildings was given a higher priority, for instance, than feeding the poor.

'I suppose I might have been happy but, by then, mine was a divided soul. I was assiduous about religious duties and observations. A certain spiritual pride drove me to outshine the other nuns, fasting often, remaining silent and alone for long periods, and immersing myself in exercises and devotions I had learnt at Hohenfeld, of which the Premonstratensians appeared ignorant. Of course, this won me few friends. But there was more to my behaviour than spiritual pride. I was lost and astray in this world without the rigour of monastic life; its astringency was a comfort to which I clung.

'Mother Magda, the Abbess, a very jovial woman, a member of an important branch of the Welf family who had, as it happened, known my father, encouraged me to cultivate other arts, in addition to my devotions. So, when I was not engaged in prayer, or manual work, I threw myself once more into manuscript illumination, music, poetry, the study of secular texts, drawing, debating and chess. I offered Mother Magda what remained of my dowry in return for a place at the Convent. She said I should stay, but that she would put the money to one side for a year, in case I changed my mind.

'Of course, in contrast to the love between the sexes, the joys of art and consolations of religion can appear pale and superficial. So it was for me, constantly possessed by my yearning for Walter. Whenever I heard tell of a singer, I would listen closely, in case it was him, and when I studied, or sang, or discussed things of beauty, it was always with him in mind, as though I were rehearsing a conversation to be shared with him.

'I realised,' she went on, 'that I would never know peace unless what had begun between Walter and myself was resolved. Perhaps you remember that song of Heinrich of Morungen: "Ez tuo vil wê, swer herzelîche minnet . . .*"

'Walter was my first love, my one true spiritual companion. This was more important to me by far than the love of the flesh, which I came to see as the distortion of something essentially truer. I understand this better now but then I glimpsed it only as the shadow of an idea. What do you think, Thomas? Is the coupling of the flesh a reunion of souls tragically separated at birth by matter? Or is it an insanity, a fury inflicted by demons made desperate and

* *It causes great pain to love with all one's heart . . .*

vengeful by the truth of human love?'

Again, I glanced towards Thomas, but he responded only with a gentle smile, refusing to be drawn into a discussion.

'I was in chapel one night,' Cecilia continued, 'and suddenly there was a vision. I saw Walter, or rather, first I heard him. His voice, his singing voice, came to me vividly, yet it was out of tune, pain-racked. Then, in my mind's eye I saw him walking through the night, poor and ragged, surrounded by blasted trees, weird clouds racing past a blood-red moon. He held his arms crossed over his chest, for his clothes were full of tiny clawed creatures, like lice, scorpions, crabs and crayfish, which tore at his itching flesh. Then in the moon I saw the writhing limbs of young women, women who saw advantage, or pleasure, in giving themselves to Walter. I saw too that Walter's face was haggard, and there was such yearning in it as, slowly, he turned towards me. He greeted me with a half-smile and I saw in his eyes the low inns, hostels and brothels where he would sing and mix with the rabble. I had no time to ask where he was because the vision faded. I only knew that it was somewhere in the German Empire, and to the west.

'That night I slept little, for the memory of the vision returned over and over. There was a real full moon outside my window, ironically pure and white. Its cold sterility came to me as a reproach since I was haunted by the idea that I had failed in my responsibility towards Walter inasmuch as we were, and are, joined.

'At last I fell into an uneasy sleep. When I woke the sun blazed reassuringly and my spirits lifted. What I should do was suddenly clear to me. I would go on a pilgrimage.

'Immediately after Mass I went to tell the Abbess of my intention. "Are you going to seek God," was her response, "or perhaps something or someone else?" I blushed at her words, sensing that she had seen through me. Still, she gave me permission to join a group of Sisters who had already made plans to leave for Santiago de Compostela.

'You might well wonder at the ease with which we, four young women, were given dispensation to leave. But you must appreciate that there was greater tolerance and understanding in those days; many noble-hearted people understood the nature of a quest. Of course, things have changed now: the eyes and ears of our times are closed, for newness frightens our leaders. Or perhaps there was another, darker reason, for there were those, in the higher reaches of power, whom it suited for me to be out of the Empire for a while.

'Early that spring, just as the first hyacinths bloomed, the Abbess gave the four of us food, money, small jewels to sell in case of emergency and letters to deliver at various houses and convents along our way. We were also given a handsome white horse between the four of us; his name was Scorpio, and we were very proud of him. The Abbess insisted it was important that I should offer to sing, whenever appropriate, in return for hospitality. I yearned to see Aquitaine, whose songs of love and chivalry I knew, their sounds radiant with the sun and nobility of the courtly life lived there. Of course, I knew of the Cathar religion, even then, but understood little enough of its true meaning.'

At this point a less patient interrogator might have quizzed Cecilia about her attitudes to heresy. Yet Brother Thomas deliberately allowed the opportunity to pass, for people respond guardedly to questions about such matters; what they tell you of their own free will is often far more damning. 'Do tell us about your journey,' was all he said.

'We set off,' she continued, 'one shimmering, incandescent spring morning and headed south-west towards Rothenburg, planning to continue to Wimpfen, Stuttgart, and then on to the Kingdom of France, where I had heard there are many admirable churches, hallowed monasteries and convents, buildings sacred to our Lord and the saints, places where Our Lady and other blessed souls have appeared to men and women, and shrines where skulls and other relics of pious saints are housed in exquisite reliquaries; people told me how warmly the sun shone, how even plants like lilies and roses were more lavish, and how creatures like scorpions, beetles, lobsters, crayfish and wolves grew to giant proportions. They told me too of the sea, which was like an immense river, in constant motion and so wide that no one could see to the other side of it, for it stretches infinite distances to places where monsters dwell, the dreadful Leviathans which are mentioned in the Bible.

'It was one thing to talk and dream of these things, but to reach them was another matter. Our progress was slow. Even before we got to Rothenburg, Madeleine, one of the Sisters with whom I was travelling, fell ill, and we had to spend two or three weeks at a small convent waiting for her to recover. This was no real sacrifice for me, since the Convent's scriptorium contained many treasures, several books in Greek, and a copy of certain poems by Ovid which were unknown to me. Moreover, there were exceptional collections of songs deposited by travelling knights, jongleurs and troubadours. I learnt many of them and sang them on Feast Day evenings to the other nuns and guests.

'As soon as Madeleine was well, we set off again, this time in the company of an elderly knight who called himself Roland von Rappenau. He was heading in the same direction and could not be dissuaded from offering to accompany us. He was a likeable, comical fellow, with a gigantic moustache and a pot belly, very proud and extremely entertaining. He could recite the old stories of the knight Parsifal and the sagas of the Nibelungen. He claimed to have fought in many battles though I, for one, was not sure whether to believe him. He treated us with the exaggerated courtliness and flattery typical, I thought, of a kind old soldier whose brains were dulled by his years and addled by wine. In any case, he appointed himself our protector, though I doubted he would have been much use if we had needed protecting.

'Imagine my shock when, one afternoon, I found him and Sister Isabel tumbling in a cornfield by the wayside. I shouted for Sarah, thinking he had taken Isabel by force. But when Isabel and Roland stood up and dusted themselves down beneath the silver birch trees, the look on their faces soon convinced me that Isabel had been a very willing party. They stood there, holding hands, staring lovingly into each other's eyes. They apologised for embarrassing us, yet they were in love, they said, and would marry at the first opportunity.

'Even more surprisingly, it turned out to be an honest match. Sir Roland's first wife had died the previous year. Apparently, he had been inconsolable until he came across Sister Isabel. He had lands nearby, and the last I heard she was happily ensconced as lady of the manor. I imagine she must be a wealthy widow now.

'Just before we reached Wimpfen, where we were to go our separate ways, I asked Roland if he had come across a singer answering Walter's description. My voice quaked as I spoke, and I could tell from the kindly look in Roland's puffy eyes that he understood. "Yes," he said. "I have heard of him, and seen him too. He is a musical prodigy. He knows thousands of songs in every style from courtly to bawdy, and in any number of different languages. But he leads a dissolute life. He drinks recklessly and drifts from one woman to the next. They seem to queue up for him, I can't think why. It never used to happen to me. Still, with men like that, you know what they say, to love them is to love one's own ruin."

'Roland's words cut me to the quick. After saying our farewells the three of us carried on south, through the wild, high mountain country towards the Cistercian Abbey of Mundfons. One night the only shelter we found was a hollow in a cliff. I sat up most of the time, keeping guard, while the other two slept. The stars in the early summer sky were brilliant, and the moon lit the wooded valley, the mountains, and the still, blossom-laden trees with such angelic light that I could feel my own soul spreading its wings, and flying over lakes and trees, church towers and mountain tops, as though it were flying home. Ah, but such moments, when you are alone, bring yearning for the one you love. If only Walter were there, I thought, and if only we could have been together as we had once been.

'I woke next morning to find the dawn sky covered with clouds, and a warm but driving rain came, from which there was no protection. By the time we reached the Mundfons Abbey, we were drenched. We asked for shelter and were directed by the monks to the small Convent nearby, likewise Cistercian, high up in the mountains just out of sight of the much larger Abbey.

'I was struck down by a debilitating fever almost as soon as I arrived. The nuns told me afterwards I was so ill they were convinced I would die. I have a clear memory of the delirium, the visions tumbling one after the other. Sometimes I would feel a feathery fluttering of angels' wings struggling to carry me to Heaven, but their plumage would only stifle me, and I would yearn for the cool earth; then I would feel myself plummeting down to dark, cavernous regions underground, where skeletal figures rowed boats of damned souls over sulphurous waters. Then I understood that I could leave my body, look down upon myself in the room where I lay, even leave the confines of the Convent, travelling through the aether to see people I knew. For example, once I saw the Graf of Leuchtenfels in a tiny country church, at prayer, begging for forgiveness. Then I would see the Gräfin, skulking through halls unknown to me. I would see Walter too, but always haggard, dirty, drinking, his arm round some girl, or lying with her, his eyes large with the horror of damnation, secretly yearning for someone, something to come to his rescue. Yet the eyes of his angels remained ever averted, and I too had failed him.

'One day, when I was recovering, but still hallucinating from time to time, my mind fixed on Walter, I saw him riding along the road from Wipfen, heading towards the Convent in which I lay. He was changed. There was an air of purpose about him now, and he bore a message for me. This dream came first thing in the morning, as I lay in bed in the infirmary, drifting in and out of sleep.

'I use the word "dream", yet these feverish states were not normal dreams, for during my fever, I had learnt, or rather re-learnt, a power many possess but few can control. I still try to incorporate such insights in my devotions, though it is wrong to trust them absolutely. You see, much of what I glimpsed was true, for Walter *was* riding towards the Convent. You may mock this faculty, Thomas, yet through it I know that you are my listener.

'Sister Rosa came for me and told me to get up, saying I had a visitor, a young knight about to set off on Crusade. She helped me to the small, vaulted room on the first floor of the gatehouse, through whose windows the morning light was pouring. There, wearing the clothes of a knight, with the insignia of holy pilgrimage on his white over-shirt, face worn, complexion shot to pieces, but still strong, and with the same light of yearning in his eyes, though deeper now, oppressed with melancholy, was Walter.

173

'The moment I saw him, I felt how much I was divided against myself. Half of me loved him so very much, wanted to give myself to him, do everything for him. Yet the other half recoiled, because of the life I knew he led. Exquisite though his singing and his songs were, he was too tainted by this world, and my love for him could never be the same.

'We sat in silence for a long while. Sister Rosa had left us but old Sister Berenice stayed in the room, as was the practice. At last, Walter began to tell me what he had done since that morning long ago when we had parted in Hohenfeld. He had returned to the Abbey near Leuchtenfels, but was forced to flee. On his travels near Offenburc, he met a blind visionary who was convinced that Walter was chosen to play a role ushering in the Last Days. Walter had flown into a rage against the self-styled seer, and left shouting abuse at him. Yet the old man's words had preyed on him. When Walter sought the man out again, intending to make amends, the man had gone, and his little chapel had burnt down. This drove Walter to such despair that he sought consolation in the life of the low people; he had lived amongst vagrants, whores, outsiders, drinkers, the scum of the earth, whom he said he had learnt to love.

'As he spoke, Walter seemed to look straight through me, as if I weren't even there. Unhappy thoughts tumbled through my mind. Could it be that, now I was paler, gaunter, and my long blonde hair cut short, I no longer had the power to please him? I thought of the other women he had known. Jealousy coursed through my veins like poison, though I knew I had no right to be jealous, since it was I who had chosen to leave Walter. I tried to tell him how happy I was as a monastic, but I broke down in tears. I confessed that my life was only emptiness without him; I chided him about his dissolute life, and begged him to change his ways for my sake.

'I remember his last words to me: "There is only one answer," he said. "I must go on Pilgrimage to the Holy Land. Believe me, if ever I do anything good, anything noble, it will be for you. You will always be with me in my thoughts."

'I recall Walter, as he said this, the ashen pallor of his skin, his avoidance of my gaze, the hunched humility of his bearing, the air of resignation with which he had borne my harsh words. His very desire to join the Crusade seemed rooted in defeat, self-loathing, as if he had lost faith with himself. For a moment, I glimpsed the terrible void which would have plunged him into debauchery. I had often wondered where his songs and his singing might have come from. Then I understood, and forgave. But it was too late. Since, I have had much time to reflect on his words, and I am convinced that, though I never saw him again, the story of our love is not yet over.'

My records for that day end at this point.

As I write now, that scent of sandalwood which used to greet me whenever I visited Domna Cecilia has returned, as if for all these years it has been trapped in these parchment pages, waiting for this moment for release. How can I explain the power Domna Cecilia had over Brother Thomas and myself? Her life seemed touched by some ideal, to embody a lost, unique beauty, as though she had access to a higher world, or had glimpsed a purity we yearn for, knowing it can only destroy. The pattern of her life has remained with me ever since, like light reflected through a shattered precious jewel, scattering shards of turmoil through my otherwise obscure existence, and awe still fills me at the thought of her.

Chapter Thirteen

THE NEXT MORNING, Brother Thomas woke ill with a fever. I thought he was sick with worry about Alyssa and his children. Outside, rain was pouring down. Thomas wanted to stay in bed until he felt better, and then visit the Prior, alone. I, meanwhile, was to go again to the Jewish quarter, in order to find out what had happened to Isaac. The next formal interview with Domna Cecilia would have to wait until the following day.

As I was walking along Mercery Lane, I saw Michael coming towards me. He was clearly anxious, and the Prior's words about him flooded back into my mind. He strode up to me and said, 'We must talk.'

I nodded. He grasped my arm, as if he were afraid I might run off, and led the way in silence out along Weterlok Lane beyond the King's Mill. We crossed the common land, reaching the edge of the city where the wall is almost entirely dilapidated, and trudged across damp grass towards a deserted house. The land immediately surrounding it was fenced off, and Michael had to force the gate open; the hinges were rusty and broken. What had once been an orchard or garden was now thickly overgrown with briar and convolvulus. The house was wooden, but for one stone wall. Next to it were the remains of a tiny stone chapel, just big enough for half a dozen people to squeeze inside, but its roof had fallen in, and it too was overrun with vegetation.

The barking of a dog rang through the damp air from

within as Michael unfastened the latches to the rickety main door and ushered me into the house. Inside was one large room with three or four other smaller areas partitioned off by wooden walls not quite reaching the ceiling. Dripping water formed a puddle near the entrance. Chained to the post in the centre of the main room, straining towards us and howling wildly at our approach, was a large sheepdog.

As soon as we entered, Michael made a small fire in the middle of the room, petted the sheepdog who soon grew less excited, and lit a few candles. In the dull, flickering light I saw a rough altar in one corner of the room, covered with a white cloth, which was stained with wax and age. The motif woven into the altar cloth was a man, a Christ-like figure, sitting cross-legged, and surrounded by foliage, from which peeped caterpillars and chrysalises. Meanwhile, the rain hissed through the foliage overgrowing the house and drummed noisily against the wooden roofboards. 'Let's sit together in front of the fire,' said Michael. 'I'll make something for us to drink.'

There was a solemnity about his movements, a calm and a grace. 'You know,' I said, 'about the arrest of Isaac?'

'Yes,' he replied, and set about piling wood on the fire. Then he rummaged in a chest and took out an earthenware pot of wine, and a jar of spices: cumin and cinnamon. He poured the wine into a brass jug with a long handle, and mixed in the contents of the jar. He gave me the jug to hold over the fire, went into the next room, and came back with a platter, on which was a loaf of bread, fruit, and onions. 'There,' he said, taking the jug from me, and pouring the spiced wine into two wooden goblets, 'now we are comfortable. You probably know that Isaac is my father.'

'He told me,' I said. 'I saw him in prison at the castle yesterday. He is as well as can be expected.'

'My father is a very fine man,' said Michael, 'though it

took me years to appreciate him. It must take courage to allow your children to ask their own questions in their own way. Some of us have to learn for ourselves.'

'He told me a little about your travels,' I said. 'It was you who took the chalice from the Prior in the Cathedral, wasn't it?'

'What makes you think that?' he said. An ironic smile played about his lips. Otherwise his features were quite impassive.

'I was there,' I said. 'I followed you and Myrrah.'

'You told the Prior?' he asked. His manner was polite, but the tone of menace was unmistakable. It occurred to me that for all his gentleness of manner, this was not a man to cross.

'No,' I said. 'But I am sure he suspects you. He is trying to blame you for the murders at Swiffeld.'

'Why did you not tell the Prior about me?' he said. 'And why should you believe I did not carry out those murders?'

'I cannot imagine you doing such a thing,' I said. 'If we are suspicious of anyone, then it is the Prior.' His penetrating eyes fixed on me and I felt uneasy, as though I still needed to convince him. 'Besides,' I added, 'there is your sister.'

Slowly, Michael's expression changed to that of a knowing smile, which was not without warmth. 'I see,' he said.

'Where is Myrrah?' I asked.

He looked at me with his head to one side, as if he were able to read my heart. 'She got away from the house before my father was arrested.' I took a long draught of the spiced wine he had made. Its warmth rushed through my veins and set my head reeling for a moment or two. 'I learnt that Osbert's men were coming and warned her. My father was more stubborn, and insisted on staying. Myrrah is travelling to a house near Saint Albans which belongs to our family. She will be safe there.'

'Do you know why they ransacked your father's house?' I asked. 'I can only assume it has something to do with the chalice. Am I right?'

'My father,' Michael said evasively, 'is a wise man. In the old days, *his* father worked closely with monks at the Cathedral Priory who had real understanding. Now most men at the Priory are like the Prior; they comprehend only force.'

'But why did you want to take the chalice?' I pressed him.

'You ask a great deal,' he said, 'and you assume a great deal. If you are to understand, then I shall have to tell you something of my story.'

He waited, as though asking my permission. 'Very well,' I nodded. Whereupon he smiled and offered me more drink and food.

'By the time I was sixteen,' he began, 'my father had already taught me a great deal, particularly, as I said, the importance of asking the right questions. But mine was a restless spirit. I wanted to go out into the world and put to the test the learning he had forced upon me, since I had little faith in it. He had the generosity to trust me. During the course of my travels, I learnt much. For example I came to understand more deeply the significance of Christian doctrines, I spent some time at the schools of Paris, and I learnt certain trades too, by means of which I could earn my living, including the arts of musicians and stonemasons. In Italy I fell in with the followers of Francis of Assisi. I never met that lovely man, but one could sense his spirit in the stories told of him by those who had, and even the rocks, trees, flowers and animals of the lands where he had preached.'

'You became a Franciscan?' I interrupted.

'Not like those who founded the Order,' he replied. 'I fear they will soon be persecuting anyone who disagrees with them, just like you Dominicans. I mean his true followers, who understand the meaning of freedom. Besides, I acquired other learning too, of which the Franciscans would have disapproved.'

'Like the parchment you used for fortune-telling,' I said, remembering our first meeting.

'That is one example,' he said. 'But that should not surprise you, since your master, Brother Thomas, is interested in such matters.' I tried not to betray my bewilderment that he should know so much about Brother Thomas. Now, with sudden clarity, I saw the connection between the pictures on Michael's parchment, the stones on the chalice he had stolen and my master's studies. Perhaps I had quite misconstrued the message he was trying to convey to me on the morning of our first meeting. 'For a while,' he continued, 'I travelled from land to land, owing allegiance to no lord, living through study, singing, carving stone and building a network of friends who shared my understanding. I settled longest in the lands of Toulouse, where many still remember the years before the armies of the French came, when there was such a great love of learning, such a profound tolerance of different understandings of the world, for here Saracen and Jew, Christian and heretic could discuss openly and fruitfully the differences in their philosophies, and learn much from one another. There are more ways of worshipping God than are written. Even the rain worships Him, in its way.'

Uncannily, just as he said these words, the rain started pouring down. Then, suddenly, there was a brilliant flash which illuminated the objects in the room, followed by a jolting crack of thunder just over the house, so loud that I cowered involuntarily. 'And the lightning,' he added. The pungent smell which follows lightning hung in the air. I remembered that Lord Rufus said Domna Cecilia had come to England from Toulouse.

'While I was in Toulouse,' Michael continued, 'I came to

understand the truth and depth of my father's teaching, so that I yearned to be with him again. To cut a long story short, when I returned to Canterbury I was reconciled with my father. This is how I know he possesses knowledge, about the chalice for example, that would interest some who are in power.' Suddenly he stopped speaking; then after a pause, he whispered, 'Can you hear?' The sheepdog grew agitated and began howling. Michael, unable to comfort him, walked towards the narrow window, then turned, his face clouding suddenly with consternation. I heard, above the rain, in the distance at first, but coming towards us with increasing urgency, the sound of shouts, harsh voices, dogs barking. 'Soldiers,' he said. 'They are coming across the open land. Did you bring them here?'

'Of course not,' I said.

He looked at me, and I could tell from his face that he trusted me. 'In that case, you are in danger too. This way you can slip out towards the town.'

He led me to a rickety door to the rear of the ramshackle house. It was overgrown with gorse, but there was a path which led towards the mill from which it would be easy to get back into town. 'Aren't you coming?' I said.

'I am beginning to realise what I have to do,' he said. 'I am sure we will meet again soon.' He grasped my arm briefly as I was leaving, in a gesture of friendship. The warmth of his touch was like a physical presence in my arm even as I walked through the chill, pouring rain towards the mill, my feet catching in the brambles.

The mill was deserted because of the season, and I hid behind an outbuilding. From here I looked back and saw a dozen or so brutal men, half of them with dogs, and three or four bearing pikes and swords, make their way towards the house. But before they reached it, Michael stepped out and offered to go with them.

They reacted with surprise and suspicion. I suppose they had been expecting a fight, but they had to lead him away towards the road where a squat man on horseback was waiting for them. I recognised this man as Sir Osbert, the Keeper of the castle, with whom we had had dealings when we visited Isaac. They set off in the direction of the castle and I followed from as great a distance as possible until I was sure that was where they were going. Then I returned to our lodgings in order to tell Brother Thomas what had happened.

Brother Thomas's fever had abated and I found him writing at the table. I told him about Michael's arrest. At first, Brother Thomas appeared to ignore me, despite my agitation. I walked closer to the table and saw that he was working, not at anything to do with the Domna Cecilia records, nor any legal work connected with the Templar murders, but on the charts and pictures relating to his own philosophical work. To get his attention, I asked Brother Thomas about his meeting with the Prior earlier that day.

'The man is impossible,' Brother Thomas erupted. This, then, was the reason for his mood. 'All he thinks about,' Thomas continued, 'is himself, his desire for power, and his frustration at not being the Archbishop, though heaven help us if he were. He thinks nothing of his monks, his vocation, and certainly nothing at all of justice. I am sure he is playing a game of cat and mouse with us, Wilfridus. He spent most of the time quizzing me about my political allegiances, as if I were guilty of treason. He asked me what I knew about threats to the King, the fall of Robert de Burgh, the situation of Peter des Roches, about quarrels at the parliament in Oxford, my opinion of King Louis of France, whether I had heard rumours that Louis might be planning an invasion, whether I thought that England would be better off as a vassal state to the Holy Roman Empire. I really do not know what he was driving at, whether he was trying to catch me out, or convince me of his own importance.'

'Did you discover anything about what he wants from Domna Cecilia?' I asked.

'Nothing specific, Wilfridus,' he replied, 'only I came away with a sense of threat. The Prior is desperate for Domna Cecilia to be condemned. And it would not surprise me if he knew where Alyssa has been taken. I have decided one thing for certain though. Whatever it costs, I shall not act against my conscience as far as Domna Cecilia is concerned. Still, the immediate problem is Michael. Wait for me at the inn in Mercery Lane and we'll go to the castle together.'

I did as Brother Thomas said, pondering his words about Domna Cecilia. I ordered myself ale, bread, salt beef, then more ale. It seemed an age before he came, well after the great bells had chimed Sext, in fact. Brother Thomas insisted on eating and drinking before we set off. His manner was congenial now, and I was the one not in the best of spirits, since my anxiety about Michael, and of course Myrrah, had subsided into resentment at being kept waiting.

Finally we set off through the drizzle towards the castle. We were soaked to the skin by the time we had run the gauntlet of obstructive soldiers. At last, we were shown into Sir Osbert's sinister chambers, with their stench of stale food and ale, and the yapping dogs tied to pillars. 'What brings you two here?' Sir Osbert snapped.

'Michael,' said Brother Thomas, in a kindly tone, though I could tell he despised Sir Osbert as much as I did. 'I presume you have him locked up with his father?'

'Then you presume wrong,' said Sir Osbert. 'My instructions are to keep the two of them apart.'

'Instructions from whom?' Brother Thomas asked.

'Now, that would be telling, wouldn't it? Perhaps you would like to guess.'

'I should like to see Michael,' Brother Thomas insisted. 'If you refuse, Lord Rufus might start asking questions.'

Sir Osbert was uncertain. 'Very well,' he said at last. 'But you will want to drink with me first. John!' he called at the top of his voice and one of the guards appeared almost immediately. 'The new prisoner. Get him respectable. Visitors.' The Keeper's breath stank of cheap ale and rotting meat. As he poured us ale, the chained dogs snarled at us, their mouths dribbling and foaming. The Keeper scolded them. Perhaps because of the mention of Lord Rufus, Sir Osbert's surliness and prevarication gave way to a sycophancy I found even more revolting. Out of politeness we each accepted a mug of his disgustingly strong ale, a real soldier's brew which curdled in my stomach. Sir Osbert talked of the part he had played in the Crusade against Constantinople some thirty years before. He had served under Simon de Montfort, he said, who later led the Crusade against the Cathars. Sir Osbert reflected on de Montfort's desertion of the Crusade at Venice. 'He was like that then,' I remember Sir Osbert saying. 'He could think of nothing but poetry and music. He had no stomach for fighting and disapproved of us attacking Zara, the reason being that it was a Christian city, of all things. That was why he went. Still, his loss! You should have seen the loot and the women at Zara, and then at Constantinople!' As Sir Osbert described the wealth and magnificence of the cities they had plundered, the booty, the fires and the women, a squalid evil hung in the air, clinging to the man's face, his eyes, his hair, his every gesture.

At last, the guard returned. He gave both Brother Thomas and me tallow lamps to light our way. We were led down the long dark staircase towards the dungeon. The lamps we carried gave off more stench than brightness. The stairs we took bypassed the ground floor where Isaac was kept, leading directly underground.

The first chamber was huge, and the prisoners were chained round the walls, men and women indiscriminately thrown together. Some were emaciated, some sat, eyes closed, motionless, neither alive nor dead. Others still strained forward when they saw us, their eyes wide, pleading. The smell was so bad I found it hard to catch my breath without retching. The guard tutted as we passed, and kicked anyone whose feet were in our way. I wondered if Hell itself could be worse than this place.

A terrible scream rose from the next stairwell, chilling me as we descended the spiral steps. The guard turned towards us, and grinned as if to fellow professionals which, I supposed, we were in danger of becoming. Assailed again by the stench, I nearly vomited. I glimpsed a long, dark corridor with cells to either side, but we hurried past, for we were to descend yet further to the lowest level. The last flight of stairs opened into a cavernous area, from which two passageways led. They were hacked into the earth and lined at irregular intervals with flat stones or lumps of crumbling masonry. We took the passage in front of us. The ceiling was so low we had to walk with our heads hunched forward. It was bitterly cold and there were puddles of freezing water on the ground. I doubted that a man or woman would be able to survive down here for much more than a few days.

Michael was in a cell at the very end of the corridor. The guard opened the latch on the rough wooden door. The cell had been in total darkness until we came. The light of the soldier's wretched tallow lamp flickered on the dull earth walls. Reaching up to a shelf he took down another lamp, which he lit for me. Michael was lying huddled in a corner on cold, water-logged ground.

Michael's eyes rolled vaguely from behind bruised lids, his cheeks cut and grazed, his top lip split and his nose puffy. Bloodstains ran from the corner of his mouth to his neck and the tattered remains of his tunic. At first he did not recognise me. 'It is not time yet,' he mumbled.

'You try first,' Brother Thomas said to me, 'since you know him.'

'Can you move?' I asked Michael. 'Can you sit up?' As I knelt beside him I noticed marks Michael must have made in the wall next to him, patterns labelled with Hebrew letters just above the dank floor.

'It is not time!' Michael repeated, oblivious of my presence. 'The dawn has not come. The souls are trapped. Not even the fire. I am not ready. Judgment is so far, we cannot even imagine it.'

He was no good to us in this state, no good to anyone. So I called after the soldier. 'Get him water and food, now!' I demanded. The guard looked uncertain. 'Hurry up or I'll tell the Keeper. We don't want to lose him, do we? I am sure the King would not be pleased.'

The soldier hesitated for a moment but went off all the same, taking care to close the door of the cell. As soon as he had gone, Brother Thomas smiled approvingly, and this meant a great deal to me. But then, in an uncanny voice, Michael began chanting: '*Wax and wane, the joy and pain, of exultation, comes again . . .*'

'Michael,' I said, taking his hand, 'you must try to concentrate. I have come to look after you. You are not badly hurt, only hungry and thirsty.'

'Another will judge me,' he went on, still groaning and rambling. 'There will be harmony between the Beasts, the Wreath. Oh, to burn, and to know it was time!'

The soldier returned with water, soup and bread. The effect was miraculous. After only a few mouthfuls, the look in

Michael's eyes changed; they focused on me and he said, 'Brother Wilfridus, it's you! Whatever are you doing here?' His words were interrupted by a rasping coughing fit, which echoed in the gloomy air.

'Can you remember what you said, just now?' I asked.

'Just now?' His eyes were blank. His old self had returned and the words he had spoken were to him as a lost dream. 'No, I was dreaming of herbs, of Saint John's wort. Who is that?' he asked, gesturing towards Thomas.

'A friend,' I said. 'Brother Thomas.'

'I am pleased,' said Michael. 'Thank you. My father, is he here? Is he well?'

'Yes,' I said. 'And you?'

'I shall be well,' he replied.

'Why did you allow yourself to be taken?' I asked.

'It had to happen,' he said as, painfully, he sat up against the wall. I helped him eat the bread and the soup as we talked. Its sweet scent was powerless against the fetid, damp smell of that cell.

Brother Thomas whispered to me, 'Ask him about the chalices.'

Michael had overheard. 'What about them?' he demanded.

'We know you took the one from the Prior that was buried in the Cathedral Crypt,' I said. Michael took another sip of the soup. He made no attempt at denial. 'Tell us why it is so important,' I urged him.

'The chalices,' Michael said, 'have power. They are symbols of something greater than themselves. You know I am Jewish by birth, yet I have studied much of other beliefs. I told you, Wilfridus, about the time I spent at Toulouse. There, I came to know a number of so-called Cathars.'

'What have they to do with the chalices?' Thomas interrupted.

'There were rumours about them. One of them was in Aquitaine, and owned by a Cathar elder. It was said to come from the time when there was a Kingdom in those lands ruled by Kings descended directly from the House of David.'

'Did the Cathars believe these rumours?' Thomas was growing impatient.

'Some did. They thought that possession of the chalice proved the truth of their religion. Others merely scoffed, claiming that such rumours were nonsense, a trick of the devil.'

'And what did you believe?' Brother Thomas asked him.

'There are dangers,' Michael said, 'as you should know. I understand something of your work, Brother Thomas.'

'How could that possibly be?' my master snapped.

'I know, for example,' Michael went on undaunted, 'that you are amongst those who have grasped the distribution of jewels of the chalice, and I know something of the system of pictures you are developing, to make comprehensible the patterns of correspondences the chalices incorporate. When I first heard of your investigations, of Domna Cecilia and the murders at Swiffeld, I made it my business to find out about you. My enquiries led me to your wife, to Alyssa. At first I was suspicious of you, Brother Thomas.'

'Do you know where she is?' Thomas had gone a deathly pale.

'Because of the danger you and she are in, thanks to your investigations, Myrrah and I gave her and the children the opportunity of living in our house at Petcotte near Saint Albans, where neither the King's men nor the Prior's will find her. You must understand,' he went on, registering Brother Thomas's reaction, 'that because of your work with Domna Cecilia, Alyssa was very vulnerable. Myrrah and I explained the situation to her. We were both impressed by her wisdom. We also talked a great deal about herbs, of which she has a profound understanding, and about your work. She went to Petcotte of her own free will, and is very happy there. Most importantly, she and the children are safe.'

'I was told she was led away by soldiers,' Brother Thomas said.

'Some of us dressed to give the impression that we were soldiers,' Michael explained. 'That was the best way to make sure no questions were asked.'

'What dangers did you warn her about?' asked Thomas.

'It began with Brother Theodor. When he was killed, I knew that my father was under threat too. You see what has happened to the Templars, and now to me. You are not immune, but it is important that you should continue with your work.'

'Why are you so sure?' Thomas asked.

'You know,' said Michael, 'as well as I do.'

Thomas remained silent for some time, weighing up Michael's words, before he said, 'Tell me about the house at Petcotte. Who else lives there?'

'It belongs to our family. It is a haven for people who are seeking new ways. Some practise herbalism and other healing arts. Some study. There are one or two painters. There is a mason amongst them. Others do simple work, like weaving, but they are known for their wisdom and philosophical ideas. Alyssa felt at home there immediately.'

'You make it sound like a religious house,' Brother Thomas commented, but he was hugely relieved, I could tell. I was beginning to sense a real affinity between the two men. Outwardly they were at odds, but at the deepest level there was much that united them.

'It is a religious house in a way,' said Michael, 'except that men, women and children live together, and there are no set observances. We practise tolerance. There are Cathar

189

refugees from Toulouse amongst those who live there.'

Brother Thomas started at this, for obvious reasons. 'They have not made a Cathar of her, surely,' he said, desperation in his voice.

'Alyssa is no more likely to become one than I am,' said Michael. 'She has too great an affinity with the things of this earth, and hopes where most would despair.'

Brother Thomas was becoming anxious again now, and our unease was compounded by the sound of other prisoners' screams which reached us down the long passageways. 'You know,' he said, almost losing his composure, 'the usual fate of such communities?'

'She will be safe,' said Michael. 'Myrrah will see to it. Your Alyssa is a remarkable woman. She is learned, yet each of her doubts is worth a hundred of other people's certainties. I know how she paints and draws. But your work, Brother Thomas, think how she must feel about your work.' Thomas blanched. It was true that Alyssa was a woman of integrity and high ideals; I wondered if it had ever occurred to Thomas that she would find it hard to tolerate the compromises his work inevitably involved. Alyssa and their children were everything to him.

'Then perhaps,' said Brother Thomas, 'you might help me regarding the wisdom which you know is important to me. Your father, and your father's father, knew something of the secret arts, and I hope their knowledge will provide the key to the problems which beset us, not least your own arrest. How can I find out more about what interested them, and about this book called the *Hermesis* ?'

'I am willing to help you,' said Michael. 'But in return, you must help me.'

'Tell me what you want, and if I can do it, then I shall,' Brother Thomas assured him.

'In that case, please use whatever influence you have in

order to let the King know about my predicament. But you must do this yourself. Do not trust others, least of all the Prior. That is all I ask. The King will understand. Now it is my turn to give you the help that you request, so that our bargain shall be complete. If you go to the inner room of my father's house, towards the rear, you will find a trap door in the raised wooden podium, which is covered with a green and purple carpet I purchased in Spain. Raise the trap door, go down two flights of stairs, and you will find yourself in a cellar. What you discover there will help you to understand. It is the place where, for three generations, my family has pursued the secret Work. I only pray that the King's men have not been there already.'

As he spoke, there was a scuffling outside the door. Sir Osbert and two soldiers appeared in the gloomy entrance to the cell, each bearing lamps whose flames lit their faces, making them look gnarled and twisted like the boughs of old trees. 'It is time to leave,' said Sir Osbert, apparently beside himself with rage.

'We have not finished,' Brother Thomas snapped back.

'The Prior,' said Sir Osbert, 'has sent for you. He says you should not be here. He has forbidden you access to these prisoners!'

'The Prior,' Brother Thomas answered back, 'is not the only power. There is Lord Rufus, and there is a King in the land.'

'I follow orders from my own lord,' snarled Sir Osbert, who had nonetheless been disconcerted by these words. 'Come along.'

We did as we were told, but not before we had assured Michael that we would do everything we could to help him. On the way up the steps towards the main gate, Thomas addressed Sir Osbert politely but firmly, saying, 'I expect this man to be kept in better conditions. Otherwise you will have to answer to the King for it.'

Sir Osbert grunted a reply. Though he was drunk and surly now, it was obvious that he did not take Brother Thomas's words lightly.

Dusk was beginning to fall as we made our way back towards the centre of town. Brother Thomas was silent, weighing up thoughts in his mind. 'It is important that we should go to Isaac's cellar as soon as possible. But it is best that we go under cover of darkness. Therefore, though it is late, perhaps we might call on Domna Cecilia first.'

'What about the Prior?' I asked.

'He can wait,' said Brother Thomas.

I told Brother Thomas that I thought one of the men present at the disinterment of the chalice might well have been Sir Osbert. My master did not seem surprised.

Chapter Fourteen

D ESPITE THE LATENESS of the hour, Alazaïs served us food as Domna Cecilia welcomed us and continued the story of her pilgrimage. Because night was falling, I recall that the candle-lit atmosphere in the room was uncanny, and there was a feeling like that of being alone in a strange church.

These are my records of Domna Cecilia's words said that evening:

'After Walter's visit, it was three weeks before I was well enough to leave Mundfons. It would have been so easy just to return to the Unterzell Convent in Würzepurc, and live out a quiet life there. In a way I even missed Martin, whose humility and stillness so contrasted with Walter's intensity. Yet I was not satisfied. Since meeting Walter, my yearning was undiminished, though now objectless, or so I thought.

'By the beginning of June, I had decided on a course of action. It was said that the German knights were assembling to embark from Marseilles. Walter would be amongst them and if I continued on the pilgrimage to Santiago, Marseilles would be on our route. Perhaps I would see him there, just one last time. I knew that my motivation was dishonest, since I was serving two masters: the pilgrimage and Walter. But then, it would have been even more dishonest to return to Würzepurc.

'Long before we reached the Rhone, something occurred

which, Brother Thomas, might interest you. We were walking in the high land near the Schouwenberc, in the Black Forest, just before the road sweeps down towards the city of Offenburc. On the road alongside us was a tall man with fiery, tawny eyes, and long silver hair. He walked with a stick, but his step was vigorous. His presence was disconcerting. My two companions fell silent and no word was spoken until suddenly, addressing me rather than the others, the old man said, "Tell me, whom do you seek?"

'The question took me aback, for Walter was constantly in my thoughts and it was as though this stranger had seen into my mind. Yet how could I admit this? He smiled knowingly and continued, "Let me put the question to you another way then. Do you still seek Walter von der Ouwe?"

' "How do you know of Walter?" I asked.

' "Ah," said the old man, "I know of many things, but I am particularly interested in this singer. Some say he will achieve much in his life."

' "Then why ask me?"

' "Because he loves you, or rather loved you."

'This unnerving old man's words were like a blast of icy air on that hot summer's day, freezing my heart. "I do not see what this has to do with you," I replied.

' "But I do. You have been a kind and lovely mentor to him. For that reason I sought you out. I see why you were chosen."

' "Mentor?" I repeated. "Chosen? What is that supposed to mean?"

' "All will become clear," he said. "Meanwhile, take this. It is from us. A sign of gratitude." He handed me a bronze chain. From it was suspended a pair of interlocking rings, one gold and the other silver.'

Falling suddenly silent Cecilia went to a chest in the corner of the room, opened it and produced from within the chain she had just mentioned. She handed it to Brother Thomas to inspect, who in turn passed it to me. The diameter of the gold and silver rings was about three finger-widths. The thickness of the bands was considerable, about that of the nail of my little finger. Both rings were intricately engraved with motifs depicting tendrils with tiny leaves, amongst which were caterpillars, chrysalises and butterflies.

'What do the symbols mean?' Brother Thomas asked her.

'I am not sure,' she replied. 'Some have said that the butterfly symbolises the risen soul, after the Last Judgment, and others say it is to do with reincarnation, in this life. But I have never been able to find out for certain. I have shown this to very few people, only to those I hoped might under-stand, or who might have been connected with the old man who gave it to me.'

'Do you know who the stranger was?'

'I never saw him again. Indeed, I might well have forgotten our meeting, or ceased believing that anything so fanciful had taken place, had it not been for this chain, which I have always had with me. I suppose it is precious to me because of the link with Walter. As soon as he had given it to me,' Cecilia continued, 'he began talking to my two companions. Just for a moment, I walked ahead, lost in thought, trying to take in the significance of what had just happened. I do not know how much time elapsed before I turned round, only to find that the stranger had gone. Sarah and Madeleine said he had headed off up a steep mountain path through the gorse and heather. As I said, I never saw him again during the course of that journey, nor have I ever seen him since. Yet I have always expected him to turn up again, any day, any moment.

'Thereafter we carried on our way, and we saw many wonders, great mountains, lakes, valleys, rivers, holy places and sites of terrible battles. It seemed in every city and every town they were building chapels or churches, or massive cathedrals in the new style, with pointed windows, high spires, and with walls so tall and thin that supports had to be added, so the buildings would not collapse. Yet I could not view these churches without a certain feeling of loss, of disappointment. Where was the old simplicity, the perfect curve of the broad, rounded arches, the broad pillars, so magnificent when painted, so harmonious when bare? The new architecture seemed to crave only virtuosity, nothing more.

'I had hoped to catch a glimpse of the crusading army assembling at Marseilles. However, the rumours we had heard on the way were only too true, that the Crusade had been abandoned. The death of Henry VI at Messina, the fear of civil war in the Holy Empire and the failure to capture Toron had led many to return to their homes. So, I spent a few days in Marseilles looking for Walter. But the streets were teeming with the roughest men, soldiers, sailors, vagrants and the lowest whores. I found no trace of Walter, and was pleased when the others persuaded me that it was time to carry on our pilgrimage towards Santiago.

'As we approached the Pyrenees, I came across two of the elders of the Good Christians, whom you Dominicans call Perfecti.'

Cecilia left a pause, and studied our reaction. She was right to do so. Thomas looked up at this point, and nodded towards me, indicating that I should note what he said in detail. 'Perfectus' is the name we give the leaders of the heretical sect also known as the Cathars. It was clear to us that whatever information Cecilia volunteered now might well be crucial.

'We were walking in the high country near Peyrepertuse,' she continued, 'where there are castles built on combs of rocks, giddyingly high above the plains. After that we followed a road zig-zagging beneath strange rocks overhanging the deep fissure of the gorge at the bottom of which the River Agly flows, so far down that it is mostly hidden from view; each glimpse of its dark waters is like a glimpse of Hades. Walking ahead of us on the narrow path, at a leisurely pace, deep in conversation, were two men. Both were dressed in black despite the heat of the day. One of them was plump and middle-aged, and the top of his head was bald and pink; I assumed that he was not used to being outdoors. The other man was younger, small of stature, slim, with short dark curly hair and the strong neck and shoulders of a peasant.

'The sun was beating down, though it was late September. We must have been walking behind them for an hour or so, and they had paid us no attention. Suddenly both turned, and waited for us to catch up, smiling the same, curious smile, warm but with an aura of resignation and detachment. I sensed immediately that these were men of religion, though the atmosphere around them had an unfamiliar quality. With practice, as I am sure you will agree, Brother Thomas, one can tell on first impression if a person is a priest or not, if he is in orders, and even which Order he belongs to. I could not place these men, however. The light suffusing them, perceptible even against the sun, had a rosy yellow hue.

'They asked if they might walk with us. We accepted, and soon I found myself in conversation with the older man, whilst Sarah and Madeleine walked a little behind with the younger of the two. The man with whom I talked was charming and attentive. He came from a noble house and spoke excellent Latin, which pleased me since I had not yet mastered the local language. It was from him that I learnt the story of Pyrene. In the days before Our Lord came, he said, even before the Great Flood, a tribe called the Bekrydes lived in the high places. Berbyx, their King, held court in a vast cave called the Lombrives. His daughter, Pyrene, was courted by all the eminent lords, but fell in love with Hercules, and lay with him. Hercules left her, to continue the work assigned him. Fleeing her father's anger, Pyrene sought refuge in the mountains but was attacked by a bear. Hercules, hearing of her fate, leapt mountains and waded through mighty rivers to be with her. But he arrived to find that she had just died. Her father, repenting his anger, had her buried in the heart of the cave of Lombrives. When he spoke at her funeral, Hercules gave the name Pyrenees to the mountains above the immense cave, in perpetual memory of his love.'

I noted even then a similarity between this story and the crow story. Thomas interrupted. 'So,' he said, 'he did not talk about the heresy?'

'He did not speak about religion,' Cecilia continued, 'nor did he attempt to convert me. He had the rare quality, which you possess, Brother Thomas, of showing a real interest in what I said, so that soon I forgot myself, and spoke quite freely to him. Nor was there any fleshly interest in his attitude, for men will often feign interest in the minds of young women, when it is really the comforts of our bodies that they crave, and this is easy enough to discern. It was as if he could see, deep within me, something of value known to few people, other than perhaps to Walter. By the time we reached Foix, I had told him about my childhood, the convents where I had lived, even about Walter and the Graf.'

'Did you not realise that he was a heretic?' I interrupted.

'It never occurred to me. This happened before the days when heretics were burnt in those lands, even before they were obliged to wear yellow crosses sewn into their clothes as a sign of penance. I had heard of heretics of course, but from the descriptions I had of them from certain priests I imagined them obviously evil and depraved, whilst this man was palpably good. Besides, in passing he had described himself as a Christian, and I did not think to quiz him (since I am neither a man nor a Dominican) as to whether he acknowledged allegiance to the Pope, if he believed in the Resurrection, or if he believed a Good Father could really wish the death of His Son. Perhaps I was too naive, or perhaps already too wise.' She smiled as she watched me jot these words down on my wax tablet, clearly aware of the effect they would have.

'So,' Brother Thomas said, 'you knew nothing about the Cathars at that time?'

'You must bear in mind that this was ten years or so before the first Crusade against the Albigensians. Then, peace ruled the land. The Pope's armies had not yet, for example, massacred every man, woman and child in Béziers, whilst the Abbot of Cîteaux called, "Kill them all, God will recognise His own!" Few had been burnt, certainly none in those lands. Oh, those lost times, Thomas; they were like the simplicity and the beauty of the old buildings: the roundness of arches and windows was like the roundness of the tolerance of different philosophies and ways of life. The breadth of the pillars was like the generosity of the life of love and joy, of which the troubadours sang.'

'So you became associated with the Cathars at that point?' Thomas interrupted.

'No, of course not,' she replied firmly. 'I carried on my pilgrimage. I could talk to you endlessly about the pilgrim road, the villages and cities, the places of worship, the relics of saints, the mountains and valleys, the hardships and joys, fellow pilgrims humble and noble, fascinating and dull, lovely and loveless; the souls, wandering like candle-flames in the night, towards the Tomb of the Apostle, each soul oddly visible, the same, yet different, striving to shine through the cloak of flesh in which it was stifled and separated; the false

199

merriment, endless stories, affected melancholy, yearnings for lost loves. I could describe to you how many tried to cope, seeking knowledge, praying, philosophising, requesting help from anyone they thought might have learnt some wisdom; others allowing their minds to set in embittered, rigid religiosity, tragically predictable, obsessively secure in their view of the world, if not their lives. I could tell you about it in detail, Thomas, but there are really only two things worth relating about my life as a pilgrim.

'The first was the impression created, particularly in the region of the Pyrenees, by those who shared the beliefs of the two Perfecti I came across on the way to Albi. No, I did not become associated with the Cathars then, but we would see the priestly Elders, men and women, wandering in groups of two or three, over high mountain passes, crossing the square of a small hilltown on some errand, or darting into the doorway of a lonely house high on a hillside late of a summer afternoon.

'When I asked about them, priests or monastics would as often as not just fall silent, as if pretending they did not exist, or else townsfolk would talk in hushed tones, referring to them as "Goodmen", "Goodwomen" or "Good Christians". Perhaps it was the mystery that haunted me as much as the atmosphere.

'The second event which had a lasting effect was not the triumphal entry of the pilgrims into Santiago when we arrived that mild September day. Though it was the moment we had worked and striven for, I remember it with a curious sensation of emptiness. Everyone, it seemed, including my two Sisters, was full of joy and rejoicing, waving banners and flags, chatting animatedly about the damage the journey had done to their feet, singing, cheering and drinking. Of course I joined in as well as I could. What else can one do? And I was happy and proud to claim my cockleshell, which I still possess. But perhaps you will understand that for me, there was no fulfilment in what I experienced. My jubilation was only on the outside.

'We spent the winter and early spring at one of the religious houses of Santiago, helping in the hospice with the welcome and care of the pilgrims, and participating in the round of services in the Cathedral. I kept expecting something to happen, some news of Walter, perhaps even that he would turn up with the next batch of pilgrims now that the German Crusade to the Holy Land had been definitively abandoned. Gradually, however, I relinquished hope, and the time came for us to head off back along the pilgrim route.

'I was pleased to start travelling again. The constant change and challenge helped me to forget myself. Besides, there was a sense of security in the simple life of a pilgrim. Those heading towards Compostela greeted me and my companions with a degree of awe, since we had already achieved what they were yet to accomplish. Our monastic clothes protected us from the advances of thieves and rogues, who were mostly superstitious about attacking pilgrims and monastics. If ever we needed money, I would sing. By then I had learnt the languages of the kingdoms we passed through, and the songs which people would enjoy. The language of the Pyrenees in particular is a beautiful language, redolent of tenderness and desire, courtly and graceful, yet witty and self-mocking too, well fitted to the expression of tales of battle, deeds of bravery and matters of love.

'The second event took place on our way home as we crossed the Pyrenees via the Roncevalles Pass, the famous valley where Roland's last battle was fought, where there are high mountains and dark glades, and where, in the morning, the mists roll down from the high places and rise up from the valleys, like ghostly armies. At the hostelry run by the monks in Roncevalles, late at night, sitting round the fire where we had been singing and telling stories, a young woman from the court of Lord Raimon of Miravel sang a song which haunted me, since it echoed my feelings of emptiness as I had walked the pilgrim route through the north of Spain without Walter:

> Se canto que cante
> Canto pas per iou
> Canto par ma mio
> Qu'es allenc de iou . . . *

'Because of the way the song affected me, I asked after the singer from whom she had learnt it. She had seen him at that very hostelry, for she often travelled backwards and forwards between Raimon's court and his relatives in the Kingdom of Aragon. He was on his way back from Spain. The young woman, whose name was Esclarmonde, described this singer as young and very handsome, with curly brown hair and piercing dark eyes. He had sung for many along the pilgrim way, his music leaving a wake of vivid impressions wherever he went. These rumours filled me both with an aching hope, and a sweet premonition of loss.

'Esclarmonde and I became friends. She lived at the court of her uncle, Raimon de Miravel, near Carcassonne, where she invited us to stay on our journey. I was drawn to Esclarmonde because of her vivacity, and her courtliness. She liked to discourse on the meaning of the word *paratge*, which they use in that part of the world to describe the ideal of the equal worth of men and women of honour. Moreover, her descriptions of her many suitors were kindly

---

* *If he sings, let him sing,/But let him not sing for me/But for my friend/Who is far from here . . . (Gaston Phébus)*

and amusing, without any hint of vulgarity.

'We were royally entertained at that court. Raimon and his wife were the epitome of refinement; compared to them the Graf and Gräfin of Stierenfurt were mere rustics, even though their wealth was comparable. I accepted the Count's invitation to sing, unaware just how distinguished Raimon himself was as a troubadour. How finely he sang after I had finished my meagre offering! However, he did not put me to shame, but rather, as the fires blazed in the brightly painted hall, and the noble guests gathered to listen quietly and attentively now that the feasting was over, he encouraged me to join him in the singing of *tenzone* and *pastorela*. His manner was so graceful that it was a source of joy to mingle my voice with his.

'At length, conversation turned to the singer of whom Esclarmonde had spoken. He was a fellow countryman of mine, and Count Raimon said his singing style bore a curious resemblance to my own. He had spent a night at Raimon's court just a month or so before. It was from Lord Raimon that I learnt for certain that the singer was Walter, that he was living at the Knights Templar house in Richerenches, and that he was about to take vows, irrevocable vows. When the fires burnt down, and I was led to the women's rooms, I lay awake, my thoughts at last my own, watching the silver moonlight pour in through the high windows. Then, silent tears came.

'As you know, Thomas, the Order of the Temple is a strict, military Order, and its members are famous for their harsh way of living, for their prowess fighting in far off lands, their readiness to die for the cause of freeing Jerusalem, and their vast wealth. It was not so much for Walter's life that I feared, for each of us must die; rather, I feared for his soul. Though Walter had mastered the arts of war, and was strong and brave, he was not a cruel man. Much in the religious life is a sublimation of baser instincts, a transformation of lead into gold. Mystics and ascetics are often by nature very sensuous. Those who help the poor, if they were not doing the work of God, would be dreadful meddlers. Contemplatives and academics would be reclusive and selfish. So it is with the military Orders. Religious discipline transforms brutality into something perhaps acceptable to God. But what if such base instincts were absent, as I was sure they were absent from Walter's innermost character? How corrupting could such a life be?

'I gave Sarah and Madeleine no choice but to follow me to Richerenches. It was a fifteen-day walk. In any case we were too late. A week before our arrival, when we were still on our way, Walter had already taken his vows. The Master of the House, a fierce-looking man with thick eyebrows meeting in a V above his nose, welcomed me with surprising under-standing and courtesy. He attempted to reassure me about Walter's vocation; Walter was to be involved with the prepa-rations for a new Crusade to the Holy Land, which would assemble in Venice the following spring. Who was I to interfere in a calling of such magnitude? I concluded that the Master was right, that I should not continue to follow Walter, that he should not even know that I had been so close to him.

'We set off, back towards Germany and Würzepurc. The others were relieved and happy. I felt numb. The sense of freedom was a melancholy one, and as spring turned to summer with all its energy and colour, I began to realise that I was no longer looking forward to taking up the religious life.

'One of the many travelling companions we had on the road was an elderly nun who, so she said, had contrived to spend much of her life on one pilgrimage or another. Her view was that there was more to discover about God on the road than in a convent. I confessed to her the dulling of my own vocation, and I recall her response to this very day. "There are some," she said, "who are called to convents and monasteries only to be drawn ever onwards towards a spiritual goal from which most, in this life, are excluded. Yet there are others who are sucked in only to be thrust out again, through no fault of their own, because the work God has chosen for them is in other vineyards. For such people, the most dangerous thing in the world would be to stay."

'Soon we had forsaken the south, the warmth of the sun, the many courts, the lovely languages and songs, and by midsummer we were back in Würzepurc. There, half-heartedly but assiduously, I took up my life as a nun once more.

'There are many ways of selling your soul to the devil. Perhaps that is what I did next. In any case, that will be for you to judge.' Her smile was disconcerting, almost malign, and in her eye was a tawny glint. 'On my return from the pilgrimage,' she went on, 'the year Richard of England died, I went once more to live in the Premonstratensian Convent of Unterzell in Würzepurc, the one dedicated to Saint Cecilia. More than a year had passed but it turned out that Mother Magda had left my dowry untouched. I suppose I had more than earned my keep copying and illuminating manuscripts, but I was surprised, and insisted that the dowry was the Convent's, and that I would soon take major vows. She smiled knowingly and said I must wait another year. She was right. I took up the monastic round again, but my heart was not in it.

'After a month or so during which I tried but failed to reconcile myself to the emptiness which was seeping into every aspect of my daily life, I received an unexpected visitor. It was a Friday, and we had just emerged from the chapel where we had sung High Mass. I was on my way to the library where I was studying the philosophical works of Hildegard of Bingen, hoping to find an answer to the questions which possessed me. An answer came, Brother Thomas – one I deserved perhaps, but not one I expected. Mother Magda, our Abbess, waved me over to her and said, grinning and winking, that a young man was asking for me, and that I should go to see him at the gate-house. Of course, like a fool, I supposed it would be Walter. I rushed across the courtyard, my feet kicking up the first autumn leaves. Yet the young man I found, sitting in a corner, head hung low, was Martin Palviezen, whose bride I was to have been. "What are you doing here?" I asked.

' "I am sorry," he said. "Perhaps I should not have come."

' "Then why did you?" In some ways his familiar presence was reassuring, comforting, yet it stirred such memories of unhappiness that I failed to see the obvious.

' "I needed to see you again. I felt that it was wrong, the way we left you that day."

' "Do not worry yourself over that," I said. "You can see that I am well enough looked after here." He looked up at me in such a way that I began to pity him, like a brother. "What do you want from me?" I asked, more kindly now.

' "I wanted to ask you to forgive us, for going away as we did," he stammered.

' "But of course," I said, perhaps too readily. "Rather it is I who should ask you for forgiveness, since I assumed you knew what had happened to me – at the court." The crack in my voice reminded me how much pain the memory of these events still caused.

' "That means nothing to me," he went on nervously. "I understand that, for good reason, you probably do not even feel friendship for me, after the way we left you. However, if it should ease your life in any way, my offer of marriage stands firm."

"But that is absurd!' I responded. "Think of your father, the dowry, my vows."

' "None of that matters." He shook his head. "I cannot understand the thoughts you think, your reading and writing, your Latin and music. But perhaps you will teach me. I have already learnt to read, since I last saw you. The local priest is helping me with Latin grammar too." He quoted the beginning of The Song of Songs. "You see the effect you have had on me?" And just for a moment, I glimpsed in his eye that spark of yearning. "There is something about you," he said, "that I must love."

' "That is ridiculous," I began, but my voice trailed away, since my own experience told me it was not ridiculous. Just a few minutes ago nothing, no one, had been further from my mind than this man; now, something inside me melted and beyond his simplicity I discerned the light of some essence which touched me. I remained silent for a while; then I said, as carefully and courteously as I could, "You are kind. However, married life is not for the likes of me. I am committed to the religious life."

' "You only say that," he said gently, "because of what happened to you. But we could live well and happily together. My father's health has not been good lately. He wants to hand over the manor to me. We could have children, and servants and friends. Marianne would love you to be with us. We have talked at length. She won't forgive herself for telling my father about you.'

' "Your father?"

' "It was Stierenfurt's deceitfulness that upset him. My father is a wise man, and he has nothing against you. He wants only my happiness, and yours."

'I remained silent for a while. Then I took a deep breath and said, "I cannot help but be moved by your kind offer. You are a good man. One day you will make a fine husband for someone. However, my circumstances are such that I could not be your wife."

' "You speak ambiguously," he replied sadly, "in order to spare my feelings. Yet I have checked, and I know that no vows, nor financial constraints hold you here." I remained silent, impressed by his perspicacity and by the clarity of his speech. "I suppose that you are still attached to the singer you met at Leuchtenfels and that is why you refuse me. Let me say that, if your feelings towards him are anything like mine towards you, then I understand. Only, I ask you the following. Let me visit you from time to time and if ever your hopes for the other man are thwarted, then allow me to repeat my offer to you."

'As soon as he left, I went to chapel, and tried to pray; I was unable to stem tears of anger. My striving seemed so stupid; suddenly, all I wanted was to be an ordinary woman and live out an obscure life of simple happiness.

'Thereafter Martin did come to see me regularly, and I began to look forward to his visits. He had changed during my absence. He had grown even more thoughtful and kind than I remembered him. It was true, he had succeeded in teaching himself to read and write passably well. He had also spent a good deal of time with priests and monastics, for his head was teeming with questions about matters of faith and philosophy which he would discuss diligently with me whenever he came to visit. I was touched by this, since I knew he had done it for me, or because of me. Besides, his questions were anything but foolish, and I began to respect the integrity of his mind. The truth was that this man I had once dared look down on as simple had moved me. Here was a generosity, a love and a forgiveness which I had rarely encountered in my life.

'In so many of the songs sung at our courts, the lady is begged to have mercy on the heart she torments. And now

I saw that I was just such a tormentor. I had lost Walter and what I mistook for a monastic vocation was fading. What was I to do? On what altar could I sacrifice myself now? In short, I decided to be merciful. Besides, I did love Martin, as a brother, as a fellow, though without the spiritual passion I had felt for Walter. I had taken no irrevocable monastic vows, and I was at an age where the flesh was making its demands felt. What point was there in resisting? I would never be happy, I thought, but that was no reason to deny happiness to another, if I had the power to bestow it. Only later did I come to understand the terrible arrogance of this reasoning.

'It is curious,' Cecilia concluded, with an unaccustomed tremor in her voice, 'that as one grows older, it troubles one most to recall times one took to be relatively calm and innocent.'

I looked up from my wax tablet; that tawny light had left Cecilia's eye, but as her black cat padded across the room, I saw it in the animal's eye instead. Cecilia herself seemed pale, ill, exhausted. We agreed to continue the next day, and as we went down the stairs, Cecilia's cat hissed at us, arching its back, tensing its claws and staring at us with something akin to hatred glowing from its eyes' black pupils.

'We'll go to Isaac's house now,' said Brother Thomas, as soon as we were out of earshot of the two men still guarding Domna Cecilia's house.

There was, in his expression, a fervour which unnerved me. It was as though that place were already drawing him towards itself. As we walked through the chilly streets beneath the starry sky, a three-quarter moon illuminating the Cathedral in front of us shone a ghostly, admonishing silver.

When we reached the Jewish quarter, from one of the houses

nearby there came the half singing, half wailing of a Hebrew lament. We approached Isaac the Jew's house from the rear. There was a guard on duty, but Brother Thomas, claiming the authority of the Dominican Order, had no difficulty in persuading him to let us in. Soon we were walking through the devastation, amidst broken pots, toppled statues and stained fabrics. Despite my horror, I felt a secret flicker of anticipation as I reflected on what might soon be revealed.

In the inner room, flamboyant tapestries and sumptuous cloth lay higgledy-piggledy over the bare floor and delicate carved objects were upturned and broken. Following Michael's instructions, we found a small trapdoor in the floorboards which had until recently been covered with magnificent carpets.

Brother Thomas raised it. In the darkness beneath was a steep wooden staircase. He took a lamp which hung just to the right of the entrance, and when he had got it alight, I followed him down the steps into a cellar. The room was completely bare, its walls built of blocks of stone and lumps of masonry. For a moment I was disappointed, but then in the corner of this room we found another trapdoor, just big enough for a man to climb through on to the ladder leading down from it. Brother Thomas went first and I followed.

Here, in the lower cellar, Thomas lit an oil lamp and a number of candles, revealing a desk, an hour-glass, a chair, and bookshelves on which parchment scrolls were neatly stacked. There was a faint scent of benjamin in the air. On the far side of the room the rushes which covered the stone floor had been cleared. Against the wall was a rough stone altar, and in front of it the remains of a fire. Above its ashes there crouched a squat iron stand supporting a glass vessel with a long neck, twisting up, and then back down, like the neck of a swan preening itself. Within the vessel, the athanor, was a murky brown viscous fluid.

When we had done with staring at this, we made our way into another room to the right, much smaller than the first. It was lined with shelves on which phials of vitriol and other substances were arranged, each a different colour and consistency in the dull light. The wall to the right was bare stone but on the left wall were mosaic tiles, depicting snakes, fish and interweaving lily-leaves and flowers; on crumbling plaster I could just decipher the faded painting of a human face. Centuries ago, perhaps this had been a dwelling place.

'Have you guessed what Isaac would have been doing down here?' Thomas asked.

'Alchemy?' I replied.

'You had not suspected?'

'I had no reason to,' I said.

'Do you think he knows how to change lead into gold?' Thomas asked.

'I don't know,' I replied, uneasily aware of a dull roaring coming from behind the cupboard where the phials were kept. 'Besides, did you not tell me once that alchemical transformations were only the outer sign of an inner process,' I added, 'and that the point of alchemy is to grow rich spiritually, not materially?'

'What we believe is less important than what others believe. It would explain a lot if the Prior has got wind of this.'

'And the King,' I added.

'The house was ransacked,' said Thomas, 'but no one seems to have been down here. We shall have to be careful whom we tell and when.'

We spent some time looking round; the sheer quantity of the books and paraphernalia daunted me. I thought it might take weeks even to begin to understand them, perhaps a lifetime. Besides, I knew that only so much hermetic knowledge is ever written, and the most important lessons are passed on by word of mouth. There is much encoded in written texts in a way which easily deceives the uninitiated. If we were going to acquire any knowledge from here, we would have to enlist Isaac's help.

We inspected the manuscripts on the shelves, hoping to find the *Hermesis* but there was no sign of it. I was astonished at the variety of languages, not only Latin and Hebrew, but Norman French, Greek and Chaldean too.

The dull booming sound came once more from beyond the shelves in which the phials of vitriol and other substances were stored. Unease gripped me, sending cold shivers through my bones. As if in a trance, I went into the adjoining room whilst Brother Thomas looked on. I ran my fingers round the back of the panel through the dust and the spiders' webs. There, I found hinges. The cupboard, as I pulled it towards me, opened like a door. The roaring sound, like that of a thousand bees, came again, followed by a dull puff of warm, subterranean air.

Edging my way into the dark space behind the shelves, gingerly at first, I found myself in a tunnel, walls reinforced by brick and ragstone botched together. I followed it for a few yards or so, the light of my lamp casting jagged shadows around me. The tunnel soon opened out; lengthy sections of walls were studded with fragments of frescoes and mosaics depicting human faces, yellow irises, white lions, red eagles and fantastic figures pouring fluid from one vessel to another. I looked back towards the entrance of the tunnel and saw Brother Thomas. His face was pale and drawn. That same roaring sound came again and I could see that it was unnerving him just as it was unnerving me.

'It is late,' said Thomas. 'Perhaps we should continue tomorrow.'

I felt relief at these words, rather than disappointment. 'I think you are right,' I said. 'There is too much to take in now. Where do you think it leads?'

'I should imagine,' said Brother Thomas, 'that there is a direct connection to the Priory. Some say it is possible to walk from here to Dover below ground.'

We climbed out of the cellar, exhausted and lost in thought, then set off through the cold, empty streets directly to our lodgings.

'By the way, were you convinced the day before yesterday,' he asked me, as we approached the Priory, 'by Domna Cecilia's description of the reasons for her pilgrimage?'

I shrugged uncertainly.

'It is curious that she told us her purpose was to seek out Walter. That is an unseemly love for a woman like her to admit. Perhaps there was some message encoded in what she told us, and she was really looking for something more.'

'If that is the case, then her quest does not seem to have been successful,' I observed.

'That is a very good point,' said Brother Thomas, thoughtfully. 'Perhaps you should settle down for the night now. I need to do some more work.'

As I made ready for bed, Brother Thomas carried on working by the light of a small lamp, sitting at the tiny window of our lodgings whilst the moon shone bright outside, casting beams about the room. I fell asleep to the comforting sound of the scratching of my master's pen.

Chapter Fifteen

T HE FLICKERING FLAME of the lamp was dull against the yellow-grey dawn light which now filled the room. I looked on through half-shut eyes, pretending to be asleep in order not to disturb my master. His pen scratched its way across the page with undiminished vigour.

At last he looked round, and though his eyes were tired, that glint of enthusiasm in them remained. 'You are awake, Wilfridus,' he said. 'That is just as well, for it is time for me to sleep now. I have completed my work on the philosophical system we have so often discussed. I believe there is great power in it, and I know that soon I shall be exhausted. Therefore I must ask you to convey this copy to Lord Rufus, for safekeeping, together with this report on our investigations of Domna Cecilia, which is a summary of our records. In it I have explained that I consider her to be innocent of heresy but I have suggested that you, Wilfridus, might disagree.'

I was taken aback at this and I sat up. 'You want me,' I said, 'to take the blame and the responsibility for her condemnation?'

'I did not say that. The letter is privately addressed to Lord Rufus. It does not signify a definitive judgment. Only we should be clear about what we believe. And of course,' he added, 'you are at liberty to disagree with my findings. But that is a matter for you. Now, please get ready to travel to Dover. When I met him in London, Lord Rufus said he would arrive at the castle there today, though on what business he would not be drawn. It should be interesting for you to talk with him, in any case. He has connections with the large Templar house at Dover. This should help advance our investigation of the murders at Swiffeld.'

'Why do you want Lord Rufus to have a copy of your philosophical writings?' I asked.

'As I said,' he replied, 'there is power in this knowledge, and the two of us, Brother Wilfridus, are vulnerable here. It would not do for it to fall into the wrong hands. I am not alone in this quest. You or Alyssa are to continue the Work if anything happens to me. Lord Rufus will not understand, but he will support you. When you return, if you do not find me here, it may be that I am working in Isaac's cellars, for there is much there which might complement these writings. Please do not seek me out there; the fewer who know about the cellar the better.'

He handed me his writings, densely written on twenty-two sheets of parchment, with illustrations of correspondences he perceived between Hebrew systems, precious stones, music, the heavenly bodies, angelic orders, alchemy, herbalism and even the hidden meanings of colours. The illustrations portrayed such things as a boy chasing a butterfly, a beautiful woman pouring liquid from one urn to another, kings, queens, wheels of fortune and a moon with scarabs reaching towards it. This system is well known now, amongst the adept, and the way each picture represents a stage of the soul's journey towards God is well established as essentially Christian and orthodox. I affirm that it was my master, Brother Thomas, who first set down this system in its truth and fullness, though the project was not a new one. Michael, for example, also understood this line of spiritual enquiry. How can I be certain that Brother Thomas was the first to release the power of this knowledge into the world? The answer is, of course, that I cannot be sure, but the fate which was to befall him supports my case, for it is written that the possession of such knowledge is never without its cost.

Brother Thomas and I ate together, and after that he settled in bed, exhausted. I took my horse from the Priory stables and headed off along the Dover road, leaving the city of Canterbury via the cattle market.

I rode hard, keeping to the pilgrim road in order to give Swiffeld as wide a berth as possible. On the way, I kept thinking about the images in Thomas's drawings, and found myself seeing parallels in people we were meeting. Thomas was like the Magician, Myrrah was the young Priestess, Domna Cecilia was the Empress, Lord Rufus was the Emperor and the Prior was the Hierophant. I supposed that, given my youth and ignorance, I was like the Fool. That is certainly how I see myself now as I was then, a Fool playing with fire. Yet I would still be hard put to say what that fire was: a glimpse of beauty perhaps, of an essential world beyond this world of change and circumstance, a world which Domna Cecilia knew better than most, and which Brother Thomas understood and was to experience in such a terrible way.

It was growing dark by the time Dover's enormous castle loomed into sight, overlooking the town from the high hills. Next to it stood the giant stone beacon, said to be a thousand years old, staring out to sea. I was tired, so I decided to rest at an inn down the road from the castle. I drank a mug of ale watching the waves curl and crash far below, as the sea-gulls swooped and circled on the powerful gusts of autumn wind. Dull lights on the distant horizon from the masts of ships made me dream of cargoes of spices and precious stones from faraway countries and noble adventures in the Holy Land. I felt then, and still feel now, cast out, adrift on a sea of time.

Mars shone low and red in the sky as I led my horse up the castle hill, winding my way along the path which zig-zagged through the ramparts, newly patched where they had been breached during the siege when John was King. At last, nervous at the thought of the powerful and courtly men with whom I was about to mix, I reached the tall keep built recently against the French, which was where Thomas had told me I would find Lord Rufus.

Within the keep courtyard, torches scattered fragments of my shadow against the high walls. There were many soldiers milling around and I felt out of place in the monkish clothes I still wore. Lord Rufus's name was like a magic key; I was led by one of the soldiers past the tiny, brightly painted chapel, built by Henry II and dedicated to Becket, up the staircase to the great hall where I was to eat before my meeting with Lord Rufus. I was shown to a draughty corner table. Exquisite red tapestries on the wall depicted courtly scenes of falconry and the arts of love; in the vaulting, crimson and gold patterns of intertwining tendrils bearing heart-shaped leaves and fleurs-de-lys glimmered in the fire and torch-light; it was like being an eye in a ruby-red precious stone, or an insect trapped in amber, trying to look out, but seeing only reflections of an encased, ideal world.

Peter des Roches, who until recently had been one of the men closest to the King, presided over the banquet. He was very much in his prime, tall, strong, cleanshaven, so graceful and so courtly in his manner that he might almost have seemed saintly were it not for those harsh blue eyes which chilled me even at a distance. He wore a magnificent green silk cloak lined with marten fur. After his fall and imprisonment the previous year he was already back on the road to power, and this evening was clearly part of his strategy. The banquet (delicate herbs flavoured the soup, saffron, ginger and other exotic spices provided sauces for the oysters and fresh fish, and two succulent young lambs had been roasted on a spit) was literally food fit for royalty, though at the time I did not realise that they were trying out the menus for the King's visit. I suddenly identified des Roches as the fifth man, the white-haired one, present at the disinterment of the chalice in the Cathedral, though I could not fathom the implications of this.

Rufus was easy to make out because of his bright red hair and freckled complexion. He wore a colourfully embroidered surcoat over a fine, striped tunic, and his boots were laced at the side, their tops lined with silk and the toes conspicuously pointed. He sat to the left of des Roches, picking at his food but looking round constantly, like a bird of prey, taking in what was going on at the other tables.

After the guests had eaten, Lord Rufus strode down from the podium and led me away from the company of itinerant knights and lesser ecclesiastics. In those days Rufus was in his late thirties. Of course I was in awe of him then, thinking him the epitome of a sophisticated man of the world, particularly since Brother Thomas always spoke well of him. Now I know his kind better. Blind loyalty to his masters and ambition would have earned him advancement at court and made him dangerous to adversaries. He greeted me warmly, for everyone to see, and then paraded me before Lord Peter and the ladies on the high table, introducing me as his 'bloodhound' who was 'snuffling round after heresy'. I noticed the unease in the eyes of the others.

Lord Rufus's red hair and quickness of movement lent him a mercurial power, and everyone but des Roches naturally deferred to him. 'Come, Brother Wilfridus,' he said ostentatiously, at last. 'It is time for our chat. Please follow me.' He escorted me out of the main hall into the network of staircases and parapets overlooking the sea. The sky had clouded and a storm was brewing. An icy wind blew in through the slit windows.

On the way down the stairs I asked Rufus polite questions about his children, whom I knew Brother Thomas had taught Latin, Greek and rhetoric. Rufus's castle in Ellethamwolde, which he had from the Earl of Gloucester, was not far from the house Brother Thomas shared with Alyssa and his own children. Lord Rufus appeared to be delighted with my conversation, and flattered me by discussing the various marriage options for Katarina, his eldest daughter, as if I were his equal. I had heard from Brother Thomas that Lord Rufus's daughter was a scholarly child. 'I do hope,' I remember saying, 'that you will be able to find her a husband who will appreciate her learning.'

It was then that I was given a glimpse of Lord Rufus's true character. Just for a moment his face set with harsh, cynical contours and he said, 'Brother Wilfridus, you of all people should have understood by now that learning is not everything.'

I heard the sea roaring in the distance as we descended to the lower chapel, and then branched off through a squat door and down further steps into a suite of three windowless rooms below ground level. Rufus lit the torches in each. The quality of the ornately carved, highly polished oak cupboards and chests, and the luxurious floor coverings, led me to conclude that these were royal apartments, for secret business perhaps, or a last refuge in war. We sat together in the furthest of the three rooms, Rufus behind the grand desk, I on a low chair in front of it.

'Well,' he began. 'Tell me about Domna Cecilia. Is she a heretic?'

'Perhaps you should read this,' I said, and I handed him Brother Thomas's records, which he thumbed through. When he had finished, it was clear that he was disappointed.

'Typical of Brother Thomas,' he said. 'Thorough, full of facts and clear analysis, but no firm conclusions, only prevarications. You were present at the interviews, Brother Wilfridus. What is your own judgment of the woman?'

I shrugged, uncertain how he expected me to reply, and not wanting to compromise Brother Thomas. 'It is too early to say,' I answered.

'Unfortunately,' he said, frowning, 'there is a degree of urgency. What sort of a life does this Cecilia lead here in England?'

'A simple, ascetic life,' I replied. 'She is kept under guard, sees few people, and claims to be a visionary.'

'Surely that is enough!' Lord Rufus sighed.

'Since saints see visions,' I insisted, 'that would not in itself be enough to condemn her.'

'You are not going to tell me she is a saint. She's not dead yet. You have to be dead to be a saint.'

'You have to be killed,' I corrected him, immediately regretting my forthrightness.

Lord Rufus, fortunately, saw the funny side of being contradicted by a nineteen-year-old novice. He laughed, placed a hand on my shoulder, poured me a goblet of wine and said, 'Well, Brother Wilfridus. Perhaps I am beginning to understand what Brother Thomas sees in you. Besides, you are right. We need something that will do for an open trial and a public condemnation.'

'May I ask why?' I said.

'You may ask, but I will not tell you,' he replied. 'Not yet.' A look of consternation which flickered across his face made me wonder if he too was being kept ignorant of the true reasons behind the investigations. 'Now, perhaps you would be kind enough to tell me what your judgments are concerning the Templar murders. You were clever, by the way, to have found the bodies in the tunnels.'

'I did not find them on my own. I was taken there by someone,' I said.

'Yes, this Michael fellow. Brother Thomas writes that he is connected to Isaac the Jew.'

'He is his son,' I affirmed.

'A prodigal son, so it would appear. What do you make of him?'

'I see no harm in him,' I replied. Thoughts of Myrrah returned, filling my mind with a sweet yearning. 'What will become of him, and Isaac, and his family, now that they have been arrested?' I asked.

Lord Rufus looked concerned. 'Who said they have been arrested? On whose authority?'

I told him about the wrecking of Isaac's house and the arrest of Michael.

'That is curious,' he said. 'No orders to arrest him came through me, and the King issued none, as far as I am aware. Still,' he went on hurriedly, 'I shall be in Canterbury in two or three days' time and we shall see then what needs doing. I am sure that no harm will come to them.'

I wondered why he was so keen to reassure me and blurted, 'I am sure it would be right to help them.' Then, seeing the look of disapproval on his face, I added rapidly, 'Provided they are innocent, of course.' I was on the verge of telling Lord Rufus about the events in the Cathedral, but then I thought better of it. I did not want anyone, other than Brother Thomas, to know that I had been there.

'Tell me,' he went on, 'about your other investigations. Who do you and Brother Thomas think was responsible for the Templar murders?'

'There are a number of possibilities,' I began, but my voice trailed away. The rich food was curdling in my stomach, and the pleasant glow of inebriation from the wine had subsided into mere nausea; I was losing the fight to keep a clear head. 'But we are not certain.'

'Has Brother Thomas seen no connections?' said Rufus. I must have looked blank. 'Between the murder and Domna Cecilia's presence in Canterbury?' Suddenly, Rufus burst out laughing. 'To think,' he chuckled, 'my dear friend Brother Thomas, who is usually so subtle, so learned, and who understands such hermetic notions as the correspondences between things – can it really never have occurred to him that there might be a link between the two investigations? Or perhaps he has not made his thoughts explicit to you, Brother Wilfridus?'

I felt humiliated and uncertain, for Brother Thomas's sake and my own. 'I am not sure,' I said.

'And the *Hermesis*,' he said, raising his eyebrows to give an impression of reassurance. 'Have you found out anything?'

I started telling him about the anti-monarchical sentiments of the gloss I had read when, suddenly, an idea formed. It was a wild idea, but I felt a desperate need to impress Lord Rufus. 'Domna Cecilia mentioned a time when she lived at the court in Leuchtenfels,' I said. 'The Graf and Gräfin were close to the Welf, Henry the Lion, and the Emperor. Cecilia mentioned that one day when she was at Rupertsburc a white-haired priest had sought her out, thrown himself on his knees before her, and told her that she was chosen; later the Gräfin of Leuchtenfels behaved towards her in a way which suggested she might have known this.'

'Chosen for what?' Lord Rufus interrupted, looking so uneasy that I began to suspect I had touched a raw nerve.

'Allow me to finish,' I said. 'Domna Cecilia also attached a lot of importance to the singer, Walter von der Ouwe, whom she knew intimately at the court of Leuchtenfels. We have found out more about him since. He joined the Templars, fought at Constantinople, and eventually became the Abbot

222

of a monastery at Bellapais in Cyprus.'

'That is well enough known,' Lord Rufus commented. 'Des Roches met the fellow when he was on Crusade with the Emperor Frederick. They stayed at Bellapais on the way. He was impressed by him. Besides, his songs are still on every singer's lips. Some used to be nervous about him. There were rumours that he had mastered certain arts which the Templars kept to themselves, and that this explained the power of his music. I still don't see what you are getting at.'

'The murder at Swiffeld,' I said, 'was at a Templar house.'

Lord Rufus breathed deeply, and the lines of worry on his freckled forehead deepened. 'So,' he sighed, 'perhaps you are making more progress than we imagined. But you must excuse me, for I have to return to my guests now. Will you pass on a message to Brother Thomas when you see him again? The King will be in Canterbury shortly, and it is probable that he will request an audience with Thomas. So he had better be well prepared.'

'An audience with the King?' I repeated.

'Don't be surprised,' said Lord Rufus. 'Brother Thomas's talents are well known.'

This was my opportunity to hand over to Lord Rufus the copy of Brother Thomas's philosophical system. 'By the way,' I said, 'my master asked me to give you this, for safe-keeping.'

Lord Rufus glanced through the pages. 'One of these days you will have to explain it all to me. But I'll find a safe place for it, don't worry. Now, however,' he said, half with regret and half with relief, 'I have other cats to flay. So if you will excuse me? And if you don't mind,' he added, 'I recommend that you should sleep down here tonight. We don't want to arouse anyone's suspicions, not at this stage. Besides, you know how Dominicans unnerve people. Someone will bring you breakfast in the morning. There is more wine for you.'

He pointed to a pitcher on the table, next to which was a loaf of bread and some cheese. In the corner of the room was a low bed with ample blankets and cushions. There was no point in protesting, for it was clear that I was not to accompany him back upstairs, so I thanked him for his hospitality, and he took his leave of me. As the door shut after him, I heard it click, ominously. I got up straight away to try it. It was locked.

I sat alone in that luxurious, empty room as the wind howled outside, and pondered his words. I drank too much wine, and slept only feverishly, getting up at regular intervals to try the door, fear welling within me, feeling as though I had been locked in the very heart of the darkness this castle exuded.

I had plenty of time to think about the people I had seen at the castle that night. They all belonged or had belonged to the King's inner circle. I thought too of the quotation from the *Hermesis*. I wondered if the time really had come for an end to be put to the dark, brooding power concentrated without justice in the hands of a few. Yet power, I now know, is the one thing over which we have no power.

That night I saw in my dreams the images Thomas used in his philosophical systems. There was the beautiful Empress, the Skeleton reaping bones, the Angel pouring wine from one urn to another, the Scarabs reaching claws towards the moon. There was something malignant about these dreams. Also, repeatedly, I would see William de Sens, high up beneath the open sky, the massive criss-cross vaults not yet having met to form the roof of the Cathedral; he would be inspecting the carving of the column heads, or considering some problem with the gigantic machines he had built for the turning of the arches; then I would see him, stepping from stone to wooden scaffolding, or reaching too far and losing his footing, then falling, horribly, silently through the shadows, himself a shadow, and it seemed that terrible fall was a punishment for divulging knowledge through the architecture.

At dawn, a young woman came with breakfast, just as Lord Rufus had promised, and I found myself free to leave. Relieved, I rode over the Downs by the burial mounds which line the way beneath the bleak skies.

Chapter Sixteen

I RETURNED TO find Brother Thomas sitting listlessly in our lodgings. Despite Michael's words, he still had no certain news of Alyssa and his children. The energy that had possessed him two days before had left him. Instead, he sat at his table, toying with a chess set he had borrowed, he said, from the Prior. He suggested we play a game to pass the time before leaving to see Domna Cecilia. I agreed, though I thought it was a foregone conclusion that he would beat me.

As we played, I told him what had happened at Dover. He nodded but made no comment, even when I mentioned the audience with the King. The chess pieces we played with were kept in a sandalwood box inlaid with pearl. The pawns were like tombstones, engraved with looping, lily-like swirls such as they once used to decorate pillars in churches and capital letters in certain old manuscripts. As to the major pieces, their most striking feature was their bulbous, staring eyes. The knights, sporting pointed beards and barbaric helmets, sat fiercely on squat horses. The bishops had flat mitres, and their vestments bore the same twisting patterns as the pawns. The kings and queens were large but also hunched, and their eyes would not leave me, exuding a power as if they had dark souls, like owls, or other creatures of the night.

As we played, I imagined I saw in the chess pieces not only the conflict between lighter and darker forces, but the intricacy of mercurial connections between the two. For once, I did not lose. The game came to a stalemate. As we got ready to leave for Domna Cecilia's house, Thomas observed that, whether one wins or loses, or plays with white or black, it is as hard in chess as in life to know whether one is on the side of light, or of darkness. Then he reminded me of the words of John Scotus, that God has engraved dialectic into the heart of every created thing. I took the opportunity to ask him his views regarding the Cathar heresy. We were still talking as we left our lodgings.

'The Elders, in particular,' he said, 'lead virtuous lives, spending much time in prayer, doing good deeds, rigorously confessing to one another their slightest sins, and adhering to a strict vegetarian diet. They are not called *perfecti* because they claim to be perfect, but because their souls are supposed to be completed, that is, ready at death to leave this world which according to them is created and ruled by an evil god.'

'They believe in the Bible, don't they?' I asked.

'Only the New Testament, though they use the Old Testament in some of their preaching. They pay particular attention to the Gospel of Saint John.'

'Forgive my naivety,' I said, 'but I have never understood why, if their lives are virtuous and they believe in the Bible, the Church has been so cruel and relentless in rooting them out.'

'There are two types of explanation,' Brother Thomas replied. 'The first is, of course, that their doctrines endanger souls. The Cathars say that there is not one God, but two. An evil god created the world, for the good God could never have tolerated the evil we experience. He could never have willed such things as suffering, illness, death, nor reproduction through coitus and the devouring of dead flesh. The only way to escape the clutches of evil, they argue, is to follow the Gospels, so as to earn the right to call the good God

"Father". Then, after death, one might be reunited with Him. Otherwise one is doomed to live again in this world.'

'They do not believe in Hell?' I queried.

'They believe that this world and the suffering here is evil enough. Therefore they count the material body as nothing. For this reason they have no graves when they die, and no funeral ceremonies – they dispose of the corpses of their fellows as if they were rubbish. Perhaps this is also why many, when prosecuted by the authorities, prefer to be burnt rather than recant. They laugh at the Holy Communion, saying the bread and the wine are material, not spiritual, and they mock the cult of the relics of Saints.'

'You mentioned another set of reasons,' I prompted him.

'Of course,' he sighed. 'Power and politics. The concentration of the heretics in the Aquitaine provides an admirable excuse for the King of France to expand his power to the lands controlled by Toulouse. And how can the Holy Church, which is of course the receptacle of all that is virtuous, maintain its influence in the face of a rival Church which, as far as its morals are concerned, takes the Gospels literally, renounces property and, worse still, maintains standards of virtue higher than the Church's own?'

'And what is your view of the heresy?' I asked Brother Thomas.

'That it is pernicious,' he said, but his tone was such that I could tell how much irony there was in that curt reply.

When we arrived at Domna Cecilia's house, Brother Thomas began by asking her about her views on alchemy, probably to test obliquely whether she knew anything about the work being carried out in Isaac's cellar.

'I know a little,' she replied. 'I admire you, Thomas, that you can ask such questions, even now. Alchemy is, to answer you, the practice of the transmutation of metals, based on the notion of the correspondence between what is above and what is below, a long, painful and perhaps futile rummaging in the realm of matter, in the hope of finding in it some spark of the divine, or gold. Am I not right?'

Thomas's next question was, 'Do you not believe, then, that the alchemical project is possible?' He asked this because certain heretics, like the Cathars, believe matter is evil and cannot bear an imprint of the divine.

'Some,' she replied, 'have argued the alchemist's picture of the cosmos is like the graven images of which the Scriptures warn us, for they are of death. Yet death is a horse which some, like Christ perhaps, might ride.'

Thomas smiled and sighed. There was no point in trying to trick her. 'Perhaps you could tell us more,' he said, 'about your life together with Martin Palviezen.'

'Very well,' she said. 'Martin and I were married in the year of Our Lord 1202, about the time that the great armies were gathering in Venice for the Crusade which ended so ignominiously in Constantinople. The wedding itself took place at Stierenfurt on a fine day in April, and a feast was held. Food was distributed liberally to the local peasants and the townsfolk, and a dance was organised for the afternoon, which went on well into the evening. Everyone was joyful, including me; only as ever I was aware of a region within myself, untouched, observing, waiting. That day I was reconciled with Stierenfurt, my uncle. "There, I told you so," he said. "I was right all along."

'Martin led me to my new home on the lands he now looked after on behalf of his father, who had grown infirm. I started when I saw the house, firstly because of its considerable size, and secondly because it seemed familiar to me, as if I had already glimpsed it in a dream.

'As Martin showed me round he explained to me how, through his careful stewardship, and through contacts he

had been careful to cultivate with the new Graf of Leuchtenfels (the old one having renounced his estates, and set off on
a pilgrimage, leaving the Gräfin to fend for herself), the
lands under his control had grown, both in size and in yield.

'Martin and I were not wealthy by the standards of the
higher nobility, but he certainly possessed more land than
many knights. Mind you, he deserved it, for he worked hard,
especially at harvest-time and in the very early spring, when
the lambs were born. Everything he touched flourished. I
was never anything but proud of Martin, and proud *for* him.
Somehow, he found the energy to read with me first thing in
the morning and late at night. We were able to afford
servants, so I was not deprived of time to study in the leisure
hours left to me when the business of the household was
done. In short, I came to know something akin to happiness.

'I lived as Martin's wife in full accordance with the pre-
cepts of the Church of Rome. I ran the household, organised
the celebrations of Feast Days and family events, I made sure
that the family was well clothed and fed, I saw to it that
proper abstinence was observed during Advent, Lent and
other seasons when fasting is prescribed, and I gave myself to
my husband at the permitted times.

'As a result of this, I bore him four children. Little Elspeth
died of fever when only a few days old, and another child, a
boy called Walter, died after only three weeks on this earth.
The two who survived babyhood were a son, whom we called
David, and who grew strong and powerful like his father. The
fourth child was a girl called Kirsta, whom Martin loved.

'I tried, in my life with Martin, to draw together the
threads of everything I had learnt: the abstinence, discipline
and reflectiveness of the convent, the playfulness and joy of
courtly love, and the practical life I had learnt on the road as
a pilgrim. I took to heart the idea that marriage is a
sacrament, and I tried to see the divine in wedded life, as I

230

had in the monastic life. I even wondered if some variant of the Benedictine rule might be lived out by married couples. But of course, if evil is to come, it will come no matter what we do to render ourselves immune from it.

'I told you about a vision I had, when I was fifteen, when I saw myself walking across a field, bountiful with dusty gold-brown wheat and blood-red poppies, a house round which butterflies played, a sick girl, lying on a low bed in a dark room, and the girl's long blonde hair woven with flowers.

'When the vision first came, as I said, I thought I was seeing my own death. For years I would not even think of it. Then the vision would return, laden with melancholy, and I would wonder where it came from. I told you how I started in surprise when I first entered Martin's house. This is why. The texture of the timber, the way the roof, with its reddish tinge, sloped down to the right almost to the ground, the dark colour of the wood inside, the hazy brightness of blossom and flowers – so much of it was hauntingly similar to that vision. Still, I did the sensible thing, and tried to put it from my mind; I succeeded in doing so for years.

'Kirsta was a lovely child. Because of her long blonde hair my uncle and his people said she was like me at her age. But I knew that was not true. She was so much calmer, so much more warmhearted than I had ever been. I taught her much of what I had learnt in the convents of my youth, and we were very close. She could read and write well, and recite many passages of the Bible in Latin, Greek and Hebrew. She was making good headway too with Virgil and with Boethius. Yet she needed none of these things to be the lovely, gentle creature that she was. Whilst learning had formed my inner landscape, it merely adorned hers. Her soul was like a quiet garden, always blooming with something fresh, pure and lovely.

'Already there had been talk of who her husband might be

231

when she fell ill, at the age of fourteen, in the first flower of her beauty. The first night of her fever I dreamt of white horses, and the next morning she already had the look of one who would die. Perhaps you know this look, Thomas. You see the face of such a person but it is as though you cannot focus on the features, only on a blurred whiteness beyond, for their spiritual bodies are already leaving them. That summer, the summer of her illness, returning to our house through the heavy-scented, flowery meadows, bearing food, or water, or medicines, to care for her, I knew with an appalling sense of oppression that I had already seen these things, this reality, in that vision years ago. Everything was the same, the colours, the textures, the presence of that poor, sick girl, so pale, her lips the colour of pomegranate, and her hair wound with absinth leaves, so soon to be replaced with rue.

'She died in the first week of July, after an illness which lasted for four months. I prepared her poor, wasted body for burial myself, rubbing her limbs with balm and scattering midsummer flowers and herbs in her coffin, Saint John's wort, saffron, marigolds and fresh daisies. The grief was terrible, yet the tormenting horror of my foreknowledge, of which I dared speak to no one, filled me with a paralysing dread. What awful gifts had been bestowed on me that had turned to such a curse? How dark and formidable was the fabric of the universe to permit such unnatural distortions in the flow of time? Perhaps it was then that I lost faith with this world.

'Martin was inconsolable, for he had so loved Kirsta. Poor Martin! Had I not always been strict about religious observances, about acts of penance small and great, had I not held forth endlessly about the need for a quest in the life of every man and woman, a quest for the life God wills for us, and had I not, in my folly, sung the praises of those who set off on

Crusade, so that the Word of God might be preached throughout the whole world, and Jerusalem freed from the Infidel, so that the Last Days might come, after which all will be well? Yes, I had spoken at length about such matters, and now I looked on in terror, as I saw the seeds I had sown come to a terrible fruition.

'Martin, who in the past had listened to such discourse with gentle good humour, and the detachment befitting a man of the land, now became obsessed with the idea of going on Crusade. Our local village priest, Father Jorst, who had called regularly throughout Kirsta's illness in the belief that he was providing spiritual comfort, talked a lot about the Cathar heresy, which he said was rife in Champagne, and near the Pyrenees. Soon, over meals, whilst out working in the fields, and even as we sat together in the evenings, Martin and David too, who was a strong lad of fifteen by then, kind and lovely in his ways, but without the love of learning Kirsta possessed, would speak of nothing else. They believed everything the narrow-minded and poorly educated Father Jorst told them, that these heretics were the spawn of the devil, that they perpetrated vile and hideous acts, that they stood in the way of the salvation of whole nations and that since they lived in Christian lands and corrupted the true faith from within, they were worse even than the Saracen.

'I did try to tell Martin and David of the gentle creatures I had once met in the Pyrenees, but they only eyed me suspiciously. For already, without knowing who the Cathars were or what they believed, they hated them as they hated death itself. I intend this as no empty comparison, for in view of the suddenness of the change that befell Martin, perhaps it was poor Kirsta's death that he hated, and perhaps he only saw Cathars where he should have seen that death; this is understandable, since death is an absence, a negative, and

233

the temptation to hate something or someone else in the place of death is too human.

'One Sunday at Mass, Father Jorst sang the praises of Conrad of Marbourg and Robert le Bougre who were hunting heretics in the Rhineland and Champagne respectively. He proclaimed with papal authority that all sins would be forgiven those who set off on Crusade against the Cathars. The die was cast. It was as if Martin had been promised, not just the forgiveness of sins, but that Kirsta would be returned to life, if only he joined the forces against heresy.

'I implored Martin and David not to take part in the Crusade. But this was no longer the same Martin I had married, nor the same Martin I had lived with for over twenty years. Grief poisoned his mind, and made him stubborn and rigid in his thinking. He said I wavered because I was a woman. His determination showed, he assured me, that now he knew best, not just about practical matters, but about things of the spirit too. As far as the running of the land was concerned, our affairs were in excellent order, and there would be no difficulty in handing them over to Andreas, his brother, while he was away. When I realised there was no hope of stopping Martin and David, I did at least manage to win one concession. I would accompany them.

'That was an appalling winter, Thomas, for I felt everything I had held dear crumbling away from me, like a castle stricken by lightning, teetering on foundations unable to support it, knowing that at any moment, my familiar world would fall apart, leaving only ruins smouldering in a shapeless void.

'During the winter, Martin and David undertook military training at Leuchtenfels under the Meraniener who, when they saw how ready Martin was to spend a fortune on war-horses, swords and military equipment, were more than happy to dub him a knight. To afford this, we had to borrow against yields from the next two harvests. Next, news reached me that Stierenfurt had died. There was not enough money for his children to continue the estate, which passed into the hands of the Bishop of Babenberc.

'Then, one day, amongst the poor people, the beggars and lepers that would come from door to door, I saw a face, so familiar to me, once so loved, so hated. She wore ragged clothes, and she was old, hunched. She took one look at me, shuddered, hid her face for a moment with hands which were horribly wasted. Then she stared at me with piercing, hollow eyes and said, in a voice so changed that I began to doubt it was hers: "It's you, the one they were always talking about. You, the *Empress*, the *Daughter of Jerusalem*, the pawn in their conspiracies. Look what they have done to me because of you! You took my husband, my wealth, my status." With that she ran away, so I did not have the chance to ask her what she meant by these words, let alone comfort her or give her alms. Martin, who by then had good contacts with the Meraniener, confirmed that I had, indeed, seen the old Gräfin. He told me that she had been reduced to begging since the Graf had left her, and she had contracted leprosy. Either he knew nothing more, or he would not tell me. That pitiful sight was only a harbinger. Worse still was to come.

'At last, the preparations were made, and the following spring, to the trilling of larksong, beneath a burning hot sun, our path strewn with flowers by the village folk who accompanied us to the edge of our estates, Martin, David and the small troop of a dozen or so men from the land who were to fight alongside them as footsoldiers, set out. They were flushed with joy, whilst I, the only woman, found my vision clouded with dark forebodings.

'Of course, the men were naive about travelling, for they had never left the confines of Franconia and Bavaria. I was an asset to them, because I was used to finding directions, negotiating prices, dealing with inopportune fellow travellers, and of course in coping with the various languages we met along our way. I used to practise herbal medicine in those days, another reason for my popularity.

'By midsummer, we had reached Lyon. French nobles took charge of the expedition from then on. I had lost none of my old talents of interpreting, singing and discoursing about knightly virtues, and I found myself much sought-after by men, mostly nobles, coming to ask my advice, to learn songs, sometimes even to sing my praises. No one, however, sensed the emptiness I felt and nothing could fill it. Martin reacted with a mixture of pride and envy. This was my element, and he must have felt like a fish out of water.

'It was at this time, incidentally, that people began to call me Cecilia, more because of my music than any saintliness, and the name stuck, even though it does not resemble my real name, which you have no doubt discovered by now.

'At last, the armies set off from Lyon. We were several thousand strong, and due to join with a much larger force in Languedoc itself. The journey was not particularly arduous, because there were so many of us, supplies were plentiful, and no one was in too much of a hurry.

'Towards the end of September we reached the outskirts of the lands of the Count of Toulouse. To begin with, nothing seemed to have changed, and I relished the wonderful climate, the radiance of the sun, and the proximity of sea and mountain. Likewise, I drank in the glorious countryside, with its hill villages, often fortified, in the centre of which new churches stood, gleaming like jewels beneath the sun and the deep blue sky, whilst along the roads emanating from the hills like spokes of gigantic wheels, or petals of delicate flowers, houses straggled and sprawled, and men and women worked cheerfully in vineyards and wheatfields, vegetable gardens and orchards. I knew from my previous visit that many men and women in those lands were free, having no feudal lord, but lived from what they owned and produced. They seemed to lack nothing.

'However, by the time we reached the area round Avignon, where the heresy was supposed to be rife, and where the terrible siege had just been lifted, the people behaved differently, hunched and haunted in their bearing, eyeing us suspiciously, scarcely looking up to mumble a greeting. Beyond Avignon, where we joined the main part of the army, there were areas which were quite deserted, and others where ragged children ran bewildered amidst burnt-out houses and through charred, barren fields. Noble hillforts where joy, song and love had once reigned supreme, were now devastated, as if hollowed out from within, leaving only speechless walls with old, tattered banners, which no one had thought to take down after battle, flapping in the desolate wind. People talked of Labécède, where the whole population had been put to the sword, men, women and children; only the Good Christian elders had been burnt. Memories of deeds during the previous Crusade were revived, like Marmande, where five thousand had been stripped, put to the sword, then their entrails cut out and left to rot in the sun. Only the Count of Astarac, the man who had led the garrison, was spared, so that he might bear witness to the holy deed of the Pope's armies.

'There was little real fighting now, for the people of the land were intimidated and many went into hiding. We rode through towns, villages and camps where only hordes of brutal young men such as I had never seen before, dressed in ragged clothes, scarcely disciplined, roamed like lions seeking whom they might devour; rape, destruction and thieving were their only entertainments. Few of the men were older than twenty, yet there was nothing youthful about them, for youth is kind, generous and abounding with happiness; these creatures, who radiated hostility through their possessed eyes, were bearers of a timeless evil. You might say that they were doing the work of God. Perhaps, but not the work of a God of love. Years before, as an unprotected young nun, when I last passed through these lands, I never felt under threat. Now, despite my advancing years, and despite the presence of my husband and his men, and our army, I felt that the danger was constant, and I understood the words of Peire Cardenal, that the courts of love had deteriorated into a house of madmen.

'We set up camp near Mirepoix; autumn came and the sunny days faded in a haze, not of golden sunsets and lush corn, but the smoke of fires from burning fields and houses.

'Seven years previously, Dominic Guzman who preached against the Cathars had died in his monastery at Prouille not far from our camp. I saw Sicart's castle where Dominic and the Cathars had publicly debated the rights and wrongs of their beliefs before an assembly of local knights and village people; I saw the place in Fanjeaux from which Dominic had witnessed a fireball descend from the skies, the place where he had shown three girls their Cathar master in the form of a terrible cat, and the place where he had thrown Christian and Cathar texts on to the same fire: the Cathar texts burnt, whilst the Christian writings demonstrated their holiness by rising up from the flames, inviolate.

'Yet your Dominic and his visions brought only death and destruction; a brooding desolation and bitter melancholy hung over the land, a tangible presence of evil. As to Dominic's miracles: the Cathars accepted them as proof of their own doctrine, that matter was ruled by the evil god, who would deliberately allow such tricks to be performed in order to deceive them from the true path. It seemed an eternity ago that anyone might have sung the well-known song:

> "Mon cors s'alegr.e s'esjau
> Per lo gentils temps suau
> E pe.l castel de Fanjau
> Que.m ressembla Paradis"*

'Nothing daunted Martin's enthusiasm for the Crusade. I tried to explain to him how the spirit of the country had changed since I was last there. But this only played to his belief that the Cathar heresy was to blame, and he would want to fight it all the more. If I suggested that our armies were at fault, he would look at me as though I were an idiot. As to David, my poor son, he only ever followed his father's lead. He had always been like that, so kind with his sister, so helpful. Even as he grew tall, handsome and attractive to women with his wavy blond hair, powerful shoulders and ready smile, he was still a little boy at heart, wanting only to please his father. If only he had been born into better times, what a fine man he would have become.

'In the right company, I was still able to tell and hear of stories of chivalry lived out in those lands: of the mysterious lady "Vierne" for example, whom Raimon, the fifth Count of Toulouse, and his troubadour, Peire Vidal, both loved; so too the many stories of Eleanor of Aquitaine and how Bernart de Ventadour was inconsolable after her marriage to Henry II of England; and my favourite, the story of the troubadour Jaufré Rudel, the Prince of Blaye in Gironde who, though he had never set eyes on her, fell in love with the Countess of Tripoli because of the many songs he heard in praise of her great beauty from the pilgrims returning

---

* *How joyful my heart is/When I see the mild weather/And the castle of Fanjeaux/Which seems like paradise. (Peire Vidal)*

from Antioch. He left his native land, sailing to see her. Alas, he fell ill on board ship, and died before he reached Tripoli; yet he died in his Countess's arms, for she had heard of his noble voyage, and sailed out to greet him. How fortunate he was, I would think, to leave this world with his ideals unshaken till the last. I told too of my visit to the court of Raimon de Miravel, the renowned troubadour with whom I had the honour to sing, and whose songs I knew well.

'Many spoke of Peire Vidal, who still lived at the court. He is the singer who claimed that his wife, whom he met in Cyprus, was the niece of the last Emperor of Constantinople. It was he who was so afflicted by the news of the death of Raimon, the sixth Count of Toulouse, in 1222 that he had his hair shaved off, and ordered his servants to do likewise. He even had his horses shorn, and he dressed only in black for a year thereafter. An old man now, he still did what he could to keep alive the spirit of generosity and courtliness, *pretz* and *paratge*, valour and noble-mindedness.

'Many spoke too of the man who was his opposite: Folquet de Marseilles. He had started his adult life as a merchant and troubadour, growing wealthy and marrying well. His songs were on everyone's lips. But in his fifties he renounced this world and entered a monastery, observing a penance of bread and water if ever he chanced to hear one of his own songs. In 1205 he became Bishop of Toulouse. By then he had grown to hate music and to hate the Cathars. He was a firm supporter of Dominic Guzman, and few rejoiced more than he when de Montfort's armies entered the land. Many blame this man for the tens of thousands of deaths that ensued.

'Here is a musical lesson, Thomas, which may explain what happened next in my life. If you take a monochord, and pluck the string, then divide it in two and pluck it again, the second note will of course be an octave above the first. Divide the string by two thirds, and the resulting note will be a fifth higher. The octave and the fifth are the clearest harmonies we have, and they are at the root of all music. If you divide the string in half seven times, the resulting note will be seven octaves higher than the first. If you divide it by two thirds twelve times over, you should end up with the same note. And yet, that is not the case. A number divided in half seven times over is not the same as that number divided by two thirds twelve times over. Nor are the resultant pitches the same. You see how even the most perfect harmony is flawed. How could a good God have allowed this? Music is said to be numbers made audible, reflecting the harmonies of the seven spheres and the beauty and majesty of God, yet here we see that music contradicts itself through number, and numbers contradict themselves through music. You may consider this observation to be abstruse or irrelevant. Yet if you grasp the appalling implications of the flawed nature of music, which I so much loved, perhaps you will better understand the course of my life.

'To continue with my story: the winter was spent in military training, in bullying acts of terror unworthy of the name of "war", and feasting off supplies plundered from local peasants, to discourage them from harbouring Good Christians. I spent much time at Vals, where there is a church that can be reached only by narrow steps in a cleft in the solid rock out of which it rises. I spent endless hours in the ancient lower chapel with its magnificent paintings of the life of Our Lord, which reminded me of the chapels of my youth, trying to recapture the stillness of contemplation which had once come so naturally to me. Little good it did me, and I even wondered if that old sense of peace I once experienced was just another illusion in a life fleeting past me like a show of shadows. Perhaps we only truly experience our lives when we suffer. Meanwhile I was haunted continually by my vision of Kirsta's death.

'My poor David, and my poor Martin. Despite the years of happiness, we did not part on good terms. I suppose we became again what we had once been. I spent much time with nobles, scholars, and churchmen of the old sort, whose minds were open to debate, and who took pleasure in meditating on philosophy, poetry and music. Martin was always busy with practical arrangements for the war. People spoke highly of his military skills and his bravery. But war is a game of chance, where valour is not enough.

'That summer, Martin and David led an expedition of about two hundred men to the area round Foix, deep in the south close to the Pyrenees. I rode with them. The Count of Foix was hostile to us, as was Count Raimon of Toulouse, but our armies were rarely attacked, both sides preferring to avoid outright battles. The local lords hoped constantly that if they left us alone, then our northern armies would just melt away, as they had done before. Sometimes the Count of Foix would even send a few troops to ride alongside the crusading armies, and just occasionally he would oppose us with a show of arms, but mostly he remained menacingly and ambiguously inactive.

'The aim of Martin's expedition was to spy out the city's defences, and to test the reaction of the locals to our presence. We set up camp near a village called Brassac, whose people were not unfriendly.

'There were rumours that Count Raimon of Foix might lead his army against ours, but no one took them seriously. One morning, as the mists rose from the mountains, my husband and a group of twenty or so men rode out to the valleys south of Foix, in order to view the land there. Our camp was on high ground and I watched them as they set off, boyishly proud in their battledress – banners, overshirts and caparisons a blaze of colour.

'Then, on the horizon, more magnificent still, we saw silhouettes of horsemen and footsoldiers, their arms glinting against the sun. Word soon got round that these were the hosts of the armies of the Count of Foix which had assembled by night in order to take us by surprise. Terror swept through our camp like a cold wind. Our leaders shouted themselves hoarse as battle lines were drawn. None of this was enough to help poor Martin and David, whose small contingent was forgotten in the rush. No one rode after them; perhaps no one dared. Only I, and a few others, looked on as they galloped down into the valley, oblivious of what lay before them.

'They did not see the opposing army until they had almost reached the top of the hill, at which point they must have been dazzled by the light reflecting from so many swords and harnesses. Shouts rang out across the valley rich with poppies and rosemary as the Count's men prepared for battle, mistaking Martin's contingent for the van of an attack. Martin and his men stopped suddenly dead in their tracks, their horses rearing and neighing.

'There was a moment's hesitation. If Martin had given the order to retreat immediately, they might have succeeded in reaching our camp. But no, they chose a vain display of valour, and rode at the opposing armies, brandishing their swords with suicidal gestures of defiance.

'Only too late did they comprehend the hopeless scale of what lay ahead as countless horsemen charged like swarming locusts over the ridge and down the valley. At the last minute, courage deserted Martin, David and their men. First one, then another, turned tail and tried to ride back, but by then their horses were too exhausted to save them.

'There was nothing noble about what followed. It was

243

slaughter. One or two of our men, I could not see who they were, turned to fight or to plead for their lives, but after a brief clash of steel and the neighing of horses they were slashed with swords or run through with lances. The rest, including Martin and David, were easily cut down from behind. How horribly the wounded screamed.

'Forgetting myself, I ran out of the camp to where my husband and my son lay. Because of the panic amongst our people no one thought to hold me back. There were lovely flowers in the grass, and a lark sang high above us, ironically oblivious of the killings. I heard men shouting from behind our lines that I should return, that it was not safe to go there. But what did I care, since I sensed already that I had lost everything? In any case, the Count of Foix's men were already returning to their lines.

'I found my son, lying on his back, a massive gash across the right side of his neck. His eyes were still open, but they had turned a ghastly red. When I closed them I saw his lips tremble, as if he wished to whisper some parting words, but there was no breath left in him, and just for a moment, before I left him for ever, he looked, despite the beginnings of beard growth, like the sleeping child I had so often held in my arms. I should like to tell you, Thomas, about my poor son, how kind he was as a boy, how shy, how full of love, the little games he would play. But to do so would pain me too much.

'Martin was still breathing. At first I thought he might not be hurt, but as I tried to take off his hauberk so that he would be more comfortable, blood drenched my hands and I saw that his stomach had been run right through. His breathing soon grew fast and uneven. I bent over him, tried to comfort him. He looked up at me, and attempted to smile. I supported his head to help him catch his breath as he gasped ever more desperately for air. At the very last, just before his mouth filled with blood, and his head sank back, he uttered the most pitiful words I ever heard from him. "I'm sorry," he whispered, "I have been a fool."

'I returned to the camp. Many tried to console me, or to offer me their protection. But the horror of what I had seen made the presence of others unbearable. I responded with a haughty silence to the kind words of those who never tired of assuring me that my husband and my son had died for a noble cause and that, surely, all their sins were forgiven.

'Meanwhile messengers rushed to and fro between the armies. Neither was really ready, or willing, to fight. The Count of Foix asked for certain concessions, and received them. A truce was agreed. The Count withdrew to the area round his castle, and our men were granted a day to return to the main body of the army in the north. The skirmish in which Martin and David had died was a chance event which had accomplished nothing.

'I remained calm. Horribly calm. That very morning, as my husband's people hurriedly struck camp, I wrote instructions for the portable possessions of my husband and son to be returned to our home, and given into the hands of my brother-in-law, Andreas, who would continue to run the estates until my return, or inherit them should I die. We headed north, stopping at the Monastery of Saint Lizier, where a solemn Mass was celebrated. Rumours were already rife about the death of King Louis on his return to Paris, and about a plague to which many in our armies were beginning to succumb. I looked at the fresco of *Christ at the Last Judgment* on the apse above the main altar; in those eyes I saw only terror and disdain, and in the carved capitals of the cloisters, where weird monsters peep from twisted acanthus and Saints suffer appalling agonies, I glimpsed a sign of the evil of creation.

'When we arrived at Pamiers, I told the army's leaders that

I needed to do penance, that I would continue on my own pilgrimage to Santiago, and thence to Jerusalem, before returning to Germany, where I would live out a life of charity, as a widow. My words filled those who heard them with awe as I had intended.

'The people of this age, as you know only too well, Brother Thomas, are either cruel, blind idealists, or else they are impenetrably cynical. There is nothing in between. Our section of the army, which was new to those lands, and new to war, was blighted with idealism, which I sometimes think of as even more dangerous than cynicism such as yours. Within a short while, news of my son's and husband's deaths and the sanctity of my intentions were to become a legend and I its heroine. Everyone, priest and lay, noble and peasant, would soon forget the reality of my past and my present. In its place they set up a graven image of everything noble, courtly and saintly. Perhaps you will do the same.

'You have done well, Brother Thomas, not to question me as to my motives. You have allowed me to speak freely, without asking me to justify myself, and I thank you for that; I thank you that you are my listener. However, if you were to ask me why I set off on my own then, why I did not return with my own people, why I have still not returned to them, I would not be able to give you a clear answer. I find it hard to explain these actions, even to myself.

'Perhaps you know the void, Brother Thomas. Sometimes you have the look of one who does. Then, I experienced it, truly, for the first time. The awareness of nothingness began to permeate my every thought, and every fibre of my body. My monastic education, my life at court, even the degradation I had experienced at the hands of the Graf of Leuchtenfels, had left me unprepared for this understanding, that all life and creation were empty, and that I was an emptiness within the emptiness.'

246

* * *

I remember that it was beginning to grow dark outside and Alazaïs was lighting the tallow lamps. Just for a moment, the deep blue light in the room pulsed with the textures of the scenes Cecilia had described. Her cat jumped up and settled in her lap. After a lengthy silence, Thomas and I took our leave and returned to the Priory. As we walked, I thought of Myrrah, and wondered if, as Domna Cecilia appeared to imply, the very essence of love in this world is that it is destined to be unfulfilled.

Chapter Seventeen

THE FIRST PERSON we saw, as we entered the Precincts by the dusky Almonry Gate, was Lord Rufus. He cut a fine figure, as he strode across the Green Court in the direction of the Palace, with his pointed shoes, and the great cloak he wore against the cold.

The moment he saw Brother Thomas he waved and walked towards us, clearly agitated. 'I am just on my way to see the Prior. Perhaps you should come with me. I need to sort out this business of the arrest of Isaac the Jew and Michael, his son.'

'Very well,' said Brother Thomas, though his reluctance was evident.

'What do you think the pretext for their detention might have been?'

'A chalice was stolen from the Cathedral,' said Brother Thomas, as the Palace loomed before us. 'They are using Michael as a scapegoat.' I tried to catch Brother Thomas's eye, wondering why he was suddenly so intent on defending Michael. But he ignored me, as he scrutinised Lord Rufus's reactions.

'How are they treating Michael?' Sir Rufus asked.

'Not well. You know Sir Osbert, the Keeper?'

Lord Rufus nodded. The Palace, as we entered, was as splendid as ever, radiant with colour and opulent shapes, but its atmosphere, in the torchlight, was chilling. The bells of the Cathedral chimed the curfew as Lord Rufus asked, 'How much do you know about this chalice?'

'We are still investigating,' said Brother Thomas.

Disregarding protests from the monks engaged in administrative work in the ante-chambers, Lord Rufus pushed his way through to the Prior's office.

John of Sittingbourne was seated behind his desk. He wore ostentatious ecclesiastical robes of red, green, white and gold; his attention was divided between a book of charts, a decanter of wine, and a large plan of the Cathedral. Next to him sat Brother Andrew, with his long eyelashes and curiously wounded expression.

The Prior's podgy face quivered with rage at the sight of us. 'What is the meaning of this?' he exclaimed. 'How dare you enter here unannounced!'

'I come from the King,' said Rufus sternly.

The Prior spluttered with fury, but contained himself at the mention of royal authority. 'Very well,' he said. 'What can I do for His Majesty?'

'The Jew called Michael you had arrested,' Rufus said, speaking in a threatening monotone. 'On whose authority did you act?'

'The man is a thief,' blurted the Prior. 'He deserves everything he has coming to him.'

'That is as may be,' said Lord Rufus through clenched teeth, 'but I am to tell you that from now on he will be questioned by Brother Thomas, to whom the King has given authority.'

I started at this as much as the Prior. 'But that is preposterous,' the Prior retorted. 'He is a criminal of the lowest sort – a traitor to the King most likely, as well as a thief. Besides, you will probably find that he has told us what we need to know already. Sir Osbert's men are nothing if not resourceful. We'll soon see.'

'This is a secular matter and it will be Brother Thomas's

job to decide. I have the order in writing and it bears the royal seal.' He took the document from within his cloak and thrust it under the Prior's nose. 'It says,' he added, 'that you and your men are to play no further part in the investigations, though you may of course be called as witnesses. Even you must agree that Thomas is more likely to be successful in discovering the truth than Osbert's butchers.'

'Very well,' said the Prior, looking up at Rufus, his piggy little eyes twinkling with anger. My impression from this was that some breach between the Prior and the King had become apparent, but the Prior would not take defeat lightly. Suddenly, he turned to Brother Thomas and rounded on him. 'Is nowhere safe from your prying? You spare neither Christian, nor Jew, nor heretic, nor do your criminal acquaintances spare the Cathedral by night. You will pay for this.' I shuddered at the cold hatred in the Prior's voice, for those last words sounded less like a threat than a resolve. His rage subsided as he said, now with sarcasm in his voice, 'You know that Michael is the principal suspect regarding the Templar murder? I thought I made that clear. You know all about his fortune-telling. You should have him burnt!'

'The chalice,' Lord Rufus interrupted. 'The King would like to know what you find so interesting about it.'

The Prior sneered. 'That,' he said, 'is a question for your Brother Thomas.'

'Indeed,' said Lord Rufus. 'In the meantime, I have an important visit to prepare for. His Highness will be staying at Saint Augustine's.'

Saint Augustine's is the name of the rival Benedictine monastery to the Cathedral Priory. The fact that the King was staying there rather than at Christ Church would be a further blow to the Prior, and Lord Rufus knew it. I remember catching Brother Andrew's eye just before we left. I had never taken to him. Nonetheless, I recognised that there was a certain sympathy between us, since we were both powerless observers of the intrigues of our superiors, of forces far beyond our control.

I followed Lord Rufus and Brother Thomas down the stairs out of the Palace and into the gloomy courtyard. 'That Prior is a pompous ass,' said Lord Rufus to Brother Thomas. 'To think that he sees himself as Archbishop. Heaven help us if he were! At least the Pope gets some things right!'

I could tell from the look on Brother Thomas's face that he had not suspected Lord Rufus and the Prior were at such loggerheads. But he did not pursue the matter further. Instead he changed the subject, asking, 'Have you heard anything about Alyssa and my children?'

'Nothing,' said Lord Rufus. 'No orders were given for her arrest. I have checked.'

'Thank you,' said Brother Thomas. Wisely, I suppose, he made no mention of Michael's house at Petcotte. He did, however, explain briefly about the cellar in Isaac's house, and asked for Lord Rufus's authority to investigate it.

Lord Rufus looked at us both askance. Then he said, without giving anything away, 'Yes, of course you have my authority. Now, if you will excuse me, I really do have to go to Saint Augustine's now. The King will be here tomorrow. He will wish to meet the two of you, by the way. I recommend strongly that by then you find grounds to condemn Domna Cecilia.'

'I have enough material,' said Brother Thomas, 'to condemn her a thousand times over.'

I was surprised at the sinister tone in Brother Thomas's voice as he said this. 'I didn't realise,' said Lord Rufus, himself taken aback.

'People never do,' said Brother Thomas, regretfully now. 'Of course, whether or not it is just to condemn her is another matter.'

'Justice and expediency,' mused Lord Rufus. 'How easy it is for those who have no power to judge those who have. My lodgings are in the stone house in the Burgate. Be there just after Angelus tomorrow and I shall present you both to the King. I shall look forward to seeing you.'

As soon as Lord Rufus had gone, Brother Thomas turned to me. There was despair in his eyes. 'Did you notice,' he said, 'the book and the chart of genealogies on the Prior's desk? They were almost certainly from the *Hermesis*.'

We walked back to our lodgings beneath a moon that had risen higher still, its brownish tinge oppressive in a night sky which weighed low and heavy. 'Are we going to stand by and see Domna Cecilia condemned?' I asked.

'There are still connections we do not understand,' said Brother Thomas. 'For example, we do not know precisely what the Prior wants from Michael, nor do we know what the relationship is between Michael and Domna Cecilia.'

'Why not ask the Prior?' I suggested.

'The Prior is not to be trusted in anything, any more than you would trust a dog baying at the moon,' said Brother Thomas.

The next morning Thomas returned to Isaac's cellar whilst I was to continue copying up notes of the previous day's interview with Domna Cecilia and then go to the library, in order to check more references regarding Domna Cecilia's lineage.

On my way back from Mass, I was stopped by Brother Andrew, who told me that the Prior wished to see me. I was reluctant at first, but realised I had no choice. Brother Andrew appeared sympathetic towards me. As we approached the Palace, which shone a brilliant white in the midday winter sun, I said, 'Tell me, what is the Prior hoping to achieve?'

'He is doing no more than anyone else would in his position. He is furthering his cause by the means that present themselves. But perhaps you can tell me: is this Domna Cecilia guilty of heresy?'

'I should imagine so,' I said.

'And Brother Thomas, what does he think?'

'He is drawn to her. I can see why,' I said. 'I am sure he would rather avoid condemning her if possible.'

'I presume you have discovered Isaac's guilty little secret by now,' Brother Andrew said next.

'I don't know what you mean,' I lied.

'His cellar. The work he does down there. It would be a shame to lose it. But then, you understand such things.' I remained silent, but Brother Andrew would have had no difficulty reading the look on my face. By then we had reached the Palace, and I was led before the Prior, who was in far better humour that day. To my surprise, Brother Andrew left immediately.

'I am so pleased to see you,' said the Prior. 'Especially after that nonsense yesterday evening. Lord Rufus can be so aggressive, and there is no need for that. Anyhow, I have a proposition for you. I am concerned for Brother Thomas. You see, I have always liked him and I would love to help him, since he does find it so hard to help himself. I am not unacquainted with the work Isaac does in his cellar, to which you have access. I also suspect that you are aware of the situation regarding the chalice. And I know exactly,' he said, with the smile of someone playing the winning move in a game of chess, 'where Brother Thomas's woman and children are. Now, I can help him in this regard. I ask only that he should help *me* – to recover the chalice and to acquire and interpret the knowledge which relates to it. I can count on you, can't I, Brother Wilfridus? Michael is sure to confess to his part in the Templar murders sooner or later – and it would be such a shame if you and Thomas were implicated.'

Until he made this last threat, I might have conceded that cooperation with the Prior was the best plan, despite the hostility in his voice. Now, though, I was not so sure. 'I must talk to Brother Thomas,' I said.

At that point Brother Andrew returned, and the Prior suddenly seemed to lose interest in me. 'Of course you must talk to Brother Thomas,' he said. 'I know you will explain to him clearly what I just told you. Some people can be their own worst enemy. Still, I must detain you no further.'

Leaving him, I made my way first to the Cathedral library, then to the one at Saint Augustine's, where preparations were already being made for the royal visit that evening. My stomach knotted at the thought of meeting the King.

I returned to our lodgings just after Nones to continue copying up my notes on Domna Cecilia. To my surprise, Brother Thomas was already there when I arrived. 'Where have you been?' he asked. Something was clearly the matter. I explained to him briefly about my meeting with Brother Andrew, then the Prior, then my work in the libraries. He waited patiently for me to finish before saying, 'Someone has been here. Do you have the records of our interviews with Domna Cecilia with you?' I shook my head. Brother Thomas pointed to the chest where we kept our papers. The lid had been forced open. It was empty but for the wax tablets which I used for taking preliminary notes. 'Tell me again,' said Brother Thomas, 'exactly what you told Brother Andrew and the Prior.'

I repeated the conversations as well as I could remember them; I was suspicious that Brother Andrew himself might have overseen the robbery while I was away at Mass and then with the Prior. I felt sick at heart. Rather than showing anger towards me, Brother Thomas tried to console me, which made me feel worse, if anything. The rest of that afternoon, we did our best to reconstitute the notes that had been stolen, growing increasingly nervous at the prospect of meeting the King.

At the appointed time, we made our way to the stone house on the Burgate where Lord Rufus was staying. He greeted us as though we were old friends and welcomed us to his rooms on the first floor, which boasted luxurious tapestries, gold and silver vessels, and a magnificent table on which food and wine were laid out for the three of us. Rufus hugged Brother Thomas warmly, and I had ample reason to believe that his affection was genuine. There was something boyish in his enthusiasm about the audience with the King.

'His Majesty,' he said, 'will be eating with a small company in the Abbey's great hall, so that he can be briefed about the matters to be brought to him the following morning. It is then, after the banquet, that we shall be presented to him. I scarcely need stress,' he went on, 'the danger of mentioning the King's presence in Canterbury to anyone, since officially he is still residing at Windsor and has travelled incognito. Can you imagine how the King must feel?' I recall Lord Rufus saying. 'Wherever he goes, grievances come before him which only he can settle.' At that stage, of course, I did not even begin to guess the true reason for the King's presence in Canterbury.

'Who else will be there?' Brother Thomas asked.

'A good question,' said Lord Rufus. 'Des Roches and his nephew are the ones to look out for. They are still close to the King in private, whatever appearances are kept up in public. Des Roches is a past master at gaining confidences, then using them against his victims. Still, you should be all right. The King likes Dominicans. You recollect the five hundred pounds per year your people wheedled out of him when they first arrived, not to mention free access to the royal forests, so they could set up a house in Canterbury.'

As Lord Rufus spoke I recalled the Dominicans amongst whom Brother Thomas once spent so much time: Gervaise with his pure eyes and ready smile, Geoffrey with his dark, curly hair and nervous laugh, and Aelryd, with his blond hair and pure skin. When we lived at Saint Albans we would spend hours debating together. Ironically, by the time I had decided to leave the Benedictines in order to join them in the Dominican house in London, Brother Thomas was already accusing them of being possessed of a subtle arrogance, and he left them for Alyssa who, he maintained, was truer, freer and lovelier than the Dominicans could ever dream of being.

When the time came for us to set off into the moonlit night to see the King, the sky was a deep translucent blue, and all the stars were out; Venus had not quite set and there was an unseasonal, muggy warmth in the air. None of us spoke. I presumed that I was not alone in feeling ill at ease. Leaving the Precincts and crossing the Burgate, it soon became clear that things were not as normal, for torches burnt on either side of the Monastery gate, which was guarded by twenty or so soldiers gathered round an open fire. Some bore pikes and others bore swords. They looked up towards us as we approached, more than ready to run us through if need be.

Their presence spurred Rufus on; his hunched demeanour gave way to the usual swagger of self-confidence. 'John, it's you, isn't it?' he called out into the cold night air, as if to an old friend.

One of the men jumped to his feet. In the toothy grin which distorted the cruel mouth from which a number of teeth were missing, I saw that dog-like delight with which even the hardest men of war greet leaders whom they like and trust. 'Yes, Lord Rufus,' he said. 'What brings you here?'

'Royal business. I have an appointment with the King in person. How was Wales?'

'We showed them, didn't we, lads?' he said. The other men grunted uncertainly.

'Back home for a while now?' While Rufus spoke, the soldier called John muttered something to one of the others, who darted inside the gatehouse building.

'Home is where there is service for His Majesty,' said the soldier, with apparent sincerity.

'That is the spirit!' said Rufus. There was a moment of unease before the younger soldier returned from within. He whispered something to the older man.

'Very well,' said the latter. 'In you go, Lord Rufus. Good luck with your business, and the same to your friend.'

We walked through the gate and into the cloisters. From inside the great hall came the sound of music and women laughing; it was unnerving to hear female voices in this place. The windows were ablaze with light. As we proceeded through cloister and corridor, groups of monks and soldiers eyed us.

We started up the staircase leading to the great hall but were stopped outside by a courtier. No one was to enter until the music was over. 'A mere singer!' tutted Rufus, annoyed. From within came a haunting melody, beautifully sung: the slow, plaintive song of a young woman who has just given herself for the first time. It was a song Cecilia had sung, and the language was the German spoken in the Frankish part of the Holy Roman Empire, different from the Saxon we are used to in England. The music finished and there was a moment's hush before applause and chatting.

We were shown in. The singer, a young blonde woman who looked just as I imagined Cecilia would have done in her youth, was leaving by the door at the far end. The resemblance was so striking that I almost ran after her.

Surely, I convinced myself, it was a trick of the light, or of my obsessive mind. I tried to whisper to Brother Thomas, but he shushed me and pointed to the interior of the hall.

The lavish fire roaring in the hearth cast strange shadows, and the torches and candles which lit the long trestle tables rendered the scene insubstantial, ghostly. I gazed in awe at the crowd of finely dressed men and ladies, as they laughed, ate and drank together.

At the far end of the hall, lounging languidly on an ornate folding stool set on a raised podium, attended by half a dozen courtiers and servants, was the King. He was tall, broad of shoulder, his skin a surprisingly pale, almost transparent hue, his features drawn. His left eye drooped slightly. Notwithstanding the warmth of the fire, his presence cast a chill as he talked to the man holding a fiddle, who had just been accompanying the singer. The King dismissed him, giving him a small bag of money; the musician smiled broadly as he left the hall. How wonderful, I thought, to have the power to bring such joy to others, but of course this power does not come without its contrary.

Another man was approaching the King. I recognised him from Dover, and of course from the Cathedral Crypt that night the chalice was removed from the tomb. He was elderly, on the plump side, but powerful in his build, even more so in his movements. Everything about him radiated distinction: pure white hair, magnificent clothes, jewelled rings on the fingers of each hand and the gold pendant round his neck, more splendid than anything worn by the King, who was dressed with relative modesty in fine dark clothes, the only jewellery he wore being a ring with a stone of black diamond. The man spoke briefly to King Henry, gestured to Rufus and then strode towards us. Many glanced in our direction. Rufus leant towards Brother Thomas and I heard him whisper, 'That is Peter des Roches, who until recently was the justiciar. Remember, be careful what you say.'

'Good evening, Rufus!' exclaimed des Roches, as he approached us. About him, despite his considerable age, was a vibrancy, an energy and a warmth which also contrasted with the coldness of the King, whose drawn features and cold eyes might well have been the mark and outward sign of the cruelty done in his name. 'Well,' he said, 'now you and your friends are here, I suppose we must conclude that the time for feasting and for joy is over, and that we must get down to business again.' But the King had noticed us already. He raised an eyebrow, catching des Roches's and Rufus's attention. To Brother Thomas and myself, the King made an ingratiating, almost effeminate gesture, tilting his head and smiling, as if we were old friends who shared some conspiracy. I am not sure whether this unnerved me or my companions more, but it was certainly effective in demonstrating that his attention was ours. We walked over and climbed the steps to the podium on which he sat.

After the appropriate formalities of greeting, which the King endured with a look of condescending languor, but never a hint that they might be dispensed with, he addressed Brother Thomas directly and said, 'So, you know a thing or two about alchemy and heresy, do you?'

'A little, Sire,' said Brother Thomas. He appeared relaxed, though I felt myself shaking with nerves. With those two words the King had shown his grasp of the two issues which occupied us, and in my view, this did not bode well. I would rather have been anywhere else. But I remained in control.

'And do you think the two are connected?'

'Not necessarily,' Brother Thomas replied, 'though in certain cases . . .'

'You know what someone told me about the Cathar

259

heresy?' the King interrupted, grinning ironically. 'That it started with some peasant from Champagne – an ignorant and vulgar fellow, by all accounts. A spell was cast on him, as a result of which a swarm of bees flew up his arse. After that, he chased his wife away, smashed up the crosses in his local church, and refused to pay his tithes.'

'It is extraordinary,' Brother Thomas said, 'what people will believe.'

'Isn't it just,' he nodded. 'One would not mind too much, but these heretics refuse to make or honour vows. How can anyone run a kingdom without vows? No one would know who owed allegiance to whom. What would monarchs do if no one swore allegiance to them? Terrible, don't you agree?'

Realising this was intended to test our reactions I forced a smile to show my appreciation of his words, and his irony. 'It would be unthinkable, Sire,' said Brother Thomas, likewise smiling carefully.

'Quite,' the King went on. 'Now, tell me honestly, do you hold out any hope that lead can be turned into gold? John of Sittingbourne does, you know.'

'It might be possible,' said Brother Thomas, 'but it is written that many long years of study are required, and afterwards one's spiritual enlightenment is such that one no longer desires material gold.'

'By God's Feet,' the King said, laughing with surprising abandon, 'whoever wrote that was certainly a wise man. But he was not a king. We kings can't do without gold. We devour the stuff. Can't get enough of it. Am I not right?' He looked round to the other two for approval, which of course they did not hesitate to bestow. 'And what do you think we should do with heretics, like that Cecilia I hear so much of?'

'That would be for yourself to decide, Sire, or a court of law, as appropriate,' said Brother Thomas. I admired him for these ambiguous answers, for it was by means of them that he drew information from others. I sensed, however, that the King had no trouble in seeing through Brother Thomas. Suddenly, he smiled broadly at us. He turned abruptly on Rufus and des Roches and said, with a harshness that sent a jolt right through me, 'Go now. Leave us alone.'

Des Roches looked for a moment as though he might object, but thought better of it and led away Rufus who was smiling nervously, clearly bewildered by the King's unexpected behaviour.

'Come with me,' the King said to Brother Thomas. I was about to bow and leave with Lord Rufus when the King turned towards me and said, 'No, you must come too. Your name is Wilfridus, so I understand. People speak highly of you. It seems you understand power well for someone so young and handsome.' I remember the tingling feeling of excitement at being singled out like this by the King, a feeling I was to experience again on future occasions, and which convinced me that monarchs are imbued with a special chemical energy. Others looked on as he stood and led us to the rear of the hall into a private chamber. A soldier stood guard outside. Within, two dogs stretched on an opulent carpet which I presumed the monks had laid specially for the King. 'My favourites,' he said. 'Don't worry, they won't hurt you.'

The dogs snarled but they were too old and tired to deal with us as they would have done in their prime. On the table, over which was thrown a delicate tapestry woven with complex Oriental motifs, stood a silver pitcher, and two goblets. In the room was a faint musky smell. The King served us personally. I had never drunk wine quite so radiant with flavour. 'By God's Feet,' said the King, 'they were very evasive answers you gave me just then. I can't say I blame you. A lot of people do the same. Sometimes I even talk like that to myself. Can you imagine? However, now, I only want your opinion, and I promise I won't hold it against you. This business of turning lead into gold. Tell me truly this time: do you think there is anything to it?'

'To be honest, Sire, I doubt it,' said Brother Thomas. 'I have always understood it as a metaphor for something else. This, moreover, is the opinion of Avicenna.' It was impressive of Thomas, I thought, to quote a famous authority of whom the King would have heard.

'You are a sceptic then?' said the King. 'Good. What about heretics? Take that Domna Cecilia for example. Do you think she is one?'

'Show me someone who isn't!' Thomas said, raising an eyebrow, but maintaining a stern face.

For a terrible moment, I thought Brother Thomas had gone too far. But the King thought this was hilarious. 'Now, now,' he guffawed. 'Don't give away the secrets of your trade. But do tell me, should heretics be burnt or not? It was not the custom in the old days, for example at the time of the pious King Edward. But now papal legates talk of nothing else. People are very keen on it. Hanging no longer seems enough.'

'I am a theologian first, Sire' Brother Thomas replied, 'and a lawyer second. I understand Church doctrine. I can tell those whose beliefs are at odds with it.'

'My word!' interrupted the King, raising his hands in mock fear. 'You are a dangerous man. You would have us all damned, me included.'

'I hardly think so, Sire. Not unless I damned myself first,' said Brother Thomas. 'And the Church's first duty is to preach forgiveness.'

'So you don't go along with burning then?'

'I do not believe,' said Brother Thomas, rehearsing an argument with which, as a Dominican, I was of course familiar, 'that it should be the Church's role to determine the punishment, only the doctrine.'

'You are a curious fellow,' commented the King. 'Tell me, what *do* you believe? Now, be honest.'

I imagined Brother Thomas had been doing rather well until then, but this question clearly shook him. There was no way out. I wondered how my master would reply. It was as if the King had sensed Brother Thomas's self-doubt and was playing on it. What was he supposed to do, recite the Creed, say sycophantically that he believed in the King of England? Perhaps the look of defeat on Brother Thomas's face was answer enough.

'Wonderful,' the King laughed again. 'You are not even sure whether you believe anything or not! You know,' he said, turning to me, 'your master is a fine fellow. I am surrounded by people who know everything: who is a heretic, who is saved, who is loyal to whom, who should be our allies, who our enemies. A king could die of a surfeit of certainty. And then they bring me the likes of Brother Thomas, corrupt, in his quiet way, but uncertain, honest. You know there are some who say that there is no Satan, only Lucifer, and that he is not the antithesis of divine light, merely its bearer and ultimate distorter. But you are learned, so you would understand that. It is true, you *are* learned, aren't you?' he said, turning again to Brother Thomas.

'I have done my fair share of study,' he said.

'And you are conversant with the philosophy of the heretics, the Jews, the alchemists, yet you don't believe any of them?'

'Not necessarily,' he began.

'There you go again,' said the King. 'You really are price-less. Of course, I admire, and sometimes envy, those who have the time and inclination to study. Take King Louis of France. Apparently he reads devotional books every day. A total bore. They'll make a Saint of him if he is not careful. As for me, I rely on others to tell me what is in books. Those who explain books to me reveal so much about themselves as they do so. Much more important. Which reminds me – those murders at Swiffeld. Do you think they were perpetrated by the Templars themselves or this Michael fellow I keep hearing about?'

'Neither,' said Brother Thomas.

'Then who?' The King's brow knotted.

'I think I know,' said Brother Thomas, 'but I might yet be wrong. I shall bring word to you as soon as I am absolutely certain. Until then, it would not be fair to name the parties I suspect.'

'Very well,' said the King. 'I appreciate your scruples – which brings me to the real reason I called you both here. Since we share many concerns, I believe the two of us should work together, Brother Thomas. I am, I confess, particularly interested in the work Isaac the Jew was carrying out in his cellar. I am not desperate to turn lead into gold myself, you understand, but I am concerned that no one else should do so without my knowing about it. Your task would be to investigate the work of those who claim to be alchemists, and tell me who is a charlatan, and who might be on to something. Would you like that?'

'It would be a great honour, Sire,' Brother Thomas said, clearly surprised and perplexed.

'Someone will bring you a letter tomorrow or the next day, explaining your role in greater detail. You will receive a pension, enough to keep you moderately well, more than you get from Rufus anyhow, and to allow you to live quite independently from him. It will help you to regularise your conjugal situation, and it will be sufficient too for you to maintain our friend Wilfridus in your employ.' The King spoke rapidly, as if bored in advance by the words he had planned.

'But this is so unexpected. I cannot say how grateful I am,' Thomas began.

'Then don't,' smiled the King. 'Your gratitude has been noted,' he said, affecting pomposity. 'You will also act as a royal lawyer from time to time, and there will be cases in which you will follow strict, secret instructions from me, as in the case of Cecilia for example. You understand?'

Brother Thomas nodded, and for the first time I thought I glimpsed the meaning of betrayal, how it insinuates itself into our hearts, minds and souls. 'You want her to burn?' Brother Thomas asked.

'Oh, there is no doubt that she will burn,' said the King. 'If you don't manage it, others will. She won't be the first.' At that moment, the King glanced ominously towards me, and I experienced a feeling like icy fingers running up and down my spine. 'You know where she came from and why she is here?' the King asked.

'Not yet, Sire.'

'You will find out in due course. The real question is the trial. The condemnation must be public and unequivocal. Am I making myself clear? I have heard nothing but good of you, and I am sure we will be able to work closely together in the future. By the way, with regard to Lord Rufus – some advice. Don't trust him. And don't tell him of anything that has passed between us. If you do, it will get back to me, and I shall know that I cannot rely on you.'

There was something about the King's manner that did not ring true, yet it was almost as though he had intended this. Poor Brother Thomas was flattered but uncertain, caught between fear and hope of a better life.

'I shall do whatever is in my power,' he said.

Unfortunately, I was not alone in detecting the ambiguity of his words. The King chuckled. 'There you go again,' he

265

said and, turning to me, he added, 'You had better keep a careful eye on him. And now we must get back to the big wide world, or tongues will start to wag.'

With that, the King's face set in its former cold expression and we re-entered the main hall. On our return, I realised that I was smiling too broadly, for I was young enough to feel pride at individual royal attention. The King strode across to his chair, and another courtier approached him, with other business. All eyes, however, were turned in our direction, as if everyone present were trying to get a glimpse of what might have passed between ourselves and the King.

Peter des Roches and Rufus both came up to us, and led us to a side table, where they plied us with food, wine and pleasantries. To my surprise, they made no reference to the royal interview. Perhaps they already knew what had been said, or wanted us to think they knew. We were treated with more respect, and that pleased me well enough. Rufus stayed with me, but Peter des Roches scurried back and forth between Thomas, the King, and other groups which had formed here and there about the room.

It was fascinating, at this late hour, as the lamps and candles began to burn down, to overhear the discussion of affairs of state in preparation for the court which was to be held the following morning. I admired the King, that he could keep so many matters in mind at once, and I felt sympathy for him too, for he has enormous burdens laid upon him, from which he is never free.

At last the time came for the King to retire. Lord Rufus stayed but Brother Thomas and I returned through the moonlit streets. Mars shone bloody red in the sky. 'It should not be difficult to use the material we have to make a case against Domna Cecilia,' I said. 'Then, with the King's patronage, we will live better. You will get Alyssa back, and all will be well.'

'It is kind of you to show such concern,' said Brother Thomas. 'However, you know as well as I that we should not act against our conscience, particularly where a human life is concerned.'

'But, what you just said to the King . . .' I began.

'I had no choice,' Thomas interrupted. 'Besides, he is suspicious of me. Not without reason.'

'You mean you will not testify against her?'

Brother Thomas did not reply and we walked on in silence. I thought about Myrrah, how important she had become to me in so short a time, then I tried to imagine how much Brother Thomas must be suffering because of his separation from Alyssa and his children. I believed that he was prepared to condemn Domna Cecilia, but I knew too that, in a way I glimpsed at the time but had not fully fathomed or rationalised, he loved her.

That night, uncertainty about the whereabouts and fate of Alyssa and Myrrah, and fears for Isaac and Michael, were an unspoken pressure which filled the space around and between us. Whilst he drank, Brother Thomas explained to me in detail the correspondences he and Alyssa had worked out between herbs, plants, the numbers, planets and precious metals. They are as follows:

0		Chalcedony	Aspen, trees of autumnal equinox
1	Sun	Mercury, opal, agate	Vervain (winter sabat incense), herb mercury, marjolane, palm
2	Moon	Moonstone, pearl	Almond, mugwort, hazel, ranunculus (buttercup), moonwort
3	Venus	Emerald, turquoise	Pomegranate, sandalwood, myrtle, rose, clover
4	Jupiter	Ruby	Tiger lily, geranium
5	Mercury	Topaz	Mallow
6	Sagittarius	Alexandrite	Orchids, pears, ripe corn
7	Mars	Amber Kephra	Lotus, onycha, watercress
8		Cat's eye	Sunflower
9	Pisces	Pearl, peridot	Snowdrops

10	Capricorn	Amethyst, lapis lazuli	Rosetree, palm, hyssop, oak, poplar, fig, saffron
11	Leo	Emerald	Aloe
12	Aries	Beryl, aquamarine	Lotus, water plants, onyca, myrtle
13	Saturn	Snakestone	White rose, lily, cactus
14	Aquarius	VITRIOL	Rush
15	Dragon	Black diamond	Hemp, musk, civit, Orchis (drug)
16		Ruby	Absinth, rue
17	Taurus	Glass, crystal	Violet
18	Cancer	Pearl	Poppy, opium
19	Gemini	Chrysoleth	Sunflower, laurel, olibanum, cinnamon
20	Scorpio	Opal	Red poppy, hibiscus
21	Virgo	Onyx	Ash, cypress, hellebore, yew, nightshade

That night, his words resonated in my mind as, lying in bed, I relived the events of the last few days, and Mars traced its eerie course through the sky outside my window. It seemed an eternity before I fell asleep, and when I did, it was to dream repeatedly of the peculiar parchments Michael had shown me that first day I saw him, and the drawings which Brother Thomas had perfected and had me deliver to Lord Rufus. One image returned with particular vehemence: that of the devil-like creature holding men in chains.

Chapter Eighteen

WE WOKE NEXT morning to one of those distempered days, when the moon can still be seen in a misty sky for an hour or so after dawn. We rose early. Brother Thomas wanted to visit Michael and Isaac at the castle prison, and then go to Isaac's cellar, but he wanted to go alone. Then, he suggested, the two of us should call on Domna Cecilia. Meanwhile I could attend offices in the Cathedral as often as I wished, he said, but otherwise I should remain in our lodgings and finish rewriting my records of our interviews with Domna Cecilia.

It saddened me that Brother Thomas did not wish me to be with him that morning, not least because of my curiosity about what he might find in the cellar.

Shortly before Sext, Brother Thomas returned and we set off towards Domna Cecilia's house. The weather was uncannily mild. Here and there, round the city wall and in the church-yards, intemperate flowers were pushing their way out of the earth, heedless of the turmoil and of winter's threat of snows, whose white oblivion might engulf them any day.

As we walked, Brother Thomas, who seemed to be in relatively good spirits, told me about his morning. Michael and Isaac were being kept in better conditions, and Isaac had given him indications regarding the work in his cellar. 'Perhaps you would like to help me,' Brother Thomas said as we approached the West Gate. 'You would be well suited to it.

Tomorrow there will probably be time for me to show you. Isaac said that a transformation had been about to take place in the retort just before his arrest. He warned against continuing with it ourselves, but I see no reason why we should not try. Who knows, we might be the first to turn lead into gold. We could tell the King and become his favourites.' Poor Thomas, I wonder how much he foresaw.

At Domna Cecilia's house we took our positions in the upper room. There was the usual pitcher of wine for us, the bread, dried fruits and other delicacies Thomas and I so much enjoyed.

Alazaïs sat next to Domna Cecilia. Both were dressed entirely in black. They held distaffs in their hands. The message could not have been clearer: these were two heretics, openly inviting condemnation, or judgment.

Domna Cecilia welcomed us cheerfully. 'I am sure you will not mind if my companion joins us today,' she said, nodding towards Alazaïs. 'I sense that this will be our last meeting here.'

There followed a silence which was broken only when Brother Thomas said, 'You were going to tell of what happened after the death of your husband and son.'

'Very well,' she said. 'The day that they were buried, I left the armies amidst great approbation, weeping, singing and excited blessings. As I took the road south to the Pyrenees, many wanted to follow me to Santiago. I was forced to explain over and over that silence and solitude were essential to the penance I had undertaken. Only a determined refusal to speak rid me of the last hangers-on, and by then I had already re-entered the territory of the Count of Foix. I walked aimlessly through the dark solace of forest glades, up into the high woods where the paths were lined with springs, then over barren, rocky highlands where lonely, magnificent eagles hovered. I ate only fruit I found along the way and drank occasionally from streams, almost unaware of my surroundings as memories washed over me like the waters of the sea, crashing with the violence of breaking waves, setting eddies and vortices a-spin, then retreating to leave a seeth-ing, frothy confusion, a semblance of calm masking the commotion beneath the surface.

'Soon, I had no idea where I was, nor did I care. Early one evening, having come across no human habitation for days, I sat beneath the bough of an old tree, deep in a valley, and watched the sun set through the branches, as a bird of prey screeched and swooped low overhead. Suddenly, I was aware of cramps in my stomach; my vision swayed and my brow burnt with fever. I must have passed out then, for I remem-ber nothing more until it was quite dark.

'As I came to, I noticed first the insistent chirping of the cicadas, then a yellowish light swaying amidst the dark boughs of the trees. The pain had left my stomach, but I was too weak to move. Two lamps zig-zagged towards me, stop-ping only when they were close enough to dazzle. For a moment I saw in that light an appalling brilliance, a choking and a burning of human flesh, but beyond and through that, a stillness, a joy. This impression faded, and I found myself looking up into the faces of two kindly women. The elder was whispering to the younger in the lovely dialect of those regions. I took them to be mother and daughter. "Here is one who has suffered," I heard the elder woman say, stroking my cheek to comfort me, tall, dark trees arching round her in the night, like a supernatural cathedral. Behind the women, and beyond the trees, an imposing pearl-yellow moon hung in the night sky.

'The younger woman helped me to sit up. Only then did I realise that they were both dressed in black from head to toe. I thanked them, in their language. The younger woman whispered, "She does not know the greeting."

' "That is of no matter," said the elder woman. "She is exhausted, and starving. It is our duty to care for her."

'This, Brother Thomas, was the beginning of my life amongst the Good Christians. The younger woman went to the village to get help. The elder stayed by my side, and gave me water from her bottle, cutting fruit into small pieces for me to suck. I must have fallen unconscious again, for the next thing I recollect was a gentle rocking motion as I was carried through the forest on a stretcher early next morning, as the first light of the sun shone through the leafy tree-tops, stirred now and then by the flurry of a bird taking to the wing.

'They bore me to a village called Antrassac. It nestled on the north side of a valley in the Pyrenees on a steep hill above a small town called Santan. It was accessible only by two narrow paths. The good people there made it their business to nurse me back to health, treating me with infusions of poppies and hemp, scented like ambergris. If ever a woman wearing black was present, anyone entering the room would curtsy three times and say, "My lady, bless me, and pray to God for me, that He should cause me to be a Good Christian and that He should lead me to a Good End." Automatically, the reply came back, "We shall pray to God for you, that He should cause you to be a Good Christian and lead you to a Good End."

'These greetings, far from arousing my suspicion, reassured me that the people amongst whom I had fallen were just what they claimed to be, good Christians. Certainly, there was nothing sinister in their manner, and the way they nursed and fed me was exemplary of Christian conduct. The visits of those dressed in black brought me the sweetest pleasure; their energy and humour restored my will to live, since they reminded me of the friends of my youth.

'My most regular visitor was called Astorgue de Lamothe. It was to her that I confided my past, as I confide it to you now, though her aim, unlike yours, was to reconcile me to life. I never associated these people, so kind and peaceful in their ways, with the enemy who killed my husband and my son.

'When I was well enough to walk, I was led to the meeting place of the Good Christians, a large stone dwelling just outside the village on the slope of the mountain. Trees overhung the house, their branches lush with leaves and vibrant with birdsong. There I met the deacon of their church, Quilhem, who claimed to know much of my life, and to admire me. He said he was profoundly sorry that I had lost my husband and my son through an act of violence committed in the name of the people of the land: he could only disapprove of such a terrible deed. It was he who told me of the death of the King of France and the epidemic gripping the crusading army. Some took this as a sign that the persecutions might stop.

'More importantly, he said that, because of my many virtues, he wished me to attend a baptism at the house of the Good Christians, and that he would be prepared, eventually, to offer me the same true baptism which Jesus Christ had passed on through His apostles. I was surprised at this, since of course I was already baptised and confirmed. Yet his manner was so vulnerable and so gentle that I did not challenge his words. Moreover, round him there was that curious rosy and yellow light which stirred memories from my distant youth. He explained too something of the structure of his Church, that he was a deacon because he had been elected, as were holders of office in the Good Christian Church; authority was not imposed from above as was the practice in the Church of Rome. I noticed that the people there did not make the sign of the cross, and asked him why this might be. "Oh, but we do," he replied. "It is a most useful way to get rid of flies."

'Before I had a chance to ask him what he meant, the guests began to arrive. It was then that I witnessed the baptism, or rather Consolation, of the two young women, called Arnaude and Alazaïs. Arnaude was Domna Astorgue's daughter. They were both about eighteen years old then, pale and very thin, with large, pure eyes. There was no perception that they were unhappy; on the contrary, though quiet, they were alive with a nervous joy, much more so than many girls I have seen on their wedding day.

'It was Domna Astorgue who took Arnaude and Alazaïs by the hand and led them to kneel in front of the small table in the middle of the room which was covered with a white cloth, and on which there was only a Book of the Gospels, a loaf of bread and two candles.

'Quilhem, the deacon, took up position behind the table, alongside his younger cousin, Peire, who was his principal companion in those days. Taking the white cloth, Quilhem wrapped the bread in it, then placed one corner over his shoulder. He began the rite with the words of Saint John: "In the beginning was the Word . . ." then he read out the Ten Commandments, and other passages from the New Testament, before blessing the bread. Next, Quilhem questioned the two girls; Arnaude replied that she wished to give herself to God, and promised that she would no longer eat food of animal origin, neither meat, nor eggs, nor dairy produce; she vowed that she would always be chaste and truthful, that she would never swear by anything which is in Heaven or on Earth, and that she would never deny the Church of Good Christians, not for fear of water, nor fire, nor death in which ever form it might present itself. From then on, she promised, she would live in community with other Good Christians, reciting the prayers, and following the Rule. Alazaïs said nothing but showed her assent by nodding vigorously.

'When they had performed these vows, Quilhem touched both the girls' foreheads with the Gospel of Saint John, and then the other Good Men laid their hands on their heads. They recited the Lord's Prayer three times with the exception of Alazaïs who merely nodded. I noted they added the words: "For yours is the Kingdom, the power and the glory, for ever and ever . . ." to the normal prayer. Then Quilhem blessed the bread with the *Deo Gratias* and distributed it, explaining that this was not "daily bread" but "suprasubstantial bread", and that it had nothing to do with the body of Christ, for Christ was spirit, he said, not fat and flour. From then on, we were told, the two girls were to be seen as Good Christian Elders, Perfect Ones. Next, the deacon and his companion kissed the Book of the Gospels, which they passed to the girls to kiss in turn. Thus the ritual greeting is shared without fear of pollution by the flesh. As the kiss was given, I became aware of the humming of bees high in the rafters of the house, and a brightly coloured butterfly straying in from outside fluttered beneath the simple beams. I often wonder what has become of Arnaude since, if she has been burnt, if her tender young face is forgotten ashes now. As for Alazaïs, you know her, for she is my companion.

'Let me tell you her story. When she was a little girl she lived in Bram. Her parents were members of the local aristocracy though they were not wealthy. Her mother often welcomed Good Christians to her house. When the armies of Simon de Montfort took the town, she saw the Parisian soldiers, the infamous Ribauts, their leader, the so-called King of the Court of Miracles, borne on a throne carved an obscene shape; this man ordered that every knight who had fought against de Montfort should be hanged outside the castle with his throat cut. As for the ordinary menfolk, another fate awaited them.

'Alazaïs saw her father dragged out of hiding, and bound with the other men. She watched as de Montfort's soldiers, leisurely swigging wine and beer, laughing and cursing, moved from one prisoner to another, sat astride them, forced their heads back, or beat them round the face. As soon as they were too weak to offer resistance, the soldiers used sword tips, knives or whatever they could lay their hands on to slit open their victims' top lips, hack off their noses and put out their eyes.

'Alazaïs saw her own father as he screamed in terror, struggling to get free, pleading and shouting as one of the soldiers butchered his way towards him; then she saw the soldier mock her father, yanking at his hair and cutting at his eyes and face with his knife. She saw the blood stream from her father, his once familiar and comforting voice reduced to an inane gurgling of pain and horror.

'Only one man was spared. His lips and nose were cut, but just one of his eyes was put out. He was left the other so that he might lead the procession of poor, maimed and disfigured men, groaning and covered in blood, as they half walked and were half dragged the full length of the road to Cabaret. Simon de Montfort chose this fate for them, so that they might act as a warning. Alazaïs walked with her father, and tried to comfort him. But he could not see her, since he had no eyes, and he could not speak to her because his lips were split and pouring with blood. He bled to death before they reached Cabaret and his corpse had to be dragged by the others.

'Alazaïs has never spoken since.

'As I lived with the Good Christian women, I heard many such stories. They often spoke of Dominic Guzman, who founded your Order, Brother Thomas. The Good Christians actually thought Dominic was a holy man, because of his life of poverty and prayer. But they could not understand why he wanted to convert them. Before he came, Catholic and Cathar lived side by side, and most believed they were engaged in the same spiritual journey, only that they were on different, albeit parallel roads. Dominic's threats of force lost him the argument, since to the Good Christians, violence is unchristian.

'They talked of the order given by Améry, the Abbot of Citeaux at Béziers, when every man, woman and child was slaughtered in the Church of the Madeleine. They talked of Minerve, of Casseneuil, of Lavaur, where four hundred alleged heretics were burnt; from the early hours of the morning until Terce, men, women and children were bound and pushed into the flames, the living on top of the dying. Cries and groaning were still heard as the pyre began to burn down in the evening, as if the fires had insufficient power to consume so many people; the porcine smell of burnt human flesh hung over the land for days. Meanwhile the Goodlady Geralda, an Elder, was thrown down the well in her garden, and stoned to death for sport. It was hours before her cries ceased.

'In view of such terrible events, it is not difficult to understand the Good Christians' belief that there is no purpose to living in this world, other than to help release other souls from the cycles of its evil, that they might be purified and reconciled with the Good God, from whom they were separated at the time of the fall of the angels from Paradise. The killings and burnings of Good Christians were, they said, as inevitable as the Crucifixion of Christ, for mankind is not redeemed by Christ's suffering, but by the proclamation of the Gospel; such deaths are not willed by the Good Father, but they had occurred because the evil world of matter cannot tolerate the presence of perfected souls, like that of Christ which was uncontaminated by matter. Therefore those who had been burnt were to be admired, since their souls too were finally cleansed from contamination by the flesh.

'I learnt much of the Good Christians' life as I dwelt with them, how they were permanently in community with one another, never ceasing from spinning, sewing, weaving or studying, other than to say the prayers, perform good deeds, visit the sick and dying, or to give their blessing to those requesting it. They always ate according to the Rule, and never failed to bless their bread. Once a week, the people would gather for the *apparelhement*, which was like the Catholic Confession, except that it was performed in a group, rather than alone with a priest, and people would speak with brutal honesty of their failings, often weeping, and tearing at their hair.

'Their faith was so honest, Thomas, so simple, that I began to wonder if the religion we were taught, with its dressing up in rich apparel, the cult of dead bones, rituals and chanting, was not perhaps absurd, or worse. When I spoke to the Good Men, I even wondered if our adoration of the cross was foolish. If your father had died on the gallows, the Good Men would say, would you worship rope? And why believe that a Good God ruled this world? In a world ruled by a Good God, illness would not just be cured every now and then. There would be no illness. And how could a Good God wish to damn people for all eternity? Surely, damnation was just an invention of the worldly powers, to inspire fear, and to oppress the people, for our souls in matter are like the Children of Israel in the desert, exiled and constantly yearning for their true home, and this is torment enough.

'I worked with the Good Christians and ran errands for them. Travelling about the high, mountainous regions of the Pyrenees, I came to know the ways of those lands: the shepherds, goat herds and vintners, nobles, travellers and singers constantly winding their way along the roads between the tiny villages nestling against the mountainsides, and the misty, otherworldly lakes like the one at Bethmale. I came to know the remote forges where weapons and ploughshares are fashioned from the red rocks hacked from the hills and mountains which glow curiously pink, orange and silver in the evening light. From these people I learnt much of the art of the transformation of metals, which you seek. I saw mysterious churches built from stones carved with images of bizarre underworlds, and secret caves too, like the Lombrives with its maze of passageways, exits and entry points; the one at Bouan, with a castle built at its mouth in front of which great tournaments are held in the springtime, but behind which are endless labyrinths of dark tunnels, receding into networks of infinity. There are other caves too, where those with knowledge can lead you to ancient paintings of human hands and of animals, and places where Stygian underground rivers run, which some say lead down to the Underworld, or to Hell itself.

'One day we were asked to deliver a message at the hillfort of Montségur, in the very south and east of the lands of Foix. Having crossed the Devil's Bridge over the Ariège, so called because of the numerous times it has mysteriously been torn down, we followed the road to the castle of Roquefixade. It was twilight, and beacon messages were being sent. The fires above the dark forests against the green, purple and crimson of the sunset made me think I was glimpsing the light of the pure, the true realm.

'The next morning, walking from Roquefixade to Montségur, the beauty of the mountains took my breath away, for their slopes are vast but somehow human. Unlike the barren peaks and plateaux further to the east, such as one finds near the castles of Peyrepertuse and Quéribus, they are fertile and green with trees and vegetation, stately and mysterious against the blue of the sky on a sunny day, yet offering comfort and solace at night-time and during the frequent storms.

'However, there is another aspect to that landscape: I was to discover how the earth, the trees, the sky, the rocks, all created things, can melt away from sensible vision, revealing a focus of evil, a dark source of loss and terror. When we had delivered our message at Montségur, and were walking down the steep path out of the village, one of the storms blew up which are so common in that part of the world. Torrential rain drenched us, and the rivulets of water streaming over the muddy paths and tree roots made it difficult to walk without slipping. Undaunted, we reached the bottom of the path and took the road towards Foix. We had only walked a mile or so when we were set upon by robbers. There was nothing out of the ordinary about them; they were brutish and selfish, like thieves everywhere. They took everything we had. The three of us were beaten. Alazaïs was mocked because she could not speak, and they tore her clothes and humiliated her, threatening to rape her, as if she had not already suffered enough. Bruised, wretched and resource-less, we returned to Montségur.

'You might think it surprising that, after so much evil, it was that one chance event which finally wrought the change in me. However, it was then, as we walked back, that sky, trees, mountains, earth melted away, merging, formless, into an all-pervading grey. So many other darknesses returned to engulf me: my loss of Walter von der Ouwe, the violence done to me by the Graf of Leuchtenfels, and the deaths of my Martin, David and Kirsta. I sensed the truth of the words of the Good Christians, that the world of matter is ruled by the evil god and that there is no hope here. I glimpsed the appalling, black heart of the void. When I returned to

Montségur I decided to fast and study in order to become a Good Christian elder alongside Alazaïs, Arnaude and my other companions.

'Montségur is a busy town perched on top of a steep hill, superficially teeming with life, yet the secret I just mentioned is always present. Its site is important militarily since it controls access to most roads thereabouts. The Count of Foix allowed Good Christians to gather at Montségur for their protection. There is a Catholic chapel, and a small garrison of the Count's soldiers, of whom most are Catholic. The Good Christians live simply alongside them, earning their keep from handiwork, sewing, weaving, making clothes, ironmongery and other such trades. Their houses are built on the steep north side; threading one's way between them along the precarious paths is not easy. The precipitous rock face forms one wall of each house, the roof jutting from it. Since there is no spring at Montségur, many of the houses are built with roofs sloping inward so that rainwater can be collected. The other walls are wooden and their shape is determined by the position of the house on the hill. Within each house are two or three flat areas, with floors either of wood or of bare stone. These are used for work, or sleeping, or preparing food and eating. Despite their simplicity, these houses can be homely, particularly at night when the day's work is done, prayers are said, the lamps are lit and the stars burn brilliantly outside. At least, life there facilitates reflection on our true home.

'A dream came repeatedly to me in those days. I would see the bodiless head of a woman, bleeding at the neck and with snakes instead of hair, cast into a massive fire as a terrible darkness fell over the land. The vision would fill me with immense sadness, for the woman's face was beautiful, despite the serpents, and the lips and eyes still smiled as they burned. I knew that something immeasurably precious was being lost, but I was not sure what this might be.

'With Arnaude and Alazaïs at my side, I spent much time in discussion with the Elders. In due course, I attended a ritual identical to the one at Antrassac, only now I was its focus. I shall not reveal the names of those who consoled me, for the majority of those Good Men are still alive, as far as I know. Having made my confession, and followed the prescribed order of the rite, I knelt for the Consolation, just as I had seen Arnaude and Alazaïs kneel some months before.

'What I experienced then was unexpected, sublime, truly consoling. I had thought that the laying on of the Elders' hands would be purely symbolic. Yet as they touched me, something fluid, a deep sensation of peace such as I had experienced in my youth, poured through me, only with such power that I heard music, Brother Thomas, a sound like a thousand choirs singing with one voice. And I saw such light; in it was the essence of my loves, of beauty and of the true music. I glimpsed their source in the Seven Heavens of God the Father, through which praises rise, which can be both seen and heard; it was as though I had borne witness to the things revealed in the book of the Vision of Isaiah, only in the timeless twinkling of an eye.

'From then, Brother Thomas, I have lived as a Good Christian, amongst the poor of Christ, fleeing from city to city, a lamb amongst wolves, blessing the bread, and keeping to the daily round of prayers, refusing any food which is the product of coitus.

'I learnt many secrets of the land, the stories of the old days when there was a Jewish Kingdom in that place, with a King of direct descent from the House of David. I learnt of the rumours of treasure beneath the ground, which had once belonged to that kingdom, like the chalice you have seen in my house. And I learnt something about myself, Brother Thomas, something that you might find surprising.

Many think I am an Empress. Not of another world, but of this. Even my father used to tell me stories of the old kings, from David to Dagobert, and of the old heroes, like Eric and Parsifal, and I am sure he believed something of the rumours. Guilhabert de Castres and Théodore de Blanchefort, who were versed in such matters, both helped me to understand that this was the explanation for the way the old priest fell at my knees when I was a young girl in Regensburg. It also explained the singular old man who, years later, gave me the insignia I showed you.

'Yet, compared with the baptism I had received, I counted this as folly. Nothing on earth, neither fire, nor water, nor glory, nor worldly power, nor any kind of death, can take away from me the peace I experienced. I understood then, as I understand now, how it is that the Good Christians have the power to accept burning with equanimity, joy even.'

At that point Domna Cecilia fell silent. Alazaïs sat, dignified, eyes wide and staring. I looked at the two women. How could despair engender such beauty? At last, Brother Thomas broke the spell of the silence by asking, 'Perhaps you could explain why you came to England. You talk of the void, Domna Cecilia, of the inherent evil of the created world, yet your journey here must have had a purpose.'

'Certainly,' said Domna Cecilia, 'an outer purpose, which I shall explain, and an inner purpose, something of a wager, which you will fulfil, with the help of your successor, for as I have said before, you are my listener.

'You know that Count Raimon defeated the French at Castelsarrasin. Yet the destruction wrought by the Crusaders as they retreated was too great for the land to bear. That is why the Count conceded to sign the Treaty of Meaux, allowing himself to be scourged in public for penance, then to be imprisoned, and then to sanction the dismantling of the defences of Toulouse, his own city, though it had never been defeated. Some say that he really had taken sides with the Catholics. Others that he was playing a waiting game. I know that, clandestinely, he had other plans, for I was part of them. This is how I came to be summoned to Toulouse.

'As a Dominican you will have heard of Guilhabert de Castres. He is still the head of the Good Christian Church. Two years ago, in the winter of the year 1233, he arrived at Montségur to take up residence there, for nowhere else was safe for him. The Counts of Foix and Toulouse themselves had placed the hill city at his disposal. He came bearing a message from the Count of Toulouse. He wanted to see me, on account of stories about my lineage, and of my allegiance to the Good Christian Church. He had, said Guilhabert, a special mission for me.

'On my way to Toulouse, I wore black, a Good Christian Elder as you see me now. Alazaïs was my companion and she has remained so to this day. Toulouse had become a dangerous place by then. The Dominicans had returned in force, and were busy setting up the so-called university, where they sharpen the logic which kills both soul and body. The first thing the Count's men told me to do, when I arrived, was to remove my black clothes and dress normally. New laws meant anyone who denounced a heretic would be given two silver marks for two years and an annual pension of one mark per year for life. In that atmosphere of terror, people felt they might be sold by their neighbour at any moment. I heard of a woman, for example, who was tried for calling on the help of the Holy Spirit rather than the Virgin when she was in labour. Even reluctance to kill a cockerel was enough to attract the attention of the Church authorities.

'Perhaps you know the new Bishop of Toulouse, Raimon de Fauga. He is typical of the new breed of religious men who organised the persecution of the Good Christians, imprisoning those who abandoned the truth in cells where they can scarcely move, and even forbidding the ordinary people from owning copies of the New Testament. Two years ago, in August, he heard about an old woman of Toulouse. She was on the point of death. In her delirium she had asked to be consoled, that is, to receive the Good Christian's last sacrament, confirming the desire of the dying person's spirit to be released from the created world, to be at one with God. The Bishop dressed himself from head to toe in black, and set off, Gospel in hand, pretending to be a Good Christian. He went to the old lady's bedside. By offering to console her, he tricked her into believing he was an Elder, and to admitting heretical beliefs which she had recanted some twenty years earlier. No account was taken of the pain which dulled the poor woman's mind, nor of the wilful deceit. On the fourth of August, to celebrate the canonisation of Dominic Guzman, he had her dragged out of her sick room, summarily tried, and burnt in front of the Cathedral. They used the slow fire to prolong her agony. Peire Sellan, one of Dominic Guzman's earliest companions, was there. After the burning, this Sellan, the Bishop de Fauga, and other dignitaries settled down to a feast of beef, mutton, wine and cheese in the Bishop's house.

'Despite such horrors, and despite the sieges only twenty years earlier, the terrible invasions in which thousands were killed and much property destroyed, many wooden buildings in Toulouse had been reconstructed, fresh timber filled the air with the scent of newness, and proud churches and palaces were being built with the brick that shines red in the morning and glows the colour of a shimmering pink rose in the early evening. To my great joy, the Cathedral of Saint Sernin still stood, its grand round arches and absidia resplendent reminders of the old days when Christian and Jew, Cathar and Saracen lived openly together, before the

Dominicans arrived with their hatred, and tolerance came to be regarded as a sin.

'At court my right to practise my faith was not questioned, though we were encouraged to attend the Catholic Mass. Why not? we reasoned. One can pray to the True God in a church as well as anywhere else.

'Amongst those interested in music was Jean de Garlande, the Master of Grammar at the new university. You might have heard his argument that universal signs are only a function of grammar, and have nothing to do with the world of matter. He was one of many who still remembered Walter von der Ouwe, and valued his songs. One fine summer's evening, in an intimate palace courtyard, where radiant sunflowers lined walls of ancient stone, still warm from the heat of the day, he and I were amongst those listening to a singer who, sitting on the steps in front of a porchway, framed by dog-tooth arches of perfect proportions, sang Walter von der Ouwe's words with such refinement and sensitivity that I almost saw Walter in him.

'When he had finished, and the torches were lit, flickering against the setting sun, I talked to this man, and asked him how it might be that, though so young, he had such a profound understanding of Walter von der Ouwe's songs. "I love his music," he said. "It is as though it knows and laments its own transience." He looked at me carefully and, smiling, tossed back his mane of long dark hair, with a movement just like Walter von der Ouwe's. Then he added, "There are affinities in this life, and I perceive an affinity between you and the writer of this music." This is how I came to meet Michael, whom you know, and whom I now count amongst those I most cherish, though he does not yet see the world as I see it.

'Nor shall I ever forget Count Raimon of Toulouse. Peire Cardenal, whom I also met, had written that chivalry streams from him, as water from a source. At first Count Raimon seems just as he is described, sated with joy, generous of spirit, surrounded by fine ladies, musicians and poets. Yet when I had audiences alone with him, away from self-righteous buffoons like the Bishop, I saw that his eyes were drawn dog-like with a sadness he could no longer hide, for inwardly he lamented the old world of freedom, of song and love, and of tolerance: the lost world, before the burnings, before the threats from Paris and Rome, and before the death of his father who had died excommunicate.

'I remember well that first evening when he called me to the private chamber, a room glittering with treasures. It was late, the business of the day, the feasting, drinking and dancing were done, and most were bedding down for the night in the various places in the castle allotted to them. Michael was present too.

' "I am asking you to travel to England," the Count said, an immense sadness, fatigue and resignation in his voice, "in the hope that you might sway the King. It is a fragile hope," he explained, "and not without danger for you."

' "Why choose me?" I asked.

' "There are a number of reasons," he replied. "The first is the story of your lineage. They say you are descended from an ancient line of Kings who have ruled in Jerusalem, at the time of the prophets, and later in these lands too."

' "There is no reason to believe such stories," I interrupted.

' "Perhaps you are right,' he said. "I know too of your father's connections with the Welf family. Both these things will make you interesting to the King of England for they undermine and threaten the legitimacy both of Louis of France and the Emperor of Germany."

' "He might well attach as little importance to such matters as I do," I replied, still unable to see the purpose of the Count's request.

' "There is a third reason. I knew Walter von der Ouwe, and I loved him for the way he understood these lands, the music, the beauty and the ideals which were born here. I heard him sing of you, Domna Cecilia, when he travelled through this territory ten years ago. He sang of you and of the years before he took part in the Crusade which ended in the burning of Constantinople in the year of Our Lord 1204. Now my land is dying too, at the hands of the so-called Crusaders. Its very soul is being consumed in their flames. You, because of the love Walter bore you, and because of your learning and music, cannot choose but to be our ambassadress. Perhaps the King of England will glimpse this truth, and come to our aid. Michael will travel with you," he said. "He understands the music, and the stories regarding your lineage, because of the knowledge he has from his own father. Moreover, his family lives in England, so they will be able to provide support. His father will help you gain access to the King."

'These words caused me to accept the mission. Not out of any vanity, but because I knew my life would be unbearable if I refused the Count, after the words he had spoken regarding Walter. The only condition I made to my acceptance was that Alazaïs should travel with us, since she is my companion, as you, Thomas, are my listener.

'I have had time to reflect on my deeper reasons for accepting this mission, Brother Thomas, and now I think I understand. I told you earlier that I thought I had glimpsed the true heart of the void. Yet those lands of Toulouse, where I had experienced it, were the home of so much that I had treasured: music, song, courtliness, freedom and beauty, both natural and human. If I can save that, I thought, by this mission, then I shall know that there *is* hope in this world.

Otherwise, I shall know, and know finally, that the Good Christians are right.'

'You were giving the world one last chance?' Brother Thomas said gently.

'This journey was a final wager, perhaps,' Domna Cecilia replied, 'against the void. In any case, we left just a few days later. As we travelled together through France, many places which might once have caused my heart to leap with joy now filled me with fear and foreboding; like the delicately carved pillars of the cloisters of Moissac which bore witness to the torture and burning of so many lovely people. What is beauty in this world but a terrible deceit? Such things as the starry, deep blue and gold enamels of Limoges no longer had the power to charm me, and the grandiosity of the new cathedrals at Chartres, Paris and Rouen seemed desolate monstrosities expressing only worldly power, devoid of any spiritual aspiration. The further north we rode, and the flatter and gloomier the landscape grew, the more I felt that I was moving towards the source of darkness. Michael would try to cheer me up, reminding me of the beauty and goodness of life and nature. Nothing he said had the power to convince me.

'Crossing from Wissant in the darkness, as we sat on deck, away from the other passengers who were singing, drinking and gaming below, the calm sea was unimaginably bleak. I thought this empty silence was more redolent of evil than any storm, fire or cruelty I had seen. For what does the Evil One want but for the sullen, lugubrious Void to extend its chill everywhere and for all eternity? The stars and the distant beacons of Calais and then of Dover made me think of the light, not of this world, for I have lost faith in it, but rather of the world beyond, where our true haven awaits.

'The midnight journey from the boat to this house, under guard of des Roches's soldiers, through the dark, flat countryside, the weird silhouettes of disconsolate northern trees arching on either side of the road, was like a journey to the gloomy heart of matter. Even Canterbury Cathedral, when its towers first appeared over the brow of a hill, looked more like a fortified receptacle of evil than a place of religion. I wondered if this dank city was not the dwelling place of the Evil One himself, and when I came to know the Norman haughtiness of its inhabitants, compared with the warmth and friendliness of the people of Aquitaine, my suspicions returned.'

'And you still think this?' Brother Thomas asked, apparently shocked.

'These were just passing impressions, for evil is everywhere in this world. It remains only for the likes of you to condemn us, Brother Thomas, and for us to burn. I know now of the impending royal marriage, that Henry's face is set against Toulouse, that we have failed, and that your King has disregarded the rumours about my birth and lineage, which the Count of Toulouse had thought was his best trump card. I am aware that I am to be another victim of the Emperor's power, of which you are the unwitting instrument. In this, at least, the Emperor and the Pope are united.'

'I know nothing of a royal marriage,' Brother Thomas told her.

'Then you are badly informed,' said Domna Cecilia. 'The King plans an alliance, through marriage, to Eleanor of Provence, which will bind him to the King of France against Toulouse.'

Brother Thomas was flushed with anger. 'So, you consider your mission a failure?' he said.

'I was denied access to the King, Brother Thomas, denied access to any normal diplomatic channels or courtesies, and placed under arrest, guarded by the men you see when you come here. But do not forget that I have seen the long processions coming down from the mountains, of those about to burn, the tall palisades, from which no one can escape. I have seen men, women and tiny children, tied hand and foot, pushed inside, locked out of hope in this world as they weep, the brushwood that will burn them tearing at their skin, some silent, others howling, mothers hugging little girls and boys, whispering as the cold sweat pours from them, that there is nothing to fear, that soon it will be over; then the long, anguished wait before the fires are lit, the agonising minutes of disbelief as the first flames are seen, but do not burn, then the smoke, the choking, the inferno licking, the blistering, searing pain. Now it is to start again.'

An uneasy silence followed. My muscles twitched and tensed as I imagined Cecilia being led into the flames. But, I reflected, no one has to suffer this fate. Even the most hardened heretic may recant, and the Church will be merciful. Perhaps Brother Thomas would find a way.

'You only have to abjure,' Thomas said. 'You do not have to die.'

Silence.

'You maintain that you have taken the sacraments of the heretics?' Thomas asked again as I struggled to note the precise words of her testimony.

'I received the Consolation,' she said, simply.

'And do you reject the Sacraments of the Catholic Church?'

'It is written,' she said, ' "By their fruits you shall know them." Can an evil tree bear good fruit? If one Church flees and forgives, and the other Church scourges and craves land and possessions, which of the two is the True Church? Surely, the True Church is the one which is persecuted.' She fell silent again.

'Do you accept the Baptism in water and the laying on of hands?'

Domna Cecilia remained silent.

'Do you believe that there are two Creator Gods, a Good Creator of the invisible world and an evil creator of the visible world?'

Silence.

'Do you accept the rites of marriage and the last unction of the dying?'

'The flesh,' she said, 'will follow the flesh.'

'Do you accept the authority of the ordained ministry of the Church, the ordination of priests and bishops?'

Silence.

'Domna Cecilia,' Thomas said in desperation, 'think of Hell, think of Eternal Damnation. I want only to save your soul.'

'I know,' she said, 'but how could a Good God permit Hell? Is not this realm torment enough? There will only be Hell when every soul has left this world, even yours, Brother Thomas. But do not think I deny Hell. I know it all too well.'

Thomas sighed. 'There is no need to continue. You know as well as I do that you have said enough for me to condemn you a hundred times over. If I wished to condemn you, that is. I can only implore you,' he said, 'to abandon a religion that is rooted in despair.'

'Think of my Kirsta, Thomas, and have courage,' she said. 'You will condemn me. You have condemned me. Not because you wish to; because you must. But there is more. I give myself to you, for you are my listener.'

Cecilia and Alazaïs stared long and hard at us; for a moment their eyes were like the mandorlas in old manuscripts, in which we glimpse the Saints in their distant, heavenly realm. Then Alazaïs left the room and Cecilia turned away, sitting hunched, a simple old woman in a bare room, that was all. It was clear that from then on she would remain silent. We had exhausted the route of questions and answers.

For the last time, albeit coldly, Thomas thanked both Domna Cecilia and Alazaïs for their hospitality. The four of us knew that Cecilia might as well have written and signed her own death warrant. At the entrance to her house, as we left, the two massively tall, brutal soldiers stood guard, like angels of death, with their cleft lips, and cut noses. I remembered the story of Alazaïs's father. One of the men held something, an animal, in his hands, pressed against him; it hissed and snarled. I realised it was Cecilia's cat.

Chapter Nineteen

Brother Thomas and I spent that evening and the following day copying up our records of the interviews with Domna Cecilia and attending the offices in the Cathedral. Domna Cecilia's only hope now was that the King would side with her, though I thought there was little chance of that. During the monastic offices the cathedral seemed to be engulfed in the ochre light of the beeswax candles; the giant criss-cross of the vaults and arches was like a massive honeycomb and the monks' chant was a hive's humming. I envied singers the unravelling of their harmonies and architects their geometric resolutions, for my mind was like a skein of knotted threads, none of which I could trace to any source.

After Nones there came a message from Lord Rufus that the King desired our presence again in the great hall of Saint Augustine's Monastery that evening directly after Vespers. There was no indication as to the purpose of the visit. The singing of the monks at Vespers was so haunting, that I wondered at the contrast between the worldliness of their lives and their ability to evoke the essence of a higher realm. I remembered Domna Cecilia's words about the flawed nature of music, and tormented myself with the fear that this beauty might be diabolic, and that the truth might be beyond even this, in a realm which, despite my attention to study and to prayer, I was yet to glimpse.

By the time we processed out of the Cathedral, darkness had fallen, and the night was cold. Stars cast a shimmering

stillness over the cloisters; tawny Aldebaran, yellow-green
Saturn and white Mercury were particularly luminous. I was
so absorbed by the intense light of these heavenly bodies that
I paid little attention to the other monks; some passed us
coldly now as though we did not exist, whilst others eyed us
suspiciously.

Thomas and I made our way out by the infirmary and then
along the Burgate with its endless rows of tiny shops, their
corbels boarded up for the night, and on to Saint Augustine's. The soldiers, huddled about their fires, scowled at our
approach. Yet Thomas's name had become a charm. He
spoke it, and door after door was opened to us. Who were
these men, these soldiers, I thought, standing guard at the
gates, playing dice in the torch-lit corridors, whose like had
slaughtered thousands in towns like Béziers and seen whores
dance naked on the Patriarch's throne in Constantinople,
that now we had power over them? To what forces had I
aligned myself? The Powers, Dominions and Thrones – were
they really angelic or were they of the Evil One? Thomas and
I did not speak on the way there. Both of us were too full of
apprehension.

There was only one table set up for feasting that night. It
stood at the far end of the hall and to the right. The King sat
on his folding stool on a raised podium, just as before. To
the left of him was his brother, Richard of Cornwall, and the
latter's dark, beautiful wife, Sanchia of Provence. To his right
were his sisters: Isabella, who had married Frederick, the
Holy Roman Emperor, but who had returned to England in
secret to be present that evening, and Eleanor who was to
marry Simon de Montfort, son of the same de Montfort who
had wrought such havoc in Languedoc eighteen years
before. They were attended by a dozen or so men and
women of the royal household, resplendent in their jewels
and other finery, including of course the ubiquitous Peter

des Roches. To the far right, perhaps somewhat excluded, was Lord Rufus.

The main body of the hall, which was bathed in the golden light of countless candles and torches, was empty. Only to the right of the door through which Brother Thomas and I entered there stood another group of men and women decked out in jewels and fine clothes just as luxuriant as those of the King and his people, only their complexion was swarthier and they spoke in a tongue I had not heard before. It was like Norman French but the words were harder to distinguish. I wondered why there was no mingling between the two groups.

When the King saw Brother Thomas he waved as if to an old friend and called out, 'Thomas! Wilfridus! Come here, for goodness' sake!' All heads turned towards us. Brother Thomas bowed gracefully and walked towards the King. Emanating from him, despite the warmth of his greetings, was that same coldness. 'You see, Brother Thomas,' he said, 'over there are our French cousins, with whom we have sometimes been at war. But tonight that is forgotten, for these gentlemen and ladies are close to Louis of France. His sister-in-law, Eleanor of Provence, daughter of the Count of Provence, is amongst them. She has travelled here, in secret, on my request. Shortly she will be presented to me and we shall see if she is fit to be my bride. You will advise me,' he added.

'You do me great honour,' my master stammered, 'but I cannot see how a man in my humble position can advise you over such a grave matter of state.'

Remembering Cecilia's words, I looked at Brother Thomas's face in the torchlight. The mask of courtly grace scarcely concealed the sudden horror he must have felt at his predicament.

'I have my reasons,' said the King. 'Besides, you are to be

my alchemist. Lord Rufus has told me of the texts you placed in his hands. You should understand the powers that lie behind such matters.'

Brother Thomas looked at Lord Rufus. He, however, turned away, unwilling to meet the gaze of the man whose secret, I now supposed, he had betrayed to the King. However, it was too late to protest. We were in the same hall as those who had overseen the raising of the armies sent against our lands and those of Toulouse, those whose advice, given lightly between pleasures, could mean life or death to thousands, sorrow or torment to hundreds of thousands.

As the King finished speaking, a hush fell. From the door to my right there entered a young woman about thirteen or fourteen years old, with long black hair, and a gaunt, fragile face, but one used to command; glittering against the purple pfellel-silk dress cut to show off the slimness of her waist were countless jewels sending shards of light like myriad stars scattering round the room. Through and beyond this light, a magnetic charge radiated from her, spanning the hall and engulfing the cold presence of the King. As their eyes met, a chemical spark passed from him to the future Queen, and there was a perceptible quivering in the magnetic fluids circling the hall, so forceful that I felt the resonance throughout my own body. I wondered if Brother Thomas was experiencing the same, for it was immediately clear to me that the King and this young woman were destined to be man and wife.

Slowly and gracefully, with a lady-in-waiting on either side of her, she walked towards the King, bowed and did homage. He offered her his hand, at which token she stood straight again. For a few minutes, he asked her, politely, about her journey, about her treatment since she arrived in England, and about the weather. Everyone in the hall listened, fascinated by the grace with which he spoke and she replied, despite her youth. Then she bowed again, and withdrew, as measuredly as she had entered, the other French attendants leaving with her.

There was silence. The King looked from one of us to another. As he caught my eye, I was taken by the luminosity in it. But it was not the lustre of desire, nor yet of joy. It was that chemical radiance, peculiar to persons of royal birth or station. 'Well?' he sighed, eventually. 'What do we think?'

No one dared speak.

'Surely someone must have a view?' he said. 'Brother Thomas, you begin.'

'Sire,' he said, speaking with more boldness, more stature and more resonance than I would previously have believed him capable, 'you know as well as I that I have been conducting the interrogation of Domna Cecilia. Allow me to plead her case. The young Duchess is lovely, and I am sure that in her person she is fit to be your wife. However, Domna Cecilia has made it plain to me that an alliance between yourself and Eleanor of Provence would mean the end of the freedoms of Toulouse, and the light, beauty and music which its way of life engendered. Therefore, Sire, I advise against this marriage so long as your lands in Toulouse are in peril.'

Brother Thomas's words were greeted with an icy silence. For a moment I wondered if he had hoped to ingratiate himself by speaking as he did. But he was no fool, and must have realised that he was bound to alienate the King and his entourage. Peter des Roches leant forward and whispered something to the King, who stood up and said, 'I am impressed, Brother Thomas, at your generosity in pleading the cause of a heretic. We were, I must confess, initially scandalised that the Count of Toulouse should send such a person to us. But now I see she has found a sympathetic ear. Would anyone else like to express an opinion?' Before anyone, even his royal brothers and sisters, dared venture an opinion, he turned to me. 'Brother Wilfridus?' he said. 'Tell us your view.'

A tremor of fear swept through me with such force that I thought my knees would give way beneath me. As his eyes fixed on me, it was as though ice entered my being through his gaze, freezing the blood in my veins. Nonetheless, I found words to speak. I remember well what I said though my motive remains unclear. Did I hope to save Brother Thomas by association with me? Or did the power of the magnetic forces I saw swirling round the room between Eleanor of Provence and the King, and the aura of joining between them somehow speak through me? 'My Lord,' I said, 'the Princess is lovely, and I know the wedding must take place.'

Again there was silence as the various members of the King's entourage glanced from one to another. Brother Thomas looked at me, not with anger as I deserved, but with a kindly resignation, and a deep sorrow, which shamed me to my very core.

'You hear that?' said the King. 'I say, this is a man to whom we should pay attention!' After a moment of bewilderment the others joined in with a chorus of praise for the future Queen, and affirmations about the usefulness of the alliance to the Duchy of Provence and thus also the Kingdom of France.

The words I had spoken could not have been more profitable to my advancement, if only that had been my desire. Lady Eleanor was called back, and there was dignified applause, followed by formal greetings and affirmations of intent, then affection, then praise for the future Queen's beauty, then laughter, music, singing, dancing and feasting, which went on well into the night. Thomas and I were offered a place at the royal table. I was fêted whilst poor Thomas was pointedly ignored.

As we ate, Peter des Roches spoke to me. 'So, you are not in league with the Count of Toulouse?'

My confusion was genuine. 'Should we be, sir?' I said.

'You contradicted your master,' he replied.

'Neither of us is in league with anyone,' I said. 'Brother Thomas spoke as he did because of something in the old woman we both value. I spoke my mind because of the energies I saw,' I said unthinkingly.

This answer was reported to the King, who referred to me from then on, not without irony in his tone, as his 'young alchemist'. Yet the mystique this conferred on me was instant, as was the raising of my status. I wondered about the impression I had had of the swirling and eddying of power in the hall as the Princess entered. Was I alone in perceiving it? How had the King grasped my sensitivity to it?

As the evening drew on, I was encouraged to stay for further dancing, drinking and merry-making. Brother Thomas observed in detached silence as Lord Rufus, des Roches and even the King chatted and joked with me. Towards the end of the evening, Lord Rufus sidled up to me and said, 'Well done, my friend. Clearly, I underestimated you. Welcome to the Game!'

Returning to our lodgings with Brother Thomas, I remember how brilliantly the stars shone, each constellation visible for those with eyes to see. In an infantile way, I was proud of my success, inwardly blaming Brother Thomas for failing to grasp the opportunity when it was offered to him. In my superficial joy, I had even forgotten Myrrah. However, the moment I thought of her again, her face, as I imagined it, was full of reproach, and in my own mouth, there was the ashen taste of future regrets.

'You did very well just then,' said Brother Thomas as we arrived in our lodgings, and he poured himself wine. 'You will make an excellent courtier. You know I have always thought very highly of you, but it seems that I too might have underestimated you. Perhaps I should recommend that you accept the position of King's Alchemist in my place, for I am not certain that I am suited.'

'That would be too much. It would be a mistake,' I replied clumsily, unable to clear my mind which was poisoned with pride.

'At least,' he interrupted me, 'something is evident to me now. They want to burn Domna Cecilia as a snub to Toulouse, and to win the favour of Louis and the Pope. I wonder what the plan is for Michael?'

I did not reply. The extent of my betrayal, involuntary though it was, of Domna Cecilia, Michael, Myrrah and my dear friend and teacher, Brother Thomas, was gradually becoming real to me, filling me with horror and nausea. I lay awake most of the night, listening to Brother Thomas snore, tormenting myself with worry and regret.

'Wake up, we must go together to Isaac's cellar,' said Brother Thomas the following morning. For the first time I could remember, he was up and dressed before me, and I was the one who had overslept. He was in surprisingly good spirits. I began to wonder if I had attached too much significance to the events of the previous evening. The sky was still streaked pink and yellow with dawn light as we made our way through the streets. Despite the biting cold, Canterbury was teeming with people because it was market day. Peasants in from the countryside, hawkers, musicians, beggars, thieves and pilgrims milled everywhere. Fires were lit here and there. Over them, some cooked slices of game, pork and salt beef, which they slapped on to pieces of bread and tried to sell as dogs snarled at their feet. Through the curling smoke and the mists, the towers of the Cathedral loomed over the city like an intruder from another realm.

As we approached the Jewish quarter, Thomas said, 'I have been giving some thought to Isaac's words regarding the transmutations in the retort. I told you he warned me against continuing the work. I am convinced I have sufficient knowledge to proceed to the next stage. It might be dangerous, of course, and you may prefer not to be present, in case Isaac's warnings turn out to have been founded.'

'Of course I want to be there,' I said. 'I wish to acquire the knowledge, whatever the cost.'

'Naturally,' said Brother Thomas, his bald head gleaming in the morning light. 'If you are to be the King's Alchemist there is much you must learn.'

I could not tell whether he felt bitter towards me after all, or if he was teasing me for reasons I could not understand, so I said nothing.

In the cellar, Brother Thomas had me sit in the room where the phials and the manuscripts were kept, whilst he stayed in the main part of the cellar. My job was to get on with the cataloguing and study of the texts that were there, whilst he lit a fire, warmed the dark, viscous substance in the retort, and carefully added other substances from the phials which he would fetch from the room where I was sitting.

I tried to work but found myself staring, much of the time, through the doorway at the glass vessel which perched, dusty and neglected for so long, leaning slightly to one side, on the metal structure above the remains of the fire, now being coaxed gently to life by Brother Thomas. The retort looked like a wounded bird of prey, dragging itself over the earth when it should have been flying through the aether. There was something pitiful about the black, viscous fluid which remained unchanged at first, despite the fire. Disappointed, I turned away and began sorting through the texts I had piled on the desk, thinking that nothing would come of this.

After a while, however, I became aware of a sweet smell,

like fresh springtime flowers mingled with olibanum or cinnamon, and when I looked into the room, it was aglow with a chrysoleth-yellow and rose hue. In the retort, instead of the black, viscous slime, there bubbled a mixture of luminous, glowing liquids, yellow, red, mauve and purple, as if performing a chemical dance.

'What is happening?' I called to Brother Thomas, who was staring, entranced, into the retort, as though he could see in it a doorway to another world. 'Tell me,' I called again. 'You must explain.'

'In due course,' he said. 'It is in the texts we gave into the hands of Lord Rufus. Perhaps, Wilfridus, you will make it your job to retrieve them.'

As he spoke, the smell coming from the retort changed, becoming acrid. Smoke began to billow from it. I found it hard to catch my breath. Then I saw that flames were spilling out of the neck of the vessel itself, licking into the air like salamanders, mingling with those below, burning with a dangerous heat.

I wanted to get up and dowse the flames, but there was a gust of cold air from the dark tunnel beyond the store-room, accompanied by a dull, roaring sound. The draught extinguished many of the candles and lamps in the room. I no longer dared move. There was an impression of someone, something, moving towards me through the swirling darkness of the tunnels beyond the room where the phials were kept. From the cupboard itself came a shaking, a banging and a rattling of glass. Brother Thomas was sitting close up to the vessel, and I watched in terror as the substance in the retort shone a dazzling white. The glass of the retort quaked like a living thing, then shattered, and fires leapt from it, engulfing Brother Thomas, and showering the room with choking ash. The blast threw me to the ground and the salamander-like flames began to lick viciously towards me.

I scrambled to my feet. The only way I might save myself was via the tunnel beyond the cupboard. I did not dare try to rescue Brother Thomas, for the fire was fierce and would soon take hold. So, I grabbed the tallow lamp for light, and a bundle of as many manuscripts as I could save, pushed at the cupboard which swung on its hinges and, choking, I stumbled into the tunnel.

I saw again the odd paintings on the walls, the human faces, the irises and lions, eagles and angels with urns. I realised how similar they were to the pictures in Brother Thomas's writings. After twenty or thirty yards the tunnel's wall fell away to the left, and I saw a large vault or cave-like structure built of stone, brick and marble not unlike amphitheatres I had seen at the Roman theatres in Lyon and Trier as a child. Here I stopped and caught my breath.

Coming to my senses I decided that it was cowardly and foolish to abandon Brother Thomas to the flames. I turned on my heels, resolving to do whatever I could to save him. I soon realised, however, that there was not just one tunnel, but a labyrinth of passageways, some lined with porphyry, and others with marble, or inset with mosaics of alabaster and turquoise. I sensed, but did not see, the presence of a vast river running nearby, dark and sulphurous.

At last, I retraced the route back to Isaac's cellar.

The fires had already burnt themselves out but the stench of burning was overpowering. The cellar was pitifully changed. All Isaac's work, his texts and phials had been destroyed. I tried to find Brother Thomas's charred body, searching carefully, blackening my hands in the warm soot and ash as I did so, until I could bear the stench no longer. Perhaps he had got away, or perhaps he had been burnt to cinders.

Sick with shock and despair, I climbed up out of the cellar. Here, nothing had changed. The interior of Isaac's house was still in the same, wrecked state, but as far as I could see, nothing had been moved or disturbed and there was no sign of the fire, other than the stench which was still in my nostrils. Outside, the guards sat around as before. None of them seemed to have noticed that anything was amiss. I hid my hands in my sleeves and hoped that my face was not too discoloured by ash as I emerged into the bright, chilly world of daylight which was more like a dream than the nightmarish place I had just left. The contour and colour of every object was sharp and clear. I was lucky to be alive. I felt like Lazarus, and thought of the words spoken to Orpheus: 'Cherish the light!'

My first thought was to see if Brother Thomas had somehow managed to escape. I went back into Isaac's house and searched it from top to bottom. Then I went to our lodgings, past the peasants bringing their fish, their salted meats, vegetables and fresh baked bread to the winter market. There was no sign of my master there.

I attended a number of offices in the Cathedral, growing increasingly desperate, then I searched the library and the scriptorium, but I could not find Brother Thomas and I did not dare ask any of the Brothers if they had seen him, because of the Prior. I crossed the Burgate and asked the Brother at the gate of Saint Augustine's if he had seen Thomas. He had not. The sun was beginning to set, and I went to Vespers in the Cathedral, giddy with fear and self-reproach. I dared talk to no one. I found myself staring at the place in the Quire where William de Sens had fallen, and I wondered if that same power which had sucked him into the void had caused the quaking and explosion of the matter in the retort in Isaac's cellar.

After Vespers, heedless of where I was going, I walked through the town's familiar twilit streets. The city was poorly guarded in those days, so I was able to walk out, through an unattended gate in the city wall, into the country. The air I breathed, the odour of excrement, the scent of the earth, the evening mist, sky, trees, voices calling, reached me as if from an impossible distance, like the backdrop to a passion play. As the sky darkened, and an opal moon rose, the earth on which I stood seemed no more than a tiny platform, spinning through a void, in which there was no good, only desire, ambition, then the inevitable destruction, confirming, through its release, the futility of our obscure acts. Surely Christ, I prayed, was always here, in this Gethsemane of a world, and surely this was the meaning of His Crucifixion, whatever the Cathars believed.

The first stars had begun to emerge. I wondered if these lights were, as some maintained, not luminous bodies, but tiny pinprick holes in the floor of the heavens, through which the faint glimmer of celestial light was permitted to shine. Or perhaps, beyond the firmament, there is nothing, only endless, cold flame, stretching for ever, and we here below are alone.

I wandered back to town; I found a tavern and ordered drink, seeking consolation.

At last, half drunk, as if driven, I found myself walking out towards the West Gate, until I reached the high stone walls of Domna Cecilia's house. I felt less like a man and more like a disembodied spirit as I approached the front door, pushed it open and walked into the familiar, sweet-smelling darkness of the ground floor where the animals were kept unslaughtered, and made my way up the wooden steps beneath the bowed timbered beams, the rough, whitened daub of the walls seeming to glow in the darkness. I realised only after I had entered that for the first time the two guards with deformed faces were nowhere to be seen. As I climbed to the first-floor room, an eerie gold and ochre light pulsed and dappled the air with a musical quality that seemed to contain voices of past lives, or gateways to other realms. The chart and the chalice were gone, and there was a chill in the atmosphere.

I climbed the stairs to Domna Cecilia's room. The room was empty. Only the side door was half open. Beyond it, I sensed pain and darkness.

There was no sign of Domna Cecilia, nor of Alazaïs. I was trying to decide whether to leave straight away, or glance into the side room, where I presumed Domna Cecilia had slept, when I heard a low, animal-like moan, followed by a whispering. Then the groaning grew louder, more pitiful still.

I tiptoed towards the door, and pushed it open. That sweet scent of sandalwood returned, now mingled with the bitter smell of hibiscus. Inside were two figures. One, wearing a Dominican habit, lay propped up on a low bed. The face was invisible because it was covered in white cloths and bandages. The other figure, with deep eyes and long, curly hair, was soaking cloths in a bucket of water over a small fire. Next to the bucket were piles of the herbs Domna Cecilia had hung out to dry in the house. Michael was waiting to apply the next rag. He nodded to me and gestured that I should sit down on the small chair in the corner of the room. When he removed the cloth and the bandages from the face, I saw only irregular blotches of red and brown peeling skin. Thomas's features were quite indistinguishable. The nose was an asymmetrical lump of flesh and the eyes were inchoate, bloody holes. The mouth was a thin, grey, lipless line. 'He is in great pain and he cannot speak,' said Michael.

From the poor, disfigured face there came another terrible moan, the memory of which fills me with anguish to this day. Before I managed to find any words, Michael put a finger to his lips. Whispering, he began to explain how, having been released from prison on the orders of the King, he had been making his way to the cellar along the tunnels which were familiar to him from his childhood, when he heard the dreadful explosion. He rushed to the cellar where he found Brother Thomas, who had been blown backwards against the steps, his face terribly burnt.

Suddenly, Michael fell silent. There was a creaking sound on the stairs below us. The door to the house had been opened, and there were slow, hesitant steps on the ladder leading to the first floor, and then low voices. I expected the worst, soldiers or Sir Osbert's louts coming to find Michael. I was scared, scared for myself, and for poor Thomas; I could not bear the thought of more suffering and terror being added to the pain which already possessed him. Anguish filled me at the thought that I, unwittingly, might have led the Prior's men to that place. Quickly but carefully, Michael finished the task of preparing the bandages and dressing for Thomas's face. Then he leant towards me and whispered, 'It is best if I go. It might not occur to them to look up here.'

Michael drew a knife from a scabbard inside his cloak. He moved stealthily towards the stairs and then, to take the intruder by surprise, crept down the steps one by one. Thomas started, allowing a brief, yelping cry to escape from his burnt mouth, but I could tell that he understood the situation from the way he forced himself to keep silence afterwards. I held his hand and the two of us waited.

I tried to understand the sounds I heard from below. There was no sign of struggle or violence. I heard only whispering, and what sounded like weeping. At last I left Thomas's side and peered down the stairs. Michael was hugging someone with grey hair and next to them was a red-haired man wearing fine clothes, Lord Rufus. As the three of them began to climb the stairs to the upper room, I realised that the grey-haired man was Isaac, Michael's father.

I returned to Thomas's side and told him what I had seen. His response was to grip my hand tightly.

Isaac was the first to see Thomas, and the first to speak. 'My poor friend,' he said. 'What has become of you?'

'Will he live?' Lord Rufus asked Michael, in a whisper. But Thomas must have heard him, for his hand trembled in mine, like a trapped bird.

'Of course,' said Michael. However, he gestured towards his eyes, in order to communicate that Thomas could not see, and never would see again.

Isaac spoke next. 'Wilfridus, Thomas, do not be afraid that Lord Rufus is here. He came to release me from prison, and he has promised to restore my goods to me. The Prior, it seems, is my enemy, not this man, or the King.'

As Michael showed us how to make and change the dressings, using honey, hibiscus, poppy and olibanum, Isaac explained how Lord Rufus had come to him earlier that day, announcing that he and his son were to be set free, and how the two of them had decided that Michael should leave the cellar by means of the tunnels, in order to confound Sir Osbert, the Keeper. As I helped dress Thomas's face I realised clearly that the burns round his mouth were less severe than those to the eyes, which had been blown in and pulped to a mess of flesh and blood.

When, finally, I did find words to speak, it was to ask Lord Rufus where Domna Cecilia was.

'The King's men came last night,' he said. 'She will be tried at the Archbishop's Palace at Loamhithe in London.'

At this Brother Thomas began groaning. The sound he made grew louder and louder. 'There is nothing we can do,' Lord Rufus insisted. Brother Thomas gripped my hand so hard I thought my bones would crack.

'What about Alazaïs?' Michael asked.

'She was taken too,' Lord Rufus replied. Thomas began

groaning again. With a terrible, gurgling voice he tried to mouth my name. Michael set about placing the cloths across Thomas's burnt face to soothe the agony, but my master grew more agitated.

At last, I understood. 'Would you like me to go to her?' I asked. At that, Thomas nodded painfully, and breathed out; then he relaxed, and the tension went out of him. 'I shall,' I said, 'at first light.' We sat in silence for a while. Brother Thomas's breathing grew more regular, and he fell either asleep or unconscious. I did not dare think what dreams he might be dreaming, or how terrible his sightless awakening would be.

With great courtesy and generosity, Lord Rufus, Isaac and Michael discussed our situation. I explained to Michael about the meeting with the King, how I had predicted the royal marriage, and how it seemed to me that the events in the cellar were somehow linked to my betrayal. They tried to convince me that this was a foolish thought, but still I am not sure. Lord Rufus said that Thomas, Michael and Isaac could stay in the house, since it was his, as long as they wished. I, meanwhile, was to set off to London the next day, to find out more about Domna Cecilia and see what the situation was regarding her trial. After all, it might be possible to save her. Then I was to fetch Alyssa and Myrrah from Petcotte and bring the two women back to Canterbury, upon which it would be decided what we might do for the best as far as Brother Thomas was concerned. As soon as the arrangements were made, Lord Rufus took his leave of us, saying he had other business to attend to.

That night I slept only fitfully. Once, when I woke, it was to hear Michael telling Thomas the crow story, to comfort him, I supposed. I understood that Michael must have had those papers placed in our lodgings in order to test our reaction to it. Now the story seemed to hold meanings I had not previously perceived.

The second time I woke, it was to hear Michael relating the old story of the Fisher King, his gloomy castle and the visit of the knight Parsifal. Michael talked so evocatively that one could easily picture the scene he conjured of the beautiful girls who served at the old King's sacred castle. As I imagined these girls, it seemed that each had Cecilia's features. It was during this description, in the pitch black of the middle of the night, that poor blind Thomas suddenly lurched forward and cried out Cecilia's name. We gathered round and tried to comfort him. The woeful noises he made might well have been sobs, but what can be said of an eyeless man's weeping?

Chapter Twenty

I WOKE NEXT morning to the smell of fresh bread which Michael had been out to fetch from a bakery nearby. He was setting out ale for us to drink and cheese to eat. Memories of the previous day came flooding back. It unsettled me to think that the platters and cups we ate from were those that Cecilia and Alazaïs would have used so often over the past few months. If only time could be reversed, I thought. If only we could re-enter the closed world of the past which was as irretrievably lost as forgotten music.

I went straight to see Brother Thomas. His face was still very sore, though the redness of the burnt skin had given way to a speckled brown and yellow. The shrivelled eye sockets were showing the first signs of healing, but Thomas was in terrible pain. Michael was sitting next to him and Brother Thomas was trying to speak. I watched the agonised movements of his scorched lips. The word he struggled to pronounce filled me with sadness and foreboding. 'Alyssa,' he said, and then repeated, 'Alyssa.'

'Can you hear me, Brother Thomas?' I asked.

His grunt signified that he could.

'I will fetch her,' I said, 'as soon as I can.' This was the only consolation I could offer.

The next words he said were clearer. 'Cecilia,' he groaned. 'Help her.'

I said that I would do everything in my power.

Isaac and Michael assured me that they would stay with

312

Thomas for as long as was necessary and that they would get more help from the town if needed. Just before I left, I remember how Isaac took my arm and said, 'Wilfridus, do not blame yourself. There are forces beyond.' This was easy enough for him to say. I thought of my arrogance in the presence of the King just two nights before. Perhaps I had not betrayed Thomas wilfully or by any specific act, but I had betrayed him all the same, and to me that betrayal had caused his injuries. Isaac looked into my eyes, as if to read my troubled thoughts, then he embraced me and said, 'You must take this, for Brother Thomas's sake. You will almost certainly need it.' With that he pressed into my hands a purse of money. I looked inside and saw coins of greater value than I had ever set eyes on before, let alone had at my disposal.

I walked out into the icy grey morning light. The rain stabbed like icicles as I made my way towards the Cathedral where I wished to fetch my horse for the journey. I remembered Domna Cecilia's words. After the presence of the gentle creatures with whom I had spent the previous night in Domna Cecilia's house it was easy enough to understand her view that material creation was evil.

I avoided the town centre, passing by Weterlok Lane and the King's Mill. I did not want to run the risk of entering the Priory, where I was bound to be recognised immediately and quizzed about Brother Thomas.

Before I reached the Priory stables, however, just as I was about to turn into Palace Street, I saw a cavalcade of four horsemen riding towards me. At first I looked on idly at the cloak of rich striped material lined with fur worn by the first rider, supposing that this was some knight or dignitary leaving the Precincts. I heard a shout, and realised that the leader of the mounted party was pointing towards me. I glimpsed the bright red hair beneath the hood. It was Lord Rufus.

It was too late to get away. He had seen me and he and his men were riding straight towards me. I felt fear because of the physical power of the horses' onrush, and more fear still at the thought of the political power Rufus wielded. 'Get on behind,' Lord Rufus called as he approached me. I suppose I must have gestured stupidly. 'There is something you must witness for the sake of Brother Thomas!' he shouted as, clumsily, I hoisted myself up on to the saddle behind him.

Soon the five of us were cantering through the city past the Palace, past the new gate, through the Forum and along the street towards the castle where Michael and Isaac had been held. Before reaching the castle, though, we stopped at an inn. 'You look hungry,' Lord Rufus said to me. Then he addressed his companions. 'You three can carry on to the castle to make sure that everything is in order.' The men rode off as instructed.

The inn was no ordinary establishment. A huge fire roared in the centre and there were tables and chairs fit for people of high office and great wealth. I felt out of place but Lord Rufus gestured to me to sit at a seat by the narrow window. He ordered us ale and meat, which smelt delicious as it was being cooked. I secretly relished the luxury of eating so well, particularly at such an hour of the morning. 'How is Brother Thomas?' Lord Rufus asked, genuine concern in his voice. I explained that he was more comfortable, but that there was no hope for his eyes. 'A very cruel fate has been apportioned to him,' said Lord Rufus. 'And he possesses such knowledge. I wonder if he would willingly exchange his knowledge for his sight. Anyhow, look out of the window.'

I did as I was told, and even as I looked, the streets filled with crowds of agitated people: ordinary townsfolk, one or two nobles, wealthy tradesmen, hawkers, whores, monks and Jews. Coming towards us, amidst much shouting, booing and jostling, was a group of soldiers. Lord Rufus looked on with superior detachment; just outside the window low women from the brothels were pulling at their hair, tears rolling down dirt-smeared faces. Rain fell in a freezing drizzle but the anger of the people was undampened. As the soldiers passed in front of the inn, I realised they were dragging someone in their midst. Now I could hear what the crowds were shouting: 'Whoremonger! Murderer! Extortionist! Userer!' At last, I caught a glimpse of the object of the anger and the hatred. It was Sir Osbert, the Keeper.

'He was arrested last night,' said Lord Rufus. 'They found bodies in the dungeon. Boys and women – in shallow graves. Half the town has grievances against him, from the Priory to the Jews. He'll probably hang tomorrow. No more trouble from him. Now, as I said, I have something that will interest you and Brother Thomas. Since your master is blind, I dare say you will be asked to act as his chief aide, perhaps you will even be his successor as the King's Alchemist. Anyhow, I should be grateful if you would read this and tell me what you think. It was given to me by des Roches.' From a leather bag he produced a large bundle of parchments, some ninety or so pages, each densely covered with fine handwriting. I thumbed through them. The papers were addressed to someone called Philip and were written and signed by the Abbot of Bellapais. This was the third manuscript I referred to at the start of this account, which I found in the box presented to me by the Dominican.

'Perhaps,' I said, 'you could tell me why des Roches gave this to you.'

'Des Roches,' he replied, 'knows Cyprus well from his crusading days; and he knew the old Abbot of Bellapais who died six years ago. A messenger brought the manuscripts to him when we were at Dover. He said they were to be delivered to Domna Cecilia.'

'So, why has that not happened yet?'

'We thought it best for Brother Thomas to see them first. You will understand that there are messages encoded in the story which only someone like Brother Thomas, with his knowledge of the occult arts, would be able to understand in full. Besides, short of divine intervention, Domna Cecilia will be burnt the day after tomorrow.'

'Perhaps,' I said, 'if Domna Cecilia were to be shown these writings, we might learn something from her reaction.'

'I am sure you are right. I have no objection to your taking them to her, provided we get them back.'

'Can she really not be saved?' I asked.

'The trial started yesterday. Your own notes contain enough information to condemn her a thousand times over. They will use them to accuse her publicly of fornication, adultery, infanticide, killing her husband, treason, shape-shifting, treachery and heresy. They will even argue that her cat was her familiar. The Pope's men were overjoyed with the copy of your deposition, Wilfridus.' Wave after wave of self-disgust flooded through me. I had betrayed the two people I most respected in this life. Lord Rufus was aware of the effect his words had on me. He was not a cruel man, but he dealt in the realms of power and was keen that this should be felt. 'Do not blame yourself,' he said. 'You had no choice in anything that happened. Rather, learn from it. Tell me what you think of those papers.'

As we drank the rest of our ale and tucked into the bread and salt pork to fortify ourselves for the journey ahead, I began reading the parchments. I soon became so involved in this study that Lord Rufus had to remind me more than once that it was time to leave.

* * *

By the time we set off, the streets had emptied again since Osbert had been led away. On the road to London the forest paths were like freezing rock, the trees jagged and livid white with frost. As we rode, Lord Rufus was generous in his explanations of the events in which I had been caught up. He told me how the Prior had come to hear of Cecilia's presence in Canterbury. Then, with the help of Brother Theodor, the Prior had found the *Hermesis*, and records referring to the time when Cecilia's father was present in Canterbury, which led him to the discovery of the chalice. His plan was to take over the investigations and present the chalice to the King, thereby winning his favour and support to become Archbishop, since he believed that the Archbishopric was rightfully his.

We spent the night at Lord Rufus's castle near Elletham-wolde. It was clearly the dwelling of a man of ambition; much that had been accumulated was there to impress: tapestries, furniture and gold and silver vessels. He was not mindlessly ambitious, however. Part of his charm was his self-awareness, his ability to mock himself, though it would have taken a braver man than I was to cross him.

As we ate together in one of his ostentatiously furnished private rooms, he got on to a favourite topic of conversation, his intense dislike of John of Sittingbourne. 'The man is quite without shame,' he said. 'He thinks no worse of murder than of lying, and seems quite unable to understand that people see through him, even if no one yet is in a position to act against him. Think of the shamefaced way he tried to win poor Brother Thomas round. It is very much to your master's credit that he resisted. Brother Thomas's judgment of others is usually excellent. It is only in his estimation of himself that he is too critical. Mind you, no one can have been more surprised than the Prior at the forces Cecilia's presence unleashed: the Templars snuffling round the secret defensive tunnels beneath Kent, Brother Theodor's discovery of potentially dangerous facts regarding Domna Cecilia's lineage.'

'Is that why the Prior had them killed?' I asked.

'There were a number of reasons,' Lord Rufus replied. 'The principal one was his fear of what the Templars might have found out about his intentions from Theodor. Though he had Brother Rainer and Sir Osbert on his side, his realisation that Isaac, Michael and Brother Thomas were beginning to understand the game caused him to grow desperate.'

'How did the Prior expect to get away with the murders?' I asked.

'His first line of defence was to place the blame on Michael,' Rufus replied. 'Osbert was to have forced or forged a confession. They might have succeeded had it not been for Brother Thomas's steadfastness, and yours,' he added. 'The fall-back strategy was that he knew Osbert was involved in espionage on behalf of the French, who wished to know about the tunnels criss-crossing Kent below ground, in case the opportunity presented itself to invade. Sir Osbert was using a pretence of counter-espionage to round up and torture whomever he pleased, including young women and boys for his own pleasure. John of Sittingbourne came to hear of this, so he was able to channel retribution away from himself, and Sir Osbert paid the penalty.'

'How was it then,' I asked, 'that Isaac and Michael knew about the chalice?'

'There are those who are entrusted with secret knowledge,' he said. 'There is always a cost.'

We spoke little after that, and I was left uncertain by our conversation, for though he had appeared so full of warmth and kindness towards Brother Thomas and myself, in everything regarding Cecilia, Rufus was harsh and inflexible. I wondered how far such a man could be trusted.

I was given a room on my own to study the manuscripts from Bellapais which described much of the early life of the man Cecilia had loved. Many details tallied with Cecilia's own accounts of him. I fell asleep before I was able to finish reading the parchments. I dreamt vividly of the man who wrote those words, and also of the strange charts and drawings Brother Thomas had entrusted to Lord Rufus, for there were correspondences between them which were impossible to ignore.

The next day, Lord Rufus insisted that I should read the Bellapais text to the end before we set off on the final leg of our journey to London. Over lunch, which we ate in the private rooms of his castle, I told him what I thought of the papers. They described in greater detail what I had already heard from Cecilia, the story of the Abbot of Bellapais's early life, his loves when he was a wandering singer and went by the name of Walter von der Ouwe, and how he took part in the Crusade against Constantinople before travelling to Cyprus. It was clear that the story was organised in a way which demonstrated hermetic knowledge of number correspondences in architecture and sacred texts.

I explained my views to Lord Rufus, who finally conceded that it would be appropriate for Cecilia to see these writings, in case we might learn from her reaction. I discovered only much later that his motivation for this must have been that he, too, was a member of the Order of Jerusalem which concerned itself with questions of lineage relating to the coming of the Last Days. We rode, practically in silence, the rest of the way to London. The content of the Abbot's writings filled my thoughts as the frosty white mists of our breath filled the air in front of us.

When we arrived, news that there was to be a royal wedding had just reached London, the great city, whose streets were brimful of life. Resplendent banners flew from each building. People rushed to and fro, smiling, and from the houses and shops succulent scents of cooking filled the air. The River Thames was alive with boats and barges ablaze with flags, and bells rang from every church tower. For a while, I wondered if this city was a foreshadowing of the Heavenly Jerusalem, where the tears of men and women are wiped away for ever. Yet the filth and cruelty of the earthly city soon became apparent once more; little enough was sacred about that place.

Lord Rufus and I took a boat together across the Thames to the old castle at Loamhithe, which was now the possession of the Archbishop. As we approached the castle gates, Lord Rufus admonished me time and again that I should do nothing to interfere with the course of events about to unfold, for to do so would be to contradict the will of the King. When we arrived, he told the guards that I was Domna Cecilia's confessor. No one thought to challenge this, so I was led past a cordon of guards and up a narrow spiral staircase to the sad little cell. It was about six feet square, and its one slit window overlooked the courtyard where preparations were already being made for her burning. The echo of wood being chopped and the crackle of twigs and branches being broken up that winter's day are sounds which still haunt me.

Cecilia, huddled in blankets at a desk where she had been writing letters, welcomed me with a grace and courtesy which transfigured her pitiful surroundings. There was no trace of resentment.

I asked her why she was alone. She replied that Alazaïs had been sent back to Toulouse. The authorities had not wished to attract opprobrium by burning a mute unable to confess her transgressions. Cecilia asked me to see that the letters she had written were delivered, and of course I accepted.

She enquired after Brother Thomas, so I explained at

320

length the events leading up to his blinding. I could tell that she was moved. 'I did not foresee,' she said, 'that he and I would fall victim to the same element.'

Next, I handed Cecilia the writings of the Abbot of Bellapais. Solemnly, she turned the pages for a few minutes, and slowly a luminous smile broke across her noble features. 'Wilfridus,' she said, 'you have brought me the greatest joy. And now you must stay and watch with me, for I do not wish to be alone. My life is complete now. I knew it was not for nothing that Thomas was my listener, and you were his companion. Indeed, you were more than just Thomas's companion, for it was you who found my father's grave in the Cathedral, and the chalice with which he was buried. Now you will be my last companion, since Alazaïs is not here. Wilfridus, neither you nor Brother Thomas must ever consider yourselves guilty of my death. On the contrary, you have always been courteous and kindly. I only regret the suffering I have caused you.'

These words, scorching me with forgiveness, made her presence unbearable to me for a short time. I excused myself and went to see the men in charge of the arrangements for the next morning. Unlike Sir Osbert, these were not cruel men, but soldiers careful to do what was right. I sensed that they were not without respect for Cecilia. The executioner himself was a tall, quiet young man, immensely strong. His name, by coincidence, was also Thomas. I begged him to ensure Cecilia would not suffer the next morning, and gave him a large part of the money Isaac had given me, a considerable sum. To his credit, he would take only what he considered his due, and handed the rest, the greater part, back to me, nodding silent acceptance. No hint of a smile crossed his powerful but still boyish face.

For hours, as the sun set, and throughout the watches of the night, Cecilia and I sat together in silence as she read the writings of the Abbot of Bellapais, over and over, oblivious now of her surroundings, and perhaps forgetting her fate as she lost herself in the past of the other. I watched with Cecilia, mostly in silence, for she was content to read, and re-read, the writings I had given her, and to pray. The quality of this night was unlike any other I have ever spent. Her stillness, her deeply lined, grave yet smiling face communicated both sorrow and anticipation. Something, an invisible brilliance, in the atmosphere around her, induced in me a feeling that we were at an interstice between worlds. When I looked at her, I was unable to focus on her features.

Not long before dawn, she addressed me, calmly and quietly, and this is my record of her words: 'It is not long now, and there are some things I should tell you. The responsibility for the death of Brother Theodor and the Templars at Swiffeld, also for the ransacking of the house of Isaac the Jew, lies with Prior John of Sittingbourne, though he used Sir Osbert as his instrument. If only the Prior's aims had been noble, but he is a man driven by the passion for advancement. He never forgave the Pope for barring his way to the Archbishopric. So when he stumbled across knowledge which, for good reason, is kept secret from base natures such as his, he tried to use it for material gain, quickly winning over the corrupt Templar, Brother Rainer, to his cause. Yet rumours about my lineage, the true meaning of the chalice, and the Templar stories of networks beneath the ground leading to rare treasures, were nothing but a source of confusion to him, and it is inevitable that he will pay the penalty. Curiously, the Prior's greed helped me with my quest, for without him I should never have found my father's grave, nor the other chalice, nor Brother Thomas and yourself.'

I asked her again to tell me what she really believed about her lineage.

'It took me a long while to understand the implications of the old stories,' she said, 'by which I had set so little store. Now these writings from Bellapais confirm the truth: the illustrious Welf family, patrons of my father, those who wished to supplant the Hohenstaufen in the line of Holy Roman Emperors, saw how these stories might serve their cause, particularly in denying legitimacy to Barbarossa, Henry VI, Philip of Swabia, and latterly Frederick II. Frederick's triumph has sealed my fate. None of this, of course, will ever be admitted openly, for such matters are left to the secret inner circles by means of which real power is wielded; I mean the power of this world, Wilfridus, which I am about to leave. But such matters are of so little importance compared with the death of my poor Kirsta, and the vision which pre-figured it.'

Just for a moment, it seemed that Cecilia was close to tears, but she fell silent, and maintained her dignity, reading and re-reading Walter von der Ouwe's words. Then she gave herself to prayer and after a while she said, 'I have one wish for you, Wilfridus. Seek out Myrrah, Michael's sister, of whom I have heard nothing but good, for she is your life's companion. Do not be foolish, as I was once foolish.'

The clear-sighted goodness of these words brought me to my feet, and I stared out of the window, hiding my emotion. Dawn was breaking. I watched as the soldiers finished the preparation of the pyre. The sky grew a foreboding grey, then streaked with sickly yellow as the sun tried to shine. Stalls were set up for traders; one or two acrobats and jesters crept from porches and doorways, but they would have been disappointed by the paucity of the crowd. After all, despite the relative novelty of a burning, only one person was to die, so there would not be much of a spectacle.

Just before they came Cecilia handed me the papers from Bellapais saying, 'You remember the trees which grew from the graves of Tristan and Isolt, their branches inter-twining at last? Such are these writings, and I offer them to you.'

As she finished speaking, a single blast on a trumpet announced that the business of the day was to begin. After the stillness of the night, what followed was a grotesque rush, the priest harassing Cecilia to accept the last rites of the Church, which to my surprise she did not refuse, the soldiers, nervous and pushy, despite Cecilia's compliance, the bustle of clerics, lawyers and nobles come to witness the burning. Rain fell as, at last, Cecilia was led out through the small crowd, which grew silent, for something in her presence, even then, commanded respect.

I looked on as she was made to kneel and tied to the stake, feet, hands and neck. Words she had spoken, memories from her life which now seemed more mine than hers, were a swirling, pulsing presence in my mind as the fires were lit. True to his promise, Thomas the executioner stood behind her until there was sufficient smoke to hide his actions, then he grasped and twisted the rope knotted round her neck, and with one quick movement spared her the pain of the searing flames.

He stood back, face motionless, his work done. I felt relief mingle with the horror. As the fires rose round her legs, and that awful stench blended with the drizzle, I felt that they were burning my own soul. Then, suddenly, the flames leapt higher, and Cecilia's frail body fell forward.

At that moment I saw, in the dazzling conflagration, jagged shapes like those sculpted in the arched portals of ancient churches; there was a faint smell of sandalwood in the air, and I glimpsed the loves and essences of Cecilia's life: father, mother, those with whom she had sung and played, Walter,

Martin, Kirsta and David, and those strange heretic friends of her latter years, amidst the mountain landscapes and sunsets of the south. I imagined her soul, pure and free at last, at one with them, suffused in a whiteness beyond the burning.

Epilogue

T HIS IS THE point at which I ended my written report for the Dominican, Brother Johannes.

A week after I finished, just as I was beginning to hope that my life might return to normal, Brother Johannes returned. As I was walking home from the church, I saw him, tall, thin, fatefully pensive as he strode up the hill towards me, his dark figure framed by the morning light shining from the east beyond the Elham Valley.

I greeted him with all the warmth I could muster, and assured him that, despite the twenty-seven long years since the events it described, I was convinced that my report was accurate.

He merely nodded.

I invited him to my house, and he accompanied me inside without further ado, but when I offered him food, he refused. All that interested him was the report. For the rest of that day he sat at my desk, concentrating fiercely, turning over the pages, scarcely looking up, only breaking to say the daily offices with me, this being our only contact. Meanwhile I tried to busy myself with routine tasks, whilst I awaited judgment, well aware of the irony that now I was to be the object of an inquisition, just like the one to which Cecilia had been subjected at the hands of Brother Thomas and myself, so many years ago. There was nothing reassuring about Brother Johannes's manner, which was kindly, but quite inscrutable.

In the evening, he allowed us to serve him food, and a conversation ensued which went on till late into the night. Here is a record of what was said:

'Tell me,' he began, 'about the events directly following Cecilia's burning.'

'It had been agreed,' I said, 'that I should set off to find Alyssa, Brother Thomas's common-law wife, in order to tell her about his blinding. Then I was to ride with her back to Canterbury, so that she should care for him.'

'How did you know where to find her?' Brother Johannes interrupted.

'Rufus's men had followed her to Isaac's house at Petcotte and persuaded her to leave. They had heard that the King's men were about to raid the house because of rumours that illegal medical arts were practised there.'

'Was this true?'

'There was a raid,' I said, 'but the business about illegal medicine was a pretext. The King was hoping to find more. In any case, Alyssa and the two children had taken refuge at the Benedictine Convent on the Port Meadow near Oxford. Perhaps you know it? It is situated on the ancient grasslands by the River Thames, at a point where it often bursts its banks, particularly during the winter.'

As I spoke, I remembered the day I arrived there from London as clearly as if it had been yesterday. There was a chill wind blowing through the matted grass and herbs, and the enormous expanses of floodwater seemed a melancholy mirror to the troubled skies. Though winter held sway and the solstice had not yet come, and despite the fact that I was still deeply distressed because of the burning, I thought I could feel an energy cracking and stirring underfoot, as if spring were already struggling for rebirth. 'I know the place,' said Brother Johannes. 'What happened?'

'I was admitted by one of the older nuns. The gate to the

Convent was bleak, but the gardens inside made a more cheery impression. They led me to Alyssa, who was busy gathering dead branches of ash and yew for the Convent's kitchen fire. She was standing near a linden tree, which reminded me of Cecilia.' As I spoke, I shuddered, as the memory of the myrrh-like scent of the smoke rising from the convent's chimney returned to me. 'It was appropriate,' I continued, 'to find her in a garden. This was very much her element, for she loved trees, plants and herbs. Her affinity with them was at the heart of her understanding of medicines. She saw in natural things the imprint of the divine which the Cathars deny.'

'Do you think that, despite what you say, she was guilty of practising illegal medicine?' asked Brother Johannes. This, I thought, was a typical Dominican trick, worthy of Brother Thomas at the time he was interviewing Cecilia. Failure to condemn a sin in others suggests guilt by association.

I answered carefully, since I did not know what his attitude might be to my own chemical researches. 'Brother Thomas used to tell me,' I said, 'how in the early days of their friendship, before the children came, she would work on her own herbarium, stitching together pieces of parchment he would bring her from monastery or chancellery, and how she would study the construction of leaves, flowers and grasses, sketching them endlessly, annotating their various properties, drawing up charts of correspondences between their names, their forms, and the astrology of their annual cycles. Her interest was in observing nature; she would have no reason to want to provoke the authorities.'

'Yet she seduced Brother Thomas,' he interrupted.

'That is one way of putting it,' I replied, and added nothing more, preferring an uneasy silence to foolish words.

'So,' he said, more kindly now. 'What was Alyssa like then?'

As he spoke, I remembered how, that day, as I walked towards her, a black cat, which looked uncannily like Cecilia's, had run in front of me, across the dewy grass, but I decided to spare my Dominican friend this detail. 'Even in that place,' I said, 'which was unfamiliar to me, just to be in her presence was like a homecoming. Despite the terrible burden of the news I bore, I was aware of all the kindness she and Thomas had shown me in the past, and it was soothing to be with her. She was a beautiful woman. She had long curly brown hair and a ready smile. There was a grace, a warmth and wisdom about her, so that I had no difficulty seeing why Thomas loved her.'

'Were Thomas's children with her?' Brother Johannes enquired.

'Yes, they were both there, playing nearby – little Benedikt who was four years old, and Katarin who was six. The thought that Thomas would never see them again pained me and I had great difficulty finding the words to explain his blinding to Alyssa.' Again, I fell silent, remembering how she looked at me as I spoke, and as I tried to console her. Her grey-blue eyes, wide open, had the same colour as the cloudy sky and the wintry water-meadows.

'So, the news had not reached her,' said Brother Johannes.

'No. She listened carefully to what I had to say, and it was typical that the first words she spoke when I had finished were words of kindness. "Let us go into the kitchens," she said. "You must be exhausted. I can serve you soup." I was very moved by the atmosphere of warmth and generosity about her; it suffused the air around us, like the sweet-smelling smoke curling from the fire of the kitchens fleeing towards the cloudy horizons beneath the dank skies. As we reached the door to the Convent, I could tell she was weeping. "So," she said, as I helped her through the door, "my poor Thomas is no longer the little clerk I first loved."

'We were alone in the kitchens, for the nuns were working elsewhere. She served me soup, and we sat together on one of the benches at the table. She regained her composure enough to tell me how she had met Michael and Myrrah not long after Thomas and I had left for Canterbury. They had come to her house in order to warn her of the danger she was in because of Thomas's investigations. She was drawn to Myrrah in particular, she said, which was why she accepted her invitation to take refuge in Petcotte.'

'Do you think Petcotte was a household of heretics?' Brother Johannes asked, still inscrutable.

'No one from there,' I replied, 'was ever convicted of heresy, though Alyssa told me, quite openly, that some questioned the Church's teaching in new ways. For example, they thought men and women should be equal and free, and all interests should be governed by the establishment of what they called Councils of Seven. Apparently, one of the walls of the house bore paintings of the lives of the Saints and Christ, intertwined with shoots, tendrils, butterflies, chrysalises and various animals. I found out afterwards that they were the work of Michael, Isaac's son.'

'How close was Alyssa to Michael and Myrrah?'

'No more than she said, at the time. They had similar interests, in the patterns which govern nature. They would have had a great deal to talk about.'

'So, she would have understood Brother Thomas's curiosity regarding Isaac's cellar?'

'Perhaps,' I said. 'That evening we sat together and I told her in greater detail about Cecilia and the events surrounding our investigations. I could not expect her to forgive Thomas and myself, only hope that she might understand.'

'And did she forgive you?' asked Brother Johannes.

'I remember Alyssa's words,' I said, 'that very evening. She was, of course, deeply upset, but she summed up the pattern of events in a way which made sense, even then. "There is a glory," she said, "in investigating the created world of nature. And there is a glory in turning one's back on this world. Tragically, the two glories are incompatible. One will consume the other." '

'And did you agree with her?' Brother Johannes asked.

'I understood what she meant,' I said, and left it at that.

'What else did she have to say?'

'From my description of the events leading up to Domna Cecilia's burning, Alyssa had grasped the depths of my feelings for Myrrah, and she was the first to help me understand that my situation was not hopeless, for there was much that I could do to change my life.'

'Like Blind Thomas,' commented Brother Johannes, 'you gave up your monastic vocation for a woman.'

'Not for any woman,' I replied. At that point, Myrrah, my dear wife, whom I still love more than anything else in this world, came into the room, and offered us food. Perhaps I am particularly sensitive to her grace and beauty, and there is no reason why I should expect anyone else, let alone a Dominican, to understand our love. Yet her presence was enough to silence him, as she served us more food and wine. I reflected how fortunate I was, to have had such a companion throughout my life. She did not just share my quest for knowledge; more often than not, she led the way. Yet her kindness towards me was never exhausted.

Next, Brother Johannes produced a scroll of parchment from a leather container which he had kept until then in an inner pocket of his cloak. 'Do you recognise this?' he said. He handed me the parchment. On it was a chart, which read as follows:

0	Fool		Aleph	Chalcedony	Aspen
1	Magus	Sun	Beth	Mercury, opal, agate	Vervain (winter sabat incense), herb mercury, marjolane
2	Papess	Moon	Gimel	Moonstone, pearl, crystal	Almond, mugwort, hazel, ranunculus, moonwort
3	Empress	Venus	Daleth	Emerald, turquoise, salt	Pomegranate, sandalwood, myrtle, rose, clover
4	Emperor	Jupiter	He	Ruby	Tiger lily, geranium
5	Hierophant	Mercury	Vau	Topaz	Mallow
6	Lovers	Sagittarius	Zain	Alexandrite [green by day, red by candle]	Orchids, pears, ripe corn
7	Chariot	Mars	Cheth	Amber Kephra	Lotus, onycha, watercress
8	Justice		Teth	Cat's eye	Sunflower
9	Hermit	Pisces	Yod	Pearl, peridot	Snowdrops
10	Wheel of fortune	Capricorn	Kaph	Amethyst, lapis lazuli	Rosetree, palm, hyssop, oak, poplar, fig, saffron

11	Force	Leo	Lamed	Emerald	Aloe
12	Hanged man	Aries	Mem	Beryl, aqua marine	Lotus, onycha, myrtle
13	Death	Saturn	Nun	Snakestone	White rose, lily, cactus
14	Temperance	Aquarius	Samekh	VITRIOL	Rush, hyacinth
15	Devil	Dragon	Ayin	Black diamond	Hemp, musk, civit, orchis
16	Falling Tower		Phe	Ruby	Absinth, rue
17	Star	Taurus	Tzaddi	Glass, crystal	Violet
18	Moon	Cancer	Koph	Pearl	Poppy, opium
19	Sun	Gemini	Resch	Chrysoleth	Sunflower, laurel, olibanum, cinnamon
20	Judgement	Scorpio	Schin	Opal	Red poppy, hibiscus
21	World	Virgo	Tau	Onyx	Ash, cypress, hellebore, yew, nightshade

'Yes,' I said, 'I do recognise it.'

'Can you explain?' said Brother Johannes.

'It is a part of the system of correspondences, in the tradition of the *Hermesis*, to which Brother Thomas gave expression in a new and unique way. It would be wrong, though, to suggest that he alone was responsible.'

'What is its purpose?' he asked.

'As you know,' I replied, 'some say there are correspondences between all things in nature, and in time. The twenty-two principles, found in numbers, the Hebrew alphabet, the heavenly bodies, music, metals, plants, animals and in the structure of the human body, are thought by some to be doorways to the understanding of the connections between all things. They argue that a profound study of such matters might give a wise man the power to transmute metals, and to move through time, divining the future, and seeing the past.'

'And you believe this?' asked the Dominican.

'I neither believe,' I said, 'nor disbelieve. A wise man would not want such power. This is what Cecilia came to understand, albeit at a terrible cost. The same is true of poor Brother Thomas.'

'You say that Blind Thomas was not alone in this work?'

'Of course not. Isaac worked with me on this system until his death three years ago, just as certain monks of Christ Church once worked with his father, before the darkness fell on that Priory. He was a wise man. His knowledge was great and his mind extremely subtle. Apart from Myrrah, he was my closest friend and companion.' As I spoke, I wondered if people still remembered us as we were at Farnham, two eccentric old men, hunched and mistrustful, with wild eyes and unfathomable ways. Or perhaps we are already like forgotten spirits amidst the aspen trees, doomed only to stir autumn leaves in the dank future of some distant century.'

'Who else was engaged in the work?' Brother Johannes asked.

'The tradition reaches back to the beginnings of time. In recent years, however, the most profound contributions were made by Walter von der Ouwe, Cecilia's old lover, and by Cecilia herself, when she was a younger woman. You see, Cecilia's years of contemplation were not without fruit. Why else should she and Walter have been drawn so powerfully to one another? The papers which I handed Cecilia on the night before her burning bore the imprint of the pattern in your manuscript. This is one of the reasons why they brought her such consolation.'

'And in the writings you gave to me,' he observed, accurately. 'Do you think,' he went on, hurriedly changing the subject, 'that others pursued Walter and Cecilia in the quest for this knowledge?'

'Of course. Yet those whose motive was greed met an even worse fate. Remember what happened to the Gräfin of Leuchtenfels, to the Graf, and to Sir Osbert, the Keeper of the castle?'

'He was hanged, wasn't he?'

'Yes, the very day after I arrived back in Canterbury with Alyssa. Amongst his crimes were the murders of Brother Theodor and the Templar Brothers at Swiffeld. It was all in vain, of course, for even if he had got his hands on the knowledge, he would never have understood it.'

'What about the Prior, John of Sittingbourne?' Brother Johannes asked.

'For the sake of the Church, he was not disgraced publicly. But the last four years of his life, after the events I have described, were bitter with regret and illness; he died, so I have heard, having confessed his sins before his Creator, so perhaps we should not judge him too harshly.'

'And how much importance do you attach,' Brother

Johannes asked, 'to the story of Cecilia's lineage?'

'As she herself said, it made her a pawn in a power game,' I replied, 'the victim of forces such as those which thwarted her mission to England and, long before, brought about the Graf of Leuchtenfels's change of heart during the course of the tournament when Walter von der Ouwe fought Johannes of Ulm.'

'Yet would she have acquired the insights she did, had that blood not flowed in her veins?'

'It was not enough to prevent her death,' I replied.

'And what do you think about her acceptance of death?' he asked. 'Was it rooted in the ugliness of despair, or in the beauty of renunciation?'

'That,' I answered, 'is a question which has haunted me from the moment I understood, so many years ago, that her death was inevitable. I have no answer.'

'Perhaps you could tell me about Brother Thomas in the days and months after Cecilia's burning,' he asked next. 'I hear that he is held by many in Ellethamwolde to have been some kind of prophet, to have had certain powers, even that he has appeared to some since his death.'

'The simple folk,' I replied, 'will believe all kinds of things.' I left a silence long enough to indicate that I had no desire to speculate on such phenomena, and continued my story from the point of my arrival back in Canterbury with Alyssa. 'It was, of course, unsettling,' I said, 'to be in the house where we had spent so much time with Cecilia and Alazaïs, especially since our purpose now was to nurse Thomas, who could not be moved. My master was transformed utterly. His skin was healing more rapidly than expected, perhaps because of the powers of Cecilia's herbs. His eyeless face and hairless head were like those of some serene oracle. He had regained the power of speech, though his voice was never quite the same again, since now it had a trembling, unearthly quality. Already, people were coming to see him, and he would set aside time each day when he would expound the philosophical systems he had developed to those who gathered around him.'

'And this was similar to the system in the parchment I just showed you?'

'Yes. And its essence could already be found in the *Hermesis*,' I explained. 'Cecilia and Walter, as I said, understood how this system could be expressed in music, and in a whole life story. Brother Thomas's genius was to express it in the form of pictures and colours. The clarity of this version is such that some use it for purposes of divination.'

'And you do not approve of this?'

'Of course not,' I said. Everyone knows there are worlds of diabolical half-truth into which only fools venture.

'And you remained with Thomas?' he asked.

'I could not leave him,' I said. 'Besides, Myrrah arrived two days later, and she too helped nurse Thomas. It would have been beyond my power to leave her. The conversations I shared with her, Thomas, Isaac and Michael were very important to me. The ideas we discussed then were to inform the course of my life thereafter. Many others came too. Brother Thomas, eyeless and snowy-skinned, was believed by many to possess supernatural powers, because of the philosophical and chemical knowledge that he had acquired. Some even believed that the explosion which maimed him was no mere accident, but that supernatural powers were involved or that magical substances were placed in the retort as a trap.'

'Tell me about Michael, Myrrah's brother,' said Brother Johannes.

I explained to him that the last time I had seen Michael was twelve years ago. I was travelling through the forests near the castle at Duningtowne, when a host of wild men rode towards me. At first, I feared they would rob and kill me, but no, they led me off in the depths of the forest to a house built into the mouth of a large cave, hidden by trees and dense foliage. There I was welcomed by a man dressed in dark green, with gleaming brown eyes, a massive beard and long curly hair. This was Michael who, despite his access to wealth, preferred to live the life of an outlaw in the forest. His wife was beautiful, and they had several children. When we talked about Cecilia, Michael said he was convinced that power struggles in the Holy Roman Empire had made her death inevitable, but that, given the dispositions of her spirit, it was remarkable that she had lived as long as she did. Michael was extraordinarily friendly. He had heard, he said, that I was passing that way, and had prepared a feast in my honour. The magnificence and generosity of his table in that wild cave were overwhelming. A number of the people who ate with us had lived alongside Alyssa at Petcotte before the community was broken up by the King's men. We conversed together at length about the lore of plants, stars, medicines and precious stones, the government of countries, and other things to do with the new learning, and ideas such as those found in the *Hermesis*, which are kept secret from those in power. Then, when we had talked enough, everyone drank, laughed and danced until late at night.'

'It seems that you are curiously enamoured of such strange people,' Brother Johannes said.

'Whenever I think that there might be hope for this aging world,' I replied, 'then it is Michael's and Myrrah's faces I see, not Domna Cecilia's. Because of her truth, her understanding, she turned her back on the universe of time and matter.'

'For a long while,' Brother Johannes said, 'during the first years of your marriage to Myrrah, you were the King's Alchemist. That is correct?'

'Indeed. I was offered the post by the King when it became clear that Brother Thomas was not fit to accept it, because of his blinding. We all moved together from Canterbury to a house belonging to Peter des Roches in Farnham, next to the great keep of the castle. Peter des Roches took a generous interest in us, and I learnt much from him.'

'How many were there in your household?' he asked.

'Myself,' I replied, 'Myrrah, Alyssa and Isaac. As you know, Brother Thomas died three years after the explosion, almost to the day. There was a strange beauty, as well as a deep sadness, watching his body gradually shed more and more of its weight, despite the care Alyssa lavished on him; it was as though he were being drawn, slowly and peacefully, into another realm. Before then, I travelled on the King's business, investigating such cases as suited my talents and insights, but I would return as often as I could to be with my family, and to consult with Brother Thomas, my teacher.' I explained to Brother Johannes how my life with Myrrah and the children she bore me was full of happiness. But it would be as wrong to write of these things here as it would to speculate on what visions might move in the darkness behind a blind man's eyes.

'And the others?' he asked.

'Only Myrrah and I have been spared. Isaac died just three years ago, and Alyssa some seven years before that. Lord Rufus is still alive. He spends most of his time on his estates at Ellethamwolde these days. Last year the King spent Christmas with him there. You can imagine how delighted Rufus was.'

'And you relinquished your post as the King's Alchemist?'

'When our children grew up and left home,' I said, 'I asked if I might be allowed to travel less, and it was agreed that I might move here, to act as curate to this quiet village, and to continue with the Work.'

'And did you succeed in changing lead into gold?' he asked, with a candour that surprised me.

'You will have to judge that for yourself,' I replied, according to the custom, for few understand that the meaning of the Work is the Work itself, rather than its end. I thought of the admixture of sulphur and quicksilver, catharism and hermeticism. The synthesis is even more elusive than the structure.

'There are many strange fates in the world,' Johannes mused, 'like that of the boy Geraldus.'

There followed a lengthy silence. I was expecting judgment, and a part of me expected this judgment to be harsh. At the same time, this man's presence, for all his inscrutability, was curiously familiar and reassuring; and his knowledge of me acted as a bond between us. Even so, I had no suspicion of what was to happen next. From inside his cloak, he produced a small wooden flute. 'Allow me to play,' he said, smiling in a way which reminded me of the old days.

His playing was interspersed with quiet singing. His voice was beautiful. I recognised the song immediately: the only one known to have been written by Domna Cecilia. Most have forgotten it now, but those of us who are involved in the Work still know it, for it contains the lines:

> 'Durchsternet was sîns sinnes himel
> glanz alse ein vimel . . .'*

'It seems,' I said, when he had finished, 'that I mistook the reason for your coming.'

He smiled, and raised an eyebrow.

At last, his visit made sense to me. Laughing inwardly, I poured us both wine, the best I had. Johannes presented me,

---

* *His mind was like a star-studded heaven/Shining radiantly . . . (FraUenlob)*

formally, with the two chalices. The first was just as Brother Thomas had described it. The stem of the second bears stones of emerald, turquoise, ruby and alexandrite; its cup is set with amber, cat's eye, pearl, amethyst and lapis lazuli.

The next day I accompanied Johannes back to Canterbury. On the way, he explained to me how he had pursued studies similar to mine for over seven years. He was a member of the brotherhood to which Walter von der Ouwe had once belonged. When he invited me to work with him, and to join the Brotherhood of Prayer of Charlemagne, I accepted. These writings are my testimony.

BETSY TOBIN

Bone House

'Wonderful! . . . poignant and gripping'
Tracy Chevalier, author of *Girl with a Pearl Earring*

Bone House is the tale of two women. The icy death of the first, a large, voluptuous and charismatic prostitute, transforms the lives of all around her: her giant son, a hunchbacked lord, his decaying mother, and a painter, whose arrival in the village threatens them all.

The second is slight and solitary – a servant, whose investigations into the prostitute's strange death result in a terrible discovery, and the beginnings of a future.

Set in 1603, *Bone House* is a novel about bodies and flesh, desire and murder, medicine, superstition and mundanity. Elegant, sensual, fiercely compelling, this is a shockingly assured and modern debut.

'A wonderful and moving novel' Iain Pears, author of *An Instance of the Fingerpost*

'Provocative (and) gripping . . . a tale shimmering with psychological depth' *New York Times Book Review*

'(Tobin) cuts through a tangle of dark and dirty secrets . . . with pearly clarity . . . A compelling story of haunted lives' *Time Out*

0 7472 6491 0

review

ROBIN MAXWELL

Virgin

Could England's 'Virgin Queen', Elizabeth I, have borne her lover, Robin Dudley, Earl of Leicester, a son? Most historians dismiss such tales as idle gossip but others speak of a young man named Arthur Dudley . . .

Set against the background of the Spanish Armada's invasion of England in 1588, two parallel tales unfold. One is Queen Elizabeth's story: her lifelong and passionate affair with Leicester; her politically dangerous pregnancy and elaborate scheme to conceal it from the world; and finally the tragic birth of her still-born son – a loss which only deepens her love for Leicester. The other is the story of Arthur, their illegitimate son, born alive but secretly swapped at birth. Young Arthur grows up a country gentleman, totally unaware of his true identity. A dreamer, a romantic and a magnificent horseman, he sets off to fight Philip II of Spain. Now, many years later, his story collides with that of his mother when, from his adoptive father's deathbed, he hears the amazing truth of his parentage.

'Fascinating' *Kirkus Reviews*

'She writes with pace and passion' *Yorkshire Post*

0 7472 6664 6

review

Now you can buy any of these other
Review titles from your bookshop or
direct from the publisher.

FREE P&P AND UK DELIVERY
(Overseas and Ireland £3.50 per book)

Hens Dancing	Raffaella Barker	£6.99
The Catastrophist	Ronan Bennett	£6.99
Horseman, Pass By	David Crackanthorpe	£6.99
Two Kinds of Wonderful	Isla Dewar	£6.99
Earth and Heaven	Sue Gee	£6.99
Sitting Among the Eskimos	Maggie Graham	£6.99
Tales of Passion, Tales of Woe	Sandra Gulland	£6.99
The Dancers Dancing	Éilís Ní Dhuibhne	£6.99
After You'd Gone	Maggie O'Farrell	£6.99
The Silver River	Ben Richards	£6.99
A History of Insects	Yvonne Roberts	£6.99
Girl in Hyacinth Blue	Susan Vreeland	£6.99
The Long Afternoon	Giles Waterfield	£6.99

TO ORDER SIMPLY CALL THIS NUMBER

01235 400 414

or e-mail orders@bookpoint.co.uk

Prices and availability subject to change without notice.